Bestselling author **Bob Shepherd** is a security advisor and 20-year veteran of Britain's elite Special Air Service. With more than a decade and a half of private security work to his credit, he has successfully negotiated some of the most dangerous places on earth as both an SAS soldier and private citizen. Shepherd is a regular media commentator on security issues and has appeared on CNN International, BBC One, BBC World, BBC Radio and SKY News. He also shares his insights on security politics through his blog; www.bobshepherdauthor.com

Also by Bob Shepherd

The Infidel

The Good Jihadist

BOB SHEPHERD

with M. P. Sabga

SIMON &
SCHUSTER

London · New York · Sydney · Toronto

A CBS COMPANY

First published in Great Britain by Simon & Schuster UK Ltd, 2011
A CBS Company

Copyright © Bob Shepherd & M.P. Sabga, 2011

3 5 7 9 10 8 6 4 2

Simon & Schuster UK Ltd
1st Floor
222 Gray's Inn Road
London WC1X 8HB

www.simonandschuster.co.uk

Simon & Schuster Australia
Sydney

A CIP catalogue record for this book is available from the British Library

Hardback ISBN 978-0-85720-880-4
Trade Paperback ISBN 978-1-84737-776-0

Printed and bound in the UK by CPI Mackays, Chatham ME5 8TD

For the fixers . . .
the *real* news gatherers.

Glossary of Terms

ORGANIZATIONS

AQI: al-Qaeda in Iraq.

BLA: Baluchistan Liberation Army. Militant group committed to the secession of Baluchistan province from Pakistan.

CIA: Central Intelligence Agency. Civilian intelligence agency of the United States government.

Delta Force: Special Forces army unit primarily responsible for US counter-terrorism operations.

ISI: Inter-Services Intelligence. Pakistan's most powerful intelligence agency.

JSOC: Joint Special Operations Command. The command responsible for conducting US counter-terrorism operations.

SAS: Special Air Service. The principal Special Forces Regiment of the British Army.

22 SAS Regiment: Unit of the SAS responsible for counter-terrorism operations.

SSG: Special Support Group. The principal Special Forces Regiment of the Pakistani Army responsible for counter-terrorism operations.

SSB: Strategic Support Branch. Intelligence Agency created by the US Department of Defense.

TTP: Tehrik-i-Taliban Pakistan. Militant Pashtun umbrella group committed to fighting the Pakistani state.

WEAPONS

AK 47: Russian-designed 7.62mm assault rifle (the most ubiquitous assault rifle in the world).

Browning 9mm: Semi-automatic pistol with a standard 13-round magazine (US and Belgian design).

CheyTac .408: US-designed sniper rifle.

Dragunov SVD: Russian-designed 7.62mm sniper rifle.

Glock 17: Austrian-designed semi-automatic 9mm pistol.

Heckler & Koch G3: German-designed 7.62mm assault rifle.

Heckler & Koch MP5: German-designed 9mm submachine gun.

IED: Improvised Explosive Device.

Lee Enfield: British-designed .303 bolt-action rifle used by British Empire and Commonwealth forces during World War I and World War II.

M4 Carbine: US-designed 5.56mm assault rifle.

RPG: Rocket Propelled Grenade. A shoulder-launched, handheld weapon that fires a warhead accurately to approximately 250–300 metres.

SIG Sauer: Swiss-German-designed pistol preferred by many Special Forces units worldwide.

Type 56 assault rifle: The Chinese version of a Russian AK 47.

VBIED: Vehicle Borne Improvised Explosive Device.

TV NEWS

BGAN terminal: Broadband Global Area Network portable satellite terminal.

B-roll: News footage.

Cutaways: Extra b-roll shot after an interview for editing purposes.

Fixer: A local producer/translator and general problem solver for foreign journalists.

IFB: Earpiece worn by on-air talent that allows them to hear live programme feeds and control room instructions.

Live Shot: A news story reported in real time.

Minder: A government official who keeps a tight leash on foreign journalists.

Stand Up: A monologue a correspondent delivers directly to the camera.

OTHER

COIN ops: Counter Insurgency operations.

The Factory: JSOC Operations Centre in Balad, Iraq.

OP: Observation Post.

Map design by Chris Olsen

PART I

Chapter 1

Baghdad 2006

The Delta lads were in good spirits. The rehearsals had gone smoothly that day despite the introduction of an outsider to their close-knit family. Matt Logan was integrating well with the twelve-man team. Waiting on a helipad in the Green Zone, there was little to distinguish the SAS soldier from his American Special Forces counterparts aside from his accent. Matt's operational kit – an M4 Carbine assault rifle, SIG Sauer 9mm pistol, assorted assault grenades, night vision and other ancillaries – was virtually identical to theirs. He'd even opted for the same camouflage pattern. But the most important parallels had nothing to do with uniforms or firepower. Delta Force was proving to be as professional as the SAS and every bit as determined. The intelligence for the operation had fed through less than twelve hours before and the Yanks were hell bent on taking down the target before the trail went cold.

A friendly blow landed between Matt's shoulders. 'Feeling good, Logan?'

Matt nodded to the Delta commander. In the British 'Green' army, officers addressed subordinates by their surname to assert authority. Matt reckoned Captain Carter's intentions were the exact opposite. The American was levelling the field. 'Yeah, boss,' he said, acknowledging Carter's rank – a courtesy he routinely denied superiors back home.

'You can hold the boss,' said Carter. 'We're all brothers here. No one's better than anyone else.'

Matt embraced the fraternal spirit. 'Whatever you say, Carter.' The reply tripped off his tongue as if he'd always addressed officers so casually. That chameleon-like ability to blend into any social group had been a deciding factor in Matt's selection as unofficial liaison to the Deltas that night. With many of Hereford's old guard chafing against the integration of 22 SAS Regiment into JSOC – America's Joint Special Operations Command – it was down to young soldiers like him to cement the new order. Matt was an ideal candidate for the sensitive mission. A newly promoted sergeant and six-year veteran of the Regiment, he could more than hold his own with the Yanks.

'So, you a sports fan?' asked Carter in his mid-Atlantic drawl.

Matt played along. 'I'm rugby daft – but that probably doesn't mean much to you.'

'Don't be so quick to judge. I played rugby in college.'

Matt was surprised. As a general rule Yanks ignored rugby. They were too obsessed with the fits-and-starts hybrid they mysteriously referred to as football. 'What position?'

'Scrum half.'

'Good man. To be fair, I've never seen a country come on in a sport as quickly as you Yanks have in rugby. The American Eagles are flying. How far do you think you'll go in the World Cup next year?'

'It's hard to say. We get paired with New Zealand, Oz or South Africa in the first round and I don't see us progressing past the group stages.' Carter nudged Matt. 'I'm hoping we'll catch a break and draw Scotland.'

Matt took the jab for what it was; a good-natured attempt to bond. 'I'm hoping we draw Japan.'

Carter laughed. 'So whereabouts in Scotland are you from?'

'Crieff in Perthshire.' The name drew a blank from Carter. Matt threw in the tourist board slogan to help him along. '"The Gateway to the Highlands."'

'So you're a real Highland warrior,' Carter enthused.

Matt slid his helmet back. 'I even have the ginger hair to prove it. What about you? Where's your kin from?'

'Virginia,' said Carter. 'But my family's originally from Ireland.'

As proud as Carter obviously was of his heritage, Matt didn't see it. Lean and angular with shorn chestnut hair, dark eyes and pale skin, the Delta captain had a self-assured, all-American optimism that defied old world labels. 'Which county in Ireland?' asked Matt.

'Cornwall.'

Matt chuckled.

'What's so funny?'

'Cornwall's in England, mate.'

A line surfaced on Carter's forehead, cracking his invincible demeanour. The last thing Matt had intended was to undermine his commander's confidence – especially on the cusp of an assault. 'If it makes you feel any better, the Cornish breed great rugby players,' he offered.

The compliment shored up the Delta captain – and just in time. Three MH-6 helicopters were closing in on the landing zone. The wasp-like buzz of the single-engine 'little birds' was barely discernible beneath the throngs of heavier aircraft criss-crossing the skies over Baghdad.

The heli pilots touched down, cut the engines and joined the Deltas for a final briefing. 'You all know the drill,' Carter began. 'Blue One will lead the assault on Tango and prosecute from the east.' He turned to his second-in-command; a black-haired, olive-skinned lieutenant. 'Hernandez and Blue Two will prosecute from the north. Bazinsky and Blue Three will be hovering to the south, ready to take out targets should they attempt to escape and/or evade capture.'

Bazinsky swung a CheyTac .408 sniper rifle around. The long barrel cut a menacing silhouette against the setting sun. 'Don't worry,' the hulking blond caressed the name he'd taped to the weapon, '*Baby Girl*'s got your back.'

'Don't forget, the regular army won't be far off,' Carter reminded them. 'Gulf will be in an over-watch position throughout the operation.' He opened the floor to his second-in-command. 'Hernandez?'

'Gulf is our safety net should anything go wrong,' the 2IC reiterated. 'But so is the Lord. God willing, we won't be calling in the regular forces until Tango is secured.'

The religious reference caught Matt off guard. Invoking God before a mission was anathema to an SAS soldier. It was the first real culture clash he'd experienced with the Deltas.

'Are there any questions?' asked Carter. The Deltas were confidently silent. 'I know this is all second nature by now, but let's not get cocky. Keep the momentum up and don't stop for anything until we've achieved our objective, not even to help a man down. Do that and the folks in The Factory will be in for one heck of a show.' He turned to Matt. 'Now as you all know, we have a guest star joining us this evening. You have anything you'd like to add before we head out, Logan?'

All eyes converged on Matt. He knew what they were after; a rousing, pre-op rallying talk. 'When I arrived here this morning, I had some idea of what to expect. Everyone knows you Yanks have tremendous assets. And believe me, my mates will be green with envy when I tell them about all the amazing kit you get to work with. But what's impressed me more than anything is your soldiering. I've been blown away watching you lot in rehearsals today. You're outstanding, all of you, down to a man. I consider it a real honour to be going on operations with you tonight.'

Matt waited for the reciprocal nods. But the Deltas didn't seem at all moved by his praise. Maybe he didn't know them as well as he thought – that or his opinion meant fuck all.

Carter resuscitated the moment. 'You heard the man,' boomed the Delta captain. 'Now let's go kick some butt!'

Whoops and cheers filled the LZ. Matt gathered his gear and headed for his heli. He was halfway there before he realized the rest of the team had hung back.

The Deltas were kneeling in a circle with their heads bowed – except Hernandez. 'Join us in prayer, Logan,' said the 2IC. It was more of a command than an invitation.

Matt raised his hand. 'You crack on with that, mate. I'll see you when you're finished.'

Hernandez glared his disapproval before launching into a passionate prayer.

The *Amen* sounded and Blue Team scattered to their respective little birds. Matt took up position in the centre heli, secured a short ladder to the D-ring on his belt, switched on his night-vision aids and checked his radio. 'Blue One Alpha, this is Blue One Bravo, radio check.'

Carter responded over Matt's earpiece. 'Roger, Blue One Bravo. Lima Charlie,' he said, letting Matt know the signal was *loud and clear*.

Matt placed his feet on the skids and gave the thumbs-up to the pilot to tell him he was good to go.

With four thumbs pointing skyward, the little bird lifted off. The cloying humidity of Baghdad dissolved as the heli climbed, the wind lashing Matt's face and body, priming his senses for the operation at hand. Through the green and black contrast of his night sight, he canvassed the steaming city below. Clusters of light dotted the power-starved capital.

Amidst the modest bonfires of generator-powered homes, the industrial furnace of the Green Zone burned. Matt slid his night aids up and looked back on the fortified enclave. He could just make out the two great pairs of crossed swords marking the entrance to the parade square where Saddam Hussein had declared victory in the Iran-Iraq war. The relics drew him back to the opening days of the US-led campaign to oust the brutal dictator. Like many Regiment lads, Matt thought the combat would be swift and decisive. After all, the politicians were saying the Iraqis would embrace the coalition as liberators. Three years on and not only was he still fighting in Iraq, he was spearheading a new era in SAS warfare.

Until now, the Regiment's Iraq operations had been restricted to targeting Saddam loyalists – old men whose power had vanished along with their patronage. But while Matt was wasting time rounding up disenfranchised geriatrics, a far more sinister enemy had crept into the nation's power vacuum. Al-Qaeda in Iraq. AQI foreign fighters and their domestic converts were doing anything and everything to stir the shit; targeting buildings with VBIEDS; sending suicide bombers into busy marketplaces; planting IEDs along the coalition's main supply routes; firing rockets and mortars at government buildings and military bases. The insurgents were as ruthless as they were indiscriminate. AQI didn't care whose blood they spilled, so long as it kept Iraq mired in chaos. For years now, Matt had been itching to take some of them out. Tonight, thanks to the Deltas and JSOC, he would finally get his chance.

Blue Team were targeting four high-ranking AQI operatives. The insurgents were due to meet in a neighbourhood east of the Green Zone shortly after dark. The location and time had been gleaned from intelligence gathered from a Delta assault on a separate insurgent position the night before. The turn-around was faster than Matt was accustomed to but he agreed with the logic driving it. Responding rapidly to intelligence was a cornerstone of JSOC's counterinsurgency strategy. With any luck, tonight's operation would yield even more intelligence, triggering yet another mission and another, until the enemy was so weakened the entire AQI network would collapse.

Some of the more seasoned operators in the SAS questioned the wisdom of JSOC's industrial-scale COIN ops. Matt's troop staff sergeant, a crusty old git of thirty-eight, warned that the Regiment risked losing the covert COIN expertise it had honed over decades. Matt dismissed this as sour grapes from a has-been who couldn't accept that his skills had passed their sell-by date. Iraq wasn't Northern Ireland. You couldn't have teams of operators doing tedious foot and mobile surveillance like the old timers had. Grey Ops were obsolete. The War on Terror was about Black Ops; speed, controlled aggression, surprise. Forget painstakingly amassing an intelligence picture. Infiltrating by heli, blowing in entry points, taking the fight to the enemy night after night – that's how the coalition would prevail.

Not only were the new tactics more effective, they suited Matt's personality. He far preferred channelling his energy into a real fight rather than bottle it up for a confrontation sometime in the future. Besides, why squander a perfectly good soldier on surveillance when technology could do the job even better? Matt may not have believed in Hernandez's God but he did have faith in JSOC's all-seeing eye. The Factory had round-the-clock aerial surveillance on Tango – the house where the AQI operatives were meeting. Special sensors were tracking the insurgents' mobile signals, mapping their locations and movements. The enemy couldn't take a dump without JSOC knowing about it.

The pilot gave a one-minute warning. Matt fixed his night sights, unhooked the ladder from his belt and surveyed the ground below. The neighbourhood looked like a toy town from above: rectangular plots; horizontal and vertical streets; a rounded mosque dome; date palms. The Humvees and Bradleys comprising the Gulf outer cordon were already in position on the edge of a vacant lot. The regular troops were six hundred yards from Tango as the crow flies, double that by road. Matt hoped they hadn't alerted any touts working in support of the insurgents. The element of surprise was crucial in an assault, especially in urban areas where prolonged fire-fights could ensnare innocent bystanders. In all his time with the Regiment, Matt hadn't experienced a single civilian casualty on operations and he was keen to keep the record unblemished.

Tango came into view. It was just as the intelligence had described; a two-storey breeze-block house, enclosed by an eight-foot-high concrete wall with a solid iron gate opening onto the street. The surrounding residences were virtually identical but Matt wasn't concerned about cock-ups. Blue Team knew which one to storm.

The heli carrying the sniper team peeled off. Matt savoured the feeling as his little bird swooped down on the target. There was no fear, no hesitation, no doubt; just unwavering resolve and unshakable self-belief. Those precious moments right before an assault when he connected with the best of himself couldn't be bought. They had to be earned. It's what Matt loved most about being an SAS soldier. Billionaires couldn't pay to do what he did.

The heli touched down with its nose facing Tango. Carter's voice exploded over Matt's earpiece. 'Go! Go! Go!' He jumped down and charged. First to the perimeter, Matt propped the ladder against the wall and placed one foot on the bottom rung to hold it steady. With his M4 ready to fire, he covered his Blue One team-mates while they scrambled up and over the wall.

Blue Two were laying explosives at the front of the house when Matt dropped into the compound. He split to the right of them to join Blue One on the eastern assault. The background buzz of the sniper team's helicopter hovering to the south and the roar of the compound's petrol-fired generator, mixed with the pounding of his heart and feet.

As he rounded the corner, a volley of automatic fire joined the adrenaline-fuelled symphony. Through the monocular of his night sights, Matt locked on an insurgent armed with an AK 47. He figured him for a foot soldier as opposed to one of the high-value targets. The man was firing away like a maniac, completely exposed.

The insurgent hit one of Matt's team-mates, spinning him around and throwing him to the ground. Matt identified his wounded man – Captain Carter. 'Man down. Man down,' Matt radioed his team. 'Blue One Alpha,' he said, relaying Carter's call sign.

Matt took evasive action and raised his rifle to take out the insurgent. He brought the central mass of the target into his sights. Suddenly, the crack of a high-velocity round flew past his ear. The AK-wielding militant slumped forward, exposing a fatal, yawning exit wound to the back. Matt held his fire. Bazinsky and *Baby Girl* had beaten him to the kill.

Matt left Carter where he lay – it was vital to maintain momentum – and carried on. His uninjured team-mates had just finished preparing a window frame for an explosive entry when a THUMP sounded from the south. The noise was music to their ears. Blue Two had blown in the front door.

Capitalizing on the distraction, Blue One initiated their charge. A blinding flash consumed Matt's field of vision as the window imploded. Fingers of incandescent light poked through a pair of shredded curtains. Matt slid his night sights up and followed his team-mates into the glimmering breach.

Three shots sounded as he jumped through the window. Matt landed with his weapon poised to fire. He immediately identified two insurgents but his Delta team-mates already had them by the shorthairs. One insurgent was down with a shot to the leg; the other was standing with his arms above his head, declaring to anyone who would listen, 'I am with America! America good!'

With his team-mates keeping watch, Matt searched the prisoners. The wounded man had a mobile phone and a knife. Matt confiscated both items before moving on to the able-bodied man who was still pleading, 'I am with America! I am with America!'

Matt recovered a pistol and examined it. The magazine was full but oddly, there was no round sitting in the chamber. He checked the prisoner's pockets and found another mobile. The screen indicated a message had been sent less than a minute earlier. It explained why the weapon hadn't been readied for firing. The insurgent had been too busy texting; alerting his AQI mates in the house or calling for back-up.

Matt gave the rest of Blue Team and the regular troops on the outer cordon a heads up. 'This is Blue One Bravo. Zone two secured. Two India's captured. Gulf 2–6 be advised. There may be additional enemy activity in the vicinity.'

The Gulf commander was first to respond. 'Roger that, Blue One Bravo. Any unfriendlies attempt to breach this cordon and we'll blast 'em all to hell, over.'

Matt winced. He hated big-timing over the radio. 'Roger, Gulf 2–6.'

Hernandez followed with a more professional update. 'Copy that, Blue One Bravo. This is Blue Two Alpha. Zone one secured. Two India's neutralized. Moving to Zone three.'

'Roger, Blue Two Alpha.' Matt left to assist on the top floor. In rehearsals, he'd practised the move with Carter. Now that the Delta captain was down he'd have to improvise. He stepped into the front hallway with his M4 in the aim. Matt could hear Blue Two's footsteps overhead, searching the rooms. He looked to the top of the staircase. There was no movement; just a black hole.

He kept his eyes fixed on the emptiness as he rounded the banister. Suddenly, an insurgent came charging out of the darkness above screaming, *'Allahu Akbar!'* God is great! The nutter was wearing an explosives vest.

Matt kept his cool and aimed for the bomber's head. Once again, the Deltas proved quicker on the draw, double tapping the insurgent twice from behind. The bomber's skull exploded, splattering chunks of brain and bone over the wall. The body slid down the steps, its deadly payload still intact.

Hernandez appeared at the top of the staircase, ready to take another shot if necessary. Matt gave him the all-clear signal and stepped over the headless corpse.

Chapter 2

Matt and the Deltas moved slickly from room to room, covering each other, rolling in flash bangs to temporarily stun any occupants, checking behind doors and underneath furniture. There were no more insurgents in the house but they did uncover two booby traps – a tripwire slung low between a window and wardrobe, and a wire strung between a chair and a bed leg. Both devices were tied to the safety pins of high-explosive grenades.

Matt marked the IEDs for the bomb disposal unit and checked his watch. Eleven minutes had elapsed since the little birds had touched down. Within that time, Blue Team had killed four insurgents, captured two high-value AQI targets alive and recovered mobiles that were potential treasure troves of intelligence. The operation was as elegant as any he'd done in the Regiment.

Hernandez declared Tango secure and gave Bazinsky's team a two-minute warning to lift off from the target area. Hanging around in a helicopter longer than necessary was an unacceptable risk in Baghdad. With the snipers preparing to head back to the Green Zone, Hernandez radioed the outer cordon troops to move in. 'Blue Two Alpha to Gulf 2–6, welcome home.'

Matt went outside to check on Carter. He found the Delta captain propped against the side of the house, pressing a personal field dressing to his neck and shoulder. 'You missed all the action, you wanker.'

The humour lifted Carter's spirits. 'How'd we do?'

Matt kneeled down beside him. 'Four insurgents dead – two captured. Not that I can take any credit for it. I didn't fire a shot. Your men were too fast for me. I couldn't keep up.'

'I doubt that,' said Carter.

Matt reached for the dressing. 'Mind if I have a look?' He peeled back the blood-soaked bandage. The bullet had entered Carter's neck and exited through his shoulder, shattering the clavicle and the joint. The wound wasn't life-threatening but for a Special Forces soldier, it was potentially worse; a career-killer. Matt pulled a clean bandage from his trauma pack and tore open the wrapper with his teeth.

'Don't sugar-coat it,' Carter winced. 'Give it to me straight.'

Matt placed the fresh pad over the old, applying even pressure to keep the wound from bleeding out again. 'The surgeons are going to try to replace your shoulder. Don't let them do it, mate. Your rehab will be long but if you stick with it and don't lose heart, you'll be back on operations.'

Carter placed his hand over Matt's. 'Thanks, Logan.'

The rumble of heavy vehicles trundling up the street announced the arrival of the Gulf regular forces. Matt helped Carter to his feet and walked him around to the front of the house, where a Bradley fighting vehicle was waiting outside the gate to take away the captured AQI operatives.

The wounded prisoner was brought out on a stretcher. While he was loaded into the vehicle, Matt scanned the neighbouring buildings. The compounds were shrouded in darkness and the windows shuttered. The gunfire from the assault had no doubt scared the hell out of the neighbours. The uninjured prisoner emerged. Hernandez had him by the elbow. The man's wrists and ankles had been bound with plastic ties, forcing him to shuffle in short, clipped strides.

An outbreak of activity at the top of the street drew Matt's eye. A white Toyota was winding its way through the Gulf outer cordon. It was a severe breach of protocol. The area was supposed to be secured – no civilian vehicles allowed. Matt raised his rifle and jerked his chin. 'Heads up, lads.'

'Blue Two Alpha to Gulf 2–6,' Hernandez barked into his radio, 'identify that white Toyota.'

The Gulf commander took several seconds to respond. 'Uh, Roger, Blue Two Alpha. Be advised, white Toyota is friendly. I repeat, white Toyota is friendly, over.'

Matt and the Deltas looked at each other. Who the hell was crashing their operation?

The Toyota parked up behind the Bradley and a middle-aged white man climbed out. He was wearing a sweat-stained collared shirt, and flashing coalition credentials. 'Who's in charge here?' he demanded. His accent was the same as the Deltas – American.

'This is a closed area,' said Hernandez.

The AQI man started babbling excitedly. 'See? See? I am with America!'

Hernandez unholstered his pistol and held it to the prisoner's head. 'Shut up.'

The gate-crasher approached the insurgent. '*Ma-fi-mushkila, ma-fi-mushkila*,' he said. *No problem.* He fronted up to Hernandez. 'Holster your pistol, Lieutenant. I'm taking custody of this man.'

'You have no jurisdiction here.'

'You're in way over your head, soldier. Now step aside or there'll be trouble.'

Carter limped forward with Matt's help. 'Is there a problem here?' asked the Delta captain.

'Who the fuck are you?' said the gate-crasher.

'Captain Nathanial Lincoln Carter.' His forceful manner belied the severity of his wound. 'What are you doing here?'

'I don't answer to you.'

'The hell you don't,' Carter snapped. 'This is a JSOC operation.' It was the closest thing to an obscenity Matt had heard from the captain's mouth.

The gate-crasher pointed to the insurgent. 'This man is *my* asset.'

The fault line reappeared on Carter's forehead; only this time it was far more pronounced. 'What agency are you with?'

Matt's eyes darted between the quarrelling Yanks.

'CIA.' The spy gestured to the prisoner. 'This man's been feeding us intel for months. He was on the verge of cracking AQI's inner circle until you meatheads blew it for us.' He got up in Carter's face. 'Do you understand what I'm saying, Captain? JSOC has fucked up royally.'

Carter's eyes narrowed with rage. Matt shared his fury. Blue Team had just risked life and limb going after a high-value AQI target who was in fact working for the US-led coalition. It was worse than a royal fuck-up. It was twelve monkeys fucking a football.

'If he's an asset then why didn't JSOC know about him?' Carter demanded.

'I don't answer to JSOC.' The CIA man was seething. 'I was operating in Iraq when you knuckle draggers were still in diapers.'

Matt wanted to deck him. The Deltas had done nothing wrong. If anyone was at fault it was the CIA. Scumbag spooks sneaking around not telling the army what they were doing. It was no way to win a war.

Matt channelled his anger into his task, quickly scanning the houses across the street. They were still dark but how long would they stay that way? The middle of a Baghdad neighbourhood was one hell of a place to get into a pissing match. 'Hey, hey!' he interrupted. 'Think maybe we can sort this out somewhere else?'

The spy threw his rage onto Matt. 'Who the fuck . . .'

A single, jarring shot silenced the spook. There was no crack – just a thump, indicating the round had been fired from the other side of the street. A fraction of a second later, the insurgent who had brought JSOC and the CIA to blows dropped where he stood, blood gushing from his throat. He'd been sniped – by insurgents.

A fusillade of rifle fire erupted from the darkened house opposite Tango. American voices collided around Matt and in his earpiece: 'Contact! Contact!'

He threw Carter over his shoulder and dropped him behind the wall of the house. 'You need me, you radio.'

'I'll be fine, Logan. Go help the team.'

Matt left Carter safely in cover and went to join the fight. He was disgusted and disheartened by the battle unfolding before him. In less than a minute, Blue Team's elegant operation had degenerated into a free-for-all slugfest. The Gulf forces were throwing everything they had at the insurgent house; 7.62 machine guns, booming 25mm cannons, hand grenades. Ribbons of incoming green tracer rounds and bands of outgoing red criss-crossed the sky. The sheer volume suggested there was no method to the targeting. The Gulf troops were firing wildly at the enemy. So was the CIA spook. He was crouching behind his Toyota, emptying a 9mm Beretta pistol into a dense wall of smoke.

The Deltas were adding their rifles sparingly to the fray, conserving their ammunition, making sure every shot counted. Matt found a separate vantage point twenty feet away to broaden the team's field of vision. Observing the house through his night sights, he counted at least three enemy weapons – two on the roof, one on the ground. How the fuck had JSOC's eyes in the sky missed them?

Matt aimed his rifle and waited for a target to appear. Suddenly, a high-explosive round flew out of the compound. A brilliant orange and black fireball erupted as the HE projectile struck the CIA man's Toyota, instantly incinerating him.

The anxious voice of the Gulf commander screamed over the radio. 'This is Gulf 2–6. Require aerial assistance. Location X-ray-charlie-eight-seven-five-four-four-seven-one-six, over!'

Typical, Matt thought. One direct hit and the regulars were calling in air support to bomb the enemy.

The outer cordon troops started withdrawing. Matt and the Deltas held their positions. The airstrike had yet to be confirmed.

A head appeared in a darkened window across the street. Matt locked on it and took up the first pressure on his trigger. Suddenly, a larger figure swooped down and whisked the target out of Matt's crosshairs. His heart slammed against his chest as he realized what he'd just witnessed – a mother pulling her child to safety. The insurgents were using civilians as human shields. The airstrike had to be aborted.

'Blue One Bravo to Gulf 2–6. Be advised there are civilians inside the house. I repeat, there are civilians inside the house,' Matt radioed.

Before the Gulf commander could acknowledge the warning, another HE bomb came screaming out of the compound. This time, it struck a retreating Hummer on the windscreen. Black smoke poured from the vehicle as it lurched to a stop. The door swung open and a charred, smoking torso fell out.

The Gulf commander screamed over the radio. 'This is Gulf 2–6, where the hell is my air support, over!'

'Roger, Gulf 2–6, this is Viper 5–8,' a pilot responded. 'We have the target in sight. Preparing to engage, over.'

The distinctive chop of an Apache gunship riding to the rescue heralded the impending airstrike. Matt yelled into his radio. 'Blue One Bravo to Viper 5–8, be advised there are civilians in that building. I repeat, there are civilians!'

Chapter 3

Four Years Later . . .
British Embassy, Kabul, Afghanistan

The auxiliary staff canteen reeked of day-old cabbage. Matt staked his claim to an empty table and poured a single serving of long-life cream into a mug of tea. A white cloud slowly engulfed the deep tobacco-stained brew, turning it beige. The transformation was more stomach-churning than the sulphurous pong in the air. Everything around him was beige; the prefab buildings in the British Embassy compound, the surrounding concrete blast walls, the rubbish-infested streets beyond. Even the snow-capped mountains overlooking Kabul were tinged with it. The hue synonymous with military life had come to signify the opposite for Matt. Beige was shit jobs in shitholes for washed-up ex-soldiers with no other options. It was the colour of civvy street.

He pulled a paper from his pocket and smoothed it open on the table. The eggshell-tinted walls receded as he lost himself in images of his native Perthshire. A photo of purple heather-speckled hillsides crowned a collection of thumbnails displaying the best of the property for sale; awe-inspiring views; lush green fields; uncut woodland; interiors and exteriors of a three-bedroomed cottage fitted with a wind turbine, rain-water harvester and solar panels. The self-sufficient smallholding was more than a distraction from the beige wilderness Matt had wandered since leaving the Regiment. His entire sense of self-worth hinged on buying it. Right now though, he didn't have a hope in hell of doing so. Sustainable living, once the preserve of ban-the-bomb hippies and other fringe liberals, had become highly fashionable with Britain's privileged classes. Demand for green properties far outstripped supply and the vendors were taking full advantage. There was no way Matt could make a competitive offer – not on his salary. All the qualities that had served him so well as a soldier were of no value outside the military. In the civilian world, money made the man.

Matt turned over the prospectus. He unconsciously rubbed a silver chain discreetly hidden around his neck while he read the handwritten note on the back. *Nathan Carter called about a job that's 'interesting' and 'pays awesome' (his words, not mine). xxx.* He refolded the prospectus. The bloody Yanks had destroyed his life once. There was no way Matt was working with them again, no matter how much money they threw at him.

A music sting from a television soon tested his resolve. The volume from the set-top was barely audible above the radio conversations flowing through his earpiece but it didn't matter. Matt was looking more than he was listening.

A still photo of a man with a straggly beard and shoulder-length dark curls appeared on screen. He was wearing a pakol – a Pashtun flat cap – and holding a rocket-propelled grenade launcher. 'Dead or alive?' asked a deep, animated voice. 'The fate of Pakistan's most wanted terrorist is in question at this hour.' The image was pushed aside by sullen-faced men and women stepping out of limousines. 'The Euro in jeopardy. Finance ministers meet to discuss the latest currency crisis.' The bureaucrats vanished, replaced by underfed women sauntering down a catwalk. 'And the controversy over ultra-thin models heats up. Is bigger more beautiful?' A video collage of war, natural disasters, celebrities and iconic landmarks flew across the screen. The montage dissolved into a shot of an aging American presenter sitting behind a desk. 'Good day. Our top story on SBC this hour; officials in Islamabad claim terrorist Abdullah Qari has been killed in a military operation in Pakistan's tribal belt. But an influential radical cleric claims the alleged mastermind of over a dozen suicide bombings, including one that claimed the lives of seven CIA employees late last year, is still very much alive . . .' The screen split into two boxes. The left held the presenter, the right a neatly groomed male correspondent with two white minarets framed over his shoulder. The banner beneath gave his location: *Live from Islamabad*. '. . . Let's cross now to Islamabad where our correspondent, Eric Riddell is standing by with the story. So, Eric, is he or isn't he?'

'Did they get him?'

Matt looked up. Steve wasn't holding a food tray – a bad sign. 'Get who?'

Steve pulled up a chair. The middle-aged ex-infantry NCO was haggard as always. Coordinating close protection at the embassy had sucked all the life out of him. 'Abdullah Qari.'

'I don't know who you're on about,' said Matt.

Steve pointed to the television. 'They were just talking about him.'

'I wasn't really paying attention.'

'Have you been living in a cave? Abdullah Qari's one of the most wanted terrorists in the world right now.'

'Is he here in Kabul?'

'No. He's the head of some Pakistani Taliban splinter group.'

'Then he's not my problem,' Matt declared.

'Don't you think you should know what's going on around us?' said Steve. 'Considering what you do for a living?'

'That's why I don't follow the news.' Matt tapped his temple. 'It messes with your head.'

'Sounds like a load of bollocks to me,' said Steve.

'I'm dead serious. The news makes you think about the big picture. Next thing you know, you're asking questions like what are we really doing here? And what have we achieved instead of concentrating on your task,' said Matt. 'One second, that's all it takes for an insurgent to whack you.'

'No good ever came from burying your head in the sand.'

'I'm burying it in my job.' Matt cupped his hands around an imaginary sphere. 'All I care about is the little picture right in front of me. That's why I haven't lost a client in four years. Besides,' he gestured to the TV, 'those news people don't know what's going on any more than we do. Hell, for all they know, this Abdullah what's-his-name could be on our side.'

'Now you're talking out your arse.'

Matt sipped his beige tea. 'I assume you didn't come here to talk about current affairs.'

'I didn't.' Steve sat back. 'I heard a rumour you're thinking of leaving us.'

Matt crooked his head and arched his brow. It was as good as verbal confirmation; he was seriously considering it.

'Don't do it,' said Steve. 'You're the only Regiment bloke I've managed to hang on to. If you leave, the whole revolving door thing will start all over again. And even if I could find someone with your skills, there's no guaranteeing they'll get on with the lads. They look up to you, you know.'

Tempting as it was for Matt to see himself through Steve's eyes – a confident ex-Special Forces soldier with an unimpeach-able air of authority – he knew it was all rubbish. 'It's nothing personal. The task's not what it used to be.'

'You may not realize it, but you've got a good thing going here.'

'This job is shite and you know it.'

'There are worse,' Steve countered.

'ShieldGroup treats us like dirt. Four years ago, the rotation on this contract was six weeks in Kabul and a month at home. Now it's nine weeks on and three weeks off at less than half my original pay.'

'So your pay's gone down. It's not like you have a wife and kids to support.'

'This isn't the army, mate. In the real world, money is respect,' said Matt. 'You want to know why I'm the only Regiment lad who's stayed with this task? Because I'm the only one daft enough to put up with ShieldGroup's shite.'

'You can't blame the company. The Foreign Office keeps putting the contract out to tender. ShieldGroup has to cut costs to remain competitive.' Steve raised his hand. 'I know it's unfair. But private security isn't what it used to be. Profits are down, competition is up and the companies that stay afloat are the ones that tighten their belts. Be thankful it's only your wages that have been slashed.'

'I bet the executives back in London are still pulling in shed-loads of cash.'

'ShieldGroup takes good care of this team,' Steve insisted. 'You have comfortable living quarters, you carry top-of-the-line weapons, all our vehicles are level B6/7 armoured with the latest countermeasures. We have great comms systems and an ops room . . .'

Matt's eyes glazed over. 'Everything we have is paid for by the Foreign Office – not ShieldGroup.'

'Who cares where it comes from? You know there are lads on the circuit driving around Kabul in soft-skin vehicles with no kit.'

'Yeah, and a lot of them are working for ShieldGroup.' Matt's disgust was palpable. 'The company sends advisors to Afghanistan armed with nothing but a visa and a plane ticket. I saw a group downtown last week buying weapons – cheap Pakistani knock-offs with crap ammo. They were looking after a building site. ShieldGroup had them living eight to a room in a guesthouse with shit and piss running down the walls.'

'You think the grass is greener elsewhere?' said Steve. 'Like it or not, mate, we're warm bodies in an industry overflowing with warm bodies. There are heaps of lads out of work on the circuit right now. Even those three magic letters after your name don't matter – except to me, of course. I know what an ex-SAS man brings to the table, but the bean-counters in human resources don't.'

Steve was right. They were lucky to be employed. Every day Matt got emails from mates with skills every bit as good as his, asking if there were any spots open on his team or if he could put in a good word for them. The best he could do was forward their CVs to a human resources manager in London who didn't have a clue. As far as ShieldGroup was concerned, all ex-military were the same – expendable. 'OK,' he conceded. 'I'll stick with the task for now. But another pay cut and I'm history.'

'Good man.' Steve rapped his fingers on the table.

Matt knew he was stalling for a reason. 'Is there something else?'

Steve bowed his head. 'Julia wants to go to Camp Phoenix.'

'When?'

'Tonight.'

Julia was a junior media relations officer at the embassy. Why would she need to go to an American military base after dark? 'Is this move really necessary?' asked Matt.

'No,' Steve admitted. 'She wants to play racketball with a girlfriend.'

'Are you taking the piss? Tell her to fuck off.'

'I know the request is out of line . . .'

'You're bloody right it's out of line. I'm sick and tired of diplomats coming here expecting to lead the same life they did back in London. This is a hostile environment, for fuck's sake, not an amusement park.'

Steve's back rounded with shame. 'I've got a wife, a massive mortgage, two kids and an ex-wife who bleeds me dry. I need my job, Matt, and I won't have it for long if I piss off the client. Neither will you.'

'Is that a threat?'

'It's a reality check. We all have to toe the line.'

'If you think you'll get sacked for standing up to the client, just wait until one of them gets killed on your watch,' Matt warned.

'That's why I want you on this one. I know full well how dangerous after-dark vehicle moves are right now. Just do us a favour and take her.'

Matt was sickened. Clients dictating unnecessary, hazardous moves; it was the tail wagging the dog. But that's what his job and pretty much every other task on the circuit had become. 'I'll need two vehicles.'

'You don't need to go all out for Julia. She's IBG.'

'Don't give me that individual bodyguard crap,' said Matt. 'Give me two vehicles or assign someone else.'

'Fine. Take Kevin with you then.'

'And I want a translator too.'

'Don't tear the arse out of it. The drivers can do whatever translating you need.'

'They're unreliable,' said Matt. 'You know how nervous the

Yanks are these days. The last thing I want is to be sat like a sitting duck outside Camp Phoenix because our drivers don't speak the same language as the Afghan guards on the outer cordon.'

'All right then. Take Ali.'

'I want Khalid.'

'Now I know you're trying to be a pain in my arse,' said Steve. 'Khalid's not even Afghan. He's Pakistani.'

'It doesn't matter. No one fucks with him. You'd know that if you ever bothered to leave the ops room,' Matt taunted.

'And get whacked?' Steve balked. 'I don't get paid enough.'

Chapter 4

Heathrow Airport

Emma Cameron opened her passport and placed it on the counter for inspection. 'I'm kind of in a hurry.'

The immigration officer didn't care. She flipped it shut and looked disdainfully at the American seal on the cover. 'What is your destination?'

'Islamabad.'

The officer reopened the passport and searched for the appropriate visa. Her lips pursed as she read the stamps; Afghanistan, Iraq, Pakistan, Yemen, Saudi Arabia. It was a veritable catalogue of global jihad. She turned back to the photo page and rotated her eyes between the picture and the live specimen standing before her. 'What is the nature of your travel?'

Emma raised her shawl around her shoulders. The pink pashmina lent a rosy hue to her pale skin. She knew what the officer was thinking. What possible business could a blue-eyed, blonde-haired American woman have in such places? 'Business. I'm a journalist.'

'What newspaper do you write for?'

'Television journalist,' Emma corrected. 'I'm a correspondent for SBC.'

The officer frowned and resumed her inspection. The reaction was like water off a duck's back to Emma. The SBC brand was as American as Coca-Cola and, thanks to the Bush years, just as vilified abroad.

'Your visa is out of date,' the officer finally declared.

'That's because you're looking at an old one.' Emma grabbed the passport, found the page she'd originally presented and slammed it down. 'Here. It was issued yesterday.'

The immigration officer scrutinized the unusual visa. Islamabad had been tightening the noose around the press corps for months. Emma had been granted six months' multiple entry. She stamped the passport and handed it back. Emma threw it into her red laptop bag and checked her watch. 'Fucking Heathrow,' she grumbled, loud enough for the officer to hear. She rushed along the moving pavement, weaving in and out of seasoned travellers and harried families. Between circling the airport waiting for a gate to open and queuing in the Non-EU Passport Holders' line, she had only thirty minutes to link up with her source before her flight to Islamabad boarded.

Emma had almost convinced herself to bin the meeting when a television gave her pause. A pretty female was reporting from a rooftop location somewhere in the world. The correspondent's voice rose and fell, punching certain words and de-emphasizing others, as if she were reading to school children. There were dozens like her all over the American news networks; interchangeable pieces of eye-candy elevating speculation to the realm of fact. Emma knew such creatures intimately because she was their queen. If she kept her appointment however, she just might lose that heavy crown.

The conveyor belt spat her out into the heart of the terminal. The cattle-class passengers were wandering in and out of duty-free shops and sitting cheek-by-jowl on impossibly uncomfortable benches. The well-heeled had retreated to the Business Class lounges. Normally, Emma refused to support the airline caste system by joining them, but on this day, she had no choice.

'Emma? Emma!'

The hairs on the back of her neck stiffened. The nasal, baritone voice was unmistakably familiar. 'Patriot Pete' Riorden.

'Emma! Emma!'

'Fuck, fuck, fuck,' she muttered. As much as she wanted to avoid a reunion, Emma's sense of decency compelled her to respond. She summoned a smile and turned. 'Riorden?' She hardly recognized the former news star. Loose skin scalloped his once trademark jaw line. His legendary hair had thinned to grey, greasy wisps.

Riorden stooped over to kiss her. 'I thought it was you.'

Emma turned her right cheek to avoid an embarrassing head joust. Riorden had always been awkward with basic social interaction even when he was on top. 'How are you?'

'I'm doing great,' he said. 'So are you coming or going?'

'Going.' Emma didn't offer more details.

'Where?'

'Islamabad.'

'Me too,' said Riorden as if the shared destination brought them level with one another professionally. 'I've got some meetings to take there and then I'm off to Quetta. Are you on the one-thirty?'

Emma briefly considered lying but dismissed the idea. Airports were fishbowls. 'Yeah.'

'I'm on standby. I'd say let's sit together but the flight's overbooked and it's not looking too promising for me.'

Emma welcomed the reprieve. Riorden was almost surely flying coach now. The last thing she wanted was to rub it in his face by comparing seat numbers.

'Does the network have a full-time bureau in Pakistan now?' Riorden asked.

'It's still a temporary set-up but it looks like it's going that way. We've had a correspondent there since last summer.'

'I saw Eric Riddell doing a report from Islamabad this morning,' said Riorden. 'You two are close friends, aren't you?'

'We went to school together,' Emma confirmed. 'That's how I got my start with SBC. Eric recommended me.'

'Now I remember,' said Riorden. 'I've been so busy lately with my new company that I've lost touch with a lot of the old gang.'

Emma raised her watch; a not-so-subtle signal that she needed to go.

'MISA,' Riorden blurted. 'It stands for Media Intelligence South Asia.'

'Sounds fascinating.'

An expression flashed across Riorden's face and vanished as quickly; a toxic combination of envy and resentment. It occurred to Emma that she must have sounded patronizing. After all, Riorden had devoted his entire life to a profession she'd been playing at for only three years. 'You are so lucky you aren't with SBC now. There's no real news on our air anymore, at least not since you left the network. Just lame-ass talking heads and conservative pundits with small penises.'

Riorden smiled. 'Better not let your fans hear you talk that way – Satellite Dish.'

Emma cringed. 'I can't stand that name.'

'Don't look a gift horse in the mouth,' Riorden advised. 'Nicknames are power, Emma. They make you a brand in your own right, independent of any network. If I hadn't been called Patriot Pete, no one would know who I am anymore.'

Emma really didn't have time for a lecture from a disgraced news personality. 'Well, best of luck with your new media venture.'

Riorden put his foot in the door. 'MISA's more than new media. I've got a network of stringers in the tribal areas of Pakistan and Afghanistan. There's nothing else like it in the region.'

'Sounds like you're onto a winner.' Emma lowered her tone to draw a line under the exchange.

Riorden barrelled on. 'We do ground truth assessments, polling, we even offer paying clients behind-the-scenes access to opposition groups and other stakeholders traditional western media rarely interact with.'

Riorden was selling MISA hard. Emma knew it had to be leading up to something.

'All we need now is a news talent with name recognition to put us on the map.'

He was trying to recruit her! God, was he delusional. 'Well, I look forward to seeing you back on air,' said Emma.

'Oh, I'm far too busy running the show behind the scenes to be the face of MISA.' Riorden looked her in the eye. 'You know, if you ever feel like leaving SBC, I've got a job waiting for you.'

'It's tempting,' Emma lied. There was nothing at all enticing about the offer – and not just because Riorden was making it. She was trying to escape her news prison, not jump to another cell.

Emma felt a vibration in her pocket. She put down her bag and checked both her handsets. The message had fed through to her BlackBerry. *Go 2 lft shower cubicle*. A complete sentence with token abbreviations; the style was definitely in keeping with her source.

'Let me guess. It's New York,' said Riorden.

Emma searched the benches behind him, looking for men or even women who fitted her idea of a Deep Throat. The faces blended together into a characterless mass. 'I've really got to take this.'

'I understand.' Riorden stepped aside to let her pass. 'But think about my offer.'

Chapter 5

Hanna Lake, Baluchistan Province, Pakistan

A shoal of golden fish circled the boat. Soheil was mesmerized. 'I thought such beauty only existed in paradise.'

'All that is beautiful on earth exists a thousand-fold in paradise, my son,' said the mullah. 'That is why Pashtun warriors and all Mujahideen do not fear death.'

Soheil stared into the turquoise water, imagining an afterlife of crystal lakes, gilded creatures and virgins. 'What if I do not fall on the field of battle?'

'Fear not,' the greying cleric removed his glasses and tilted his face to the sun, 'Allah shall give you the death you deserve.'

The words dissolved Soheil's vision. A smack on the water swept the last of the palette clean. The boat's third occupant, a bushy-bearded Baluch youth, was attempting to bludgeon a fish with his foot. Soheil tried to be patient with the simpleton, reminding himself that they were brothers-in-arms now. True, the Baluch were less pious and sophisticated than his own Pashtun tribesmen, but at least they were brave and obedient. It was more important than ever that Mullah Maulana be surrounded by such men. The great cleric had many enemies. This trip to Hanna Lake was the first outing he'd taken in months.

Even with the Baluch in tow, the day was surpassing all of Soheil's expectations. Mullah Maulana had been exceedingly generous; buying them lunch and renting a paddle boat to explore the reservoir. The young Pashtun took it as a good omen. Surely Allah had forgiven his sins for him to have received such gifts.

Soheil placed his feet on the pedals and started cycling. They'd have to return to the madrassa soon and he wanted to get a closer look at the irrigation dam on the lake's eastern shore. Soheil marvelled at the great wall rising out of the water. He'd once dreamed of engineering such remarkable structures; great monuments that would bear witness to his life long after he'd passed. Now he knew there were more noble paths to immortality.

Soheil gazed at the taupe hills overlooking the reservoir. The patchwork of cracked earth reminded him of his native village in Kurram Agency. He recalled the life he'd left behind to become a Mujaheed. Even by the standards of the tribal areas, Soheil had been born into a very poor family; ten mouths to feed – seven of them female. He and his older brother should have contributed to the family purse as soon as they could work, but their father, a good man and devout Muslim, wanted more for his sons. When a madrassa opened near the village, he insisted they attend. It was the only formal schooling available.

Back then, of course, Soheil found reciting Koranic verses very boring. He wanted to be an engineer not an imam. But like many privileges that are given rather than earned, he didn't value his education until it was taken away. When his father died, Soheil's older brother insisted he quit school and take a job in a brick factory to support the family. The young Pashtun worked from sun up till sun down, stoking fires with old tyres to heat the ovens. He'd return home, covered in black soot with one hundred rupees in his pocket; the equivalent of one American dollar. Even that pitiful compensation passed through his hands like water.

Custom dictated that he turn his wages over to the family patri-
arch – his older brother.

Soheil longed to escape his brother's hold and become master
of his own house. He dreamed of taking a bride; a beautiful,
round-hipped, full-breasted beauty who would cook his meals,
wash his clothes and do as he ordered. But how could he marry
when he hardly earned enough to put food on the table, let alone
amass dowries for six worthless sisters?

In the summer of his eleventh year, his life changed forever. An
old classmate from the madrassa told him about a camp in
Waziristan, a place where young Pashtun of exceptional character could learn about Islam. His brother objected and a terrible
row ensued. Soheil accused him of placing money before Islam.
His brother called him a fool and warned that he'd end up dead.

Certain Allah would approve of the soul-saving pilgrimage,
Soheil left home with only the clothes on his back. When he
arrived at the camp, he promised the amir he would find some
way to pay. But Abdullah Qari had no interest in money. He
asked only that Soheil study Koran and learn how to become a
true Pashtun Mujaheed. 'Allah has called you here for a reason,'
Amir Qari told him. 'Prove you are worthy of his grace. Learn
about your people and the true Islam.'

Soheil quickly embraced all the camp had to offer. It was great
fun running through an obstacle course shooting a rifle. He
imagined his enemies cowering in fear as he picked them off one
by one. He felt most invincible during explosives training. The
bombs he was learning to build were highly complex; not even
the infidel armies with all their technology could defend against
such advanced weapons. But of all the lessons Soheil received,
none inspired him more than the daily lectures delivered by Amir
Qari.

Before the camp, Soheil had known little of his people and

their struggle for independence. Amir Qari explained how over a hundred years ago, when the British Empire ruled South Asia, a man named Durand had hatched an evil plot to weaken the Pashtun tribes. He proposed a treaty that would divide them between what are now called Afghanistan and Pakistan. The resulting Durand Line was a disaster for Pashtunistan and for Islam. No good Muslim could ever recognize such a travesty. Yet the wicked government in Islamabad, in its desire to keep the Pashtun at heel, insisted on preserving the infidel's creation. Soheil had always believed Pakistan's army and its government defended Muslims. Amir Qari opened his eyes. Islamabad's support for the West's crusade against their Pashtun brothers in southern and eastern Afghanistan proved that Pakistan cared nothing for its Muslim brothers. A true Islamic nation would *never* support the infidel.

Soheil grew fanatical about reuniting his people and creating a true Islamic nation that would liberate Muslims throughout the world. The Emirate of Pashtunistan would be a model state, governed not by democracy, a western abhorrence, but by Sharia law. He tackled his lessons with the devotion of a zealot, determined to earn the privilege of fighting for Amir Qari. But in his eagerness to please his leader, Soheil had committed a vile sin. Now he feared he would never become a true Mujaheed.

'What troubles you, my son?'

The young Pashtun did not want to reveal his true thoughts to Mullah Maulana. Nor did he want to sin further by lying. 'I was thinking of Amir Qari,' said Soheil. 'They say he is dead.'

'Do not allow the infidels' lies to weaken your faith. Allah watches over Amir Qari. Pray for him and all warriors of Islam.' The mullah raised his arm for assistance.

Soheil helped the old cleric sit up. 'When shall I be allowed to fight?'

The mullah donned his gold-rimmed glasses. 'A Mujaheed's strength lies not in his sword but in his faith. That is why you were sent to me.' Soheil bowed his head in shame. 'Take pride in all you have achieved,' said the cleric. 'I have seen your faith grow strong.'

Soheil took heart from the mullah's words. 'Do we have time to see the great wall?'

The mullah raised his eyes to the dam. 'Do you admire this?'

'Very much,' said Soheil. The mullah appeared disappointed with his answer. 'The engineering is most fine, is it not?'

'Do not admire this work,' the mullah reprimanded. 'The British built it when they occupied this land. All marks left by the infidel must be erased; whether a dam or a line on a map. Until that day comes the Pashtun shall never be free.' He placed his hand on the Baluch's shoulder. 'Your people have suffered as well, my son. That is why we have joined forces. Together we shall defeat the infidels and make our nations whole again.'

The Baluch answered the call to arms. 'We shall fight for our homeland!'

Soheil was fuming. How dare that donkey try to show him up. 'Our struggle shall set all Muslims free!'

The mullah stared through the young Pashtun. 'Do you say these words to court my favour?'

'No,' Soheil insisted. 'I would lay down my life to liberate my people. For only when Pashtunistan is liberated shall all Muslims taste freedom.'

The cleric beamed with approval. 'Amir Qari shall hear of this, my son.'

Chapter 6

British Embassy, Kabul, Afghanistan

'Let's go then,' said Julia.

Matt blocked the door of her living quarters. 'You can't go out like that. You need to change.'

Julia glanced down at her outfit – a pair of white Lycra mini-shorts and a matching cardigan. 'What on earth for?'

'Because you're dressed inappropriately.' Matt picked up a set of body armour. The neglected flak jacket was covered in dust. 'And put this on too while you're at it.'

'We're taking an armoured car,' Julia sniffed.

'As your security advisor I'm asking you to please wear your body armour and cover up. You need to respect the environment in which you're operating.'

'You make it sound like we're sitting in a foxhole.' Julia looked past him to the courtyard outside. It was snowing. 'Though you may have a point.' She grabbed a coat from a wall hook and threw it on. The thigh-skimming parka gave the impression she was naked underneath.

'You do know this is a *Muslim* country,' said Matt.

'We're going to an *American* base, not a mosque.' Julia picked up her racket and waved it in his face. 'Step aside. I have a court reserved.'

Matt slung the flak jacket over his arm and followed her outside. The ground was fast disappearing beneath a blanket of white. 'What if we have an accident on the way to Camp Phoenix? Do you really want to be standing on a street corner in Kabul freezing your arse off?'

Julia turned around. Her ponytail lashed her face before swinging back into place. 'Isn't that why you're here? To make sure things like that *don't* happen?'

Matt gave up. There was no reasoning with the likes of Julia. He'd seen too many diplomats just like her come and go over the years.

A pair of white Toyota 4×4s were fuelled up and waiting with the engines running. Kevin and Khalid were standing beside them. Like Matt, the two men were cleanly shaven and dressed in the standard uniform of the embassy's non-diplomatic staff: cargo trousers, heavy-soled hiking boots, fleece-lined Gortex jackets over body armour. They all appeared interchangeable, save for two key differences rarely detected by the casual observer. Matt and Kevin were concealing German-made Heckler & Koch 9mm pistols and had hand-held radios strapped to their belts for one-to-one communications. As a 'local' hire, Khalid wasn't permitted to carry weapons – or listen in on the security team's conversations.

The translator recoiled as Julia rounded the corner. 'Which one is for us?' she asked, oblivious to Khalid's reaction to her.

'We're taking both,' said Matt.

'All this is for me? I should always travel after sundown,' she remarked.

'You're riding up front with me and Khalid.' Matt shoved the body armour at her. 'I'm not going to ask you again.'

Julia took the flak jacket reluctantly. 'Hurry up. I don't want to be late.'

While she headed to her vehicle, Matt briefed his team. 'I

checked all the medical packs. They're good to go.' He looked at Kevin. 'Do you have your personal trauma pack?'

Kevin confirmed with a nod.

Matt turned to Khalid. 'Have the drivers been fully briefed?'

Khalid didn't answer. The translator was still staring at the spot where Julia had been standing. 'She is naked.' He said this as if no one else had noticed. 'Does she think she is in England still? Does she think she is Lady Godiva?'

'Technically she's not naked – at least not from the waist up,' Kevin chuckled.

Khalid was not amused. 'I could see her bloody fanny. I am a Muslim. I cannot drive a naked woman through Kabul.'

Matt was caught out by the objection. Khalid had encountered worse and never complained. 'Don't go pulling the Muslim card,' he said. 'I've seen you cheating during Ramadan.'

Kevin laughed. It infected Matt and finally Khalid. 'I may not be the most devout Muslim,' the translator conceded. 'But I am not stupid. She is dangerous, Matt. You cannot take her to Camp Phoenix. If we are stopped and someone sees her, there will be a riot.'

'That's why I asked for you,' said Matt. 'To make sure no one stops us.'

'Can you not take another translator?'

'Sorry, mate.' Khalid opened his mouth. Matt stopped him before he could say any more. 'End of discussion.'

Matt took up position in the front passenger seat and kept the door open while he performed his final checks. He unzipped a canvas bag stashed at his feet. A Heckler & Koch 5.56 assault rifle was nestled inside, ready to be grabbed at a moment's notice. He reached his arm around the back of the seat to make sure his trauma pack was close to hand. Instead of a small, spongy lump, he felt the hard rounded edge of a Kevlar-covered plate.

He turned. 'Enough's enough now,' he said, picking up the flak jacket. 'Put it on.'

Julia crossed her arms defiantly. 'No.'

Matt gave up and shoved the body armour between her seat and the door.

'What are you doing?' she protested.

'Giving you an extra layer of protection in case we're attacked,' he grunted. He faced forward again and picked up a handset from the dashboard. 'Hello, Zero, this is Bravo 1–5. Radio check.'

Steve's crackling response from the embassy's ops room filled the cab. 'Roger, Bravo 1–5. Zero Lima Charlie.'

'Bravo 1–5 Lima Charlie, towards Charlie Papa,' Matt continued.

'Roger, towards Charlie Papa,' Steve confirmed.

Julia edged over the invisible line dividing her and Khalid. The translator went rigid with disapproval. 'Do you know what they're saying?' she asked.

Khalid refused to respond.

Matt returned the handset to its cradle and shook his left wrist. A pressel switch dropped from his cuff. The line was attached to his hand-held radio. 'Bravo 1–9, this is Bravo 1–5, radio check.'

Kevin's voice responded over Matt's earpiece. 'Bravo 1–9 Lima Charlie.'

Julia tapped the back of Matt's shoulder.

'What?' he said, annoyed.

'Who is Charlie Papa?' she asked.

'It's not a who.' Matt didn't elaborate.

'Tell me what it means,' Julia hounded.

Matt twisted around. 'Charlie Papa is code for Camp Phoenix, not that it should concern you.'

'Don't be so sure.' Julia smiled coyly. 'I'm writing a book.' She waited for Matt to follow up with a question. When he didn't, she gave him an answer regardless. 'It's about my time in Afghanistan.'

Matt couldn't give a toss what Julia got up to in her off hours. But he didn't want her book coming back to bite him on the arse. 'I'd appreciate it if you left me out of it.'

'Don't flatter yourself. Besides, I'm not using real names. It's a *roman à clef.* That's a fictionalized account of a real-life experience.'

'I know what a *roman à clef* is.'

Julia doubted the claim with a patronizing smile. 'The book chronicles a year in the life of a fun-loving English girl who takes a posting in Afghanistan.'

'Sounds gripping,' Matt deadpanned.

'My publishers think so. They had no idea what a fabulous social life women have in Kabul. The "Tarts and Taliban" parties, the restaurants . . .' she shielded her face with her hand, a hollow gesture to avoid shocking Khalid. '. . . the men,' she mouthed. 'My publisher calls it "Bridget Jones meets body armour".'

Matt was lost for words. It was bad enough Julia had zero regard for the real hazards of operating in a hostile environment without glamorizing her recklessness to others. Six years in the most elite military regiment in the world and for what? To look after a bunch of clueless, condescending prats who thought Kabul was one big party.

Chapter 7

Heathrow Airport

The din of the terminal faded as Emma entered the sound-proofed sanctuary of the Business Class lounge. Her fellow travellers averted their eyes, pretending not to notice her; though she could feel them on her back as soon as she passed – leering, inspecting, measuring her against her expletive-free, televised doppelgänger. Normally she tuned out unwanted attention, but on this occasion Emma noted every glance, no matter how innocuous. She was checking for reactions or even a lack of reaction; anything that breached the boundaries of common curiosity. She was searching for her source.

She followed the signs for the showers into a corridor. The orange, convex walls rose up on either side, blinding her to anyone approaching from the front or the rear. She thought she heard footsteps closing in from behind. Panicked, she rubbed her neck to calm herself but all she found was bare skin. The good luck charm that normally assuaged her anxiety was protecting someone else now.

Emma whipped around. No one was there. The empty space taunted her. Who was she kidding? She wasn't a real journalist. All she did was regurgitate wire copy and the *New York Times*. She couldn't even take credit for her 'exclusive' interviews. Local fixers and other behind-the-scene producers set those up. The sad truth was, Emma had never handled a news source in her life, let alone an anonymous one claiming to have classified information. For all she knew, he – or she – could be a fantasist or worse, a stalker. Whoever it was, they didn't seem particularly savvy. Google Mail accounts under different names, cryptic text messages and now dropping information in a Business Class lounge. It all smacked of a Walter Mitty trying to look like an insider. Then again, maybe all whistle-blowers were this amateur. How would she know?

An illuminated arrow pointed right down a hallway where the showers were located. Emma steeled herself and carried on. As she rounded the bend, she was beat to the turn by a man walking from the other direction. With his heavy, unkempt blond beard he cut a strange figure among the clean-cut suits in the lounge.

Emma followed him down the off-shoot, searching for an opening. His shoulders were massive. When he reached for the door to the shower room, she had no choice but to press her red laptop bag to her chest and duck under his arm.

'Excuse me,' she said, pushing the door open with her back. She locked it behind her and raised her bag like a shield; as if Italian leather, a computer and make-up would offer any sort of protection. Emma tiptoed through the changing area, eyes pivoting left and right. She was certain she glimpsed a shadow moving inside the shower cubicle. She cracked open the door and jumped aside, prepared to slug whoever emerged with her laptop case. No one came charging out. Emma peered inside. The shadow had been cast by a soap dispenser.

She put down her bag and got to work. The most obvious place to begin was a stack of towels resting on an overhead rack. One by one she shook them out, discarding them into a heap on the floor. There was nothing folded inside. She pushed the wall tiles, hoping one would give way to a secret compartment. They were all cemented in place.

A shower bench was the only remaining possibility. She tried pulling it away from the wall but it was bolted in place. She ran her fingers beneath the seat. Six inches in she hit a patch of sticky residue. 'Gross,' she muttered. Her disgust vanished when she felt a hard lump.

Emma crouched down and looked up at the obstruction. It was a data storage stick. She ripped it free of its taped cocoon and examined it. The mark on the cap stopped her cold: SBC's logo.

A sickening thought occurred to her. Had all the cat-and-mouse been a set-up? Was someone at SBC trying to destroy her credibility? It wasn't out of the question. Riorden had always claimed he'd been undone that way.

She tapped the stick against her hand. If it was a hoax, some-one had gone to an awful lot of trouble to make her look incompetent. The information on the storage device might just reveal the person or persons responsible. She took her laptop from her bag, fired it up and plugged in the stick. A compressed file with dozens of documents appeared on the screen. She opened one at random. A picture slowly rendered; an aerial shot of buildings with convex roofs surrounded by barren land. Judging from the airstrip running next to them it was probably some kind of military installation but that didn't prove anything. Classified images were easily downloaded from Google Earth.

She tried another file to see if it would prove more definitive. A written document unfolded. It appeared to be some kind of payment authorization. The more Emma read the less convinced she was of its authenticity. Then she saw the signature.

Emma's heart nearly flat-lined. She ripped the stick out of the port and jumped back from the computer, panting. She looked at the screen. The document was still burned on it.

Terrified, she grabbed the laptop, raised it over her head and slammed it down on the bench. She kept pounding until the motherboard spilled from the casing.

Chapter 8

Kabul, Afghanistan

Julia drew up her parka around her neck. 'Could you please close your door? I'm freezing.'

Matt pulled the handle and braced for the dreaded double click of the heavy armour locking into place. It was like sealing himself in a coffin. He wrestled his claustrophobia back into his subconscious and concentrated on the dangers ahead. The snow was coming down in piles now; the last dump before the spring thaw. The flakes streaking past the embassy's perimeter lights had gathered on the razor wire, burying the teeth beneath fluffy, undulating mounds. The beauty was misleading. It was hard enough bumping through Kabul in a three-ton armoured 4×4 in clear conditions, let alone on slick, icy roads that were never gritted or ploughed. Matt checked the sky. The clouds were thick and low, the worst conditions possible. If they were targeted by an IED the accumulation would tamp the explosion, intensifying its destructive power.

The driver pulled between two Victorian-era cannons and turned left. Matt kept his eyes peeled as they looped their way through the secured enclave. Most of the local Afghan guards and ex-Gurkhas working in support of the various embassies in the area had taken shelter in wooden shacks. Too bad the Taliban didn't take snow days as well.

They cleared the ghost town and headed onto the open road.

The weather had thinned the traffic considerably. There were no bicycles or donkey carts; just a handful of lorries, 4×4s and cars. The lack of vehicles heightened Matt's suspicions towards those that were braving the storm.

A lorry with brass chains strung along its chassis drove toward them. The jingly was a local vehicle, the type used to haul and deliver goods. Matt scanned the tin-roofed shops lining the road. They weren't accepting deliveries tonight; all the shutters were drawn. 'Bravo 1–9. One hundred up on the right; large lorry. Be aware,' he radioed to Kevin.

He kept eyes on the lorry until it passed. VBIEDs topped Matt's list of security concerns during vehicle moves. Roadside bombs and nutters in explosive vests deploying on foot ran a close second and third. The so-called countermeasures on his 4×4 that promised to disrupt mobile signals initiating IEDs did nothing to allay his fears. As he'd learned in Iraq, no amount of technology can stop a determined insurgent.

Matt checked in with the ops room. 'Hello, Zero. This is Bravo 1–5, towards green one seven.'

'Excuse me,' Julia bellowed from the backseat. 'What's a green one seven?'

'Roger, Bravo 1–5, towards green one seven,' Steve responded.

'It's a map coordinate,' said Matt.

'What kind of map?'

Matt's irritation was fast turning to anger. 'A spotted map,' he explained, hoping it would shut her up.

'Do they differ from regular maps?'

Matt snapped. 'It's not my job to furnish you with material for your book, Julia. My job – my sole job right now – is to deliver you to Camp Phoenix unharmed so you can play racket-ball or whatever leisure activity it is that you found so pressing that you had to risk your life and mine and the rest of the team's by dragging us through a snow storm at night. So unless you have a question that pertains directly to your immediate safety, I'd appreciate it if you would stop yapping and let me get on with my work.'

'How dare you speak to me like that.' Julia was indignant. 'You wouldn't dream of taking that tone with a man.'

'You're right,' said Matt. 'If you were a man, I'd chin you.'

Khalid stifled a laugh. Julia became more enraged. 'I have more of a right to be here than you . . .'

Matt tuned out Julia and honed in on a taxi idling on the edge of a lot. There were no passengers in the vehicle – just a single driver. It couldn't have just dropped someone. The JCBs, cranes and other building equipment for hire were chained down for the night. He radioed Kevin. 'Bravo 1–5 to Bravo 1–9. Eighty up on the left. Yellow taxi, one up. Be aware.'

Julia talked over him. '. . . I read Central Asian history at Oxford. I've studied Dari . . .'

'Your fancy degree won't keep you alive,' said Matt.

'You're just jealous. I bet no one in your family has ever been to university.'

The comment riled something deep within Matt. His face contorted into a superior, patrician scowl that rendered the young diplomat dumb. 'You know nothing about my family, Julia.' He caged his Mr Hyde and radioed their position back to the ops room. 'Zero, Bravo 1–5, one mike from Charlie Papa,' he said, indicating they were one mile from Camp Phoenix.

The Afghan guards manning the camp's outer security cordon pointed them toward a holding area. Matt scanned the queue of vehicles. It was the exact scenario he had feared. Insurgents could take their good, sweet time assessing the line, deciding how best to attack. He radioed an alternative plan to Kevin. 'Bravo 1–5 to Bravo 1–9, we're going foxtrot to Charlie Papa.

Turn around and wait for us down the road.' He grabbed his trauma bag from the backseat. 'Tell the driver to wait with Kevin's vehicle,' he said to Khalid. 'We're walking Julia the rest of the way.'

'I think it is best if I stay with the driver,' said the translator.

Matt threw the bag over his shoulder and checked his 9mm with his right hand to make sure it was tucked discreetly under his shirt and coat. 'You're coming with us.'

'But Kevin may require my help.'

'Forget it.' Matt gestured to the Afghan guards outside the inner cordon. 'I need you to get us past those blokes.' He stepped into the open air and assessed the security. The fortifications were typical of a military installation. Double rows of twelve-foot-high concrete blast walls interspersed with Hesco baskets lined the perimeter of the camp. A chicane of low concrete barriers paved the final one hundred yards to the front gate.

Julia got out and started practising her swing. She'd left her flak jacket in the vehicle. 'If you're not going to wear your body armour at least carry it with you,' said Matt.

She pointed with her racket. 'Camp Phoenix is right there.'

'Yeah – and it could be mortared, it could be rocketed, or fifty angry Taliban could come climbing over the walls,' Matt argued.

Julia rolled her eyes. '*Please.*'

'You do realize this is a war zone?'

Julia ignored him and kept swinging, unaware of the Afghan soldiers ogling her bare legs.

Khalid asked the ANA guards a question in Dari. One stopped leering at Julia long enough to answer.

'They are only allowing American vehicles inside the base,' the translator explained to Matt. 'No exceptions.'

'I figured as much. Tell them Julia's a British diplomat and that we'd like to walk her up to the front gate.'

Khalid put the question to the guards. They objected. Matt unearthed two credentials from his coat – an identification card from the British Embassy and a security pass issued by ISAF, NATO's International Security Assistance Force in Afghanistan. Neither impressed the Afghans.

'Allow me,' said Khalid. The translator produced a worn photograph of himself and another man standing in front of the Afghan national flag. The guards immediately stepped aside.

'Who is that in the picture?' asked Matt.

'My uncle.' Khalid flashed a cagey grin. 'He is the head of criminal investigations for the Kabul police.'

Matt laughed. No wonder no one fucked with Khalid.

The snow crunched beneath their boots, drowning the ambient noise from the base. Matt stepped over the first chicane and held out his hand to assist Julia. She brushed it aside and mounted the barrier herself. As they worked their way toward the entrance, Matt periodically checked the blast walls to the right. Calculations flashed through his head; force per square metre and other formulas that allegedly measured how great an explosion the walls could withstand.

A woman waved to them from behind the gate. She too was wearing a parka over a tennis skirt. 'Be with you in a second,' Julia called. Her expression soured when she turned to Matt. 'I'll take it from here.'

'I can't leave you until you're inside the base,' said Matt. 'Then you're the Yanks' problem.'

'Spare me the ridiculous protocol,' Julia moaned. 'I'm more than cap—'

A barrage of rifle fire from the outer cordon shut her up. Matt reacted immediately, seizing Julia by the shoulders and dragging her toward a blast wall. Gunfire mixed with Kevin's voice in Matt's earpiece. 'Contact! Contact! Get into cover!'

A white Toyota saloon came barrelling through the Afghan checkpoint. Matt knew exactly what they were up against: a VBIED targeting the front gate of Camp Phoenix. He threw Julia behind the blast wall and dived on top of her. 'Cover your ears and open your mouth,' he commanded, pressing her hands to the side of her head. He checked behind him to make sure Khalid had taken cover. The translator was nowhere to be seen.

Matt climbed off Julia. 'Hold your position,' he ordered. He looked between the two rows of defensive walls. No one was hiding in the empty spaces. He crawled to the edge of the blast wall and poked his head out. He hoped Khalid wasn't crouching behind a chicane. The barriers would fly like toothpicks once the bomb detonated.

The sight that greeted him was even more disturbing. Khalid was still in the chicane but he wasn't cowering. He was standing behind a barrier, aiming a Glock 17 at the oncoming VBIED. How the hell had he got his hands on a pistol? 'Khalid!' Matt yelled. 'Move to cover!'

Khalid ignored the warning and fired fast double taps at the VBIED. The bullets ripped through the bonnet and shattered the windscreen but they failed to disable the vehicle or the insurgent behind the wheel.

The back tyres spun out as the bomber turned into the chicane. 'Move to cover, Khalid!' Matt called again. But the translator refused to give up. With the cool head of an experienced marksman, he re-aimed his weapon but before he could operate the trigger, bursts of automatic fire erupted all around him. The US troops inside Phoenix and the ANA soldiers on the outer cordon were both trying to take out the VBIED. Khalid was trapped in crossfire.

'Get down!' Matt yelled. But Khalid had pressed his luck too far. A bullet struck him, tearing a chunk out of his thigh. He crashed to the ground, wounded, exposed and unable to move.

Matt's eyes shifted to the VBIED. It was less than twenty yards from the gate. With no thought for his own safety, he jumped into the maelstrom. The crack and thump of high-velocity rounds circled him. Bullets ricocheted off the concrete barriers, spewing fine concrete dust over the virgin snow. He reached Khalid and dragged him toward cover. The wounded translator was still clinging tenaciously to his Glock.

A chilling crash signalled the moment of truth; the bomber had breached the final chicane. With a Herculean heave, Matt pulled Khalid behind the blast wall.

The VBIED detonated with a blinding flash. The overpressure from the explosion moved through Matt, boxing his ears with a painful WOOMPH. The ground trembled and a THUMP sounded. It was the VBIED's engine block slamming into the spot where Khalid had fallen.

A cloud of debris swept the area, obscuring everything. Matt's traumatized ears echoed with muted cries from US soldiers: *Man Down! Man Down! . . . It's a fucking come-on!* He looked at Khalid. The translator was alive but his leg was haemorrhaging severely. The femoral artery had been hit. He could die within minutes.

Matt shoved his knee in Khalid's groin to stem the flow of blood. 'Hang in there, mate.' He wrestled a bandage from his trauma pack with one hand and radioed Kevin with the other. 'Bravo 1–9, this is Bravo 1–5. Man down. Man down. Kilo has arterial bleeding to a leg wound.' He shoved the bandage into Khalid's thigh. 'Don't worry. Phoenix has a great medical facility. The Yanks will fix you right up.'

Khalid grabbed Matt's forearm. 'I shall never forget what you have done.'

Matt's face flooded with guilt. He should have resigned before agreeing to the vehicle move. Now Khalid was paying for his lack of integrity. But when he looked the translator in the eye, he didn't see a helpless victim, but a warrior full of defiance. 'Nice Glock by the way.'

'It was made in Austria,' Khalid said through clenched teeth. 'Not a cheap copy.'

'Keep a hold of it because if that VBIED was a come-on, I'm sending you back out there.' Matt looked over his shoulder to check on Julia. She'd wandered off. He looked around frantically. He spotted her walking through the ruins of the chicane, covered in white dust, her coat missing. 'Julia!' he called to her. 'Get back behind the wall!'

She turned in circles, trying to pinpoint the voice. Matt needed to retrieve her but he couldn't let up the pressure on Khalid's leg. 'Julia! Julia!' he shouted. She stopped. For a brief second, he thought he'd got through to her. But she wasn't responding to him. Something was blocking her path. Julia's expression morphed from wonder to confusion as she tried to decipher the obstacle, turning to horror when she finally realized what it was: the dismembered torso of a soldier. She started screaming: short, ear-splitting shrieks like a siren wailing. The high-pitched cries agitated the US troops who had formed a human barrier around the blast site. Their faces were taut and their weapons poised to shoot. Matt feared Julia would be shot if she didn't shut up.

Kevin came running out of the haze carrying a full medical pack. 'Are you injured?' he called to Julia.

'Over here!' Matt shouted. Kevin ran to assist. 'It's his femoral artery,' Matt explained. 'Take over here. I'll get Julia.' He swapped his knee for Kevin's and ran to his screaming client. 'You're all right,' he said to Julia. 'You're safe. Don't worry. I'll get you out of here.' But there was no consoling the hysterical diplomat.

The woman who had waved to them from behind the gate barged through the line of soldiers, cursing. Though also covered in dust, unlike Julia she was in full command of her faculties. She took the young diplomat in her arms. 'It's OK, honey, it's OK.' She threw her venom on Matt. 'What's wrong with her?'

'What do you think?' said Matt. 'Go back to your base. I'll take care of her.'

She held Julia at arm's length and looked at her eyes – the pupils were pinheads. 'She's in shock. I'm taking her to the infirmary.'

The woman pushed past Matt. A soldier stopped her from going further. 'Ma'am, you need to get back inside camp now,' he ordered. 'We're shutting down.'

The woman wrapped her arm around Julia's shoulder. 'I'm going there now, you idiot.'

The soldier raised his hand. 'Your friend has to stay here.'

'Like hell she does!'

The soldier was not intimidated. 'She's not permitted inside the gate, ma'am.'

The woman lost it. 'You let an Afghan suicide bomber waltz up to our front door and now you're telling me you won't let a clearly traumatized *British* woman into camp? Your priorities are totally fucked, you know that!'

Matt pulled Julia back. 'I'll take care of her,' he said to the soldier. 'But my translator's badly wounded. He needs medical attention right away or he'll die. I'd like to take him to your infirmary.'

'Is he American?' asked the soldier.

'Local. He's a civilian attached to the British Embassy. He has full security clearance . . .'

'Forget it, man. We're on lock down. US military personnel only.'

'He's on *our* side,' Matt argued. 'You can't just let him bleed to death.'

The soldier's conscience pricked his tough stance. 'I'm sorry, man. I'd like to help him out but orders are orders.' He turned to the woman. 'Back inside the gate – now.'

She stuck by Julia. 'I won't leave her here.'

'Just go,' said Matt.

'But . . .'

'They won't let her inside and the longer she stays out here the worse she'll get. Go back to your base.'

The woman finally relented and left with the soldier. Matt took off his coat and wrapped it around Julia. She immediately went limp.

He scooped her up and carried her over to Kevin. 'I radioed the ops room,' Kevin informed him, as he circled Khalid's leg with a bandage. 'They know there's been a contact and we have one man down.'

'How's his leg?' said Matt.

Kevin showed him an empty packet of clotting agent. It conveyed the urgency of Khalid's condition. The agent had stopped the haemorrhaging but if they didn't get the translator to a hospital soon and flush it out to restore circulation, he'd lose his leg.

Matt handed Julia off to Kevin. 'Get her back to the embassy. I'm taking Khalid to Karti Wali hospital.'

'Karti Wali?' said Kevin. 'There's a medical facility two hundred yards from here.'

'The Yanks won't have him.'

'Are you taking the piss?'

'I wish I was.' Matt pulled the coat tighter around Julia. 'Get her out of here. I'll see you back at the embassy.' He kneeled beside Khalid. 'Change of plans. We're going to Karti Wali.'

Khalid was close to losing consciousness. 'Then I must be a lost cause.'

'Don't worry. I'll show the doctors your family photo. They'll be too scared to let you die.' Matt tucked his arms under Khalid's torso and legs and stood up. The silver chain he kept hidden beneath his shirt flew out with the upward thrust. A matching cross dangled on the end.

Khalid grabbed the religious pendant and let it go. 'My life is in the hands of a Christian,' he said, as if it were a tremendous irony.

'What?' Matt looked down. The cross was bouncing against his chest. He balanced Khalid on his knee. 'Don't worry, mate,' he said, returning the charm to its hiding place. 'It's not.'

Chapter 9

United States Embassy, Islamabad, Pakistan

The baby-faced marine stood across the table holding a plastic bag. 'Please remove any cell phones or other electronic devices.' Emma deposited her BlackBerry and private handset. The marine handed her two numbered claim chips in return. 'I apologize for any inconvenience.'

'Don't worry,' said Emma. 'I know the drill.'

'For what it's worth, I don't think you'd use yours to set off a bomb.' The marine blushed. 'I watch you all the time, ma'am.'

Emma smiled politely, her default response to such compliments, especially those tagged with ma'am. She walked to the foot of the metal detector and emptied the contents of her pockets into a plastic tray; a notebook, two pens, a lip gloss and the item which had prompted her visit to the US embassy in Islamabad.

Before passing through, she swept her hand over the back of her neck; force of habit from years of removing her silver cross and chain at security. She smiled as the naked flesh reminded her of the promise her charm was now keeping . . .

She'd given it to Matt just two weeks earlier, on London's Millennium Bridge. The couple's mood had grown as grey as the Thames below. Emma's career was taking a toll on their relationship and the demands were about to get worse.

'It might be a while before we can meet up again,' she told him.

'Where are they sending you now?' asked Matt.

'New York for a few days. Islamabad after that.'

'Why don't you fly through Dubai and we'll hook up?' he suggested.

'I can't this time.' Emma raised her collar against the wind. 'I've got to connect through Heathrow.'

Matt looked out over the river. Emma knew he suspected something. She caressed his face. 'I'm working on a story – an important one.'

Matt pulled away. 'You're *always* working a story.'

'This one is different. If it pans out, it could change everything and not just for me – for *us*.' She retrieved an inexpensive handset from her bag. 'I got a new phone yesterday. Let me give you the number.'

Matt scorned the throw-away mobile. 'What about your precious BlackBerry? Or your private email. When are you going to share *those* with me?'

'You know why I don't.'

'Why are you keeping me at arm's length?'

Emma didn't blame him for being paranoid. What man wouldn't be, given the circumstances of their relationship; long separations, constantly changing phone numbers, stolen weekends in airline hubs. Nothing was settled. Everything was transient. Except her feelings for him. 'I told you, New York goes over my BlackBerry invoices with a fine-toothed comb, numbers, texts, everything. I don't want some nosy desk assistant prying into my private life.'

'That's just an excuse and you know it.'

'Don't be ridiculous.'

'Disposable phone; disposable relationship.'

'You know that's not true.'

'Then prove it,' he challenged. 'Give me your BlackBerry number. I won't abuse it.'

Emma couldn't give Matt what he was asking for – not with her source texting the number. She couldn't allow him to get caught up in her world. 'I know the situation is frustrating but please be patient . . .'

'No more lies, Emma,' he snapped. 'Stop fucking me around, and come clean.'

'What do you think I'm hiding from you?'

'Admit it. I was never anything more than a distraction. Someone to keep you company during layovers. And now that the penny's dropped, you're cutting me loose.'

'What penny? What are you talking about?'

'The property,' said Matt. 'You thought I could buy it for you, and I can't. You're finally seeing me for what I really am – a broke ex-soldier living pay cheque to pay cheque.'

'Fuck the property.'

Matt turned from her. 'I can't give you the life you want. You should be dating some rich City boy.'

'I don't *want* a City boy.' Emma reached for him. 'But I do want a new life . . .'

Matt resisted her. 'Yeah, one without me . . .'

'Would you shut the fuck up and listen to me!' She lowered her voice. 'The story . . .'

'Don't be so gutless! You know you want to break it off so just come out with it.'

Emma slapped him across the face. 'You fucking bone-head. I'm not trying to break up with you. I'm in love with you. Can't you see that I want to marry you and grow old with you and wipe the drool from your face when your teeth fall out?'

The rant struck Matt like a thunderbolt. 'You want to marry . . . *me?*'

Now it was Emma's turn to feel insecure. 'I'm not so sure now. You are an ill-tempered git . . .'

Matt grabbed her and kissed her. Emma tried to convey through the embrace what she couldn't confess out loud. He was the only thing genuine in her counterfeit life.

'Will you marry me, Emma?'

'Of course I will,' she beamed.

'I'll get you the farm . . .'

'Forget the farm.' She kissed him again. 'I just want you.'

'No. You deserve a new life. We deserve a new life. I'll find a way to get us to Perthshire, I promise.' He laced his fingers with hers. 'I'm going to get you a ring too. A big diamond to let the world know you're mine. Who am I fooling; a wee diamond, very wee . . .'

'We don't need a diamond.' Emma untangled her hand and removed her silver chain. 'There,' she said, draping it around Matt's neck. 'Now everyone will know *you* belong to me.'

'I can't take your good luck charm.' Matt looked down at the cross. 'Besides, don't you have to believe in it for it to work?'

'I'll feel better knowing you have it.' She pressed the cross to his chest. 'Promise me you won't take it off until we say *I do.*'

Emma stored away the memory and searched for a place to sit down. It was the last day of the Muslim work week and the US Embassy's reception area was filled to capacity with Pakistanis anxious to learn whether their visa applications had been approved. An assembly line of Foreign Service Officers toiled behind a wall of bullet-proof glass, trying to complete the forms before the close of business. Every minute or so a buzzer went off, a number flashed and a hopeful soul rose to collect their passport. The pleas and tantrums that often followed spoke of lost business deals, missed reunions and shattered dreams.

As bad as she felt for those denied entry, Emma couldn't help but sympathize with the youthful FSOs charged with delivering the bad news. Most of them had probably gone to work for the State Department hoping they'd see the world and foster understanding between nations. Instead they'd ended up locked behind an impenetrable barrier, rejecting the huddled masses for being too tired, too sick, too poor and too brown to grace the land of the free.

A beep sounded. Emma checked her ticket against the display. Her number was up.

A young woman walked up to the glass. She was very striking – raven hair, voluptuous lips, athletic figure – though like many physically blessed female FSOs, she'd neutered her looks with unflattering glasses and hair pulled into a severe bun. She still stood out. She seemed less disenchanted and more full of purpose than her colleagues. Emma assumed she was new to the job.

'Mr Joiner is ready to see you now. Please go to the door on the left and I'll buzz you through.' She greeted Emma on the other side. 'How do you do, Ms Cameron, I'm Bethany Saunders.'

'Nice to meet you, Bethany.'

'I must confess I'm a big fan of your work,' Bethany gushed. 'Will your camera crew be following shortly?'

'Oh, this isn't a formal visit. Ted and I are old friends.'

'Ted?'

'Mr Joiner,' Emma clarified.

'Of course. Please, follow me.'

The embassy's inner sanctum was representative of many US

diplomatic compounds – white walls, dated furniture, flags, tacky patriotic art. The understatement was deliberate. The State Department would much rather appear tasteless than project wealth and power.

'So how long do you plan being in Islamabad?' asked Bethany.

'Tough to say,' said Emma. 'It could be a day, it could be a month. It all depends on the news cycle really.'

'Is this your first trip here?'

'No. I've been in and out for the past two years.'

'So you must be familiar with the embassy. I imagine you spend a lot of time in diplomatic compounds, given your line of work.'

'Not as much as I used to,' said Emma. 'I was an FSO before I started doing this job.'

'Really?' Bethany lit up. 'When did you serve?'

'2002–2006.'

'So you were part of the post nine-eleven recruiting wave.'

'I was indeed,' Emma confirmed. 'How long have you been with the service?'

'Oh, I plan to make a career of it.'

The fact that Bethany had dodged the question didn't escape Emma. If there was one thing she'd learned from her time as a correspondent, it was that people loved to talk about themselves – unless they had something to hide. She tried a less direct tack. 'How long have you been posted in Islamabad?'

'Long enough to know not to eat the melons,' Bethany joked.

Another evasion. Emma's suspicions grew. 'Did you request this posting specifically?'

'I just go where they tell me,' said Bethany. 'So how does being a TV correspondent compare to the life of an FSO?'

Emma had misjudged Bethany completely. The brunette

bombshell was no Foreign Service neophyte. She didn't even work with the State Department. No wonder she was so bright-eyed and determined. Bethany was Ted's gal. 'Every job has its good and bad points,' said Emma.

Bethany stopped outside a door and knocked before entering. Emma searched for a nameplate. There wasn't one. Ted didn't trust her enough to see him in his real office. She should have anticipated as much. It had been years since they'd seen each other and their parting words hadn't exactly been kind ones.

'Emma. How are you?'

Ted's greeting was very staid given the history between them. Emma mirrored his detachment. 'I'm fine. Thanks for seeing me on such short notice.'

'Not at all.'

'Can I get you something to drink before I go?' Bethany offered.

'Nothing for me,' said Emma.

'That will be all for now, thanks,' said Ted. Bethany eyed the pair like a chaperone before closing the door. As soon as they were alone, Ted threw his arms around Emma. 'It is so great to see you!'

Emma's concerns abated. Ted was too good a guy to bear a grudge. 'You too,' she said, hugging him in return. She stood back and had a long look at him. Her old friend had sprouted a few wrinkles and his hairline had receded slightly but his eyes still held the glint of a man who believed wholeheartedly in his vocation. She should have listened to him.

He showed her to a scruffy sofa. 'Boy, I haven't seen you since . . . was it Baghdad?'

'Amman.' Emma took a seat and had a quick look around. The office was definitely temporary. There were no commemorative paperweights on the desk, not even the ubiquitous stack of

Russian dolls. But Ted had thought to introduce one personal effect; an old photograph of herself, him and Eric Riddell in their graduation gowns, proudly displaying their diplomas. The picture was his way of saying *I told you so*.

'Now I remember,' he feigned. 'That was right before Eric lured you away to the glamorous world of television.'

'Have you seen him at all?'

Ted shook his head. 'Eric and I haven't seen each other in years.'

'Surely you've been *watching* him,' Emma pressed.

Ted shrugged. 'I see him on TV now and again.'

Emma changed subject. 'How's Stephanie, by the way?'

'She's good.' Ted nodded. 'Still working for the World Bank.'

Emma recognized the tick from their school days. Ted was hiding something. 'Maybe we could all get together for a drink while I'm in town?' she suggested.

Ted's head stopped bobbing. 'Stephanie and I split up,' he confessed.

'I'm sorry.' Emma fished for an appropriate platitude. 'You were a good couple.'

Ted nudged her. 'You never liked her.'

'She never liked me either.'

Ted took Emma's hand and squeezed it. The gesture conjured the old passion they'd once shared but never consummated. 'She was jealous of you.'

'She shouldn't have been. You were never the cheating kind.' Emma pulled her hand away. 'So what happened?'

'She gave me an ultimatum: her or my work. The rest, as they say, is history. But enough of my sob story; what about you?' Ted looked hopefully at Emma's empty ring finger. 'Still a free agent?'

'Actually, I'm seeing someone.'

'Good for you.' Emma detected a shift in Ted's mood but she couldn't decipher it exactly. Disappointment? Concern? He leaned in, as if impatient to be taken into her confidence. 'Is it serious?'

The body language was a con. Ted had obviously thought her visit would reignite the old flame. 'We're getting married.'

'Wow. Married.' Ted digested the blow. 'I hope he's more understanding about your work than my ex was about mine.'

The warning didn't offend Emma. Ted was just trying to get some of his own back. 'Work won't be an issue,' she said. 'I'm quitting.'

Ted raised his brow. 'Far be it from me to throw cold water on your impending nuptials, Emma, but as your friend, not to mention a recent divorcee, I should caution you; if this guy's asking you to give up your career, you'll probably end up resenting him.'

'He didn't ask me to give up anything. It's my decision.'

'Oh, I get it.' Ted nudged her playfully. 'The old biological clock ticking loudly?'

Now she was offended. 'No louder than your testicles.'

'Touché,' said Ted. 'Seriously, Emma. Is this guy really worth it?'

'It's not just him. I'm tired of the bullshit.'

'I thought you couldn't wait to inform people of world events.'

'Come off it, Ted. You know I'm not a real journalist.'

'Three hundred and forty million viewers would disagree.' He took her hand again. This time the gesture was strictly platonic. 'Is it really that bad?'

'It's worse.'

'There's a lot invested in you,' Ted cautioned. 'Do you honestly think they'll just let you walk away?'

'It depends.' Emma released her hand and pulled the storage stick from her pocket.

'What's that?'

She gave it to him. 'I was hoping you could tell me.'

Chapter 10

Quetta, Baluchistan Province, Pakistan

The soldiers were a grainy, green blur. They crept toward the house with backs bent and rifles raised, like hunters stalking prey. One peered inside a window. What he saw through the bulbous goggles Soheil could only imagine. The supple curve of a naked breast? A wife pleasuring her husband?

The video cut to probing head torches. The soldiers were now inside the house, ransacking rooms and rounding up men. A group of women cowered in a corner, their hands reaching vainly for their husbands, brothers and sons as the infidel soldiers led them away. Soheil's sexual fantasies fused with his righteous anger, creating a feeling more potent than either. His rage intensified as the American soldiers bound the men's hands with plastic ties and forced them down on their stomachs. 'The infidel has no respect for the sanctity of the Muslim home,' said an authoritative narrator. 'Like thieves they creep in under cover of darkness.'

The video dissolved into a series of still photographs – a hooded man standing with his arms spread, another crouching like a dog while a western whore held him by a leash. 'The infidel imprison Muslims without cause and force them to endure all manner of torture and humiliation. Yet it is the infidel who are the criminals.' Another still appeared on the screen; a photograph of a smiling schoolgirl. 'Abeer Qasim Hamza was fourteen years old when American soldiers entered her house and violated her repeatedly. They then murdered her and her family to conceal their heinous acts.' A montage of distraught, veiled women wailing over dead bodies flashed across the screen. 'Western crusaders and their Zionist masters have unleashed a wave of death and destruction across the Muslim world. They wish to subjugate all Muslims and control our resources to enrich themselves.' The funeral scenes were pushed aside by UN footage of doctors and nurses inoculating children. 'The infidel come in many guises. These medical workers claim to be administering polio vaccine. They are in fact injecting poison that will make Muslim boys impotent.' The mass vaccination gave way to children in a hospital burns unit. Soheil recognized the location: Gaza. His fury boiled over. Of all Islamic resistance movements, none moved him more deeply than Hamas's struggle against the Zionist occupiers. Not even the plight of his Pashtun tribesmen had as profound an effect on him. 'In 2009, in its campaign to steal more Palestinian land, the Israeli government dropped bombs of white phosphorus on the Muslims of Gaza,' said the narrator. The video zoomed in on a child's exposed bone. 'It is against international law to use white phosphorus against civilians, yet not a single Israeli has been charged with war crimes. The Zionist puppets of the West refuse to condemn the Jewish state. The infidel will not rest until they have destroyed all Muslims,' the narrator continued, 'but Mujahideen from around the globe are rising to defend Islam.' A *nasheed* – Islamic vocal music – flooded the room as the atrocity video culminated in a flurry of martyr scenes; a plane slicing through the World Trade Center, IEDs obliterating military vehicles in Iraq and Afghanistan. Soheil's wrath turned to elation. The infidel could never triumph in the face of such sacrifice. He felt as if his soul would rise out of his body and float to heaven.

A jarring snort brought him back to earth. The Baluch who'd ruined his outing to Hanna Lake was fast asleep. Soheil looked at him with contempt. The Baluch had no sympathy for their fellow Muslims. All they cared about was their own parochial struggle.

The DVD finished and another was loaded. Soheil settled in for more stories of infidel crimes, but this video was different from the others. It opened with a *nasheed* playing over an image of a bearded man – a fellow Pashtun riding in a car with his hands bound behind his back. His eyes were full of terror and he was mouthing protestations of innocence. The scene changed. The Pashtun was now sitting in a dark room with a blindfold wrapped around his head. Soheil's heart wept for his fellow tribesman. The infidel dogs treating him so horribly would pay.

The video jumped to a new clip of the Pashtun man lying outside on gravel. A large hand was forcing his head to the ground. The shot tilted up to reveal another hand tossing a knife. Soheil was aghast. He'd never seen a man killed before – not even on DVD. When the picture zoomed out, his shock grew greater still. It was not a man wielding the blade but a Pashtun boy! The child was dressed in a combat vest and white trainers that swamped his feet. The masked adults – also Pashtun – were cheering him on in his grim duty.

The *nasheed* faded out as the young executioner described the crime the man had committed. 'He is an American spy who betrayed his Taliban commander,' the child declared in a voice not yet broken by manhood. 'Those who do this kind of thing will meet the same fate!' He bent over and started sawing the man's neck. Soheil wanted to turn away, but he couldn't for fear of being labelled a coward by his fellow students. He watched, horrified, as the child severed the traitor's head from his body then kicked it aside like a football.

The study room erupted with applause. Soheil tried to join in but was too stricken with fear. Was that really how the Taliban dispatched traitors?

He was still in shock when Mullah Maulana entered the room. The cleric beckoned to him and pointed to the Baluch to join him outside. 'I have wonderful news,' said the normally dour holy man. 'You have been called to arms.'

Soheil forgot all about the horrible video. '*Al hamdu lilah*,' he cried. *Praise be to God*.

'Come,' said the mullah. 'The field of battle awaits you!'

The young jihadists followed the cleric into the compound's central courtyard. The potted fruit trees were just beginning to bud. Soheil inhaled the grassy air, committing the smell to memory. He'd enjoyed his time at the madrassa. It was far more luxuriant than the spartan camp he'd abandoned in Waziristan. It even had Wi-Fi. But leaving such comfortable surroundings was a small price to pay for the privilege of becoming a true holy warrior.

Two men were waiting for them inside the front gate, rifle barrels visible beneath their khameezes. Soheil took comfort from the clandestine security. He'd never ventured outside the compound after dark.

'I must leave you here,' Mullah Maulana apologized.

'We understand,' said Soheil.

The cleric kissed the jihadists on the cheek. 'Remain faithful and you will find glory, my sons.'

Soheil and the Baluch stepped into the street. The metal gate locked behind them. The empty darkness was frightening; it was so barren compared to daytime. A car with the headlights switched off pulled up and four men got out. Soheil tried to run, but they were too strong. They grabbed him and dragged him to their car, banging his head on the frame as they pulled him through the door.

Soheil's heart was racing. It was just like the video. 'Have faith, brother,' a voice whispered. 'This is for your own protection.'

A blindfold was placed over his eyes. Soheil's senses heightened. The car's upholstery reeked of jihad – rancid nicotine, sugary plastic explosive, musk. The combination drew him back to the terrible sin he feared would damn him for all eternity . . .

Soheil had been at the camp in Waziristan for a little over a month when Amir Qari asked to see him – alone.

'I am disappointed with your progress,' Qari declared. 'You have a great appetite for the arts of war but your faith is weak. You cannot remain here.'

Soheil threw himself at his master's feet. 'Do not send me away,' he pleaded. 'I cannot go back to my home.'

'You are of no use to me.' Qari kicked him. 'Be gone!'

Soheil crawled after him, sobbing. 'Please. I beg of you. Find some use for me.'

Qari grabbed Soheil by the chin and rubbed his thumb around his mouth. 'I do require the services of a *chai* boy.'

That night and for countless nights afterward, Amir Qari engaged in *batch bazi* with Soheil – boy play. The pain and humiliation were excruciating. He felt unclean and worthless, but the attention Amir Qari bestowed on him was also disturbingly empowering. The whole camp knew Soheil was the great warrior's favourite. He could not understand how being a whore had won him such respect.

The abuse came to an abrupt end when the Pakistani army invaded Waziristan. Amir Qari fled to the mountains with his most trusted fighters, while those considered not ready for battle were sent to Mullah Maulana's compound in Quetta. The cleric's sermons left Soheil convinced that Allah had sent the army to punish his deviant behaviour. The mullah warned that those who engaged in homosexuality would be buried beneath a wall.

The car stopped. Soheil tried to keep his fears in check. Surely Allah would not have made him a Mujaheed had his sins not been forgiven? 'Keep your blindfold on,' a voice whispered. 'You are almost there.'

Soheil and the Baluch were led out of the car and up an uneven walkway. The sounds and smells filtering past reminded the young Pashtun of the carefree days before his father's death; snippets of Indian soap operas, boiling rice, petrol fumes.

The comforting odours faded as they were pushed inside a building. The guides departed, leaving the two young jihadists alone. Soheil took a deep breath to steady his nerves but unlike outside, the scents trapped by the walls were completely foreign to him. He wondered into whose hands they were being delivered.

The door opened, drowning the strange smells with familiar cologne. Soheil's body stiffened with terror. The call to arms had been a ruse!

The agonizing touch of a thumb to his lips confirmed it. Amir Qari had returned for him.

'You may remove your blindfolds now,' the jihadist leader instructed.

Soheil obeyed his abuser. Weeks in hiding had not weakened Amir Qari. If anything, he appeared to have grown stronger. His black curls were lustrous. Even his beard was fuller.

Qari embraced the two jihadists and bade them to join him on the carpet. 'How have you been?'

Soheil bowed his head to hide his loathing. 'We have been well. Every day we pray that Allah give you strength to defeat our enemies.'

'Your prayers are appreciated,' said Qari. 'My enemies are many and my presence here is proof that your hearts are pure and your prayers worthy of Allah's consideration. So tell me, are you getting all you need? Are you eating well?'

An image of past abuse flashed in Soheil's mind. 'Koran gives us all the nourishment we require.'

'I understand you've made excellent progress with your studies. Mullah Maulana tells me your piousness is exemplary. And you,' Qari turned his attention to the Baluch, 'you are a true credit to your people and to Islam. That is why I have asked you both here tonight. Mullah Maulana feels you are ready to contribute to our struggle.'

Soheil raised his eyes. Amir Qari had not brought him there for sex. He truly had been called to battle.

'As you know, we have suffered many setbacks in recent weeks,' Qari continued. 'The Pakistan army has invaded our homeland, destroyed our camps and slaughtered our people. Nothing is sacred to the whores in Islamabad – not even your beloved madrassa here in Quetta.'

Soheil and the Baluch looked at each other, alarmed. 'Surely they would not violate the sanctity of a holy place of worship and study,' said Soheil.

'This is the darkest hour of our struggle,' Qari brooded. 'Those who are pure of heart and strong of will are needed now more than ever. We must show the devil whores in Islamabad that we will no longer accept their tyranny. We must make our enemies fear us!' He paused to lock eyes with each boy. 'Tell me, my brothers. Are you prepared to lay down your lives for our struggle?'

'I am ready, Amir Qari,' the Baluch declared.

Soheil felt the moment deserved grander language. 'I am ready to die for my homeland and for Islam!'

Qari beamed with approval. 'I knew from the moment Allah led you to us that there was greatness in you . . . both of you, which is why you have been chosen for the most sacred and glorious of missions . . .'

The most sacred and glorious of missions. Soheil's heart stopped. Allah had not forgiven him. He would indeed be buried for his sins.

Chapter 11

Makran Coast, Baluchistan Province, Pakistan

A blossom of daylight sprang from the horizon. Tansvir crouched in the cutting, waiting for his men to come ashore. In twenty minutes, the ghostly mist swirling off the silvery waters of the Arabian Sea would burn away, robbing them of their camouflage.

The old commander's knees howled in protest. He'd been squatting for two hours waiting for his target to appear. He picked a sprig of wild herbs from the bush beneath him and rubbed it between his fingers. The soapy oils fused with the salty air, silencing his aching joints. He kept inhaling the elixir while he looked over the land he loved. Of all Baluchistan's treasures – the ancient juniper forests of Ziarat, the almond groves of Loralai, the gorges of the Harnai Pass – none was more breathtaking or vital to his nation's future than the Makran Coast. It was the jewel in the crown of Baluchistan, one Tansvir was determined to keep for his people.

The hum of outboard engines floated over the jagged cliffs. Tansvir searched the empty shoreline below. A two-man craft emerged from the fog, followed by another. Angry waves tossed the tiny vessels, threatening to capsize them, but Tansvir was unconcerned. The coxswains were the sons of fishermen. They knew how to tame the sea.

The crafts cleared the danger zone and landed safely in a

sandy cove. The boats were in position to receive the cargo. It was now down to the ambush party to seize it. Tansvir alerted the killer group hiding in a crag twenty metres further up the road. The initiator raised his grenade launcher. Like his commander, Sobhat wore a white turban that blended with the sun-bleached rocks.

Tansvir gave him the signal to ease down. If the missile were deployed prematurely, it would miss the target and alert the guards accompanying the cargo. Sobhat still had much to learn about guerrilla warfare. But what the eager young warrior lacked in experience he made up for in courage and commitment. It comforted Tansvir no end to know that the next generation would fight to the death for freedom.

Sobhat's retracting launcher beckoned to Tansvir, conjuring memories of the sacrifice that had enlisted it to the Baluchistan Liberation Army's struggle. The RPG had been part of a cache stolen from a Pakistani army depot three years earlier. The daring raid had claimed the life of Tansvir's last surviving son. Such ghosts were attached to many weapons in the BLA's arsenal. There were Chinese Type 56 assault rifles taken from Pakistani forces during the clashes of 2006; Russian-made AKs recovered from skirmishes with Iranian soldiers in the 1990s; Soviet PPS submachine guns – a gift from Iraq to aid the Baluch during the uprising of 1973. But the weapon with the oldest, most distinguished provenance belonged to Tansvir himself: an English-made Lee Enfield .303 bolt-action rifle his great grandfather had wrested from a Pashtun mercenary fighting for Britain's Civil Armed Forces. The year of the encounter was engraved in the butt – 1919.

Vibrations rumbled the earth. Tansvir cased the winding coastal road through his binoculars. The undulating hills had yet to give up the trucks but he was confident they were the ones he and his militia were waiting for. For the past two months, every Friday before dawn a two-vehicle convoy would drive east along the Makran Coastal Highway to where heavy earth-moving equipment lay idle for the Muslim day of rest. The diggers and lorries were clearing the way for a pipeline that had suffered many acts of sabotage and the Chinese engineer over-seeing the project needed to ensure they were adequately secured. No doubt, he would have preferred to send a lackey given the fate of other foreign workers in Baluchistan, but stand-ins would not suffice for a project of such vital importance to Pakistan and its most important ally.

The pipeline was the culmination of a project that had started ten years earlier with the development of the deep water port in Gwadar. The once sleepy peninsula on Baluchistan's western edge had long fired the imaginations of empires that dreamed of building a sea outlet for Central Asia's fossil fuel wealth. The Soviets had eyed it as the final prize in their doomed conquest of Afghanistan. From the ashes of Russia's failure, China's rising commercial power had given birth to an even grander vision. Gwadar was to be the hub of a new Sino Silk Road; a conduit for Middle Eastern crude oil and natural gas shipped from Gulf nations across the Arabian Sea and pumped in from Iran. The liquid currency would be transported through Pakistan via a trans-Himalayan pipeline into Western China while Chinese consumer goods would circulate back along Pakistani highways and railways to be loaded onto Gwadar's ships for distribution around the globe.

The trading hub and its various tentacles should have ushered in an era of prosperity for the Baluch. Instead, it launched the greatest land heist in the history of Tansvir's people. Hundreds of thousands of acres of ancient Baluch property were summar-ily hijacked by elites in Punjab and Sindh who used their influence to falsify deeds and place the land in the public domain. The stolen real estate was then sold off cheaply to developers in Karachi, Lahore and Islamabad who kicked-back proceeds to the generals and politicians who'd made the land-grab possible. As the profits mounted, more outsiders joined the gang rape. Chinese and Singaporeans migrated to Baluchistan to oversee engineering and building projects, pushing skilled local workers out of management positions. Dispossessed and barred from their country's future success, native Baluch were reduced to selling manual labour to the occupiers for a pittance.

Tansvir checked the local guards overseeing the pipeline equipment. They were wrapped in blankets, fast asleep beside a long-dead fire. Soon they'd be extinguished as well. Like other collaborators, they'd sealed their fate when they'd betrayed their people. Crying poverty was no excuse. Better to suffer an empty belly than starve the soul of freedom.

Two trucks rounded the bend. Tansvir tracked the lead vehicle through his binoculars. It was packed with armed Pashtun, employees of a security company based in Quetta. The guards had no affiliation with the Pakistani Taliban, Tansvir's new allies. They were Afghan refugees, locusts who now outnumbered the Baluch in their own nation.

The rebel leader raised his arm to signal the killer group. He paced the advancing vehicle before letting it fall . . . *five, four, three, two . . .*

Sobhat responded on cue, launching a rocket-propelled grenade at the lead truck. The missile hit the target, exploding on impact. The killer group leapt out of their hiding place and charged the burning truck.

The sleeping Baluch guards abandoned their post and ran into the desert. Tansvir relished the hunt as the distance widened between him and the fleeing collaborators. He raised his antique rifle, brought the slower target into his sight and slowly operated the trigger. A .303 round flew out of the barrel and into the back of the guard, killing him instantly.

Tansvir pulled back the bolt to eject the empty case and pushed it forward to feed another round into the chamber. His palm tingled with anticipation as he locked the bolt down into place. The second guard had crossed the three-hundred-metre threshold – a genuine challenge with an iron sight.

Confident in the accuracy of his ancestor's prize, Tansvir aimed the Lee Enfield and fired. The guard's skull exploded as the round took his head from his shoulders. Another direct hit, another collaborator dispatched without mercy. That was how freedom was won.

The killer group had dealt with the Pashtun security force with equally ruthless efficiency. Those who hadn't perished in the RPG explosion had been shot on sight. The ground around the burnt-out lead truck was littered with blackened and blood-ied bodies.

Tansvir stepped over the corpses to join his fighters. They were waiting for him near the backing vehicle. The truck was still pristine. 'Show me the cargo,' he ordered.

Sobhat pulled the Chinese engineer out of the cab and presented him to his commander. The hostage was crying and pleading in his native tongue. Tansvir inspected him for injury. He'd sustained a few bruises in the attack but was otherwise unharmed. 'What of his driver?' asked the rebel leader.

Sobhat led Tansvir around to the back of the truck. The captured Baluch driver was lying face down on the ground with his wrists bound behind his back. 'You've done well,' said Tansvir. 'Go prepare the cargo for transport.' While Sobhat left to wrap the engineer in blankets and ropes for lowering onto the boat, Tansvir dealt with the driver.

He drew a knife from his waistcoat and kicked the collaborator onto his back. The man yelped with terror when he saw the armed commander standing over him. 'Do you know how the BLA punishes traitors?' Tansvir asked, dropping to his knees. He shoved two fingers into the driver's nostrils and drove the knife forward. The man howled as the nose was cut from his face.

Tansvir wiped his blade clean on his victim's kameez. 'Wear your shame,' he scowled, planting the severed nose in the collaborator's bleeding sinus cavity, 'as a warning to others.'

Chapter 12

Islamabad, Pakistan

The office was a tip. Old wire copy, empty beer bottles and over-flowing ashtrays littered the dining-table work space. A waste basket in the middle of the room stood surrounded by crumpled wads of DAWN newspapers, Pakistan's most popular daily.

Emma took a seat in front of the bureau's editing terminal and cleared the rubbish from the keyboard. She wanted to see what Eric had been working on the day before. The encrypted double-screened computer connected directly to SBC's library server back in New York. Every live and taped story that aired on SBC could be accessed through it along with all the raw footage that ended up on the cutting-room floor: male correspondents applying make-up and hairspray, botched stand ups, video deemed too graphic for public broadcast.

She hit the space bar. Instead of a dialogue box requesting a user name and password, the screensaver gave way to a webpage featuring one of her SBC publicity photos under the banner *Rate This News Babe*. Though she loathed such sites, Emma's curiosity compelled her to scroll down and see how her colleagues had scored her. She'd been awarded a five out of a possible ten. The accompanying comment explained the point deduction. *Hot face, huge ass. That's why you never see her below the neck.*

Emma closed the browser and rebooted. It wasn't the first time she'd been slated by a male colleague. SBC's foreign news bureaus were run like college fraternities. Burping, farting and misogynistic comments were positively encouraged. Women like Emma who voiced their distaste were written off straight away as bitches. But even those who suffered in silence were treated as unwelcome interlopers, unless they drank like Russian sailors and fucked the crew with abandon – in which case they were considered 'fun to work with'.

She checked the assignment board to see which of her co-workers had been trashing her this time. There were three names written in columns along with hers. One of them, Smudge, she didn't recognize. Eric Riddell, the correspondent she was taking over for, was a friend, not to mention the last person on earth who would harm her public image. That left one culprit: Jerry Fitzwilliam, the bureau cameraman.

Emma walked across the room and opened a window to clear her head. The scent of stale lager, cigarettes and old sweat dissipated as she inhaled the fresh air. She reminded herself that all the back-biting and bullshit would soon be behind her. Ted had asked for twelve hours to authenticate the documents she'd given him. If they checked out – and Emma was almost certain they would – she'd be through with this life forever.

She cast her eyes over the city she dearly hoped would mark her swan-song. Islamabad was the perfect place to call it quits. With its wide boulevards, marble-faced buildings and flawlessly manicured public spaces, Pakistan's capital was as staged and soulless as her career. The neighbourhoods were so characterless, they were named by grid number. The upscale area housing the rented bureau-cum-living quarters she was standing in was known simply as F-6.

Like other privileged areas of the capital, F-6 had been largely silenced by the upsurge in terror activity. On this morning, there were no maids hanging out washing or children frolicking beneath the paper mulberries and billowing eucalyptuses, just police checkpoints, unsightly blast walls and private security guards watching over properties vacated by wealthy locals who'd fled to safer pastures.

A Pakistani guard crossed beneath Emma's window and headed for a staircase on the western side of the villa. The local hire was holding a long stick in one hand and dragging a fold-up chair with the other. Emma reckoned he was going to patrol the roof terrace – that or take a nap.

Halfway up the staircase, the guard's radio crackled. He looked back toward the front of the property. Emma followed his line of sight. The other guard on duty was opening the gate.

A late 1980s model gold Mercedes Benz pulled in and parked beside the bureau's crew vehicle – a shiny, black 4×4. Emma recognized the car. It belonged to Naj, SBC's local fixer. Though somewhat of a slacker, Naj-i-pedia as the crews called him was indispensable, a walking database of Pakistan's complex history, who could navigate the country's labyrinthine bureaucracy to secure visas and travel permits.

Suddenly, it hit Emma what day it was: Friday. Wild horses couldn't drag Naj into work on his day off. She ran back to the dining table and pulled up the newswires on one of the bureau's back-up laptops. A dispatch at the top was marked *Flash*.

RAWALPINDI: THWARTED SUICIDE BOMBER CLAIMS QARI IS ALIVE

According to the lead-in, the Pakistani authorities had a suicide bomber in custody who claimed to belong to TTP-Q, the Pakistani Taliban splinter group led by Abdullah Qari. 'Fuck me,' Emma muttered. The London morning shows would definitely want a live shot. She read on. The failed bomber had been caught outside a mosque in Rawalpindi – the garrison city right next door to Islamabad. 'Fuck me hard,' Emma moaned. London would also want b-roll – news footage of the scene – not to mention blogs, tweets and all the other frivolous first-person point of view 'enriched content' crap the network insisted she file. And as soon as London was fed, New York would wake up and demand she do it all over again. Emma was in no mood to stand on a rooftop past midnight, filing reports and banging out 140-word updates between live shots. Not when Ted was waiting with an answer.

She considered making a break for the embassy. No one else was awake yet. But what if she was wrong about the files and had to return to the bureau with her tail between her legs? She would have a very uncomfortable time explaining her absence.

She checked the assignment board again. Eric wasn't scheduled to fly out until eight o'clock that evening. Emma grabbed a marker and started delegating coverage duties. If she could convince Eric to one-man-band the live shots for the morning show, it would free her up to go to Rawalpindi with Naj and Jerry to shoot the b-roll. Once the video was in the can, she could send the crew back to the bureau while she diverted to the US embassy to get 'official reaction' – or at least, that would be her excuse.

She had just finished writing *Live Shots Solo* next to Eric's name when a foul stench crept up behind her, the same mix of cigarettes, booze and body odour she'd just purged from the room.

'Coffee,' moaned a gravelly voice. 'I need coffee.'

Jerry looked like he'd just crawled out from under a rock. His hair was matted and he hadn't shaved in at least three days – or showered, judging by the smell of him. 'There isn't any,' she told him.

'Where's the cook?' Jerry fell into a chair. 'The lazy fucker should be here by now.'

Yet another aspect of international news reporting Emma wouldn't miss; slovenly westerners complaining about domestic staff in third world countries. 'It's Friday,' she reminded him.

'Backward ass-fucking country,' Jerry rubbed his head, 'why can't they have a normal weekend like the rest of the world?' He looked to Emma for sympathy. 'I don't suppose you could make me some coffee?'

'Nothing would give me greater pleasure,' said Emma. 'But I'm afraid my ass won't fit through the kitchen door.' She turned her back but kept tabs on Jerry's reaction through a darkened monitor screen. He was giving her the finger and mouthing the word *cunt*. Even she drew the line at the 'c' word.

Another man twice the size of Jerry and equally worse for wear dragged himself into the office. 'How do you do,' she said, extending her hand, 'you must be Smudge. I'm Emma.'

Smudge took her hand and dropped it.

'So,' she persevered, 'what do you do?'

Smudge collapsed next to Jerry. 'I'm your security advisor.'

If Emma had a match, she could have lit his breath. Matt would be appalled. 'Do you always get shit-faced with the people you're looking after?'

'Smudge served with the 82nd Airborne in Baghdad,' Jerry interrupted. 'He knows what to do if we get in the shit, don't you, man.' He raised his fist, an invitation to punch the point. Smudge left him hanging.

Naj appeared in the doorway. The fixer was as classic as his car – yellow-tinted sunglasses, polyester suit, tufts of white hair sprouting from his ears. 'Emma! My dear girl, it's been too long.'

'How have you been, Naj?' she said.

Naj pressed his hand to his chest. 'As soon as I heard the news this morning, I knew I must come in.'

'Do you know anything about the mosque that was targeted?' she asked.

'I know this neighbourhood well. Many army officers live there. They and their families all pray at that mosque.'

'What about the bomber?' she probed. 'Did he really confess to being TTP-Q or is that just wishful thinking by the police?'

'I phoned a source of mine,' said Naj, 'a very high-ranking police officer. He told me they can prove that the bomber was groomed by Abdullah Qari.'

Before Naj could elaborate, Eric Riddell bounded into the room. As always, the correspondent was groomed to within an inch of his life; freshly shaven face, clean fingernails, hair locked in place with gel, razor-sharp creases down his trouser legs. 'Good morning, everyone. Isn't it a beautiful day?'

'You're chipper,' said Emma.

'That's because I'm outta here.' He stopped to give her a kiss on the cheek. 'Thanks to you.' Eric's exuberance faded when he saw Naj. 'What's going on?'

'A suicide bomber was apprehended in Rawalpindi this morning,' Emma explained. 'Apparently, he belongs to TTP-Q.'

'He tried to bomb a mosque used by the military and their families,' Naj added.

'Jesus,' said Eric. 'Qari's martyrs are really upping their game.'

'We must report on this,' Naj insisted. 'It is vital.'

'I was thinking that if you could do the morning live shots, I could head over to Rawalpindi with the crew and shoot some b-roll,' Emma suggested.

'Are you dreaming?' said Eric. 'There's no way London or New York will want me doing lives with you here.'

'They will if we present a united front,' Emma argued. 'Come on, Eric. You know that as soon as you leave I'll be tethered to that dish 24/7.'

'Sorry,' Eric said without sympathy. 'That's the gig you signed up for.'

'Come on,' she pleaded. 'Even felons get work-release.'

Eric considered her request. 'OK. But if you're going to Pindi you should do the blogging . . . and the tweeting,' he haggled.

'Deal,' said Emma.

Eric looked at Jerry. The shooter was near comatose. 'We better get some coffee in that one before you head out. Why don't you come help me make it?'

Emma followed Eric into the adjoining kitchen area. It was even dirtier than the office: dishes encrusted with food, counter tops laden with crumbs, bottled water in various stages of empti-ness. How Eric, king of hygiene could tolerate such filth was a mystery.

He pulled a tin of coffee out of the cupboard. 'So where were you yesterday?'

Emma had her excuse at the ready. 'Shopping.'

'How many rugs can one person own?' He slid the filter out of the coffee machine and grimaced. No one had emptied the used grinds. 'You should take Smudge with you as well.'

Emma looked back at the security advisor. His head was hang-ing between his knees as if he were about to vomit. 'I'll leave him here. You might need the extra set of hands.'

'It's a live shot, Emma. What could go wrong?' Eric glanced at Smudge. 'Besides, it's about time he started earning his keep around here.' Eric dumped the grinds onto an overflowing bin. 'We haven't left the bureau in weeks.'

'You must be climbing the walls,' said Emma. 'Have you tried to do any travel?'

Eric fitted a new filter. 'I've had Naj working on permits for Quetta,' he said, filling it with fresh grinds. 'They haven't come through so far.'

'What story are you chasing?'

'I want the permits in the bag in case Mullah Maulana grants us an interview.'

'Abdullah Qari's spiritual guide?' Emma balked. 'He doesn't talk to the western press. It's not his MO.'

'That may be about to change.' Eric started the machine. It gurgled to life. 'Word around Islamabad is the government's getting ready to take him down. I bet he'll talk to any journalist to get his story out before that happens – western or not.'

'Should I follow up while you're gone?'

'Sure.' Eric's BlackBerry rang. The tone was a digitized version of the old 1990s anthem *You're Unbelievable*. 'Good morning,' he said. 'Yeah, we saw it . . . Rawalpindi? It's right next door to Islamabad . . . yes, I'm sure.' He rolled his eyes. 'Twenty minutes to two hours depending on traffic . . . OK . . . OK . . . yeah. I'll let her know.' He hung up and gave Emma an exaggerated frown.

She knew it. London wanted her to do the lives. 'Shit-mother fucker-shit.'

'Sorry,' said Eric. 'Tell you what. When I get back from Rawalpindi, I'll pick up some of your shots – give you a chance to get out of the bureau before I leave tonight.'

Emma threw her arms around him. 'You're a life-saver.'

He squeezed her tightly. 'I wouldn't go that far.'

Chapter 13

Heathrow Airport

Matt stared at the revolving door, thinking of the events that had spun him from full employment in Kabul to hustling for work on the outskirts of Heathrow. He wondered how Khalid was holding up. It gutted him to leave the wounded translator at Karti Wali.

A jet buzzed the hotel. The downwash rippled through the windows and struts into the pavement beneath Matt's feet. His resolve wavered as he contemplated the choice he now faced. If he went through the door, he'd sacrifice what little integrity he had left. Turn back and he'd lose the only thing in the world he cared about.

He pulled the prospectus from his pocket to remind himself why this compromise was worth making . . .

Emma knotted her pink shawl around her waist. 'I've been dying to show this to you,' she said, reaching for her bag.

Matt studied the naked curve of her back. 'It can wait,' he said. 'Come back to bed.'

She retrieved a piece of paper and bounced down beside him. 'Just read this, will you?'

Matt took the paper half-heartedly. 'Hold on,' he said, sitting up.

'I knew that would get your attention.' Emma pointed to one of the thumbnails. 'Look, the cottage even has a wind turbine. You still remember how to fix them?'

Matt kissed her and read on. The property was perfect; exactly like the one he'd grown up on. 'Bloody hell,' he exclaimed when he saw the asking price. 'You've got to be joking.'

'I know it's steep but it's not impossible,' said Emma. 'I called my accountant. If I cash in my retirement savings I'll have three-quarters of that covered. We'll get a loan for the rest.'

'You can't blow your entire pension,' said Matt. 'Think of your future.'

'Think of *our* future,' she said, nuzzling his neck. 'Imagine waking up to that view every morning . . .'

Matt ran the sums. Even if he pooled his meagre savings with Emma's lump sum, they'd still have a stonking huge mortgage.

'I'm sorry,' he said, peeling her off. 'I can't buy this for you.'

'I'm not asking you to. We'd be buying it together.'

'Get real, Emma. No bank is going to lend you money if you quit your job and move to Scotland. And they won't give me a look in. I'm a security advisor with no assets working in hostile environments.' He threw the paper down and climbed out of bed. 'I have bad risk written all over me.'

'Where are you going?'

'The shower.'

Matt heard his mobile ring as he turned on the water. 'Mind answering that?' he shouted. 'It might be work.'

A minute later, Emma appeared in the doorway.

'What did they want?' asked Matt.

She untied her shawl and let it fall to the floor. 'It wasn't work. It was an old friend of yours.' She stepped out of the pink, pooling fabric and joined him in the shower. 'He was calling about a job – one that pays well.'

*   *   *

The door delivered Matt into a vast, stone-floored lobby. His echoing footsteps clashed with the soothing baroque music piping over the hotel's PA system as he made his way to the hotel bar.

Carter was sitting on a sofa, nursing a beer and watching the news on a 42-inch television. The ex-Delta captain had grown his hair and beard since the Baghdad raid but his taste for state-of-the-art kit hadn't changed. The suitcase resting on the floor next to him must have cost eight hundred dollars.

'Logan!' he said, grabbing Matt's hand. He reeled him in for a one-armed hug. 'Man, it is good to see you.' The sincerity of the sentiment lingered on Carter's face as he let go. He was close to tears. 'Damn, Baghdad seems like it was just yesterday.'

Matt hadn't come to talk about the past. He was there to secure his future. 'Thanks for delaying your connection to meet me.'

'Anything for you, brother. Hey, have you been watching the Six Nations?'

Matt had forgotten they'd bonded over rugby. 'I've been in Kabul. You can't get the games there.'

'It's probably for the best,' said Carter. 'Looks like Scotland's in for the wooden spoon this year.'

'We have to win *something*.'

'Sit down. Take a load off. Let me buy you a pint – that's what you say here, right?'

Matt sat down. 'No, thanks. I never mix drink with business.'

'Neither do I really, but since I'm not flying now 'til later this afternoon, I thought one couldn't hurt,' said Carter. 'Besides, it'll help ease me into Islamabad time.'

'Islamabad?' Matt perked up. 'That explains the ferret on your chin.'

'You like it?' Carter stroked his beard. 'I've had it since Afghanistan. I did a tour there before I left the Deltas. Those were some good times, let me tell you.'

'So why'd you retire your black kit?'

Carter grinned. 'Who says I retired it?'

Matt pointed to the expensive luggage resting at Carter's feet. 'Can't afford that on a soldier's wage.'

'Can't afford it on a regular contractor's pay either,' said Carter. 'I'm guessing that's what finally convinced you to get back to me?' He punched Matt playfully. 'You're terrible at staying in touch, you know that?'

Matt cut to his bottom line. 'You said the pay is awesome. Is that true or were you flannelling me?'

'It's all true, brother. The question is – are you still worth it?' Carter shifted into the role of interviewer. 'What have you been up to since you left the military?'

'Close protection in Kabul.'

Carter didn't hide his disappointment. 'So you've been baby-sitting civvys.'

'Diplomats,' Matt corrected. 'I haven't lost a single client in four years.'

'What about a member of your team?'

Matt thought of Khalid. 'Not to the best of my knowledge.'

Carter cocked his head. 'You like your job, Logan?'

'Think I'd be here if I did?'

Carter's detachment faded. 'I'm glad to hear it. Because if there's one thing I can't stand it's seeing a great soldier go to waste.' He rubbed his hands together. 'What if I told you I'm having more fun now than I did in the military?'

'I'd say it sounds too good to be true.'

'Well it isn't,' said Carter. 'Not when you work for 7M.'

'7M?' said Matt. 'Never heard of them.'

'Yeah, you have.'

Matt deciphered the acronym. 'Bloody hell – you mean Seven Mountains Security?'

'Like the corporate rebrand?' Carter joked.

Desperate as Matt was to build a new life with Emma, the infamous security firm was a compromise too far. He stood up. 'Sorry to have wasted your time.'

'Just hear me out,' said Carter. 'I promise you won't regret it.'

Every fibre in Matt's being was screaming *leave now*. But how could he face Emma without a job? He sat back down. 'You have one minute.'

'I'll have you convinced in thirty seconds.' Carter launched into his pitch. 'There's no denying 7M's had some bad press . . .'

'You think?' Matt interrupted. 'Gunning down civilians at checkpoints, torturing detainees . . .'

'A lot of those stories have been blown out of proportion.'

'Really? Which one?' Matt challenged.

'I'm not going to sit here and analyse everything that's been written about 7M,' said Carter. 'You of all people should know that liberals control the media. And now they control Washington too. 7M's become a whipping boy for all the pansies who've lost their nerve in the War on Terror. Hell, you can't even say *War on Terror* since a Democrat moved into the White House . . .'

Matt tapped his watch.

'I'm the first one to admit that 7M isn't perfect,' Carter continued. 'It has its share of cowboys just like every other private security company.'

Matt recalled some of the dross who'd rotated through the British Embassy over the years. 'That's a fair one, I guess.'

'Do you think I'd work for 7M if I didn't believe wholeheartedly in the company and its mission?' Carter didn't give Matt a chance to answer. '7M does right by its clients and the people who count know it. That's why we're a global leader in private security. Governments, energy companies, mining, engineering, banking, telecoms, media; if it's a player, we look after it.' Carter pointed to the television. 'They're a 7M client.'

Matt turned. SBC was on the screen.

Chapter 14

Rawalpindi, Pakistan

The neat rows of traffic started to bottleneck. 'What's the problem?' Eric asked from the backseat.

'It is the goddamn auto-rickshaws.' Naj hit the horn. 'They hold everything up.'

'I thought those were banned from Islamabad.'

Naj pointed to the highway sign.

Eric read the name emblazoned on the green background. Rawalpindi. No wonder peasants were ruling the road. 'Pindi' as the locals called it was the real Pakistan; an organically grown, sprawling mass of teeming humanity, winding streets, stinking markets, decaying Hindu temples and trashy mosques financed with Saudi oil money.

The correspondent buried his head in a reporter's notebook. The bedlam outside the 4×4 receded as he meditated over the parallel lines dividing the clean white space. He reminded himself there were indeed laws that gave order to the universe; fixed principles that somehow shoehorned even the most violent excesses into harmonious endings.

Naj turned off the main road and slowed for a police checkpoint. 'How much further?' Eric asked.

The armed policeman manning the makeshift barrier waved them through without asking for credentials. 'We shall be there soon,' said the fixer. 'Two, three minutes tops.' He turned up a side street, into a neighbourhood of densely packed concrete buildings. Some of the balconies were practically touching.

Smudge rolled down the front passenger window and looked out. 'Jesus, this takes me right back to Sadr City.'

'Do you want to turn back?' asked Eric.

Smudge retracted his head but left the window open. 'No,' he said defensively.

'You sure?' Eric challenged. 'Because if you don't think it's safe . . .'

'I can't say it's one hundred percent safe here any more than a doctor can tell you you're in one hundred percent good health,' Smudge waffled. 'I gotta throw in some sort of qualifier for insurance reasons.'

Naj drove over a pothole. Jerry came to with a snort. 'Are we there yet?'

Naj pointed to a round dome rising from a tangle of power lines. 'There is the mosque now.'

A half dozen 4×4s identical to SBC's lined the alleyway leading to the square where the mosque was located. A beat-up minivan with an odd antenna shaped like a helicopter rotor was nestled among them. Eric pointed to it. 'Try squeezing in next to that one,' he said.

'But there is no room,' protested Naj.

'Then block them in,' Eric ordered. 'I don't want to lose time hunting for a parking space that doesn't exist.'

'Are we pressed for time?' asked the fixer.

'I want to get some sound bites from the locals when prayers let out,' said Eric.

'I doubt there is anyone in the mosque,' said Naj. 'The security services will have evacuated them.'

'I'm sure there are plenty of people praying somewhere around here,' Eric countered.

Naj manoeuvred the oversized vehicle behind the minivan. As soon as he threw the car into park, a gaggle of children descended on Smudge's open window.

The security man swatted them back and shut it. The urchins were undeterred, pounding the glass to demand a handout. 'Where the hell did they all come from?' said Smudge. 'Go away!' he yelled through the glass.

'They will not leave empty-handed,' said Naj.

A child pressed a mangled limb to the window. Another pointed to a missing eye. Smudge grimaced. 'Are they war orphans?'

'Hardly,' said Eric. 'Their parents maim them and then send them out to beg.'

'That's some sick shit,' said Smudge.

'It happens all the time in this country,' said Eric. 'The more pathetic the child, the more money they earn.'

A boy no more than four years old broke off to return to his mother. She smacked him on the back of the head and sent him back to work, tears streaming down his dirty face.

Smudge reached for his wallet.

'What the hell do you think you're doing?' said Eric.

'Where's your heart, man?'

'I wouldn't do it,' Jerry warned. The cameraman shoved his right hand between the seats. 'See that?' He pointed to a thick raised scar on his thumb. 'I got it in an Iraqi refugee camp. I thought I'd be nice and give my spare change to the kids. I may as well have stuck my hand in a tank of piranhas. Those little shits nearly shredded it. I couldn't work for a month.'

Smudge re-evaluated the flesh-eaters outside his window. 'Maybe I should hang back here and keep an eye on the vehicle,' he suggested. 'We don't want them stealing the tyres.'

Naj opened the glove compartment. 'You can give them these when we leave.' He passed Smudge a box of individually wrapped chocolates. 'Open the window no more than one inch,' he cautioned.

Smudge distracted the beggars with candies while the rest of the team headed for the square.

The police had erected a security cordon to keep journalists and curious locals at bay. Jerry shouldered his camera and climbed on top of a car bonnet to shoot over the corralled horde.

'Is there any activity near the mosque?' asked Eric.

'Not much.' Jerry kept his eye to the lens as he spoke. 'Just a bunch of soldiers standing around an SUV.'

'What does it look like?'

'Same as every other SUV in this country – black. Wait,' he paused. 'I think someone's coming to make a statement.' The cameraman jumped down and started pushing his way through the crowd. Eric and Naj followed behind.

An army officer in a green beret and sweater stepped inside the cordon. The press descended on him with camera lenses and fuzzy-sleeved microphones. 'I am Colonel Saeed Suleiman.'

'Could you spell your name for us?' Eric shouted.

The colonel smiled. 'S-U-L-E-I-M-A-N.' He read directly from a prepared statement. 'At approximately 8.30 a.m. local time, the security forces apprehended a terrorist attempting to detonate a vehicle-borne improvised explosive device. The terrorist was taken into custody and army explosive disposal experts defused the bomb successfully. Due to the vigilance of our army and police, a tremendous tragedy has been averted this day. Our security forces will not rest until the terrorists who threaten the peace and unity of Pakistan are defeated.'

The journalists screamed questions at the colonel. 'Can you tell us more about the bomber? Was the army the intended target?'

'It is too soon to comment on these matters,' said the colonel.

Eric shoved a microphone in his face. 'Was the bomber groomed by Abdullah Qari?'

The question sparked a frenzy among the press corps. 'Is TTP-Q behind this? Does this mean Qari is alive?'

The colonel raised his hands for silence. 'I have no further comment at this time . . .' The journalists kept shouting. 'We now invite members of the press to photograph the explosive device. I would ask you to please remain orderly and respect the barricades we have erected for your safety.'

The colonel remained tight-lipped as he led the journalists out to the 4×4. The soldiers surrounding the vehicle parted, revealing a decommissioned explosive device in the boot. The bomb was massive – five artillery shells interspersed with wires and blocks of plastic explosives.

'Damn,' said Jerry, zooming in on a warhead. 'I wouldn't want to be around when that thing went off.'

Eric checked his watch. 'Neither would I.'

Chapter 15

Islamabad, Pakistan

Emma was sweating like a pig. She'd been circling the white-tiled roof for ten minutes, attempting to establish a signal with the portable satellite dish. The green connection lights on the laptop-sized Broadband Global Area Network terminal were stubbornly dim. She checked the angle of the dish against a larger one fixed on a neighbouring rooftop at the back of the villa. It didn't make sense. The BGAN was pointing in the same direction.

She banged the terminal with the heel of her hand. The local guard laughed. 'You think you can do any better, be my guest,' she challenged. The guard lowered his eyes sheepishly.

She tucked the terminal under her arm and pulled a tissue from her pocket. Emma's makeup was sliding down her face and she didn't have time to reapply it. As she dabbed, she gazed absently past the guard. At last, the problem was clear. All the satellite dishes at the front of the villa were facing east. She looked over her shoulder. The one she'd been using as a reference was pointing south. No wonder she couldn't make a connection.

Emma realigned the BGAN to match the dishes to the front and waited. Beeps sounded as one by one, the lights ignited. With the satellite finally up and running, she finished setting her shot, mounting a video camera on a tripod and pointing the lens west. She looked through the viewfinder. Two minarets were visible screen right. London and New York would be creaming themselves.

She set the auto-focus, walked five paces out toward the edge of the roof and marked the position on the tiles with two strips of black duct tape. The last step was to tie it all up by running a firewire from the camera to the laptop and a cable from the computer to the BGAN.

The bits of kit linked and talking, she opened a dialogue box on the laptop and hit connect. A channel number popped up on screen. She pulled out her BlackBerry and rang the control room in London. 'It's Emma calling from Islamabad. I'm on channel 438. See you in a second.'

She walked over to the X and squared her body to the camera. The viewfinder filled with her image. 'Good morning,' said a tired director over the phone. 'Can you move a little bit to your right? I want to see more of that mosque.' Emma swayed and came back to her original position. 'Much better,' said the director. 'Um, you're a little shiny. Can you take care of that?'

Emma stepped off camera. She hated being ordered to powder her face. It was so demeaning. Male correspondents could look like a bag of shit but God forbid female reporters appear anything other than airbrushed.

She popped back on screen with her face sufficiently matted. 'Much better,' said the director. 'We'll call you on IFB three.'

Emma fixed her earpiece. The sound of two voices – a chirpy female and a dulcet-toned male – fed through the IFB. The London-based morning show anchors were engaging in 'banter'; news speak for mind-numbing bullshit. 'Can you hear me?' the director cut in on the signal. Emma gave him the thumbs-up. 'Good. Can we get a mic check?'

Emma clipped a microphone to her lapel. 'One, two, three, four, five . . .'

'Got it,' said the director. 'Stand by; we're coming to you in five.'

With five minutes to kill, Emma reviewed the script she'd prepared earlier that morning. Like all her live shots, the entire exchange from introduction to the follow-up questions had to be meticulously choreographed in advance.

Anchor Lead-In: Talk about a close call. An alleged suicide bomber in Pakistan was apprehended this morning while attempting to kill dozens of innocent bystanders. The arrest is a rare victory for Pakistan's security services who've been struggling to contain home-grown terrorists wreaking havoc in that country and in neighbouring Afghanistan. Joining us now live from Islamabad with all the details is our very own Emma Cameron. Emma, what have you been able to find out?

Emma: It was an attack aimed at the very heart of Pakistan's establishment, Kiki. The alleged car bomber was apprehended early this morning local time in the garrison city of Rawalpindi – home to Pakistan's main army headquarters. The intended target: a mosque popular with the country's military elite and their families.

Senior Pakistani officials confirmed to us that the bomber was recruited and trained by TTP-Q, the breakaway Pakistani Taliban faction led by Abdullah Qari. The terrorist leader is believed to be behind dozens of suicide bombings, including one that claimed the lives of more than half a dozen CIA employees in Afghanistan last year. If you recall, reports were circulating that Qari was killed during a military offensive in Pakistan's tribal belt last month. But the evidence gathered from this morning's terror scene suggests that the Taliban leader is still very much alive.

Kiki: Emma, why all this confusion about Abdullah Qari?

Emma: Well, Kiki, as you know, Qari is from Pakistan's tribal belt which for years now has provided a safe haven for Taliban operating both in this country and across the border in Afghanistan. At the urging of the United States, Pakistan finally began taking steps to dismantle this Taliban mini-state through a series of military offensives but after nearly three years of fighting, the terrorists seem to be getting stronger. Pakistan is desperate to show it is making progress in this war. And indeed last month, the army claimed that it had finally killed Abdullah Qari. But an influential Muslim cleric closely associated with TTP-Q has maintained all along that Qari escaped unharmed. From what we know of this morning's failed attack, that would seem to be the case.

Kiki: Why is Abdullah Qari so tough to kill?

Emma: Qari may have enemies in Islamabad but he has a lot of supporters in Pakistan's tribal areas where he's leading a secessionist rebellion of ethnic Pashtun; hence why TTP-Q has focused its campaign of terror on the government in Islamabad and not coalition forces in Afghanistan.

Kiki: But Qari was responsible for killing all those CIA employees in Afghanistan last year. I mean, come on – there was even a martyr video that showed him sending off the bomber.

Emma: You're right, Kiki. Qari is responsible for that notorious attack. But bear in mind that the CIA base he targeted was being used to launch pilotless MQ-1 Predator drones over the border into Pakistan to bomb TTP-Q training camps. After the CIA attack, Pakistan assured the United States it would do everything in its power to capture and/or kill Qari. But they're having a tough time making good on that promise. Not only has Pakistan failed to stop the terrorist mastermind, he's attacking the army where it lives and worships.

Kiki: It certainly sounds like Qari can strike wherever and whenever he pleases, Emma, which raises a disturbing question: if the army can't protect their homes how can they keep Pakistan's nuclear arsenal from falling into the hands of terrorists?

Emma: That is the question on everyone's minds right now. Pakistan insists it has measures in place to keep its nuclear warheads safe *but* it refuses to allow the United States or the United Nations to verify those safeguards independently.

Kiki: So what then? We're just supposed to take their word for it that the nukes won't fall into the wrong hands?

Emma: Islamabad has really dug in its heels on this issue, Kiki, stating it will never allow any country to have direct or indirect access to its nuclear facilities.

Kiki: So what's the best- and worst-case scenarios, Emma, especially after this morning's near miss?

Emma: Many are hoping Pakistan will bow to international pressure and open its nuclear programme to outside scrutiny. Until that happens, we'll just have to hope that the safeguards work and the terrorists don't get anywhere near the nukes.

The ominous report was sure to be a ratings winner. Few viewers would realize of course that Emma hadn't actually bothered to visit the scene or speak to a single official herself. But the biggest con of all was the 'impromptu' follow-up Q&A with the anchors. There was no way the talking mannequins in London could wrap their heads around Pakistan's myriad complexities, let alone make the leap from thwarted suicide bombing to nuke-wielding terrorists. That kind of scaremongering had to be spoon-fed.

'Two minutes,' said the director. 'And don't forget Twitter.'

Emma pulled out her BlackBerry. Damn social networking

bullshit. She poised her thumbs over the keyboard and let rip: *Landed in Islamabad yesterday. Haven't seen a fucking thing. Don't have a clue what's really going on so I made up a load of shit to report.*

She deleted the entry. Tempting as it was to salt the earth before she left, some truths she'd have to take to the grave. She searched her mind for something innocuous to send out. Eric's words to her that morning came to mind: *About to go live from Islamabad. What could go wrong?*

A plagiarized tweet. It was the perfect ending to her bogus news career.

Chapter 16

The tweet fed through to Matt's phone. 'So SBC's a client of yours, eh?'

'That's right,' Carter confirmed.

Matt read Emma's tweet and glanced at the television. 'So have you ever done close protection work for SBC?'

'CP work's for bottom feeders,' said Carter. 'Not ex-Special Forces.'

'Last I checked, CP was the top of the food chain in private security.'

'The industry is evolving.' Carter grew more discreet. 'Have you ever heard of an outfit called ICON?'

'We're coming to you in less than a minute,' said the London director. Emma lowered her clipboard and looked into the camera. 'Can you tie your hair back?' the director badgered. 'It's blowing everywhere.'

Emma stepped off camera. If that asshole insisted she preen at the last second, he could goddamn well sweat while she did it out of view. She tilted her head back and gathered her hair up. As she looped it into a ponytail, she noticed a vehicle driving through the checkpoint at the top of the street: a black 4×4. Eric was back way ahead of schedule. At least something was going her way.

'Thirty seconds!' the director screamed.

'Fuck off,' Emma hissed.

The London control room went berserk. 'We can hear you! Your microphone is on!'

Emma couldn't give a toss. After this, she'd never be on air again.

Matt tuned an ear to the television . . . *Talk about a close call* . . . 'Can't say I have.'

'ICON's a new division of 7M,' Carter explained. 'An elite division. We only employ ex-Special Forces.'

'That is the oldest bluff on the circuit, mate,' said Matt. 'A company hires a few ex-SF to kick things off and then replaces them with cheaper ex-infantry lads as soon as they're up and running.'

'Not ICON,' Carter insisted. 'Only elite soldiers cut it on our team. And believe me, we know who's who in this business. Your name's in the database.'

Our very own Emma Cameron . . . Matt glanced quickly at the telly. His heart skipped a beat as his future wife appeared. *It was an attack aimed at the very heart of Pakistan's establishment* . . . 'Because you gave it to them,' he retorted.

'They had it before I even started with the company. ICON knows everyone worth recruiting. Sign on the dotted line and you'll be well looked after. I promise.'

Senior Pakistani officials confirmed to us that the bomber was recruited and trained by TTP-Q . . . 'What about the rest of 7M?' Matt challenged. 'The bottom feeders as you so generously refer to them. I bet the company doesn't look after them too well.' He stole another look at Emma.

'7M is professional across the board,' Carter assured him.

'Every employee is considered a valuable member of the fam—'

A white flash engulfed the television screen. The blood drained from Matt's face. The sight was sickeningly familiar. For the briefest moment, he clung to the vain hope that it was just a technical glitch. Then Emma's head snapped to the left, the screen shook and the dreaded BOOM confirmed the worst: a massive bomb had detonated right behind her.

'Jesus, Mary and Joseph!' Carter exclaimed.

Matt watched helplessly as the woman he loved dropped from the frame. The picture turned sideways and cracked. Emma was visible in the background, lying motionless in a pool of blood.

A cloud of debris rolled in behind her. Matt leapt out of his seat and crouched in front of the television. He reached for the screen as if he could touch her. The picture dipped to black. Emma was gone.

Chapter 17

It seemed like an eternity before the screen reanimated. Matt sat motionless, struggling to process what he'd just seen. Emma had been murdered before his very eyes – yet she was thousands of miles away.

The London studio anchors looked like deer caught in headlights. 'We seem to be having some difficulties out of Islamabad . . .' the female anchor stammered.

'Ha!' Carter blasted.

'. . . we'll be right back after this commercial break.' The signal reverted to an SBC promotional video.

'Now that's taking reality TV to a whole new level,' Carter joked. 'Abdullah Qari definitely outdid himself this time.'

Matt turned to him. 'Who?'

'Abdullah Qari,' said Carter. 'You know, the terrorist who kicked the CIA's butt in Afghanistan and exposed them for the clueless pen-pushers they really are? That reporter chick was talking about him right before she got whacked.'

A face rendered through Matt's trauma – a man with long hair holding an RPG. 'Abdullah Qari,' he repeated.

Carter resumed his ICON pitch. 'I realize this doesn't exactly make a strong case for 7M's across-the-board professionalism but you know even the best laid security plans can't anticipate every . . .'

Professionalism . . . The word punched through Matt's shock, urging him into action. 'You don't have to say any more.' He stood up. 'I want a job with 7M.'

'Awesome,' Carter declared. 'I'll put in a call to ICON HQ right now.'

'I didn't say ICON,' Matt corrected. 'I said 7M.'

'I'm afraid I don't follow,' said Carter. 'If you don't want to work with ICON then what the hell do you want to do?'

'I want to start at the bottom. Put me on the SBC contract. I'm guessing there's an opening now.'

Carter was baffled. 'That task is so beneath you, Logan.'

Matt scrambled for an excuse. 'If 7M is professional across the board, that should hold true for all its contracts, including SBC,' he challenged. 'Get me on it. If I like what I see, I'll join ICON.'

Carter pulled out his mobile and started dialling. 'Consider the job yours then.'

PART II

Chapter 18

Shin Warzak, South Waziristan, Pakistan

Cars and trucks festooned in bright plastic flowers convened on the compound at the end of the cul-de-sac. Indian pop tunes, honking horns, pistol and rifle fire added another layer of merriment to the festivities. The wedding had been going on for several days. Tonight, though, was the main event, the final celebration of a union that promised to heal the ancient rift between South Waziristan's feuding tribes. The groom was Wazir; the bride Mehsud. The arrangement was not compensation for a murder or other slight. Both parties had entered into it peacefully. Even more auspicious, the husband was rumoured to be taken with his new wife.

A brother of the groom came out of the compound to film the arrivals. Women in blue and gold burkas dodged his camera and disappeared into the main house to help prepare the wedding feast. A few male guests were just as shy but most of them played to the lens, showing off weapons and offering testimonials of brotherhood before adjourning to the courtyard for their exclusive celebration.

A black 4×4 pulled up beside a white-washed tree. The photographer rushed to greet it. Such vehicles were status symbols in Pakistan's tribal areas. The occupant had to be a man of tremendous importance.

The doors flew open and three men in pakols climbed down.

All of them had bandoliers strung across their chests and rifles slung over their shoulders. The photographer went ashen as the faces registered in his viewfinder. 'Forgive me,' he said, lowering the lens. 'I did not know it was you.'

Abdullah Qari motioned to one of his henchmen. The loyal guard seized the camera. 'Why do you take Amir Qari's picture?' he demanded.

The photographer trembled. 'It was not my intention.'

'Are you a spy?'

'I am not! I swear before Allah.'

'Liar!' barked the henchman.

The youth dropped to his knees. 'I am your most loyal and humble servant, Amir Qari.' He kissed the Taliban leader's feet. 'I would give my life to defend yours.'

Qari brushed him aside. The grovelling of a youth was not half as satisfying as the fawning that awaited him inside the compound.

He was pleased to see the host had spared no expense on the wedding feast. A large awning had been erected over the court-yard to conceal the festivities from hostile eyes looking down from the heavens. A rubab player was tuning his instrument. Qari searched for a drummer. Without percussion there could be no dancing and without dancing, the evening would lack the proper climax.

The guests parted for Qari and his entourage. Low-ranking labourers and gangsters bowed reverently before him. Wealthy merchants, crime bosses, warlords and educated bureaucrats stepped forward to kiss him on both cheeks. All declared their undying gratitude to Pashtunistan's would-be liberator.

Qari basked in the adulation. It didn't matter that the tributes were offered out of fear rather than respect. In his mind, the sentiments were interchangeable.

He made his way to the most powerful men at the gathering, aside from himself: the tribal chiefs sitting in a circle, discussing the future of their realms. Many were the same age as Qari; late twenties, early thirties. Their fathers and grandfathers had lost their heads for daring to defy him.

One of the chiefs stroked his chin and laughed as Qari approached. The Taliban leader wondered whether they were mocking his beard. He was very self-conscious about the patchy wisps on his face. He tried to compensate for this humiliating blemish on his manhood by wearing his hair long over his shoulders, but it was not always effective.

The chiefs rose. 'Amir Qari,' said the elder who'd made fun of his beard, 'you honour us with your presence this evening.'

'The honour is mine,' said Qari, assuming the detractor's seat.

The chief snapped his fingers. A young boy rushed over with another chair. 'Have you news from Mullah Maulana, may Allah's grace be upon him.'

'Mullah Maulana is well,' said Qari. 'He believes it will not be long now before Islamabad agrees to discuss our independence.'

'Once that is achieved, the western forces in Afghanistan will surely see the folly of their efforts and agree to split the country between north and south,' another chief offered.

'Pashtunistan will be reunited soon,' Qari said confidently.

The chiefs nodded in agreement – except the detractor. 'But your last attack was not entirely successful,' he said. 'One of your martyrs was captured alive.'

Qari was enraged. How dare that donkey criticize him? 'Our success that day far overshadowed any failure,' the Taliban leader insisted. 'We slaughtered a western whore before the eyes of the world. There is not a general or politician in Islamabad who does not fear us now.'

'By all means, laud your victory. But unwise is the warrior who fails to learn from his mistakes. There is weakness in your organization.'

Qari deflected the criticism. 'Surely you are aware that we have taken on a new ally.'

'This alliance with the Baluch concerns me,' one of the chiefs interrupted. 'They are not good Muslims.'

Another agreed. 'Their lack of piousness has infected our warriors.'

Qari moved to quell the backlash. 'Our alliance with the Baluch is not ideal. But if we sever it now it will only strengthen our common enemy,' he argued. 'How long have Wazir and Mehsud been weakened by turning their swords on each other?' The chiefs looked at one another. 'We need to fight alongside the Baluch until Islamabad is defeated,' Qari declared. 'Be patient, my brothers. Today we embrace the Baluch, but tomorrow we shall conquer them. Their lands and their riches shall be ours.'

'Is that what you would have us be?' said the detractor. 'Occupiers?'

'I would have us be strong,' Qari answered.

'We are not Punjabis. Tyranny is the way of the weak.' He drew his pistol. 'This makes us strong.'

Qari and his henchmen drew their pistols in return. 'Indeed it does,' said the Taliban leader.

The sound of celebratory gunfire defused the stand-off. The sun was setting. It was time to leave the courtyard to allow the women to lay the wedding banquet.

Darkness had descended over the russet mountains when the men returned to their feast. Steaming platters of flatbread, spiced rice, roast mutton and stewed meat had been placed on large plastic

sheets along with bottles of soda and pots of sweet tea. The meal
was sumptuous, but no one, including the fathers of the bride and
groom, dare touch a crumb before Qari broke bread.

He assumed the place of honour and tucked in. Qari gorged
himself until his face glistened with fat and his belly was near
bursting. His hunger, like all his appetites, was voracious.

Young boys brought out more platters piled with pomegran-
ates, almonds, pistachios, candied fruits and sesame confections.
Opium pipes and flasks of whisky began making the rounds.
Though both were strictly forbidden by Islam, indulging such
vices was accepted if not encouraged at such events. Qari partook
of both and reclined on a cushion, listening to the soulful plucks
of the rubab.

The sound of a drum roused him from his drug-induced slum-
ber. The plastic sheeting had been cleared. Qari sat up. The real
entertainment was about to begin.

A boy dressed in women's clothing appeared from behind a
curtain. He spun across the carpet, ringing bells tied to his wrists
and ankles. The dancer was not to Qari's taste; a shadow from
shaving was evident on the child's upper lip.

A second dancer joined the show, his face hidden beneath a
sheer pink veil. The unknown aroused the Taliban leader.
Though less talented than the bearded youth, this one could
prove more to his liking.

The melody changed and the dancer removed his veil. Qari
was pleased. The boy had not yet been ruined by puberty. He
turned to his henchmen. 'Bring him outside.'

The guards did as they were bid and left their master to his pleasure. Qari opened the door of his 4×4. 'Get in and undress,' he
ordered. He waited outside while the child prepared himself.

Drunk and high, the Taliban leader swayed back and forth, trying to keep his balance. The feeling of cold metal at the base of his skull quickly restored his equilibrium.

'Call out and you die,' warned the man holding the pistol to Qari's head.

The Taliban leader was certain it was the chief who had challenged him earlier. 'Why so impatient, brother? I shall finish with the boy quickly.'

The pressure subsided. Qari turned to confront the chief whose death he would now surely order, only to be blinded by a fist. He fell to the ground, dazed. 'You take him then,' the Taliban leader panted. 'I'm not in the mood now.' The offer invited more blows. Feet set upon Qari from all sides. He tried calling for his guards, but his cries could not penetrate his own shielding hands.

The attackers scooped Qari off the ground and loaded him into the boot of a truck. The rebel leader was barely conscious when it screeched out of the cul-de-sac and headed downhill, tossing him about like a boat in a storm. As he went under, he heard cannons firing in the distance – thousands of them.

Chapter 19

Matt stared at the document on his tray-table. He'd developed calluses, he'd thumbed through it that many times. If only his heart could harden as well. 7M's post-incident report of the attack on SBC's Islamabad bureau may have been written in the dry language of corporate arse-covering, but there was no white-washing Matt's guilt or anguish. The post-mortem was a constant reminder of how he'd failed Emma – first as a provider and then as a protector. There was only one thing he could do for her now. Find and kill the man responsible for her murder.

Matt didn't underestimate the obstacles that lay ahead. Abdullah Qari had managed to elude the Pakistani army and a fleet of US drones. Evasion that effective required a well-resourced and loyal support network, one Matt would have to learn inside and out if he were to have any hope of getting near the terrorist mastermind. That's why he'd asked Carter to put him on the SBC contract. It was the perfect cover for operating covertly in Pakistan. As a security advisor to a recently targeted network, Matt could easily pass off any probing into TTP-Q as background research for his job. There was so much about Qari he needed to learn. What drove the Taliban leader? What was his agenda? Who inspired him? Who backed him? How did he select his targets? And most crucially, who had helped him pull off the spectacular attack on SBC's bureau?

Matt may not have known why of all the western networks in

Islamabad, Qari had set his sights on Emma's, but he was certain of one thing: TTP-Q had someone on the inside feeding them information. It was no coincidence that the VBIED had detonated when Emma was live, on-air. Qari had wanted the world to see his handiwork uncensored. That level of precision required an accomplice who could access SBC's schedules well in advance. Whoever the traitor was, Matt would find him soon enough. He'd be meeting his new clients in a matter of hours.

Before he said hello, Matt was determined to tackle the post-incident report with a clinical eye. 7M had published it just two days after the attack; a lightning turn-around for a security company. He knew there were holes in the findings, mistakes that had been glossed over, omitted details that were preventing him from getting to the truth. But though he'd spent the last forty-eight hours scouring the pages, Matt had found nothing so far. Emma's loss was still too raw to allow him to read with any degree of objectivity.

He opened the document. As usual, the stated Aim of the report provoked instant fury.

> The purpose of this report is to extract lessons that may be applicable to current and future 7M operations.

The only 'lessons' Matt could identify were how to conceal colossal lapses in professionalism. The flannel started with the opening Background section. The bullet points listed the date and time of the attack; the method (VBIED); the type of explosives used (military artillery shells, plastic explosive); client casualties (1); cause of death (lethal shrapnel wounds sustained during the attack); and collateral damage (2 local nationals employed by client). Nowhere was Emma named specifically. She and the rest of SBC's employees were referred to anonymously as

Clients A, B, C and D. The identity of the 7M advisor on duty at the time was similarly concealed – Contractor S.

There was, however, one strategic exception to the single-letter aliases. Written in bold type at the bottom of each page was the following disclaimer:

Post incident, 7M Ltd in accordance with company policy and operational SOPs, enlisted an external assessor to conduct a comprehensive review of the incident. The assessor, Emilio J. Hernandez, is a full-time employee of ICON, a separate but wholly owned subsidiary of 7M Ltd. Mr Hernandez has extensive Special Forces operational experience in the United States military and has worked as a civilian contractor in hostile environments for more than two years. Having spent November 2007 to present in Pakistan, he possesses a thorough understanding of the specific security challenges of the country. This report is the only official 7M Ltd report in regards to this incident.

As far as Matt could tell, the Bible-thumping 2IC who'd given him shit in the Green Zone hadn't been brought in to shed light on 7M's mistakes but to cover up the close protection bottom-feeders' mess. Few would have the expertise or the balls to argue with the findings of an ex-Special Forces soldier.

Matt turned to the section marked Incident. The blow-by-blow was a mildly embellished version of the Background section. His frustration welled. He still couldn't find the smoking gun.

Whatever hint of impartiality he'd mustered abandoned him completely when he turned to the final page. Nestled below the Conclusion was a passage that made him want to put his fist through someone's face. Though it was tempting to skip over it,

Matt knew he shouldn't. He needed to ingest the obscenity and build up his tolerance before he met the clients. If anyone suspected he had an ulterior motive for working with SBC, he'd be booted off the job.

* 7M CP performed a security audit of SBC's Islamabad bureau prior to the clients taking occupancy. Though various security issues were highlighted, the clients opted for occupancy, citing cost considerations for rented residential accommodation v hotels offering a comparable level of security in Islamabad.

Tears of fury streamed down Matt's face. SBC had knowingly housed Emma in a vulnerable location just to save a few quid. And 7M, the network's money-grabbing security advisors, let them get away with it in order to keep the contract.

He closed the report. The only way he was going to find the missing pieces was see the incident area and make his own assessment.

'Headset?' asked a flight attendant.

Matt wiped his eyes. 'No, thank you.'

The attendant noticed Matt's tray-table wasn't lying flush. 'Can I help you with that, sir?' The stiff smile concealing her monotony fell when she noticed what was blocking the table: a large bulge beneath Matt's shirt.

He knew what she was thinking: there's a suicide bomber on board. The truth was less explosive, though it would still raise eyebrows. Matt had half a million dollars in client money strapped to his waist.

'I changed my mind.' He took a headset to calm her fears. Martyrs spent their last minutes praying, not watching in-flight entertainment.

Matt put on the earphones and switched on his console. Clips of soundtracks synced with the pictures flickering on the tiny screen embedded in the seat in front of him: cartoons, reruns of sit-coms, movie previews. The vapid fragments had a soporific effect. Matt hadn't slept since Emma's murder and the four nights of insomnia were finally catching up with him.

He was drifting in the space between consciousness and dreaming when the words *Abdullah Qari* rattled him. The SBC news update had been pre-recorded earlier that day. Correspondent Eric Riddell was reporting from Islamabad.

. . . local witnesses claim at least twenty-seven members of the wedding party were killed in the drone strike. Senior Pakistani officials insist no Taliban militants were sheltering in the area at the time, including Abdullah Qari.

The contentious attack has further strained relations between Pakistan and its western allies. This morning, Islamabad announced it will be closing its borders to NATO convoys supplying coalition forces in Afghanistan until further notice . . .

The details of the dispatch faded as Matt was drawn back to Emma's final, violent live shot: the flash of light, her head snapping to the left, the shaking camera, her blood streaming across the roof. He'd replayed the sequence in his head a thousand times, trying to reconcile it with Hernandez's conclusion that Emma had died of shrapnel wounds. Matt could have sworn he'd seen Emma's head snap *before* the bomb detonated – not after. If he was right, she couldn't possibly have been killed by flying shrapnel.

But if it wasn't the bomb, then what had killed her? Matt knew his attachment made him an unreliable witness to her on-screen murder. He tried searching for the clip on YouTube to confirm his suspicions. But by the time he'd thought to look for it, the graphic video had been red-flagged and pulled.

Comments left by mourning fans flashed through his head as he succumbed again to exhaustion. If it hadn't been for Emma's admirers, he never would have met her . . .

Matt was minding his business in the cattle-class queue when he felt the nudge on his shoulder. 'Dude,' said the passenger standing behind him. 'Check it out.'

Instinctively, Matt scanned the Dubai airport terminal for warning signs of an attack: abandoned luggage, young men in loose-fitting clothes mumbling prayers. Only one thing stood out as unusual: a very fit blonde woman loading black cases onto the baggage belt at the KamAir Business Class counter. She was struggling with the heavy load and her male travelling companion was doing nothing to help. The lazy git was just standing there holding a camera.

'It's the Satellite Dish,' said the fan.

Matt started searching for comms equipment. 'Where?'

The fan pointed to the blonde. 'Right there, dude.'

Matt gladly refocused on the damsel in distress. 'Who is she?'

'Emma Cameron. Don't you watch the news?'

After those stolen glances at the ticket counter, Matt doubted he'd ever see Emma again. She was a class above him and the wheat never waited with the chaff in Dubai Terminal 1. He was knocked for six when he saw her sitting in the Irish bar with her camera-toting companion.

Matt ordered a Coca-Cola and took a seat across from them. He quickly discovered he wasn't the only man in the bar taking an interest in the news beauty. Emma was bombarded.

Businessmen handed her their cards, private security contractors passed her cocktail napkins with their details. She didn't enjoy the attention at all but handled it well enough, smiling for pictures and gracefully declining phone numbers. The best moments for Matt though were between barrages when Emma would let her guard down. There was something in her solitude drawing him to her, a longing he knew intimately. Emma Cameron was disillusioned with her lot.

Two businessmen walked toward her. Matt eavesdropped on their conversation. *Nice tits . . . I'd fuck her . . .* they joked to one another. His protective instincts aroused, he kept an eye on the pair. Sure enough, they crossed the line and started harassing Emma outright.

She looked to her travelling companion for help but he was too drunk to care. 'Hey!' Matt shouted. 'Don't you fellas have wives at home?'

The shamed duo backed off. Emma acknowledged Matt's help with a grin; the most sincere she'd offered anyone so far. He wanted to parley his small act of chivalry into a conversation but by the time he'd worked up the courage, it was time to go.

When they landed in Kabul, Emma had a twenty-minute head start off the plane. Determined to introduce himself, Matt exploited his knowledge of the third world airport to narrow the gap. He knew passport control would be manic; five rows of irritable travellers convening on a single kiosk. There was, however, one that was always wide open.

Matt grabbed a policeman and shoved a twenty-dollar bill into his hand. The officer promptly whisked him through the empty kiosk reserved for ISAF personnel into the baggage area. He spotted Emma at the front of the customs queue. There was a hold-up. Her travelling companion's camera had been impounded.

'I've got the paperwork right here.' The cameraman searched his coat pockets. 'Shit.'

Daggers flew from Emma's eyes. 'What the fuck, Jerry?'

Matt was surprised to hear her swearing. The earthy language made him like her even more.

'I left the forms at the bar in Dubai,' said Jerry.

'You fuckwit!' Emma turned to the customs officer. 'We can't locate the paperwork right now but if you switch the camera on you'll see that it works.'

The officer handed her a slip of paper. 'Go upstairs. Pay fine, then you get camera back.'

Emma crumpled up the paper. 'You mean bribe,' she challenged.

The customs officer called the police. Matt could see where this was headed. Emma's defiance was going to land her in an Afghan jail. He stepped forward. 'They're with me.'

Emma turned around.

Matt knew she recognized him from the Irish Bar. 'Name's Matt,' he said, extending his hand.

'Thank you for your concern, Matt, but . . .'

'Shut up and let me help you.' Matt waved to the arrivals area where Khalid was waiting for him. He called the translator over. 'These people had their camera confiscated.'

'Afghans have grave concerns about video cameras,' Khalid explained. 'The Northern Alliance leader Ahmad Shah Massoud was killed by assassins posing as journalists. They hid the bomb in their camera.'

Matt gestured at Emma. 'I don't think she's an insurgent. Come on,' he whispered to Khalid. 'Be a mate. Make me look good.'

Khalid got the camera back in short order. He handed it off to Matt. 'Good luck.'

Jerry swooped in and grabbed it. 'Thanks, man.'

Emma waited for the cameraman to move from earshot. 'That's twice you've come to my rescue today,' she said to Matt.

'I can't bear to see a lassie in distress.'

Emma raised a brow. 'Lassie?'

'Cameron's a Scottish name,' Matt pointed out, 'or do you prefer Satellite Dish?'

The familiarity bred instant contempt. Emma's barriers flew up. 'Well, thank you for all your help. Goodbye.'

She turned and walked away. Matt was ready to call it a day. Who was he kidding? Emma was famous and he was just another loser on the pull. Then, out of nowhere, the motto that had encouraged him through so many impossible odds went up like a flare. *Who Dares Wins* . . . 'Hey, lassie!'

*   *   *

The plane slammed down on the runway. Matt tucked away the precious memory. Sentiment and distraction were luxuries he could no longer afford. He had a terrorist to hunt.

Chapter 20

'You've been putting us off for days,' Ted complained down the secure line. He glanced at the newspaper headline which had prompted the latest phone call to his Pakistani counterparts.

CRISIS IN US INTELLIGENCE:
CIVILIAN DEATHS THREATEN TO UNDERMINE
CO-OPERATION WITH PAKISTAN

'We have every right to interrogate the suspect and you know it,' Ted fumed, 'a United States citizen was murdered.' He knew the comment would backfire before it even left his lips and not because his drone had just killed more than two dozen innocent Pakistani civilians. High or low, morality carried no weight with Inter-Services Intelligence, Pakistan's spy agency. In Ted's experience, the ISI responded only to hard-nose tactics – blackmail, extortion, threats – things at which they themselves excelled. 'Well, as soon as you remember that we're supposed to be sharing intelligence and not hoarding it, give me a call. In the meantime, I'll be compiling a full report for the Senate Intelligence Committee which I'm sure they'll find useful when it comes time to review the 7.5-billion-dollar aid package that pads your Swiss bank account!'

Ted slammed the phone down and looked at Bethany. She was holding fast to her files. 'The ISI claims we have no authority to interrogate the suspect,' said the spy chief. 'But I'm guessing you figured that out.'

'Perhaps we can get the State Department to lean on them?'

'No one at State's going to stick their necks out for us.' Ted picked up the newspaper. 'The sharks are circling, Bethany.'

'For what it's worth, sir, the article is rather vague. US intelligence could refer to the Defense Intelligence Agency, the Strategic Support Branch . . .'

'It doesn't have to name us specifically. Whenever there's an intelligence failure, people automatically assume it's the CIA.' Ted threw the newspaper down. 'It was bad enough when people thought we were evil. Now we're evil *and* incompetent.' He picked up a paperweight and started tossing it.

Bethany laid her files down on the desk and took the orb from his hand. Ted searched for another object on which to vent his frustrations. His windowless office was full of paraphernalia: snow globes from various postings, a Newton's cradle, photographs. A plastic bin came into his crosshairs. Ted kicked it to the wall but the physical exertion offered only momentary relief. He slumped behind his desk – dejected. 'I may as well just tender my resignation and get it over with.'

'But you were just promoted, sir.'

'On the back of failures which we now know were beyond the control of my predecessor. Our agents in Afghanistan, the Detroit bomber . . . neither of those were the agency's fault. But this wedding debacle is on my head,' said Ted. 'I ordered that strike. It's my responsibility.'

'But Abdullah Qari was at that wedding,' Bethany pointed out.

'Not when the missile hit. And that's all that counts.'

'Think of all the good that's happened,' Bethany encouraged, 'all the terror attacks that have been prevented as a result of work that's happened on your watch.'

'The public never sees the successes.' Ted slipped further into his funk. 'They see correspondents getting blown up on live television. And we can't even interrogate the one suspect in custody who could lead us to the culprit.'

Bethany sat down across from him. 'May I speak candidly, sir?' Ted surfaced from his gloom long enough to give her a nod. 'Does it really matter whether or not we interrogate the suspect? We know why Emma Cameron was targeted. If we inform the Director, he can take it to Congress.'

Ted wondered whether he'd made a mistake allowing her to work on such a delicate case. She hadn't been exposed to this world of duplicity long enough to appreciate the minefield they were navigating. 'The Director doesn't want to bring this to Congress – especially now. It will look like we're trying to blame our mistakes on another agency.'

'But, sir . . .'

Ted raised his hand. 'The laws of physics apply as much to the CIA as they do anywhere, Bethany.'

'I don't follow.'

'Shit rolls downhill, not up,' Ted explained. 'The Director expects us to contain the damage, wrap it up in a package, tie it with a silk bow and present it to him as a problem solved.'

'I understand,' said Bethany. 'So, how would you like to proceed?'

Ted gestured at the newspaper. 'That article quoted senior Pakistani officials. They could give a rat's ass what happens to civilians in the tribal areas. That story is a shot across the bow. Pakistan is looking for any excuse to sever intelligence co-operation with the United States.'

'Is it possible they're just sabre rattling? It wouldn't be the first time Islamabad cried wolf to milk more money out of Congress.'

'I don't think so,' said Ted. 'They sense an imminent threat to their state. It's our job now to figure out how much they know. The suspect can tell us that.'

'But he's nothing but a foot soldier. He'll know nothing about Abdullah Qari's inner circle.'

'It doesn't matter. The suspect is a window into the ISI's thinking. They'll work him over until they get the confession that fits their version of events. God knows, I've seen it happen before.'

'The ISI isn't known for their soft touch,' Bethany commented.

Ted wondered at her naivety. If she was going to realize her potential as an intelligence agent, the scales would have to fall from her eyes. 'I was talking about us.'

'Sir?'

'When I was a young case officer – not much older than you actually – I was part of a team assigned to take over an FBI interrogation of a high-profile terror suspect,' Ted explained. 'To their credit, the FBI didn't really need our help. They'd managed to obtain informed, actionable intelligence from the suspect almost immediately. In fact, he was proving to be quite the resource – until we screwed it up. You see, the CIA team consisted of one token, wet-behind-the ears, full-time company man,' Ted pointed to himself, 'and two outside *contractors*.' The word still left a bad taste in his mouth.

'Contractors?' asked Bethany.

'Hired guns. Neither of whom had a background in intelligence. In fact, neither of them had ever conducted an interrogation in their lives. They were shrinks, if you can believe it.'

'But why bring in two psychologists when there were experienced interrogators inside the agency?'

'Experience was a liability during the Bush years.' Tempted as he was to elaborate, Ted was equally loath to digress. 'The contractors' credentials didn't matter. They were hired because they were willing to do whatever was necessary to justify their pay cheques.'

Bethany looked at him curiously.

Ted spelled it out for her. 'Get the answers the Pentagon and the White House were hoping to hear. So these numb nuts blew into town, waving some executive order and basically told the FBI to take a hike. After that, the interrogation fell apart. The contractors didn't believe in the Informed Interrogation Approach. Their techniques were straight out of KUBARK,' he said, referring to the infamous 1960s CIA torture training manual. 'After twenty-four hours with the contractors, the suspect shut down and stopped talking.'

'Did they waterboard him?' asked Bethany, as if such practices belonged to an ancient era.

Ted was oddly comforted that his protégée would never have such a dark shadow cast over her service. 'No,' said the spy chief. 'All it took was a little sensory deprivation for the suspect to clam up. When he did start talking again everything out of his mouth was complete fiction, but the contractors didn't care. As long as it kept their paymasters happy they passed it on as gospel. The impact on our operations was devastating. We were tied up for months, years even, chasing down bullshit leads that the suspect had manufactured just to please those contractors. In the meantime, real terrorists were plotting real attacks.'

'Did you file a complaint?'

'You bet,' said Ted. 'And I wasn't the only one. The Director of Counterterrorism was furious when he learned what was going on. He took it all the way to the White House.'

'Did the President take action?'

'Oh, he took action all right. He fired the Director and handed half our portfolio to the Strategic Support Branch.'

'So the contractors were never held to account?'

'They're still working for the government as far as I know.'

Bethany was indignant. 'They violated the Geneva Convention. They should be in jail.'

'At least episodes like that are behind this agency,' said Ted. 'Thank God we were called to the carpet by Congress and forced to disclose all of our activities during the Bush years. But as long as there are elements of the US intelligence community operating without oversight, deniable resources like those contractors will never be short of work.'

Bethany pushed her mannish glasses back into place. 'There's certainly no shortage of them in Pakistan.'

The comment reinvigorated Ted. 'Enough history. Did you bring the files I asked for?'

Bethany grabbed the stack of folders and handed him the top one. 'This is a list of all US journalists currently working in Pakistan. Most of them are staying at the Serena in Islamabad.'

Ted scanned the names quickly. 'Let's hope none of them stray too far afield.' He closed the file. 'Next.'

Bethany passed him the second folder. 'These are the phone records you requested.' Before Ted could read them, she laid the third folder over it.

'What's this?' he asked.

'Another journalist.'

Ted opened the file. The name was familiar but he hadn't heard it in years. 'OK,' he said. 'I'll bite.'

'He's not here on a press visa,' Bethany explained. 'He's travelling on a *business* visa.'

'How'd you find him?' Bethany gestured at the phone records folder lying on the desk. 'Excellent initiative,' said the spy chief.

Bethany basked in his praise. 'I've already taken the liberty of putting surveillance on him. You'll be interested to know that we're not the only ones watching him.'

'Don't assign too much significance to that,' Ted warned. 'He's probably caught in the ISI's Islamabad dragnet with his old press buddies.'

'He's not in Islamabad, sir.'

Ted reassessed her. 'So where is he?'

Bethany smiled. 'Quetta, sir.'

Chapter 21

Benazir Bhutto International Airport, Islamabad

'Anything to declare?'

Matt distanced his thoughts from the bricks of cash strapped to his waist. 'No.'

The customs officer oscillated a greedy eye between Matt's face and the cheap nylon duffle shielding his torso. 'Open it,' he ordered. Matt slid the duffle onto a grimy countertop and stood by passively while the officer ransacked his belongings. The neatly rolled clothing bundles were shaken and discarded into a heap, the contents of the toiletry bag tipped out onto the filthy counter. When the initial search produced nothing, the officer delved further, running his hands along the bottom of the bag to check if it was false.

Matt prepared himself. If the half a million dollars he was smuggling for his clients were confiscated, he'd be held liable for the lot. And this bastard wasn't going to let up until he'd found something undeclared.

The officer's attention shifted abruptly. Matt looked over his shoulder. A group of Chinese businessmen was making its way up from the baggage claim. Their suits were as ostentatious as their matching leather suitcases. The officer grunted and jerked his chin; a signal for Matt to collect his things and move on. There were richer foreigners to shake down.

*   *   *

Multi-generational families and drivers holding white-boards were gathered behind the barriers in arrivals. Matt searched for his name among the Arab, Iranian, Asian and Chinese extractions. He couldn't find it. Figured. Contractor S – the useless advisor he was taking over from – was supposed to be his point of contact.

Matt walked into the main terminal. Policemen armed with automatic rifles were patrolling the open space. With their overt display of firepower, they should have been the most conspicuous figures in the airport. But a lone man in a tan shalwar kameez had managed to eclipse them all. It was Carter. The ex-Delta captain looked like he'd come from a fancy-dress party.

'Welcome to Islamabad,' he said in an unusually tempered voice.

'What are you doing here?' asked Matt, surprised.

'You didn't think I'd let you come to Pakistan without saying hello.'

'Isn't running a CP bloke from the airport a bit menial for you?' It sounded like a joke, but Matt was serious.

'I don't mind slumming it for you, brother,' said Carter. 'Come on.'

A group of soldiers armed with Heckler and Koch MP5s came barrelling along the pavement outside. Stacks of luggage tumbled down as people with carts swerved to avoid them. 'Are the security forces always this heavy-handed?' asked Matt, side-stepping a split bag.

'They're nervous about the protest tomorrow,' said Carter.

'What protest?'

'Against the drone strike.'

Matt looked at him blankly.

Carter stopped. 'You do know about that, right?'

'I've been sitting in the Pakistan Embassy for three days

waiting for my visa to be approved.' Matt could tell Carter was reluctant to fill him in on the details. 'What happened?'

The ex-Delta captain looked around before speaking. 'The CIA dispatched a Predator to a house in South Waziristan. Abdullah Qari was supposed to be attending a wedding there. Turns out he wasn't and a bunch of civilians got whacked instead.' He bowed his head. 'You know how these things are, Logan. Fog of war and all.'

Matt nodded. 'Fog of war,' he repeated. It was all he could do not to choke on the words.

Carter continued walking. 'Every Taliban sympathizer in the tribal belt is up in arms over it. The government tried throwing them a bone by closing the border to NATO supply trucks bound for Afghanistan, but it didn't work. Come this time tomorrow, Islamabad will be overrun with tribal-belt hillbillies.' Carter slapped Matt on the back. 'And you, brother, will have a ringside seat. The protestors are marching on the Presidential Palace which is just a stone's throw from the Serena. That's where your clients relocated after their house was bombed.'

Matt recognized the five-star hotel name from Kabul. His anger bubbled. Now that Emma was dead, SBC was finally loosening its purse strings. 'Fancy digs.'

'Don't get too used to it,' said Carter. 'When you get tired of baby-sitting journalists – and you will get tired of it – I'm moving you right over to ICON.'

'Let me get through this task first.'

'Come on, Logan. You know it'll be a cakewalk.'

'I bet the laddie I'm replacing thought so too,' said Matt. 'Where is Contractor S anyway?'

'He blew town the day of the incident.'

Matt felt robbed. He was looking forward to having a heart-to-heart with Contractor S. '7M sacked him straight away, eh?'

'Oh, he wasn't fired,' Carter corrected. '7M CP reassigned him in case some money-grubbing lawyer at SBC got it in his head to sue us down the road. It's like I told you back in London: the company takes care of its own.'

Matt's anger spiked. Contractor S and everyone above him needed hanging for what had happened to Emma.

Three men smoking next to a red Toyota came into Matt's crosshairs. Immediately his professionalism kicked in. All were dressed in identical black suits and none carried luggage. 'Red Toyota. Three up.'

Carter shielded his eyes. 'Where?'

'Could you be a little more subtle?' said Matt.

'Relax, brother. I'm sure it's nothing.'

His suspicions heightened, Matt searched for other incongruities. A vehicle sitting on the edge of the car park soon caught his eye. To the layman, the tatty minivan with the garland of red and gold pom-poms would seem unremarkable; a local cab resting between passengers. But there were clues that the vehicle and its occupants were far from humble. The minivan was parked in such a way that no one could pull alongside, leave and detonate a bomb or sneak underneath an adjacent vehicle to plant a magnetic IED. The dead give-away though was the propeller-like antennae on the roof. The beat up minivan was decked out with a sat comms system worth more than the vehicle itself.

'Keep your eyes forward,' Matt instructed Carter. He tracked the black-suited men's movements through his peripheral vision as he and Carter walked past. As soon as they were clear, he heard the doors slam and the engine start. 'Can you tell if they're pulling out?'

'No,' said Carter. 'My eyes are forward, remember?'

'It's no joke,' said Matt. 'They looked pretty heavy to me.'

'Everyone in Pakistan looks heavy. Don't be so paranoid.'

'Better to be paranoid than get caught out, especially when we're outnumbered.'

'But we're not.' Carter gestured to the minivan on the edge of the car park.

Matt should have known. The Deltas and their fancy kit.

Carter slid open the back door. A beige shalwar kameez and black zip-front flak jacket were resting on the seat. 'These are for you,' he said, handing them to Matt. 'Body armour's your call but we'd appreciate it if you put the clothes on. We like to keep a low profile at ICON.'

'I'm not ICON,' Matt reminded him.

'You are 'till you get to your hotel.' Carter ducked inside. 'You ride shotgun, start getting your bearings.' Matt climbed into the front passenger seat. 'You remember Hernandez, don't you?' said Carter from the backseat.

The 2IC was behind the wheel. Like Carter, he'd grown a beard and opted for local clothing, though Hernandez's swarthy features made the disguise more convincing. 'Good to see you, mate,' said Matt.

The Bible-thumping 2IC responded with a cold nod.

Matt gathered up the long kameez. 'If it's all right with you lads, I'd like to swing by the incident area before I meet the clients.'

Carter and Hernandez exchanged glances through the rear-view. 'Didn't you read the post-incident report?' asked the ex-Delta captain.

'I did.' Matt poked his head through the shirt. 'I'd still like to see the house.'

'Something wrong with the report?' Hernandez challenged.

Much as Matt wanted to rubbish the 2IC's work, insulting him would be counterproductive at this point. 'I know you lads don't think much of close protection work but don't lump me in with that meathead who was here before me.' He pulled the local trousers over his western pair. 'I want to see where the incident took place and make my own assessment. It's no reflection on the quality of your work, Hernandez. It's just how I do things. I'm sure you'd do the same in my position.'

Carter opened the door. 'I'll phone the ops room and let them know we're making a diversion. Finish briefing him, will ya?' he asked Hernandez before closing it.

The 2IC grabbed a map from the dashboard. 'Airport,' he said, stabbing it with his index finger, 'hotel, SBC's old house.' He shoved it at Matt. 'You keep it.'

Matt quickly studied the map. It was a standard grid with no unique markings. 'Don't you use spotted maps?'

'CP folks find them too confusing,' said Hernandez, as if Matt were one of the bottom feeders. He pulled a black gym bag from beneath Matt's seat. 'Vehicle weapon . . .' Matt reached for it. The 2IC blocked him. 'That's for Carter's use only. I'm just letting you know it's there.'

Matt didn't relish the idea of sitting on his hands during a contact. 'Fine. I'll make do with a personal weapon.'

'Foreign CP teams aren't licensed to carry weapons in Pakistan.'

Matt gestured to the bag. 'What the fuck is that? A water pistol?'

'ICON doesn't do CP,' Hernandez reminded him. He leaned across Matt's lap and knocked on the window to get Carter's attention. 'Do we issue him with a homing beacon?' he shouted through the glass.

Matt tensed. The one thing he didn't need was a beacon tracking his every move.

Carter shook his head no.

Matt tried to seem annoyed. 'What about comms?'

Hernandez tossed him a mobile phone. 'If you get into trouble, 7M's ops room in Virginia's on speed dial.'

Matt flipped the phone open to check the battery life. 'What about the ops room in Islamabad?'

'We got one, but you don't,' said Hernandez. 'All CP tasks are coordinated out of 7M HQ in Virginia.'

Matt tallied his deficits: shit comms, no spotted maps, no ops room and no weapons. If Steve could see him now, he'd have a right laugh.

Chapter 22

There was no system to manage the traffic exiting the airport car park, just honking horns, recriminations and vehicles punching their way into a snaking queue. Matt spied the red Toyota idling ahead. 'Red Toyota, three up,' he warned.

'What's that?' asked Hernandez.

'Logan's feeling a bit on edge,' Carter explained.

The Toyota waited until they passed before joining the exodus. Matt reached into his day sack and took out a portable suction mirror.

'What you got there?' asked Hernandez.

'I want to see who's coming up behind us,' said Matt, attaching the mirror to the windscreen.

'Put that away,' said Hernandez. 'Me and Carter can handle any counter-surveillance.'

Matt adjusted the mirror to bring the Toyota into view. 'This was SOP in my last job.'

'You're out of date, man,' said Hernandez. 'I took an SAS counter-surveillance course in England. All the Deltas do now.'

Matt doubted Hernandez had studied with the Regiment. The course the 2IC was referring to was nothing but a money spinner for a private security firm. 'Does it bother you at all that those courses have a one hundred percent pass rate?'

He kept his eyes glued to the mirror as Hernandez pulled

onto the highway. The red Toyota quickly disappeared behind a wall of 4×4s, pick-ups, saloons and riotously decorated lorries.

A mile on, Matt spotted a streak of solid red bolting up from the rear. 'Eighty metres behind us; red Toyota. Three up.'

'You realize this is the main road from the airport into Islamabad?' said Hernandez.

The Toyota was holding steady three cars behind. 'Well then maybe you should consider varying our route,' Matt suggested. 'Especially if you use the same one all the time.'

Carter was watching the ego clash with tremendous amusement. 'We have several back-up routes,' he assured Matt.

'You'll get to know them soon enough,' Hernandez taunted. 'Most of your time will be spent chauffeuring journalists to and from the airport.'

Matt kept track of the Toyota's movements. 'Have there been any incidents on this road lately?'

'A few but none of them insurgent related,' said Carter. 'Kidnappers and car jackings mostly.'

'A thief would hit the jackpot with me right now,' said Matt. 'I'm a walking bloody hole in the wall.'

'You signed up to be a cash mule,' said Hernandez.

Matt had no comeback. 'I can't wait to hand it off and get a receipt.'

'You don't need to bother with a receipt,' said Carter.

'What if some of it goes missing?' asked Matt. 'I don't want it coming out of my pay cheque.'

'Don't worry. It won't.' Carter handed Matt a magazine. 'Just give it to this guy when you see him.'

The magazine was opened to a photo of a thirty-something man with a mouth full of straight white teeth. Matt read the headline above it.

STICKING WITH THE STORY
ERIC RIDDELL VOWS TO CARRY ON
EMMA CAMERON'S LEGACY

The correspondent was using Emma's murder to advance his
career. Matt was incensed. A thought suddenly struck him: was
this Eric Riddell character calculating enough to want her dead?
It seemed unlikely that a western correspondent would collabo-
rate with an Islamic terror organization but ambition did make
for strange bedfellows. And there were only three SBC employees aside from Emma working in the bureau at the time of the
attack; a very narrow field of suspects. 'What does a correspondent need with all this money?' Matt asked.

'You can't wipe your butt in this country without greasing a
palm,' said Hernandez.

'It's the same in Afghanistan,' agreed Matt. 'But half a million?'

'That's petty cash in Pakistan.' Carter laughed.

'You better get with the programme, Logan,' Hernandez
warned. 'You're playing in the big leagues now.'

'What Hernandez is trying to say,' Carter intervened, 'is don't
underestimate Pakistan.'

Matt wasn't about to be lectured by two Yanks who knew
fuck all about counter-surveillance. 'I just did four years in
Kabul. I think I can handle myself here.'

'No one's saying you can't. But believe me when I tell you that
Pakistan's on the brink of a war that will make Afghanistan look
like a playground tiff.' Carter's mood turned dark. 'There are a
hundred and seventy million people in this country – eighty
million of them under the age of twenty. That is one sizeable
recruiting pool for Islamic jihadists and, Lord knows, they have
plenty of gripes to exploit. Name the social problem and Pakistan
has it in spades: illiteracy, unemployment, racial discrimination,

ethnic strife. The President and his cabinet are so corrupt, they make African dictators look like choir boys. Do you know what they call President Zardari?' he asked rhetorically. 'Mr Ten Percent. On account of all the kickbacks he gets.'

Hernandez raised his hand like a preacher. 'When the righteous are in authority, the people rejoice. But when a wicked man rules, the people groan.'

'Amen to that,' said Carter. 'The last President of Pakistan – Musharraf – he was even worse. Did you know that when we were in Iraq, Pakistan was cutting deals with Taliban operating out of the tribal areas?'

'Deals?' asked Matt.

'Musharraf agreed not to go after them so long as they didn't cause trouble here,' Carter explained. 'Basically, he gave the Taliban carte blanche to use Pakistan as a staging area for attacks against our forces in Afghanistan. Meanwhile, he refused to allow us to pursue them back across the border. Talk about a rigged game.'

'And our troops still don't have permission to operate here,' Hernandez added. 'CIA drones is all Pakistan will allow and you know how effective they are.'

Matt hated to admit it but the Deltas' knowledge of their operational area put his to shame. 'At least Pakistan is going after the Taliban now.'

Carter and Hernandez were astonished. 'Not the Taliban that matters,' the 2IC scolded.

'Not the *Afghan* Taliban,' said Carter, 'Mullah Omar and the Haqqani network and the rest of the terrorists killing our boys in Afghanistan.'

'Christ almighty, don't you know the difference?' Hernandez hit the steering wheel. 'Damn it. Now you've gone and made me take the Lord's name in vain.'

'Do you know who *created* the Afghan Taliban?' asked Carter. 'It was Pakistan, brother. After nine-eleven, they promised to cut 'em loose but Islamabad didn't keep its word. Sure as I sit here now, Pakistan is funnelling weapons to the Afghan Taliban, giving them training, logistical support, refuge. I mean, it ain't for nothing that they call Mullah Omar's gang *the Quetta Shura*.' Carter reined in his emotions. 'But now all that terrorist coddling has come home to roost. There's a new Taliban in town; TTP-Q and it doesn't have its sights set on Afghanistan. Abdullah Qari wants to take down the government in Pakistan . . .'

Carter's voice receded. Having avoided politics for years, Matt had always thought *Afghan* and *Pakistani* were nothing more than geographic designations for the same group of terrorists. But there was in fact a world of difference between the two Taliban. Abdullah Qari had a totally separate agenda from the insurgents who'd attacked Camp Phoenix.

Matt surfaced from his thoughts and checked his mirror. A lorry dripping with silver and green tinsel had taken the Toyota's place. He couldn't see the red saloon anywhere. Matt cursed his lapse of concentration. One second – that's all it took to get whacked.

'. . . Pakistan's days are numbered,' Carter concluded. 'The question now is: who's going to benefit when it all comes crashing down? Imagine what would happen if al-Qaeda was allowed to gain a foothold here like it did in Afghanistan? They'd have their very own nuclear bomb. We can't let that happen.'

'We *won't* let that happen,' said Hernandez.

The tinselled lorry pulled off the highway and the red Toyota came back into view. Matt had caught a break. 'Red Toyota, three up.'

'Chill out,' said Hernandez.

'If you don't believe me, slow down,' Matt barked. 'I bet you they don't try to overtake us.'

Carter nodded to Hernandez. 'Go on. Give it a try.'

The 2IC rolled his eyes and slowed to fifty miles an hour. Cars and lorries started flying past them – but not the Toyota. It was holding steady eighty yards behind.

The Deltas grew uneasy. 'Now accelerate,' said Matt.

Hernandez did as instructed. The Toyota adjusted its speed to keep pace. 'I'll be darned,' said the 2IC. 'You're right, Logan. They're definitely tailing us.'

Carter pulled out his mobile. 'I'm on it.'

Matt kept track of the vehicle through his mirror. He wondered who the trio were. They looked more like bureaucrats than insurgents, but that didn't mean they weren't dangerous. 'Who would be taking an interest in your movements?'

Hernandez shrugged.

'Don't fob me off. I'm riding with you. I have a right to know.'

'Well,' said the 2IC, 'the ISI don't take too kindly to foreigners – especially security contractors.' He paused. 'I'm sorry I gave you grief.'

'No worries,' said Matt.

'I have a hard time trusting folks who don't accept Jesus Christ as their saviour,' Hernandez explained.

A black 4×4 with no plates suddenly came screaming up the shoulder of the highway. 'Black 4×4,' said Matt. 'Two up.'

Carter turned. He was still on the phone. 'Relax,' he said. 'They're with 7M Close Protection. They were nearby so the ops room sent them to check out the Toyota for us.' He spoke into his phone. 'Yeah, I see them.'

The 4×4 swerved out off the shoulder and tucked in right behind them. Matt was fuming. 'You bang on about being low profile and you bring in these fuckers? Call them off.'

Carter covered the receiver with his hand. 'What's wrong?'

'We have the drop on that Toyota but they don't know it yet,' said Matt. 'If we play our cards right, we can evade, double back and find out who they are. Get those CP fuckers off our arse. They're compromising us.'

'Disengage,' Carter ordered into the phone. 'Yeah, I'm sure.' He hung up. 'I'm sorry. Counter-surveillance is your strong suit – not ours.'

'You know, Logan,' said Hernandez, 'we could really use you on our team – even if you are going to hell.'

The black 4×4 pulled off. Matt checked his mirror. The red Toyota had vanished.

Chapter 23

F-6, Islamabad

Matt paced the freshly laid asphalt. 'Can you remember how deep it was?'

Hernandez stroked his beard. 'Roughly ten feet, maybe?'

Matt surveyed the ground around him. The VBIED blast crater wasn't the only thing that had been covered over. The whole incident area had been washed down with pressure hoses. 'So how big do you reckon the bomb was? A thousand pounder?'

'That sounds about right. The blast wave covered a two-hundred-metre radius.' Hernandez waved his hand like a referee. 'The front of the house caught the brunt of it.'

The depth of scorched vegetation supported the 2IC's conclusion. So did the scars on neighbouring properties – missing walls, boarded-up windows, patches of bare mortar where the tiles had been blown off. Matt retracted his eye. Shrapnel pocks were visible on the jagged remnants of the villa's courtyard wall.

He replayed Emma's final moments against the canvas: the blinding light, her head snapping left, the shaking camera. A question started to take shape. 'Did the autopsy confirm the client died of shrapnel wounds?' he asked. 'Your report never mentioned the results.'

Carter answered him. 'That's because there was no autopsy.'

Matt was stunned. 'Then order one now. SOPs mandate independent corroboration,' he added hastily.

'Too late,' said Carter. 'The body was cremated.'

'What!' Matt grappled with his emotions. 'What if there's a follow-up investigation?'

'Relax,' said Hernandez. 'I saw the body. The back of her head was blown clean off.'

An image of Emma's maimed corpse filled Matt's mind.

'Something wrong?' asked Carter.

'Jet lag.' Matt pulled it together. 'What about the other victims? The Pakistani nationals?'

'Those dudes were hamburger,' said Hernandez. 'The police had to order DNA tests to make positive IDs.'

With all of the bodies reduced to ashes or mince, establishing another cause of death for Emma other than the official one would be nearly impossible for Matt. 'What kind of fragments did you recover from the scene?' he asked.

'Artillery shell casings,' said Hernandez. 'Traces of det cord, PE.'

'Pretty much your bog standard IED,' Carter concluded.

A minivan with an ICON telltale sat comms antenna appeared at the top of the street. The driver rolled down his window and handed what appeared to be a stack of credentials to the policemen manning the barrier. Matt's vision tunnelled as another piece fell into place. 'Was that checkpoint operational at the time of the attack?'

'Affirmative,' said Hernandez.

The clue brought more omissions to light. The report never explained how the VBIED had breached the checkpoint, or even what type of vehicle it was. 'How did the bomber get past it?' asked Matt.

Hernandez looked to Carter for guidance.

Matt eyed the two Deltas. 'What's going on?'

Carter took the lead. 'The VBIED was a Trojan Horse.'

'What, like an army or police vehicle?' asked Matt.

'Neither.' Carter paused. 'It was a civilian vehicle; a black SUV with no plates to be exact.'

The description was a dead ringer for the 4×4 that had compromised them on the highway. 'Are you telling me it was a 7M vehicle?' Matt was incredulous.

'It was *not* one of ours,' Carter insisted. 'But it was the same model that 7M CP uses in Pakistan. An identical VBIED was apprehended in Rawalpindi the morning SBC was attacked.'

'Why wasn't this mentioned in the report?'

'It wasn't pertinent,' said Hernandez.

'The hell it's not,' Matt challenged.

Carter defended his second-in-command. 'Hernandez was only following orders. I know it sounds bad but you gotta get some perspective here, Logan. The company looks after a lot of VIPs in Islamabad: diplomats, businessmen, the type of people that don't like to be inconvenienced by security checks, even when they're for their own good. So 7M CP made an arrangement with the police to let them by-pass checkpoints. TTP-Q obviously cottoned on to that and took advantage.'

Matt was ready to take a flame-thrower to him. 'You laid the groundwork for the suicide bomber to drive right up here,' he accused. 'Why didn't you just cut out the middle man and kill her yourself?'

Carter stared right through him.

The sudden chill extinguished Matt's fury. He'd shown far too much emotion. 'I'm sorry. I didn't mean you lads. It just winds me up when contractors don't do things by the numbers.'

'It's forgotten,' said Carter. 'Just don't mention it again.' He turned his attention to the arriving minivan.

Four men dismounted the vehicle. The quartet were clones of Carter and Hernandez: westerners with beards and local clothes.

Matt recognized one of them from the operation in Baghdad – Bazinsky. The blond sniper resembled a Viking in pyjamas.

A leader stepped from the pack, a wiry, disciplined character with light-blue eyes and thin lips. Matt figured him for a retired commander. He definitely had the swagger of one. 'You must be the blade,' said the commander.

Matt bristled at the SAS moniker. He'd never cared for it. 'Not since I left the Regiment.'

The commander squared up to Matt. 'Carter said you know how to take one for the team. That still hold true, boy? Or has civvy street made you soft?'

'Logan's in the middle of a recce,' Carter interrupted. He turned to Matt. 'Why don't you finish up and I'll introduce you to everyone when you're done.'

Matt turned his back to the crew. He could feel Carter's eyes on him as he stepped over the courtyard wall. Having pushed his luck with the ex-Delta captain, he figured it best to wrap up his investigation quickly. His top priority was the roof – where Emma had been slain.

Matt searched for a way up. The villa's façade was entombed in plastic sheeting that rippled with the wind, suggesting there was little left standing behind it. He walked around to the side of the house and found an outside staircase. It was badly damaged; held in place by a thin tendon of metal.

Matt placed his foot on the lowest rung to test its resilience. The staircase creaked and pulled away from the wall. He looked for windows he could crawl through but, like the door, they too were swaddled in sheeting.

Throwing caution to the wind he started to climb. Halfway up, the staircase began to give way. Matt ran to the top step and jumped, just as the metal snapped. The staircase collapsed with a thunderous crash.

The ICON men drew their weapons and aimed at the twisted heap. Matt called to them from the rooftop. 'Stand down, lads! Wankers,' he muttered beneath his breath.

'Need some help gettin' down?' the commander yelled.

'I'm fine.' Worried that the cavalry might come charging up any second, Matt wasted no time. He scanned the roof. Any major debris had been cleared but, unlike the ground, it hadn't been pressure washed. Two bloodstains still bore testament to the grisly event; one on the southern edge near the front of the house, the other on the western.

Matt tried to establish which one belonged to Emma. He rewound the video of her last report in his head and froze it. Emma blurred as the background details came to the fore: two thin, white minarets and a sloping roof.

He stood on the southern stain. Positioning his thumbs at ninety-degree angles, he raised his hands as if looking through a viewfinder and swivelled until the grand white mosque in the distance came into view. He adjusted the imaginary lens to bring two minarets to the right of the frame, and pictured Emma standing in the centre. From that angle, the roof of the mosque was entirely blocked.

Matt moved to the bloodstain on the western edge and performed the same exercise. This time, the framing was a perfect match for the live shot: two minarets to the right of the screen with part of the roof protruding left. He was standing on the exact spot where Emma had died.

Matt bent over and touched the stain with his fingertips. The surface was uneven. He crouched down and brought his eye level with the tiles. Two pieces of duct tape in the form of an X had been left behind.

As he peeled off the strips, Matt could feel Emma's energy curling around him. A shudder travelled down his spine. He was still missing something.

He stood up and looked to the mosque in the distance. The setting sun was creeping over the white space, turning it a brilliant pink. Matt imagined Emma standing in front of him, filing her report. He replayed the sequence of her death again; the burst of light, her head snapping left as the shrapnel hit it . . .

It finally dawned on him what he was doing wrong. He was studying the crime scene's 'television' mirror image – not the real thing before him. He turned 180 degrees to mimic Emma's stance during her live shot and dropped his head onto his right shoulder – which to a viewer would be the left side of the screen. Matt's eyes widened. Emma's head had snapped *into* the blast wave, not away. It was physically impossible for flying shrapnel from the VBIED to have killed her. Something else had cut her down, something unleashed *before* the bomb had detonated.

Chapter 24

Matt looked out over the neighbouring rooftops, imagining an alternative scenario to the one in Hernandez's report. He envisioned an assassin nesting behind a satellite dish; Emma's head coming into the crosshairs; the round leaving the rifle; the bullet striking right before the suicide bomber detonated his payload. The theory was plausible but the more Matt considered it, the less it held up to scrutiny. He had no definitive proof of her head snapping left and such a highly coordinated attack would require skills and organizational discipline on par with the Regiment. TTP-Q had proven themselves capable – but not *that* capable. Until Matt could see a replay of Emma's live shot, he had to acknowledge the possibility that his theory was nothing more than deep denial.

He knelt down and caressed the bloodstain. 'I'll get the bastard who did this to you, Emma. I promise.'

'What are you doing, Logan?'

Matt withdrew his hand. Carter was stepping out of a plastic-covered window onto the rooftop. 'Nothing.'

'We found a way down if you're about ready to finish up here.'

'Be there in a second.' Matt composed himself as Carter ducked back inside. He couldn't afford another sloppy display of emotion.

He walked over to the window and peeled back the plastic sheeting. Suddenly, everything went black. Matt panicked as the sensations of drowning overwhelmed him. He couldn't see or breathe. Sounds were distant and distorted. He broke through his phobia and focussed. There was a bag over his head. Hands, two – no three pairs were restraining his arms and legs.

Matt flailed violently but his struggling was purposeful. He freed an elbow and threw it back with all his might. The hard joint collided with cartilage.

A pair of hands fell away. 'Motherfucker!' cried a Yank voice.

It was the Deltas. They'd ambushed him! Motives ran through Matt's head. Maybe Carter and his mates wanted the money. He knew men who would kill for less. It didn't fit though. Special Forces didn't fight for treasure. Honour, duty, that's what mattered to them. Matt's mind raced. His outburst. That had to be it. Carter knew he was hiding something and he was making him pay.

Matt reached for the bag around his head only to have his arm smacked away. Straitjacketed, he swivelled his wrist. His knuckles brushed against something hard and cold; the butt of a pistol. It was strapped to a thigh.

Matt cupped his hand, thrust it into the ICON lad's crotch and squeezed as hard as he could. The man let out a howl. Banking the lad would cover his groin against further injury, Matt performed one more compression and went for the pistol.

He unfastened the holster and pulled the weapon free. The hands restraining him released all at once. He fell to the ground with a thud, pulled the bag off his head and surfaced with the pistol ready to fire.

'Whoa, whoa, whoa!' the ICON team shouted. 'Stand down! Stand down!'

Matt held the weapon firmly. Carter, Hernandez and the rest of the Yanks had their hands raised. 'Are you off your bloody heads!'

The Deltas looked at each other and erupted with laughter. 'Welcome to the family!' Carter exclaimed.

Matt slowly lowered the pistol. The ambush had been nothing more than a juvenile initiation ritual.

'You put up one hell of a fight,' said the commander.

'I told you he was a real Highland warrior,' Carter boasted. 'Let me introduce you to everyone, Logan. You already know Hernandez and Bazinsky.'

Matt nodded to the sniper. 'Where's *Baby Girl*?'

'Don't worry,' said Bazinsky, 'she's never far.'

Carter moved on to the commander. 'This here is Colonel McKay. He was our CO in Delta, now in charge of ICON Pakistan.' He gestured to the rest of the team. 'That's Dietrich and Ginta. They were Navy Seals but we try not to hold that against them.'

McKay pumped Matt's hand. 'Carter's been bending my ear about you for years,' said the commander. 'It's good to finally meet you, son.'

'What the hell . . .' all heads turned to Hernandez. The 2IC was looking down at the floor. He bent over and picked up the silver chain and cross Emma had given Matt.

Matt shrank. The damn thing must have snapped during the fight. It didn't say much for his security credentials – wearing a Christian symbol in a Muslim country.

'Is this yours?' Hernandez asked him.

Matt briefly considered not owning up to it but the ICON team was too close-knit not to figure it out. 'Yeah. It's mine.'

Hernandez walked toward him, swinging the cross. 'Are you familiar with Pakistan's blasphemy laws? Proselytizing is a crime

here, punishable by death. You've endangered all of us by wearing this on your person.'

'Let me explain,' said Matt.

The ICON team closed ranks around Hernandez. 'There's
nothing to explain,' said the 2IC. 'I've got your number, Logan.
We've all got your number.'

'It's not what you think,' said Matt.

Hernandez's scowl spread to an all-consuming smile. 'You've
been saved!' cried the 2IC.

'Glory be! . . . Praise God!' the team bellowed.

Hernandez bear-hugged Matt. 'There's no need to hide your
light under a bushel. You're amongst friends here.'

Matt hadn't a clue what had just happened.

'I knew it,' said McKay. The team parted to let the commander
through. 'As soon as I laid eyes on you, Logan, I said to myself,
that man – he's an agent.'

The team hummed their agreement.

Matt was even more confused. 'I assure you, Commander, I'm
no agent.'

'You're an agent of change,' McKay declared. 'You didn't come
to us by accident, Logan. Everyone under my command has been
called here by God. I come from a long line of God-fearing warriors. My great granddaddy fought in dubya; dubya two. My
granddaddy in Korea and my daddy – he served in 'Nam.
Soldiering is in my blood just as sure as Jesus Christ is in my
heart. That's why I've been blessed with leading this sacred
mission.' He paused. 'Ever wonder why we're losing in
Afghanistan, son?' The ICON team lowered their chins, as if it
was their personal failure. 'Because while we've been fighting for
ground our enemies have been fighting for something far more
precious: their immortal souls. Eternal damnation is one hell of
a motivator – one our forces have been sorely lacking. We ran

away from Nuristan, we ran away from the Korengal and we're holding on in Helmand by the skin of our teeth. Now, some will tell you it's a question of manpower – that all we need is more boots on the ground and everything will come up roses. Well, the Russians tried that and they ran away with their tails between their legs. Some say we don't have enough resources. I call bullshit on that too. We can flood Afghanistan with soldiers and weapons but none of it will make an ounce of difference until we stop acting like a bunch of politically correct pansies and start fighting the same war our enemies have been fighting all along.' He got up in Matt's face. 'I'm talking Jihad, son. Holy war.' McKay's eye turned to Hernandez. 'Romans 13.4,' he barked.

The 2IC stepped forward. *'For he is the minister of God to thee for good. But if thou do that which is evil, be afraid; for he beareth not the sword in vain: for he is the minister of God, a revenger to execute wrath upon him that doeth evil.'*

'It is our duty as Christian soldiers to restore God's dominion on earth,' McKay said solemnly. 'We must eradicate Islam, eliminate the scourge of terrorism and bring the light of Jesus Christ to this land.' He placed his hand on Matt's shoulder as if knighting him. 'Is your faith strong enough to answer this sacred calling?'

Matt knew there was only one answer that would get him out of there in one piece. He nodded.

'Hallelujah!' cried the team.

'Let us pray,' said McKay. The team closed their eyes and bowed their heads. 'Lord, we thank you for bringing our brother Logan to us,' the commander began. 'We commit him into your hands in Jesus' name and ask you, Father, to protect and guide him. Give him strength, o Lord, to defeat our enemies, so that the King of Glory may come into this land and shine his grace upon them. Amen.'

A refrain of amens followed. Matt searched the men's faces. All were deadly serious. This was no joke. Carter and his mates were bona fide Christian jihadists. And, as far as they knew, so was Matt.

Chapter 25

Gwadar, Baluchistan Province, Pakistan

The falcon perched regally on its master's glove. Tansvir removed the bird's hood and thrust his arm inside the mews. The falcon dug in its claws. 'More stubbornness,' he chided. 'I should have sold you to the Arabs.'

A figure stirred in the corner of the adjacent cage. The falcon's glistening brown eye pivoted. Abdullah Qari stepped forward. The Taliban leader's face was bruised and swollen, his wrists rubbed raw by the oily leather straps Tansvir's fighters had used to tie them together. 'Release me,' he growled.

The bells on the falcon's tail feathers rang as it nervously beat its wings. Tansvir tightened his grip on the leather jesses tied above the bird's talons. The restraints were identical to Qari's. 'There, there,' the rebel leader cooed. He reached into a satchel and pulled out some raw meat. The bird calmed and took the reward.

Qari laced the tips of his fingers through the chain link. 'Free me now!'

Tansvir released the falcon to its mews perch and closed the door. An accomplished jailer, the rebel leader knew the worst form of torture was silence.

Qari shook his cage. Tansvir failed to acknowledge him again. The Taliban leader's fury gravitated to the feasting falcon next door. 'Go ahead. Leave,' he warned. 'As soon as you are gone I shall snap that bird's neck and eat her for dinner.'

The threat pricked Tansvir's paternal instincts. He turned and faced his captive. Standing toe-to-toe, the physical differences between the men underscored their radically polar agendas. Tansvir was a veteran of his cause; grey, fearsome, battle-hardened. His face was lined with all the determination and sacrifice of a commander resigned to fighting for a future he would never live to see. Qari's by contrast had no scars or blemishes to suggest a warrior's history. Aside from the beating he'd suffered at the hands of Tansvir's militia, the Taliban leader's corporal narrative was one of self-gratification; well-fed, clear skin, thick hair. The only thing wanting was his unmanly beard.

'She is a saker falcon,' said Tansvir. 'An Omani sheikh offered me a hundred and fifty thousand dollars for her. If any harm should befall her in my absence, you shall pay a much higher price.'

'What about him?' Qari gestured to the cage across from his. The Chinese engineer was on the floor, rocking back and forth in the foetal position. His hair and clothes were thick with grime. 'How much is he worth to you?'

Tansvir regarded his commodity without pity. 'His value is currently being negotiated.'

'He stinks,' Qari sneered. 'You need to bathe him.'

'Damp is fatal to falcons.' Tansvir ran his hand along the top of Qari's cell. 'The worthy master nurtures his birds of prey.' His eyes turned to daggers. 'The unworthy master destroys them.'

It was clear to them both that Tansvir wasn't speaking of falconry. 'You are too sentimental,' said Qari. 'Such creatures exist to serve their master. It is our prerogative to dispose of them as and when we see fit.'

'Falcons are born to hunt. Take away that instinct to survive and you defile the very essence of falconry.'

Qari laughed. 'No wonder your people live in chains.'

'The Pashtun may have no regard for the lives of its warriors but the Baluch find suicide missions repugnant. Do you understand!'

'Jihad demands sacrifice,' Qari said with mock piousness. 'We are all Muslims, brother.'

'Muslims have been killing my people for sixty years.' Tansvir spat. 'I curse the day I allied my army with yours.'

The remark fed Qari's impertinence. 'Oh, but we are allies, old man.' He pressed his forehead against the cage, daring Tansvir to strike. 'At least until one of us dies.'

Tansvir pulled a knife from his waistcoat and grabbed Qari's beard. The terrorist's flesh spilled through the hollow galvanized diamonds. 'That can be arranged.'

'Kill me and your people shall pay for it,' Qari warned.

Tansvir pressed the tip of the knife to Qari's face. 'My people shall celebrate your death!' he cried, slicing the blade up.

Qari fell backward as his beard parted from his chin. 'I shall have your head for that!'

Tansvir threw down the wispy tuft and ground it in the dirt with his heel. 'You and your Taliban are no threat to me.'

'It won't be me who comes for you, old man.' Qari was shaking with rage. 'Our benefactor shall hear of this!'

Tansvir laughed. 'Do not believe what the newspapers and the television say about you, Qari. Everyone is expendable.'

Qari ceased trembling. Rather than intimidate, Tansvir's words had emboldened him. 'The name Abdullah Qari is now feared throughout the world. Everyone knows who I am. No one outside this province has heard of you or your pathetic cause.'

The comparison was as cutting as it was accurate. For decades the Baluch had tried to garner international support for their struggle against the Pakistani occupiers. But the wider world didn't know or care to know about the forced annexation of Tansvir's homeland and the abuses committed against his

people. Baluch independence had been an orphaned cause –
until Tansvir entered into an alliance with TTP-Q, a compromise
he now bitterly regretted. 'I have never sought fame,' the old
warrior insisted.

'That is why your people are slaves.' Qari toyed with the chain
link. 'Just look at what has been invested in me. My fighters are
well funded. We have all the latest technology of warfare at our
disposal.' He nodded at Tansvir's Lee Enfield. The rifle was
hanging on a hook in the corner of the mews house. 'The BLA
carry antiques into battle.'

Another devastating observation. The BLA had been promised much by their mutual benefactor, but had received nothing
so far. Tansvir feared his fighters were being deliberately denied
weapons so that when Islamabad did fall, the Baluch would be
subordinated to TTP-Q.

'Harm me further and your people shall pay for your folly,'
said Qari.

It took every ounce of Tansvir's strength not to kill him. But
he couldn't risk incurring the wrath of their benefactor. He
unlocked the cage.

Qari stepped out and presented his wrists. 'Untie me,' he
ordered.

Tansvir slipped off his falconer's glove, drew it back and
slapped the gauntlet across Qari's face. The Taliban leader
cradled his stinging cheek. 'You shall regret that!'

Tansvir drove his fist into Qari's stomach. 'Fight me if you
have the courage but know this. The sons of Baluchistan are not
yours to martyr.'

Chapter 26

Matt was running on fumes. ICON's bizarre welcoming cere-
mony had depleted the last of his physical and emotional
reserves. 'How much further?' he asked.

Hernandez pulled onto the shoulder. 'This is you.'

Matt looked at the stretch of empty road. 'Where's the hotel?'

'About half a kilometre up. We'd take you all the way if it
weren't for the security checks,' Hernandez explained. 'We can't
have the Serena's rent-a-cops tearing our vehicle apart.'

'You'd best ditch your local gear,' Carter advised. 'Rock up to
the Serena in a dusty hajji suit and they'll think you're a terrorist.'

Matt removed his shalwar kameez and opened the door.
'Thanks for the lift, lads.'

'Hold on a second.' Carter climbed out to have a private word.
'You really impressed Colonel McKay back there, you know.'

'I'm sure that's down to you building me up.'

'No, it's not. The colonel called you an *agent of change*. Do
you know what that means?'

Matt still had no idea. 'I wasn't expecting it, that's for sure.'

'The colonel will be watching you closely on this task. Keep
your nose clean and you'll be writing your own ticket.' He
embraced Matt. 'Take care, brother.'

Carter climbed in the front seat and the minivan sped away.
Matt legged it. Five hundred metres along, the hotel came into
view. The four-storey building was set far back from the road

and surrounded on all sides by landscaped gardens – a modern-day version of the medieval moat. His disgust with 7M and SBC was at an all-time high. The security of the villa he'd just come from was in no way comparable.

The guards on the hotel's outer cordon eyed Matt warily as he approached. He knew he looked strange arriving on foot, so to allay their fears he handed over his bag without being asked.

They finished searching it and brought out a hand-held metal detector. Standing with his arms and legs spread, the death-beetle click washing over his body, Matt reflected on how far he'd strayed from his comfort zone. From the Regiment through the embassy, he'd always worked as part of a well-supported team. Now he was alone, unarmed and, for the moment at least, a rich target. It was becoming increasingly clear that if he was going to survive, let alone achieve his objective in Pakistan, he'd have to adjust his mindset as well as his tactics. The lightning strike predatory instinct that had made him so effective at Black Ops had suddenly become a liability. Matt needed to be patient and carefully gather intelligence on his target before even considering taking it down. The covert Grey-Ops virtues he'd once arrogantly dismissed as inferior were now essential to his success.

The guards let him pass through the hallowed gates. It was like stepping into a gilded fortress. The long driveway leading to the hotel's entrance was lined with meticulously clipped shrubs. Architectural trees in terracotta pots encircled a hexagon-shaped external foray; a final barrier to potential bombers.

The glass doors parted, lashing Matt with a blast of frigid air. He laid his duffle and day sack on a conveyor belt and watched them disappear under a hooded cover. The guard on duty was not nearly as vigilant as the ones outside. He didn't even bother to look at the x-ray.

The scent of money enveloped him as he entered the opulent

lobby; crystal chandeliers, polished marble floors, dark expensive wood. Traces of human sweat were discernible beneath the stony base notes. The hotel staff were dashing about like gazelles, serving the same spoilt international riff-raff Matt had seen living it up in Kabul; diplomats, UN officials, military officers, journalists and CP teams with a handful of corrupt, well-heeled locals thrown into the mix. How they could sit there, sipping pomegranate juice in an oasis of luxury while the country imploded around them, was a mystery. Carter was right. Pakistan's days were numbered.

Reception directed him to a premier suite on the second floor; SBC's temporary bureau. Matt took one last look at Eric Riddell's magazine spread before knocking on the door.

'Can I help you?' Eric answered.

Matt gave the pretender to Emma's throne the once-over. 'You shouldn't open the door to strangers, you know.'

Eric's megawatt smile dimmed. 'Excuse me?'

'You're a public figure. Anyone could be looking for you.' Matt slapped the magazine in Eric's hands and pushed his way into the suite. The Serena's rarefied air retreated as the noxious smell of burnt plastic hit him like a closed fist. The room was filled with damaged equipment.

'Who are you?' Eric demanded.

'Matt Logan.' He turned but didn't offer his hand. 'I'm your new security advisor.'

'Do you always scare the shit out of the people you take care of?'

'Only when I want to make an impression.'

'You've got an odd sense of humour.' Eric flashed a cautious smile. 'I guess we could use some comic relief around here. As you can imagine, we've all been a bit on edge.'

He didn't seem on edge to Matt.

Eric held up the magazine. 'Obviously, you've heard about our tragedy.'

'You seem to have done all right out of it.'

Eric's face turned to granite. 'I'll have you know that Emma Cameron was more than just a colleague of mine. She was a very old, very dear friend. No one is more devastated by what happened to her than me.' He shielded his face with his hands.

Matt was sure the tears were an act, but when Eric surfaced it was like looking in a mirror. The anguish on the correspondent's face was every bit as genuine as his own. 'I'm sorry. That was out of line.' Matt offered his hand. 'Why don't we start over?'

Eric wiped his eyes and returned the gesture. 'I guess I can't blame you for thinking I'm a total dick. That article is beyond tasteless. I had nothing to do with it. Some idiot in our PR department planted it to try and boost the network's ratings.'

He even sounded a bit like Emma. Matt suspended Eric's name from his list of suspects for the time being. 'How are you holding up?'

Eric sighed. 'I'm taking it day by day. You never dream anything like that can happen until it actually does.'

'That's always the case,' said Matt.

'I haven't left the hotel since we were moved here. But I can't hide for much longer. There's a demonstration tomorrow the network wants us to cover.'

'I heard. Are you sure you're up for that?'

'I gotta get back in the saddle sometime. If I don't, the network will find some way to fire me. Cowardly war correspondents aren't of much use,' Eric explained. 'Our fixer Naj can brief you on all the details in the morning.'

'Fixer?'

'Our local producer/translator/driver – you know, a jack of all trades.'

The description raised Matt's suspicions. 'Was he working with you when the bureau was attacked?'

'Naj has been with us for donkey's years,' said Eric.

Matt's suspicions heightened. A local employee with intimate knowledge of SBC's operations; the MO certainly dovetailed with a Taliban collaborator. But there was still one more possible suspect Matt had yet to suss. 'So it was just you and Naj here with Emma Cameron?' he asked, teasing the identity from Eric.

'My cameraman was here too.' Eric paused. 'You haven't worked with television journalists before, have you?'

'You're my first media client.'

'Don't worry. It's not brain surgery,' said Eric. 'I'm sure you'll catch on quickly.'

Matt looked around the suite. 'Your kit's in a hell of a state.'

'We salvaged what we could from the house,' said Eric. 'Let me give you a quick rundown. There's the shooting equipment: lights, camera, tripod, gels, cables . . .'

Matt noted the pieces as Eric ticked them off. An item missed from the tour came into view: a singed, red bag stashed behind a pile of black cases. Emma's laptop case.

'. . . and last but not least, the basic office stuff,' Eric continued. 'Computers, editing terminal, assignment board. You're welcome to use any of the laptops but the editing terminal's off limits.'

Matt prised his eyes from Emma's computer bag. 'I'm sorry, the what?'

Eric pointed to the double-screened computer. 'The editing terminal. It connects directly to the New York library server. Everything the network shoots is archived on it so we can't afford to have viruses invading the system.'

Emma's final report flashed through Matt's head. 'Do the archives include live shots?'

'You bet.'

Finally, Matt had a way to confirm or deny his theory.

'So you do know some of our lingo,' Eric observed. 'You sure you haven't worked with the media before?'

'Just diplomats in Kabul.'

'You must have a military background. Infantry?'

'Special Forces,' said Matt.

'Wow. Our last guy was just a grunt.'

'You'll probably find I operate very differently from him.'

'Good,' said Eric. 'We need to shake things up around here.'

'Oh, I'll shake things up.' Matt looked around for basic breaches. He honed in on the assignment board. The names *Riddell* and *Fitzwilliam* were written on it along with two room numbers. 'That'll have to change for starters.'

'We've got a new crew board on order,' said Eric.

'I'm not talking about the physical board.' Matt rapped his knuckles on the room number column. 'You and your co-worker are staying on different floors. We should all be on the same floor, preferably at the same end of the hallway, so if there's an incident I can round you up quickly and move you to safety.'

'Then we'll move,' said Eric.

Matt had never had a client accept his advice so unquestioningly. 'I can explain this all in more detail.'

Eric shook his head. 'There's no need. Let me tell you something about war correspondents, Matt. A lot of us think we're bulletproof, especially the so-called "seasoned" ones. I thought I was Teflon. And then Emma died.' He paused. 'It could just as easily have been me on the rooftop that morning. I was all set to do the live shots. The only reason I'm standing here is because the producers wanted her instead of me.'

Matt could see Eric was grappling with survivor guilt. He

struck him off his list of suspects. The correspondent had never had it in for Emma.

'I don't know if anything positive will ever come out of her death,' said Eric. 'But at the very least, I know now that it's only blind luck that's kept me alive. You're the security expert, Matt, not me. So from here on out, assume that whatever you say goes.'

'Then we should get on like a house on fire.'

'What floor would you like us on?' asked Eric.

'This one's ideal.' Matt threw down his bag. 'I'll stay here.'

'You don't want to sleep with the gear.'

'Someone should keep an eye on it. It's worth a lot of money. Speaking of which . . .' Matt unfastened the money belt and handed it to Eric. The correspondent looked at the cash as if it were a yoke destined for his neck. 'If you're uncomfortable carrying that much cash around, I'm happy to do it,' Matt offered.

'I have no intention of carrying it.' Eric walked to the closet and opened the safety deposit box.

'I wouldn't put my trust in a hotel safe,' Matt warned. 'Seriously, let me look after it.'

Eric fiddled with the combination. 'You have enough to do without being our banker.' He withdrew a stack of papers and deposited the belt inside.

'I know this hardly seems a fair trade,' he said, handing Matt the paperwork. 'It's a welcome pack from SBC human resources . . .'

Matt flipped through it.

'. . . waivers, disclaimers, insurance forms,' said Eric. 'There's no hurry to fill them out.'

Matt tossed them. 'Then I won't.'

'Jerry and I were about to head up to the roof for some barbecue—'

'Jerry?' asked Matt.

'My cameraman.' Matt's heart skipped a beat. It couldn't be the same Jerry from Kabul Airport? 'You're welcome to join us.'

'Thanks, but I'm knackered.'

Someone knocked. 'That'll be Jerry now.'

Eric opened the door. Matt's heart stopped. It was the same Jerry – the only person in the whole bloody network who could connect him with Emma.

The cameraman made a beeline for the minibar. 'I need a few brewskis before we go.'

'Aren't you going to say hello?' Eric berated. 'This is Matt. Our new security advisor.'

Jerry opened the fridge door. 'How do, Matt.' He didn't turn to look at him. 'Want a beer?'

The cameraman was as rude and useless as Matt remembered. 'No, thanks.'

Jerry grabbed a bottle from the fridge and opened it. 'Just as well,' he said, taking a gulp. 'All they sell in this dump is local shit.' The poor review didn't stop him from stuffing two more bottles in his pockets.

'Do you plan on paying for those?' said Eric.

'It's the *bureau* minibar. Bill it to operations.' Jerry looked at Matt, listed and blinked.

Matt wasn't sure whether the cameraman was trying to place his face or simply focus. He smelled like he'd been drinking all day.

'Have you worked with us before?' asked Jerry.

Matt put on his poker face. 'No, mate.'

Jerry lingered.

'Matt's tired.' Eric pushed the cameraman toward the door. 'Let him get some rest. See you at ten a.m. tomorrow?' he asked Matt, as he opened the door.

'Ten a.m.,' Matt confirmed. He locked the door behind them and jumped onto the editing terminal. A dialogue box requesting a user name and password appeared on the screen. He typed in *Emma Cameron* and filled in the password with his own name: *Matt Logan*. The combination was rejected. Frustrated, he tried other variations: *eCameron* and *mlogan; emma* and *matt*. The computer locked on the third attempt. Matt was shut out.

He stormed around the room, cursing. If he couldn't find a file on a computer, how the hell was he going to find Abdullah Qari?

He collapsed beside Emma's laptop case and opened it. Her pink shawl was resting on top. Matt buried his face in the material. It still smelled like her. But the scent was fading.

Chapter 27

'I must make a phone call before we go,' said Naj.

Matt didn't like the sound of that – his primary suspect sneaking off right before they left for the demonstration. 'To who?'

'A source,' said the fixer.

Eric looked up from his notes. 'Don't be too long. I want to leave here in five.' He called to Jerry. 'Is all your gear loaded?'

Jerry slammed the boot shut. 'Yeah.'

Matt picked up a set of body armour and walked it over to the cameraman. 'Don't forget to put this on.'

'You put it on,' said Jerry.

It was déjà vu: a car park, a flak jacket, a clueless civvy. Matt peeled back his shirt. 'I'm wearing body armour under my clothes.' He nodded to Eric and Naj. Both men were wearing blue flak jackets with the words PRESS written on the front and back panels. 'The rest of your team's wearing theirs too.'

'I'm not like the rest of the team.' Jerry started punching the air. 'I'm a prize fighter when I shoot, bobbing and weaving, fast on my feet.'

'A member of your crew was killed not a week ago,' Matt argued. 'Do you want to be next?'

The cameraman kept shadow boxing. 'Ain't nothing gonna happen to me. I got the moves and I got the karma.'

'Karma?' said Matt. 'Are you taking the piss?'

'What goes around comes around.' Jerry stopped jabbing.

'Emma didn't buy it on account of some random act of fate. That bitch wouldn't piss on you if you were on fire . . .'

Matt's hands balled into fists.

'Jerry!' Eric snapped his neck at the vehicle. 'Get in.' The cameraman did as ordered. 'Naj!' The fixer looked up from his call. 'You too. We need to go.'

Matt's fingers uncurled as logic distilled through his rage. Maybe he'd been too hasty judging Naj.

Eric approached him. 'Don't worry about the body armour,' said the correspondent. 'If Jerry gets shot it's his own damn fault.'

'He smells like a bloody pub rag.'

'Jerry always smells like he's had a few too many,' said Eric. 'Acts like it too.'

'How do you put up with him?'

Eric sighed. 'Believe it or not, he's an artist with that camera, tenacious too. You'll see. As soon as Jerry rolls tape, he's a different man.'

In any other circumstances, Matt would have cancelled the shoot. But there was no way he was going to let a pisshead stand between him and a prime intelligence-gathering opportunity. The demonstrators gathering down the road were from Pakistan's tribal belt – Abdullah Qari's territory.

He climbed into the front passenger seat next to Naj and called the ops room in Virginia to let them know they were en route. 'This is Logan with SBC in Islamabad. We're leaving our hotel and going up Constitution Avenue to the roundabout that intersects with Jinnah Avenue . . .' The proper names felt like boulders in his mouth. '. . . we expect to be in situ for a couple of hours.' Naj missed the turn for Constitution. Matt covered the receiver. 'Where are you going?'

'The source I called is with Islamabad police – very senior,' the fixer explained. 'Constitution is sealed off. The demonstrators are now gathering at the intersection of Jinnah Avenue and Ataturk. From there they will march to the Presidential Palace.'

'Change of plan,' Matt said into the phone. 'We're taking Ataturk to the roundabout. I'll check in when we arrive.' He hung up. 'Next time you want to deviate from the agreed plan, run it past me first.'

'I am the driver,' the fixer answered back. 'I plan our routes.'

'Just do as Matt says,' Eric ordered.

Matt consulted his map. 'What makes you so sure the demonstrators are going to the Presidential Palace? That intersection is within striking distance of the US Embassy as well.'

'This is not my first demonstration,' said Naj. 'I started with this network in 1988, the year General Zia was assassinated.'

'Zia wasn't assassinated,' said Eric, his tone implying he'd argued the point many times. He looked at Matt's reflection in the rear-view. 'Take everything Naj-i-pedia tells you with a grain of salt, especially when it comes to General Zia.'

'I don't know who you're talking about,' said Matt.

'Zia was a fundamentalist army general who took power in a coup,' Eric explained. 'In a way, he's responsible for the story we're covering today. He funded and supported the Mujahideen in Afghanistan. Without Zia, the Taliban would probably never have come into existence.'

'He is also responsible for arming this nation with nuclear weapons,' Naj countered. 'Hence, why he was assassinated. Pakistan had grown too powerful under Zia.'

'Enough with the conspiracies,' Eric moaned.

'He was a great man,' Naj insisted.

Matt digested the seemingly innocuous quarrel. Naj had very high regard for a dead fundamentalist, Taliban-nurturing dictator. He also had foreknowledge of where the demonstrators – men who could very well be tied to TTP-Q – would be gathering. Forget Jerry. Naj was definitely his man.

The fixer slowed ahead of an intersection and pointed east. 'There is where the demonstrators will march to.'

Matt looked up the sweeping stretch of asphalt. Behind a roundabout sealed by police barricades, three white buildings stood on a carpet of green grass. Though influenced by the same Mogul-Stalinist architecture – naked columns, long windows, sharp angles – the structures lacked any sense of unity, as if they were co-existing under duress.

'The building in the centre is the Presidential Palace,' said Naj. 'Cabinet House is to the left, Parliament to the right. It is the nerve centre of Pakistan's body politic.' He pointed straight ahead. 'And there are the demonstrators,' he announced, 'as I said they would be,' he added smugly.

Matt retracted his eye along the avenue and over the inter-section. Abdullah Qari's brethren were congregating in a car park on the north-east corner. The bearded, long-shirted tribesmen were streaming off painted buses, old saloons and pick-up trucks with gypsy caravan tops. 'It looks like a Taliban convention.'

Naj smiled. 'It is.'

Matt searched for crowd-control measures. A small group of uniformed police officers was keeping watch over the demon-strators from the south-east corner of the junction. The security services were throwbacks to an earlier era: epauletted blue shirts, old-fashioned berets, long sticks with one end entwined in black leather, steel shields studded with rivet welds. It was a bad sign. Dated gear implied dated crowd-control tactics. At least they were keeping their distance and trying not to be provocative.

Matt gestured to the corner adjacent to the police. 'Pull up over there.'

'Dude,' said Jerry. 'Are you fucking blind? The story's across the street.'

'I know where the demonstrators are. I'd just rather not go barrelling in there and start a riot.' Matt looked over his shoulder. 'I'm not armed, you know.'

'I am,' Jerry raised his camera, 'with the ultimate weapon.'

'Do you see any other 4×4s in that car park?' argued Matt. 'If we approach on foot we won't seem nearly as threatening.'

'Matt's got a point,' said Eric. 'We're doing it his way.'

Naj pulled onto the kerb and they all got out. Jerry retrieved the tripod from the boot and dropped it in front of Matt. 'Here.'

Matt looked at the ungainly piece of equipment. 'Here what?'

'Security guys carry the sticks,' said Jerry.

'I'm not a Sherpa, mate. Carry your own gear.'

'It's not like you're doing anything else,' Jerry countered.

'Really, mate.' Matt pulled a pair of binos from his day sack. 'I'm watching your arse.'

Eric hoisted the tripod onto his shoulder. 'I've got it, Jerry.'

The sticks wobbled. Eric was already hauling his own day sack in addition to wearing body armour. 'You sure you're all right with that?' asked Matt.

Eric was struggling to find the fulcrum. 'I'm fine. Just do what you need to do.'

Matt recced the car park through his binos. Some of the protestors were unfurling banners. The signs were written predominantly in a language he couldn't read, but a few were targeted at foreign eyes.

THE BLOOD OF THE PASHTUN IS ON YOUR HANDS
PRESIDENT ZARDARI!

ZARDARI AMERICA'S PUPPET!

Matt lowered his binos. 'I think you should keep your distance from that lot.'

'If that's your call, I'll go with it,' said Eric. 'But the network's going to want sound bites from the protestors. If you could find some way for us to get them, I'd really appreciate it.'

Matt didn't want to drop Eric in the shit. He re-assessed the crowd. There was definitely an undercurrent of defiance flowing through the protestors but they didn't appear to be overly agitated. Hugs and kisses were flying. 'Tell you what. I'll hang back here . . .'

'Man, you are one lazy fucker,' Jerry interrupted.

'I'm being proactive.' Matt spoke directly to Eric. 'While you're gathering your sound bites, I'll be back here, watching for trouble. But if I call you and tell you to get out of there, I don't want any arguments. You move.'

'Understood,' said Eric.

While the crew left to gather their elements, Matt widened his surveillance area, searching for stragglers or others who might be hatching trouble on the fringes. He swung his binos due west. Two minivans parked off the road with the passenger curtains drawn came into his sights. Both had propeller satellite antennae. ICON was in the vicinity.

Matt remembered Carter's parting words. *The colonel will be watching you closely* . . . He pushed north to see if he could find the ex-Delta captain and his mates. There was no sign of them but there was another sight from the day before: a red Toyota saloon hidden behind a tree. The ISI was spying on ICON again.

Matt feared guilt by association. He needed to get ICON off his tail before they landed him on the ISI's radar. He hit speed dial on his phone.

'7M operations,' answered a woman in Virginia.

'It's Logan in Islamabad again. I need to speak with someone from ICON.' He couldn't tell her more than that. Anyone could be listening in on the call.

'We don't have access to that information, Logan. I suggest you put in a request with corporate during regular business hours.'

'It can't wait,' Matt insisted. 'I need to speak with them now.'

'Like I said, you can put in a request . . .'

'Listen,' Matt said sternly, 'this is an urgent security matter. Find that number ASAP and call me back.' While he waited, he split his attention between his clients, the ICON team and the ISI spooks in the Toyota. His mobile rang. 'What's the number?'

'Um, hello.' Matt didn't recognize the voice on the other end. 'I'm looking for a Mr Matthew Edward . . .'

Matt was startled to hear his middle name. 'Who is this?'

'I'm calling from SBC human resources about an insurance . . .'

'I don't have time for this.' He hung up. 'Fucking paper pushers,' he mumbled. Matt checked again on the ICON vans. They had no idea they were being watched.

Chapter 28

Quetta, Pakistan

'Our reporting and research network extends throughout the region . . . yes, that includes the tribal areas. We have more than a dozen stringers there . . .'

Ted listened to the conversation feeding through his earpiece, not that he needed state-of-the-art eavesdropping equipment to hear what was being said. Pete Riorden was speaking so loudly the whole street could hear him.

'The subscription website will cover most of your needs. But you may want to consider MISA's Strategic Communications service,' Riorden pitched. 'It's proving extremely popular with clients who require more targeted message strategies . . .'

Targeted. Journalists like Pete Riorden were the worst kind of thorn in Ted's side, pseudo spooks who thought covering wars had qualified them to wage it. The disgraced newsman was so out of his depth, he was speaking on an unsecured mobile. Every intelligence agency with a stake in Pakistan's future was listening to his conversation, not to mention all the touts hanging around the hotel, marking targets for kidnappers. How he'd managed to survive an hour in Quetta let alone a week was beyond Ted.

'. . . Our personnel know how to handle the unique challenges of operating in disputed areas . . . Our list of services? Well, let's see, we compile reports, conduct opinion polls, umm, atmospherics, metrics . . .'

Ted knew the big reveal couldn't be far off. Riorden had used his apartment in New York City as collateral on his MISA start-up loan. If the newsman didn't close this deal today, he'd be homeless.

'We have many exclusive sources . . .'

Ted pressed the receiver to his ear. 'Come on, dumb ass, spit it out.'

'Yes, that includes members of the opposition . . . Taliban and other hostile actors . . .'

And with that statement, Riorden crossed the line from news gathering into intelligence gathering.

'It would of course entail an additional charge on top of the standard private client subscription fee, plus an upfront retainer. I can get my lawyers to draw up the contract and email it to you before close of . . . Now? I do have a copy of our standard contract which I could amend . . .'

The other party was laying the trap.

'I'm booked pretty solid,' Riorden bluffed. 'But I might be able to do some rearranging and eke out an hour or so to come see you . . .'

The party on the other line suggested they meet at Riorden's hotel. It was a nice touch. They knew the newsman would never agree to it. Even by Quetta's frontier standards, the place was a dump. The sheets were stained and the complimentary bottled water in the mini-fridge had broken seals from tap refills. The gas-fired heater was the sort that if the fuel supply cut in the night – which it *always* did – you'd die of carbon-monoxide poisoning.

'I'm on the other side of town,' said Riorden. 'It would be faster if I came to you.'

The other party offered an alternative venue. Ted checked his map. There were any number of places they could abduct Riorden in transit – provided no one else grabbed him first.

'Yes. I know the restaurant . . . Forty-five minutes? Let me check with my assistant.' Riorden paused for effect. 'No problem. I'm on my way.'

Ten minutes later, Riorden emerged from the hotel. A boy carrying a wooden shoeshine box ran up to him. The child's face and hands were stained with black polish. 'Mister, Mister—'

'Go away,' said Riorden.

'Five dollar. I shine shoes too good.'

'I said get lost.'

'Three dollar,' the child haggled.

Riorden raised his hand to hail a minicab. The lack of a dedicated car and driver was further evidence of his desperate financial straits.

Two taxis nearly collided as they vied for Riorden's business. The shoeshine boy tipped the scales, running into the street and blocking one of them from advancing.

The child ran back and opened the door of the winning cab. He shoved his hand at Riorden for a tip. The newsman swatted him away and slammed the door. Undeterred, the boy ran around to the driver's window. The cabbie slipped him fifteen hundred rupees.

Riorden took no notice of the princely gratuity. Had he bothered, he may have realized that the child had been paid to set him up.

The losing taxi followed Riorden through the winding, dusty streets. A mile into the journey, a white 4×4 joined the chase. Ted made no attempt to conceal his western features. He was wearing sunglasses and a baseball cap. The spy chief would have stood out like a sore thumb had it not been for his vehicle; an SUV stencilled with the bright blue logo of UNHCR – the United

Nations High Commission for Refugees, Quetta's most ubiquitous international aid agency.

Wrapped in his favourite cover, Ted savoured the stealth pursuit. He'd vowed when he'd been promoted to Station Chief that he wouldn't let his human int craft go to pot. After all, it was skill erosion that had catapulted him up the CIA's ranks in the first place. His predecessor had made the fatal error of thinking that espionage had evolved into a video game. Had the agents under his command in Afghanistan spent more time scouting, recruiting and interrogating instead of sitting in briefing rooms looking at live feeds and analysing charts, they might have realized that the asset they'd invited into their base was a suicide bomber. But they couldn't see the traitor in their midst. Technology had dulled their instincts.

Ted kept tabs on the conversation taking place between Riorden and his driver. The cabbie was straight out of central casting: talking politics, offering to be on standby 24/7 for a 'small retainer'. It was a bit over the top in the spy chief's view, but the distraction techniques were definitely working. Riorden had yet to take issue with the driver's ridiculously circuitous route.

When they reached the Liaquat bazaar, Ted pulled off. Following the cabs through the crowded marketplace could tip them off. He continued listening to the conversation as he drove around to the far side.

'Where are we?' asked Riorden.

'My uncle has shop here,' said his cabbie. 'You come. Have tea.'

'I don't have time for fucking tea. I've got a very important business meeting to get to.'

'My uncle give you very, very good price on rug . . .'

'Stop,' Riorden demanded. 'I'm getting out.'

'Wait, wait,' said the cabbie.

'Get me to that meeting now or you won't see a dime,' the newsman threatened.

The cabbie relented and continued on. Ted checked his watch. All told the detours and distractions had tacked an extra thirty minutes onto Riorden's journey. The timing was near perfect.

Riorden's cab and the taxi tailing it emerged from the market. Ted followed them onto a dual carriageway. When they reached a level crossing, Riorden's driver stopped abruptly. Horns and screeches sounded as vehicles ground to a halt behind him: the losing taxi, two lorries, a saloon, Ted's 4×4 and an auto-rickshaw carrying two men with shawls wrapped around their faces.

Ted looked south. The Chaman Passenger Express train was approximately forty-five seconds away; a close shave by western standards but a wide margin in a country of accomplished train matadors. The auto-rickshaw swerved out of the queue and travelled up the shoulder. Ted could hear the tuk, tuk of the two-stroke engine as it passed beneath his window. It reminded him of the playing cards he'd put in his bicycle spokes as a child. Here he was, all grown up and still playing games. He loved his job.

The train was now approximately twenty seconds from the crossing. Someone was going to have to make a move – fast.

The rickshaw passengers cast off their shawls and rushed Riorden's cab. Both men were holding pistols. Riorden dived beneath the window when he saw them coming. His cabbie remained tall behind the wheel.

The armed men brandished their pistols, threatening to shoot the cabbie if he didn't open the door. He didn't flinch.

The men stepped back and fired at the window. Rather than shatter the glass, the metal jackets encasing the lead bullets shredded and bounced off the ballistic surface. The pair dived for cover to avoid being struck by the flying projectiles.

The driver of the losing taxi got out and ran forward. He too was holding a pistol. With three armed men bearing down on him, Riorden's cabbie made his move, hitting the accelerator and heading into the crossing. The men shot at the smoking, spinning tyres to try to stop the cab from escaping. The bullets punctured the wheels but it made no odds. The run-flat tyre rims simply cast off the damaged rubber and skipped over the tracks.

The armed men looked on helplessly as Riorden disappeared behind a wall of train carriages. They'd have a tough time explaining this one to their superiors back in Islamabad. The ISI had been counting on questioning Riorden. Too bad Ted's agent had grabbed him first.

Chapter 29

Islamabad

By morning's end, more than six hundred protestors from the tribal areas had convened on the car park. The police had swelled their ranks as well. Forty black-shirted riot officers were now gathered behind the western barricade sealing the roundabout in front of the Presidential Palace. Like their blue-shirted counterparts down the street, the riot squad's kit was archaic. The only upgrades Matt could indentify were mesh visors, hard helmets and padded vests.

The rumble of heavy vehicles hailed the arrival of yet more security reinforcements, but they weren't police. The column heading north up Constitution Avenue was comprised of military APCs and tanks.

The soldiers took up position on the southern and northern barricades of the roundabout. Unlike the police, they weren't counting on leather-wrapped sticks for crowd control. The soldiers were armed with automatic rifles.

Matt examined the weapons through his binos. As far as he could tell, none of them had been modified to accommodate rubber bullets. He searched for tasers, tear-gas canisters and other non-lethal tools for keeping protestors in order. There was nothing. The deficit was disconcerting. If the police failed to contain the demonstrators with batons, it was straight to the soldiers' live rounds.

Matt called his clients. Eric had been in the car park for nearly an hour conducting interviews and he didn't want the correspondent pushing his luck – especially when there was a potential TTP-Q collaborator translating. 'You about ready to finish up?'

'Almost,' said Eric. 'Ten more minutes and I'll have all the sound I need.'

Matt assessed the protestors. Their energy levels were elevating. 'Make it five.'

Two tribesmen with megaphones called the demonstrators to order. The march was about to get underway. Matt watched as Abdullah Qari's brethren split into two distinct groups. As a belt and braces, he did a quick survey of the vehicles in the car park as well. Though he hadn't seen any weapons among the demonstrators, there was still a chance some could be offloaded at the last minute.

A young, bearded laggard emerged from a bus. He was empty handed but something about him rubbed Matt the wrong way. He tracked him to see which group of demonstrators he'd fall in with. Instead of taking sides, the man circulated among the crowd, selecting random recruits to bring onto the bus.

The first recruit re-emerged with a bag slung over his shoulder. Matt's alarm bells sounded. He phoned Eric. 'You lot need to get back here, ASAP. Serious trouble's brewing.' He split his attention between his retreating clients and the bus. Matt wanted to see if the man handing out goody bags had any mates helping him. He imagined a group of dark-complexioned, pakol-wearing Taliban shit stirrers. But when the door opened, the opposite emerged: a tall, lily-white blond – Bazinsky. Matt was knocked for six. What was the ICON sniper doing there?

He checked the minivans across the street. One of them pulled

out, collected Bazinsky and sped away. The other held its position. Matt searched the area in earnest. There had to be other
ICON lads still hanging about. Maybe one of them could tell
him what the hell was going on.

'Everything OK?' Eric puffed.

Matt relieved him of the heavy tripod. 'Someone was passing
out bags to the demonstrators,' he explained. 'I don't know what
was in them but I didn't want you near it.'

Naj looked back at the car park. 'Can you show me this agent
provocateur?'

'He's gone.' Matt was no fan of ICON, but he wasn't about to
give them up to Naj. 'I think we need to call it a day, lads.'

'No,' Jerry butted in. 'The protest hasn't even started. Eric
hasn't done a stand up . . .'

Matt turned to the correspondent. 'Stand up?'

'It's a monologue to camera,' Eric explained, 'sort of like a
video signature.' He pulled Matt aside. 'I don't want to
contradict you – especially in front of Jerry, but I'm kind of in
a bind. If I leave before this thing even starts, New York will
have a fit.'

The smart thing to do was to pull the plug. But Matt didn't
want to get Eric in trouble. Maybe it was the correspondent's
connection to Emma, but Matt felt obliged to go the extra mile
for him. 'OK. We'll stay but we need to play it safe.' He searched
for a position that would give them a bird's-eye view of the
action. 'There,' he said, pointing to a small rise south of the
roundabout. 'If we stand off to that flank we should be able to
shoot everything without being too exposed.'

Jerry lit a cigarette. 'So now you're a director of
photography?'

'Come on, Jerry,' said Eric. 'You've worked harder angles than
that.'

'Why are you taking his side?' The cameraman pointed his cigarette at Matt. 'He's fucking security.'

'Which is why we're listening to him,' Eric retorted.

Matt walked his clients up to the grassy hillock. From a security perspective, the rise was ideal: a hundred metres directly across from the riot police manning the western barricade and slightly ahead of the soldiers guarding the south and north.

A unified chant went up. The first wave of protestors marched out of the car park. Banners and posters bearing the image of an old, grey-bearded man with wire spectacles rose above the sea of heads, along with red flags embellished with a circular crest set against a black stripe.

Jerry planted his sticks, pressed his eye to his lens and hit record. The cameraman's fingers danced over the levers and buttons, as he manipulated the shot. It was like watching a world-class pianist in action.

Eric sidled up to Matt. 'See what I mean. And Jerry's just getting warmed up.'

The cameraman introduced acrobatics to his routine – tilting, panning, squatting – capturing the advancing horde from every conceivable angle. Matt was amazed. Jerry the pisshead really was a different man when the tape started rolling.

The second wave of protestors began marching. Like the first, they too were carrying banners, red flags and posters of an old man in glasses. 'Who's the old bloke in the picture?' Matt asked.

'Mullah Maulana,' said Eric. 'Abdullah Qari's spiritual guide.'

Matt committed the cleric's image to memory. 'What about the flag? I've never seen it before.'

'It's the Pashtun national banner,' said Eric. 'The Waziristan tribes fought under it against the British last century. They've resurrected it in recent years to show Pashtun unity against the government of Pakistan.' He pointed. 'The demonstrators out front – they're Mehsud, the largest tribe in South Waziristan. Behind them are the Wazirs – the Mehsuds' sworn enemy.'

'They seem to be getting along now.'

'Both tribes lost members in the drone strike,' said Eric. 'Just give it a few months. They'll be at each other's throats again, I'm sure.'

Matt studied the two-bodied beast snaking its way toward the roundabout. 'Does Abdullah Qari belong to one of the tribes?'

'Qari's Mehsud,' said Eric. 'Pakistani Taliban leaders are always Mehsud.'

Matt checked the car park with his binos. A small contingent of white-turbaned men was bringing up the rear of the protest. Their flags were different from the Pashtun banner; green and red with a sunburst set against a blue triangle. Matt handed his sights to Eric. 'Who are the men in white?'

The correspondent adjusted the focus and returned the binos. 'They're Baluch. They're pissed off at the government too.'

'So they're Pashtun as well?' asked Matt.

'No,' said Eric. 'The Baluch are a totally separate ethnic group. They're more Arab than Asian.'

A chorus of counter-chants suddenly rose up from the south. Matt turned to find another group of protestors rounding the corner of Constitution Avenue. The new contingent had even less in common with the Pashtun than the Baluch. The men were mostly beardless and wearing western clothes. There were also females in the mix, wealthy women in expensive silks and sunglasses encrusted with designer logos. Their posters were different as well. Instead of an old man, they were marching under the image of a middle-aged, dark-haired woman in a white veil.

'Jerry!' Eric pointed south. 'Get some b-roll of this.'

Jerry swivelled the tripod to shoot the new arrivals.

'Who are they?' asked Matt.

'Sindhi,' Eric explained. 'The woman in the posters is Benazir Bhutto. She was head of the PPP – the Pakistani People's Party. A Pakistani Taliban suicide bomber assassinated her in 2007 during a Presidential campaign. After she was killed, public sympathy swung behind her husband, Asif Ali Zardari, the current President of Pakistan.'

'Is that the bloke they call Mr Ten Percent?'

'He is indeed,' said Eric. 'It looks like a few Sindhi nationalists have tagged along too.' Eric pointed to a banner with foreign script. 'See that sign. It says *we don't want Pakistan.*'

Matt plotted the trajectories of the two groups. The security services would have their hands full keeping the Sindhis and Pashtun apart. 'Are you expecting anyone else or is this it?'

Eric jerked his chin north. A third group of demonstrators was advancing on the roundabout. Like the Sindhis, they were urban and westernized, only their poster boy was a middle-aged, clean-shaven man with thinning hair. 'They're Punjabi,' Eric explained, 'the most powerful ethnic group in Pakistan. Punjabis control the army – and the government when Nawaz Sharif is in power.'

'Is that the bald guy?' asked Matt.

'Yeah,' Eric confirmed. 'Sharif is head of PML-N, the opposition party.'

'It's like alphabet soup. How do you keep it all straight?'

Eric laughed. 'Just remember "N" stands for Nawaz, just like "Q" stands for Qari.'

'So it's all personality led,' Matt observed.

'Personality *and* pedigree,' Eric added. 'A charismatic figurehead helps but what really counts in Pakistan is ethnicity. The biggest ethnic group is the Punjabis and they're dominated by the Sharifs. The second biggest ethnic group is the Sindhis. They're dominated by the Bhuttos. The Bhuttos are big land owners who control Sindh province and southern Punjab. The Sharifs are industrialists with a stronghold in central and northern Punjab. For the last forty years, one of these two families has controlled the government – except when there's a coup and the head of the army takes over.'

'Like General Zia,' Matt observed.

'General Zia, Pervez Musharraf . . .'

Matt remembered the Deltas' politics lesson on the drive from the airport. 'Isn't he the one who cut deals with the Taliban?'

Eric was impressed. 'So you didn't just fall off the turnip truck.' He nodded at Naj. The fixer was standing off to the side, observing the crowd with increasing trepidation. 'Naj was a *huge* fan of Pervez Musharraf's,' Eric explained. 'They're both Mohajirs; Urdu-speaking Muslims who migrated from India during the partition. When Musharraf left office, Naj was inconsolable.'

The personal nugget cemented Matt's suspicions. Naj was definitely in cahoots with the Pakistani Taliban.

The Pashtun were within striking distance of the roundabout and the Sindhis and Punjabis were closing fast. 'Shoot your stand up now,' said Matt. 'If those barricades give way, there'll be hell on.'

Eric alerted Jerry and fixed a wireless microphone. The cameraman framed the shot and raised his thumb. 'I got speed.'

'Stand up, take one.' Eric straightened his back and stared down the lens. 'Pakistan is a key ally in the War on Terror. But increasingly, the civilians on the front lines of that war are losing patience. With an insurgency growing more powerful by the day and popular support for the government at an all-time low, this nuclear-armed Islamic power has never appeared more vulnerable.'

The stand up captured in a nutshell the scenario Carter had described to Matt the day before. Pakistan was disintegrating. And its nuclear weapons hung in the balance.

Chapter 30

The police behind the western barricade locked shields as the Pashtun reached the roundabout.

A minute later, the Punjabis and Sindhis convened on their respective ends. The Punjabi soldiers immediately yielded to their baying brethren, raising the northern barricade to allow them to flood into the circle. Not to be outdone, the Sindhis pressed their rights until the soldiers capitulated to them as well.

Cosseted by the security services, the elite protestors flaunted their position. They jeered at the excluded Pashtun, mocking them with threatening gestures. It reminded Matt of public-school toffs puffing their chests at working-class boys from behind the school gates. He doubted the privileged groups would be as brazen if they had to confront the country's disadvantaged on equal terms.

The Pashtun chanting grew deafening as they demanded to be allowed into the roundabout. A United States flag rose over their heads. The crowd cheered wildly as it was set alight.

Matt honed in on the arsonist. He had a satchel around his shoulder. 'Get down!' Matt ordered.

Eric and Naj ducked onto one knee. Jerry moved – not for cover, but to slide the camera off the tripod and keep filming.

The arsonist pulled a Molotov cocktail out of his bag, lit the crude rag wick and hurled it at the police. The petrol ignited as the bottle shattered against a shield. Another Molotov flew over the police line and landed in the centre of the roundabout. The fireball caught the hem of a woman's shalwar kameez. The fine, diaphanous material flamed like moth's wings.

Jerry looked up from his lens. 'I'm going in!' he announced.

Matt grabbed him. 'Do you have a death wish?'

Jerry yanked his arm free. 'Touch me again and I'll sue, you motherfucker.'

'Let him go,' Eric warned. 'He means it.'

The cameraman pushed and shoved his way into the centre of the Pashtun rioters. Matt washed his hands of him. The mad-arse wasn't worth it.

'Uh-oh,' said Eric.

'What's wrong?' asked Matt.

'I think the competition is trying to get a leg up on us.' Eric pointed north. 'That building. I think there's a cameraman on the top floor.'

Matt zoned in on the area with his binos. 'Which window?'

'Third from left.'

Matt panned to the open window. He strained to interpret the shadows stirring inside. A long unmistakable line materialized: the barrel of a rifle. 'That's no fucking cameraman. There's a sniper in there.'

'Are you sure?' said Eric.

'Positive.' Matt tried to establish some form of ID but the sniper was well hidden. He shifted his surveillance west. The ICON vehicle was still in situ. He wondered – was that *Baby Girl* at the window?

The crack of a high-velocity round sounded over the mayhem. Matt swung his sights back to the open window. The rifle barrel had withdrawn into the darkness.

'Holy shit!' Eric pointed to the western barricade. A Pashtun tribesman lay collapsed in front of the police barricade, his head split by a bullet.

'We've got to get out of here now,' said Matt.

Enraged by the death of one of their own, the Pashtun scrambled over the barricade and hurled their bodies against the police shields. An officer lost his footing and fell backward, breaking the phalanx. The tribesmen exploited the weak link to push their way into the roundabout.

All-out civil war erupted as Pakistan's ethnic groups collided. Caught in the current of chaos, Jerry raised his camera above his head and allowed himself to be swept into the centre.

Matt waved his arms. 'Jerry! Jerry! Get out of there!'

'He won't listen,' said Eric. 'I'm sorry, Matt, but we can't leave him behind.'

'Fuck!' Matt fumed. 'Naj.' The fixer was still kneeling down. 'Get up. We're going in there.'

The fixer regarded the rioters with horror. 'Are you mad?'

'Do as Matt says or you can kiss your pension goodbye,' Eric threatened.

Matt dragged the reluctant fixer to the southern barricade. The crush of humanity was impenetrable. Jerry was completely enveloped by protestors. Matt needed a diversion to create an opening. 'Tell the soldiers to fire some warning shots over the crowd.'

Naj ran to a soldier, slipped him a bribe and cowered behind him. The soldier raised his rifle and discharged four rounds into the air.

Everyone in the roundabout stooped – except Jerry. The cameraman remained upright – filming.

A Pashtun protestor seized upon the westerner in their midst. He pointed at Jerry and screamed: 'Death to America!' Others joined the indictment, chanting 'Death to America!' Jerry turned in circles, filming the accusers as if he were merely an observer of their hatred and not the focus of it.

Matt tucked his head down and rammed his way into the crucible. The putrid stench of sweaty armpits and bad breath battered him as he thrust toward Jerry. 'I'm getting you out of here!'

'Fuck off!' said the cameraman. 'I'm working.'

'They want to kill you!'

A Pashtun armed with a police stick rushed them. Matt kicked the legs out from under the tribesman and wrestled the weapon away. He fenced Jerry with his back. 'Stay right behind me!'

Swinging the stick from side to side, Matt slashed his way forward through the rioters. With the edge of the roundabout in sight, he checked behind him to make sure Jerry was still there. The cameraman was exactly where he'd left him – and still rolling tape.

Enough was enough. Matt jousted his way back in, stepped into Jerry's blind spot and chinned him. The shooter collapsed into his arms – out cold.

Chapter 31

The click of a round feeding into a chamber pierced the still darkness. 'Is that supposed to frighten me?' said Eric.

McKay switched on the light. The ex-Delta colonel had exchanged his Pakistani costume for a conservative blue business suit. 'Just keeping you on your toes.'

'How long have you been here?'

McKay re-holstered his pistol. 'About two hours.'

'You should have contacted me first. What if I was with someone?'

'I sent you a message,' said McKay.

'I've been busy today. You should know. Your men were there – working.' Eric emptied his pockets onto the dresser. The loose coins rattled and spun on the polished mahogany.

'I don't mind waiting. It gave me a chance to catch up on my reading.' McKay picked up the magazine Matt had given Eric. '*Having narrowly escaped the suicide bombing that claimed the life of Emma Cameron,*' the ICON commander quoted, '*Eric Riddell vows to carry on the newswoman's legacy.*' He closed the magazine. 'Aren't you gonna thank me?'

Eric turned. 'Thank you? For what?'

McKay tossed the magazine onto the coffee table. Emma's picture was on the cover beneath the epitaph *Dying to Tell the Story*. 'For clearing the decks. Now that that bitch is out of the way, there's no limit to what you can do.'

Eric stared at the image. 'Don't be obscene. Emma wasn't my competition. I recruited her for Christ's sake.'

'She was a threat to national security.'

'You should have told me what you were planning to do,' Eric snapped.

'Remember who you're talking to, boy,' McKay warned. 'And don't play dumb. You knew damn well what was going to happen. She could have compromised everything we're trying to achieve here. Don't you dare shed a tear for that traitor.'

Eric looked down at the dresser. The coins were a mess. 'It must be a luxury – seeing everything in black and white.'

'It ain't rocket science,' said McKay. 'You're either with us or against us.'

Eric met the ICON commander's eyes in the mirror. 'How dare you question my loyalty.'

McKay backed off. 'Just making sure. You're about to get a whole lot more responsibility, boy.'

Eric shuffled the coins like a shell game. He couldn't decide whether to organize them by size or value. 'I've got enough on my plate right now, thank you.'

'Don't be so modest,' said McKay. 'You're the best banker we ever had. Now that that bitch is history, we can move you into other tasks. Heads of state, rebel leaders, they'll all be lining up to talk to Eric Riddell.' McKay mulled the possibilities. 'That's how Massoud got whacked, you know.'

Eric stopped shuffling. 'That was a suicide mission.'

'I wasn't suggesting you kill yourself,' said McKay. 'We aren't the ISI.'

Eric assessed the vertical row he'd created. Organizing by value had been a mistake. The coins were all out of kilter. 'Keep killing our own and we will be.'

'We kill when we have to,' McKay warned. 'The ISI kill for

sport. They're overrated thugs. Hell, they can't even keep track of a few contractors operating in their own backyard.'

'Speaking of contractors, my new security advisor is suspiciously competent.' Eric faced McKay. 'Did you really think you could send one of your men to spy on me and I wouldn't know?'

'Who, Logan?' said McKay. 'He's not one of mine – not yet at least.'

'Bullshit.'

McKay held up two fingers. 'Scout's honour. How's he gettin' on?'

Eric didn't buy it. McKay didn't trust anyone who wasn't Special Forces. 'He broke my cameraman's jaw today.'

McKay chuckled.

'If you want to keep Logan in Pakistan, you better rein him in. My cameraman wants him fired. I just spent the last hour convincing Jerry that it was a protestor who clocked him.'

'I appreciate you looking out for him,' said McKay. 'You may redeem yourself yet.'

'What's that supposed to mean?'

'It means if Logan works out here, it would go a long way toward restoring confidence in your ability to run a tight operation. That whole business with Cameron was sloppy.'

'What makes you think I can control Logan?'

'Good point,' said McKay. 'If he gets out of hand again let me know and I'll have a quiet word with him.'

'You can start by telling him to back off about us changing rooms,' said Eric. 'It took me two days to clean this one.'

'He's just being thorough,' McKay placed a small metal object the size of a watch battery on the coffee table, 'which is more than I can say for you.'

Eric stared at the listening device. He was off his game. Way off. 'So is that why you dropped by? To check up on me?'

'No,' McKay stood up, 'we got us a situation in Quetta.'

Chapter 32

Quetta, Pakistan

Matt didn't need to harness his counter-surveillance skills to know he was being watched. The government minder was practically smothering him. He shoved the fat bastard with his hip. The minder sucked in his gut only to collapse back into a blob. Fitness levels notwithstanding, with Naj driving and the minder sitting between them, it was always going to be a tight squeeze in the hired saloon. Matt would have preferred to ride in the back between Eric and Jerry but the bloody camera was taking up the middle.

He checked the passenger mirror. Their police escort was half-asleep. There were eight of them riding in the open cab of a pick-up truck, their chins resting on the butts of their Type 56 assault rifles. The safety catches on some of the Chinese-made AKs were set to fire, indicating there was no round in the chamber. Fat lot of good they'd be in a contact.

The ill-prepared security detail had greeted them right off the plane; ostensibly to deter Quetta's myriad kidnapping gangs from targeting SBC. Matt feared the police would have the opposite effect. The overt escort made him and his clients that much easier to mark. The whole safety argument was a bluff. Eric had alerted Matt in advance that the Pakistani government was much more interested in managing SBC's coverage in Quetta than protecting them from criminals and insurgents. The portly minder had already taken the liberty of arranging an interview with the newly appointed Governor of Baluchistan later that evening. Though not expressly stated, he left no doubt that the meeting was mandatory.

The drive from the airport explained why the government was so keen to keep journalists on a short leash. The capital of Pakistan's largest and most sparsely populated province was as rough as Islamabad was polished; a wild west of crumbling mud brick walls, stewing garbage, sludge-filled canals, beggars, drug addicts and burka-clad women. The similarities with Kabul were striking; only instead of one Taliban, Quetta hosted two.

The minder belched, filling the confined space with sour stomach fumes reminiscent of the British Embassy canteen. The discomfort underscored the conclusion Matt had started to draw in Islamabad: it was time to ditch the civvies and cast his lot with ICON. For two days he'd sat in the Serena, trying to figure out what ICON was doing at the demonstration. Then it clicked. Carter said he was having more fun now than he'd had in the Deltas. He and his mates had to be working some sort of outsourced US military task; a counter-terrorism operation targeting TTP-Q. The Molotovs were incentives to cultivate assets that could lead them to Abdullah Qari. The sniping was damage control until they made the big kill. It all made perfect sense. The Pakistani army couldn't stop Qari. With US troops barred from operating in the country and CIA drones killing everyone but militants, it was down to the private sector to eliminate the terrorist mastermind.

ICON had the inside track to Qari and Matt wanted in. There was nothing left to gain from working with SBC. He'd found Emma's betrayer, he could settle the score later. What mattered most now was decapitating TTP-Q. But before Matt handed in his resignation to SBC, he had one more assignment to complete with the network – one that could prove an intelligence bonanza. Eric had landed an interview with Mullah Maulana, Abdullah Qari's spiritual puppet master.

Eric had briefed him on the plane about Maulana's rise to infamy. Apparently, few had even heard of the cleric until his most famous disciple decided to blow up the CIA. Islamabad wanted him silenced but the options for doing so were sorely limited. The Pakistanis couldn't arrest Maulana without incurring the wrath of locals who regarded him as a man of faith. Bombing the cleric's compound was a non-starter due to the presence of a mosque and madrassa. A ground assault was possible but according to press reports, Pakistani intelligence sources claimed Maulana was stockpiling weapons; arms that could fuel a bloody and protracted stand-off should the army invade.

Naj turned off the main road into a pleasant, tree-lined street. A day market was in full swing. Sellers were romancing prayer rugs and tables full of incense while potential buyers haggled for deals. But Matt knew this was no retail heaven. Across from the lively commerce, a sprawling complex brooded in the shadow of a speaker-swamped minaret. This was Mullah Maulana's turf.

Naj drove around the eastern wall of the compound. The waste ground surrounding the complex was packed with lorries and trucks. He pulled in between two vehicles and parked with his nose facing the wall of the fortress.

'Turn around and back in,' said Matt.

'Why?' said the fixer.

'We may have to leave in a hurry,' said Matt. 'If that happens you don't want to be shifting . . .' The police escort rendered the point moot by parking behind them. Matt turned to the minder. 'They're going to have to move.'

'They are here for your protection,' said the minder.

'Well then they should start acting like it.'

Eric piped up. 'I'm sure the police know what they're doing.'

Matt waited for the minder to leave the car. 'What was that about?'

'We're going to have a lot of battles to fight today,' said Eric. 'Let's choose them wisely.'

Matt helped Jerry unload the gear from the boot. He didn't mind pitching in now that the cameraman's mouth was wired shut. Eric walked around, carrying his body armour. 'Good man,' said Matt, 'better safe than sorry.'

The correspondent fed his arms through the body armour. 'I plan on giving the mullah quite a grilling,' he said, zipping it closed.

The minder donned a pair of sunglasses and led them around the corner to the compound's entrance. An old man fondling prayer beads rose from a chair as they approached.

A brief exchange ensued between the minder and the ancient gatekeeper. They were speaking in a local dialect but the raised voices and sharp looks were universally comprehensible.

'I'm afraid they will not allow us inside to interview Mullah Maulana,' the minder announced. 'I know this is disappoint- ment for you. But do not despair. You will have the opportunity to interview the governor tonight.'

Eric looked to Naj as if to say, *do your job and put this right*. Naj responded by staring at his feet. 'We're not allowed inside,' said Eric, 'or *you're* not allowed?'

'I cannot guarantee your safety unless I am with you,' said the minder.

Eric smiled but the gesture dripped passive aggression. 'We've come all the way from Islamabad to interview Mullah Maulana . . .'

'But now you will interview the governor,' the minder inter- rupted. 'He is very, very important man in Pakistan. This is much better for you.'

'You have to understand that my network flew me here to do a story on Mullah Maulana. But I'll tell you what,' Eric stepped into the minder's space, 'why don't I interview you instead? We'll do it right now.'

'But I am just a humble servant of my people,' the minder floundered.

'Who better to explain to our viewers – that's over 200 countries worldwide by the way – why the government of Pakistan is afraid to let us talk to Mullah Maulana.' Eric turned to Jerry. 'You ready to roll tape?'

Jerry shouldered his camera. The minder shook his head. 'No, no, no . . .'

'I'm sure you'll be a natural,' said Eric.

'It is not my place.'

Eric gave the signal for Jerry to stand down. 'Then let us go inside. We'll do our interview and if we're not out in say, three hours, you can send in the police after us.'

The minder was not pleased to have a compromise forced on him. 'One hour. Then we shall come for you.'

Eric smiled again. 'Make it two.'

Chapter 33

The sedate old man with the prayer beads belied the siege mentality inside Mullah Maulana's lair. The moment the gate shut, a scrum of masked guards in black turbans charged Matt and his clients.

The security ordered them to drop their gear and spread their arms and legs. Matt leveraged the search position to scan the rooftops: they were alive with rounded backs scrambling beneath ramparts. Maulana's compound was literally crawling with sentries.

The guards finished the body searches and moved on to the equipment. Jerry switched the camera on and held up the view-finder. 'He has to prove the camera isn't a bomb,' Naj said to Matt. 'That is how Ahmed Shah Massoud was assassinated.'

'I know,' said Matt.

'The timing of Massoud's death is most curious,' said the fixer.

'That's enough, Naj,' said Eric.

The fixer lowered his voice. 'Ninth September 2001 . . .'

'Put a sock in it,' Eric hissed.

Satisfied their intentions weren't hostile, the guards led them to their leader. The call to prayer blasted from the loudspeakers as they entered a southern block of buildings. Matt stole glimpses through the open doorways lining the hall. Mullah Maulana was stockpiling more than weapons in his compound. There was thousands of dollars' worth of computers, radios, boxes of medical supplies and tinned foods. The cleric and his followers could hold out there for weeks if attacked.

They emerged into a courtyard filled with blossoming fruit trees. Men were gathered around an ablution pool, washing their hands and feet in preparation for worship. A mosaic of leather sandals paved the way westward toward the mosque.

Matt peered through the archway into the beating heart of Maulana's fortress. Rows of fighting-age men were busy performing the calisthenics of their faith: kneeling, bowing, pressing their foreheads to the floor. A row of backs rose at the front, triggering a wave. Matt caught a glimpse of black curls falling on shoulders before it was swallowed by the swell. He superimposed the snapshot onto the picture of Abdullah Qari he'd seen splashed across the television screen in the embassy canteen. His senses sharpened. Was the terrorist leader hiding in plain sight?

The guards whisked them into a northern block of buildings; the only two-storey structure in the compound aside from the minaret. The deep baritones emanating from the mosque gave way to the high-pitched buzz of children reciting Koranic verses.

Matt quickly tallied the children in the classroom. There were at least four dozen adolescent and pre-adolescent boys rocking back and forth like the moving parts of a machine. Further down the corridor, the older, nearly completed products of Maulana's jihadist assembly line were watching videos.

The guards deposited Matt and his clients in an office upstairs and told them to set up for the interview. Maulana obviously channelled his funds into defence. The place was humble: peeling walls, a desk littered with paperwork and DVDs, one chair, a few prayer rugs and cushions. The only luxury Matt could identify was an air-conditioning unit cut into the brickwork below the level of the window.

Jerry made the best of the limited resources; positioning two pillows on a carpet, adjusting the tripod to its lowest setting and arranging a triangle of lights.

A boy came round with sweet tea and sugared almonds. Matt declined the refreshments but Naj scooped a handful of nuts. 'It is an insult not to eat. Take something before you offend our hosts.'

Matt hated the idea of heeding Naj's advice as much as he did taking food from the man who'd inspired Emma's killer. But Eric had a point about choosing battles. There was nothing to be gained from fighting over tea. He took a glass and nursed it by the window overlooking the courtyard. It was an excellent vantage point for observing the worshippers leaving the mosque. Matt knew it was a long shot, Pakistan's most wanted terrorist holding up in the compound of its most controversial radical cleric. But he couldn't shake the feeling that Qari was there with them.

A guard entered the office. Though his face was covered, his shalwar kameez was different from the group who'd escorted them from the gate. The material was much finer, more like a gentleman's smoking jacket than a uniform. 'I am Mullah Maulana's security chief,' he announced in heavily accented English.

Eric extended his hand. 'Eric Riddell. SBC. Thank you for inviting us here today.'

The security chief snubbed the correspondent. 'Turn on your camera.'

Jerry hit record and stepped away. The security chief's sleeves fell back as he adjusted the viewfinder. Matt noticed the raw wounds on the man's wrists.

The chief tampered with every conceivable button and left to fetch his master. Jerry was still performing triage on the camera when Mullah Maulana arrived with the chief and half a dozen guards.

Despite the entourage, the cleric was not at all as Matt had imagined him. Maulana was positively elfin in stature.

'So good of you to come to see me,' the cleric gushed. 'Please, sit,' he said to Eric. He made small talk with the correspondent while Jerry finished setting his shot. Matt could not reconcile the cheery boffin discussing cricket scores with the face of fanaticism he'd seen towering over the crowds of the tribal protestors. How could such a tiny, soft-spoken man inspire people to martyrdom?

Jerry raised his thumb, indicating they were good to start. Eric cleared his throat and put on his game face. 'Mullah Maulana,' he began. 'The government has accused you of trying to Talibanize Pakistan. Is that a fair charge?'

Matt was rubbing his hands. First question and Eric was going for the jugular.

'Who is the Taliban? What is the Taliban?' Maulana asked in a nasal voice. 'I shall tell you. Anyone who opposes the govern-ment in Islamabad, anyone who opposes the army in Islamabad and anyone who opposes the intelligence services that control the army and the government. I have made it my business as a man of faith to expose the crimes all of these institutions committed against the Pashtun people and against all good Muslims. If that makes me guilty of trying to *Talibanize* as you put it, then so be it.'

Matt adjusted his snap assessment of the cleric. Maulana was no pushover. The way he'd manipulated the question to stake the moral high ground betrayed a sharp strategic mind. Eric had his work cut out for him.

'What crimes exactly?' the correspondent probed.

'The politicians in Islamabad steal from the public purse. The army in Islamabad slaughters the innocent. The ISI kidnaps and kills anyone who dares speak out against these crimes,' Maulana answered.

'Those are some very serious charges,' said Eric. 'What proof do you have?'

'Look what happens when the Pashtun make a legitimate and peaceful protest against the indiscriminate bombing of their homes. The President of Pakistan orders the army to shoot them. This is irrefutable fact.'

'Now, the tribal areas . . .' Eric continued.

Maulana raised his hand. 'That name is a British fiction which the oppressors in Islamabad have adopted.' He sounded like a professor correcting a student.

'What name would you prefer I use?'

'Pashtunistan.'

'Exactly what do you mean by Pashtunistan?' asked Eric.

Maulana looked into the distance as if imagining a dream. 'The land where the Pashtun people have lived and died for centuries.'

'Yes, but what do you consider to be the borders of that land?' Eric pressed. 'There are Pashtun in southern and eastern Afghanistan. Do you consider those areas part of Pashtunistan?'

'It is *all* Pashtunistan,' said Maulana. 'The Durand Line is a foreign creation the Pashtun people will never accept.'

'By Durand Line you mean the border between Pakistan and Afghanistan.'

'Yes,' Maulana confirmed. 'No good Muslim recognizes this abomination. Our brothers living under the heel of the northern Afghan tribes should be reunited with us. Allah demands it.'

Matt was starting to understand the cleric's game. No wonder he didn't come over as a raving fanatic. Maulana was simply using Islam to bolster a nationalist agenda. As jihadists went, Carter and his mates were more legitimate.

'It sounds like you're proposing Afghanistan be split in two,' said Eric.

'That would be the best solution, yes.'

'Then what would happen to the rest of Afghanistan?'

'It would be free to determine its own destiny.'

'And if that destiny lies with the United States and the NATO coalition,' Eric challenged. 'Would you still be as supportive then?'

'We do not care to rule over the northern Afghan tribes,' Maulana insisted.

'Let's talk about the tensions between your movement and Islamabad. There has been a very violent campaign waged by TTP-Q against the government of Pakistan. In response, the army has invaded Pashtun areas to weed out terrorists . . .'

Maulana talked over him. 'The only terrorists in Pashtunistan are the foreign armies occupying it.'

Eric returned the volley. 'Yes, but the Pashtun are undeniably using violence to achieve their aims, violence targeting innocent civilians – including one of my colleagues.'

Matt was loving it. Eric was holding Maulana's feet to the fire.

'Islamabad is waging genocide on the Pashtun people,' said the cleric. 'Any citizen of any country which supports that genocide is not innocent.'

'So you consider all allies of Pakistan fair game?'

'Yes. That is why I urge those nations to reconsider their positions.' Maulana paused to sip his tea. 'If the government in Islamabad would give us the freedom we desire, there would be no more bloodshed, no more violence.'

'But Pakistan is a democracy,' Eric pointed out, 'a system that allows for non-violent change through majority vote.'

Maulana's affable façade slipped. 'Democracy,' he scoffed. 'A hollow and blasphemous ideology. How can you expect Muslims to submit to a system that accords homosexuals, Jews and other deviants a say in who governs them?'

'But some Pashtun nationalist parties are achieving results by working within the system. Take the ANP for example. Thanks to their efforts North-West Frontier Province will soon be called Khyber Pashtunistan,' Eric argued.

'Which only reinforces the division of our people,' Maulana countered.

'But there are Pashtun in the Pakistani government. There are Pashtun in the army – the same army that has launched offensives in the tribal areas and the north-west frontier.'

'Those men of whom you speak are no longer Pashtun,' Maulana declared. 'They forfeited their birthright when they joined forces with our oppressors. They are Durvand – non-Pashtun. And the Durvand in Islamabad have but one concern: enriching themselves at their people's expense. The political party masters, the officers who rule the army, the ISI – all of them hoard the country's resources. They raid the public treasury and hide their ill-gotten gains in blasphemous western banks that profit from usury. Now that they have bled those reserves dry, the Durvand have found a new source of wealth . . .' he raised his finger, 'the fatted calf of American aid money. This is why the army is trying to crush Pashtunistan. So they may fill their purses with America's gold.'

'Do you consider Afghan President Karzai Durvand?' asked Eric.

'Of course,' said Maulana. 'The world knows the Karzai family is in the service of the CIA.'

'But Karzai is in reconciliation talks with the Taliban.'

'The Taliban of whom you speak are proxies of Islamabad,' said Maulana. 'They have nothing to do with my followers.'

Eric paused to reset the conversation. 'If the government in Islamabad relented and allowed Pashtunistan to become an independent emirate, would you lay down your arms and cooperate with non-Islamic countries – specifically the United States and its allies?'

Matt's delight turned to alarm. Where was Eric going with this?

'There are many Muslim nations that have found accommodation with the West. Kuwait for example, or Qatar. We would not be opposed to following those examples,' said Maulana.

'So you're saying Pashtunistan could be a friend of the United States?'

'If we are treated with respect, we shall reciprocate in kind,' said the cleric.

Matt was devastated. In one question, Eric had gone from portraying Maulana as a dangerous, hard-core jihadist to a reasonable man the West could do business with. How could the correspondent have allowed himself to be manipulated like that?

'You're asking America to take a big leap of faith,' said Eric. 'When the Taliban were in control of Afghanistan they let al-Qaeda take over. How can we be sure the same thing wouldn't happen in Pashtunistan?'

Matt took heart. Eric was trying to put the interview back on track.

'Again, the Taliban of whom you speak are Islamabad's proxies,' said Maulana. 'As for my followers, I can assure you that it is the obligation of every Pashtun to defend his nation against foreign incursion. That includes foreign al-Qaeda fighters.'

'If the government in Islamabad does not relent, how long will you continue to fight?'

'We shall never surrender,' Maulana declared. 'But the longer our struggle continues the more chaotic it will become and then we cannot guarantee what will happen.'

'What do you mean *can't guarantee?*'

Maulana bowed his head. The studied gesture imparted an air of foreboding. 'We have resisted efforts by foreign fighters to infiltrate our struggle because we know they wish to exploit us for their own agenda . . .'

'What agenda?' Eric cut in.

'Pakistan has weapons al-Qaeda would like for themselves,' said Maulana, 'nuclear weapons.'

'Are you suggesting that if Islamabad does not agree to a free Pashtunistan, al-Qaeda could gain control of Pakistan's nuclear arsenal?'

Matt couldn't believe it. Eric was playing right into Maulana's hands!

The cleric hesitated before answering. 'We would not like this to happen. But if the international community continues to support the status quo, it will.'

'Thank you for sitting down with us today, Mullah Maulana.' Eric broke character. 'I think that's a wrap.'

Matt was astonished. Not only had Eric blown the interview, he'd left out the most important question. 'Wait!' he shouted.

Eric shielded his eyes against the camera lights. 'Something wrong?'

'I have a question,' said Matt.

'Can we talk about it later?' asked Eric. 'We still need to do cutaways.'

Matt stepped out of the shadows. 'It's for Mullah Maulana.' He pushed past the ring of security and stared down at the cleric. 'Where is Abdullah Qari hiding?'

Chapter 34

Eric turned ashen. Naj choked on an almond. The only person not shaken by the question was Mullah Maulana. The cleric appeared amused. 'Why, Amir Qari is among us, of course.'

Matt lunged. 'Where!' The guards seized him by the arms and shoulders. The security chief took advantage, sucker-punching him in the stomach.

Eric leapt to his feet. 'That's enough!'

Matt rebounded from the blow. 'Tell me where you're hiding Qari!' he demanded again.

Eric turned to the mullah. 'Order your men to stand down.'

Maulana nodded calmly to his guards. 'Unhand our guest. I'm sure he means no harm.'

The guards released Matt at once. Before he could launch into a tirade, Eric grabbed him and pulled him to a corner. 'What the hell is wrong with you?'

Matt was rabid. 'You heard him. Qari is here.'

'If Qari was here do you really think the mullah would disclose that on camera?' said Eric. 'Get a hold of yourself.' He left Matt and reclaimed his seat across from Maulana. 'You still rolling, Jerry?' The cameraman pointed his thumb skyward. Eric resumed his interview. 'Mullah Maulana. I want you to be absolutely clear with us. Is Abdullah Qari in this compound right now as we speak?'

Maulana smiled serenely. 'Amir Qari is in the hearts of every Pashtun.'

'But is he *physically* here?'

Maulana sighed. 'Sadly, I do not know where Amir Qari is but I am certain Allah watches over him.'

The answer slapped Matt back to his senses. He should have realized Maulana hadn't been speaking literally. Once again, he'd allowed emotion to infect his judgement. Only this time Matt hadn't just endangered himself, he'd put his clients at risk as well. It was an unforgivable lapse of professionalism.

'Thank you, Mullah Maulana.' Eric exhaled. 'Kill the lights, Jerry.'

Ted observed Riorden through the closed-circuit video. The newsman showed no signs of physical abuse. His face was clean shaven and his legs and hands weren't shackled. He would have looked like a willing informant if it weren't for the Gitmo chic orange coveralls. Ted would have preferred to have kept him in street clothes but that option was eliminated during the grab when the newsman shat himself.

Riorden started humming to fill the silence. For someone who'd been in custody less than forty-eight hours, he was coping poorly. The newsman's eyes had more bags than a Shar Pei. Good thing the conditions of his confinement were being meticulously documented as per Ted's orders. Riorden had spent the night in a heated holding cell with a bed, sink and toilet. Fresh linens had been provided along with brand name toiletries. His loo roll was two-ply.

Bethany entered the observation room. 'I'm ready to begin, sir.'

Ted beamed with pride. He knew his protégée was nervous and excited. Who wouldn't be for their inaugural solo interrogation? But you wouldn't know it to look at her. Bethany was thoroughly composed; a company gal through and through. 'If you feel like you need help, give the signal. It won't be held against you.'

'I know, sir.'

Ted examined the subject again. Riorden was as fragile as an eggshell but cracking him was no sure thing. If Bethany came on too strong, he might shut down or start telling a pack of lies in the hope of earning his freedom. The last thing the spy chief wanted was for the interrogation to drag on for weeks. Move thoughtfully. Move fast. Stay a step ahead. That's how he ran his operation. 'Remember. This guy may have dabbled in intelligence but he's no pro. He's just a scared civilian.'

'A civilian with some very dangerous contacts,' Bethany pointed out.

Ted's brow furrowed. Maybe Bethany wasn't ready. If insecurity got the best of her, she might make the rookie mistake of aping male aggression. A female interrogator's biggest asset was her natural empathy. If Bethany played to her strengths, Riorden would be putty in her hands. 'He's probably expecting a tough guy off the TV, you know.'

'We can only hope,' said Bethany.

Ted's fears abated. She was ready.

'We'd like to get some pictures of the compound before we leave,' said Eric.

'Of course. We have nothing to hide.' Mullah Maulana turned to his guards. 'My security team will show you whatever you like.'

The chief cut in. 'I shall remain by your side, Mullah.'

The cleric smiled at Eric. 'He worries too much.'

The guards filed out the door. Jerry and Matt gathered the gear and joined them in the hallway.

Eric lingered. 'It was a great honour . . .'

'Please, stay and talk with me, Mr Riddell.' Maulana sat down on a rug. 'May I offer you more tea?'

Matt looked in from the hallway. 'We need to stick together,' he reminded Eric.

Maulana appealed directly to the correspondent. 'I would be most interested in learning your views on our situation.'

'You go ahead,' Eric said to Matt. 'I'll catch up later.'

Matt mustered his limited diplomacy reserves. 'We might miss something important if you're not with us.'

Eric bowed to Maulana. 'Excuse me a moment.' He joined Matt in the corridor. 'I don't think it would be wise to shun the mullah's hospitality, especially after that scene of yours.'

Matt didn't have a leg to stand on – not after the way he'd behaved. 'Don't move from this room until I come back.'

'I won't.' Eric closed the door on Matt. 'Let's do this quickly,' he said, peeling off his body armour.

'Who is that man?' the security chief demanded.

Eric laid the flak jacket on the desk and ripped open the Velcro on the front and back plate panels. 'None of your fucking business.'

'How dare you!' The security chief picked up the jacket and threw it across the room. Bricks of freshly minted US currency spilled from the opened pockets.

Eric looked at the dishevelled piles of bills. 'You're counting them.'

'You do not give me orders!' The security chief ripped off his scarf. 'Who do you think you are talking to?'

Eric was not at all intimidated. 'Wind your neck in, Qari.'

Chapter 35

Eric couldn't help but take pleasure in seeing Abdullah Qari's battered, bruised and shorn face. If anyone deserved to be taken down a peg, it was the monster he'd helped create.

'I shall have your head!' Qari threatened.

'Amir Qari,' said Mullah Maulana. The cleric's voice was full of deference. 'Our friend has come a long way. And he has come quickly. This shows your concerns are taken seriously.'

Qari spat at Eric's feet. 'Give me my money.'

Eric side-stepped the puce phlegm and picked his flak jacket off the floor. 'It was in twenty-thousand-dollar bundles,' he said, depositing the jacket and loose bills on the desk.

Qari ploughed through the cash, counting and discarding the bills in a disorderly heap. 'It is not enough,' he declared when he finished.

'There's a hundred and twenty thousand dollars there,' said Eric. 'That was the agreed amount.'

Qari raked his arm through the piles, sweeping them off the desk. 'Give me more!'

'I'm not authorized.'

'Do you know what that Baluch dog did to me?' said Qari. 'He locked me in a cage. He beat me with his dirty glove. He cut off my beard! No one does that to Abdullah Qari and lives!'

'Do you ever get tired of saying your own name?' asked Eric.

Qari seized the correspondent by the collar. 'Crawl back to

your masters and tell them that if they do not give me more money I shall extract my revenge in blood.'

Eric refused to show fear. 'I'll be sure to give them the message.'

Qari tossed him aside. 'Worthless errand boy.'

The insult meant nothing to Eric. He picked himself up and reached for his flak jacket. 'You better take your money and go. My crew will be returning for me soon.'

Qari grabbed him from behind and pulled a knife. 'Why does that servant seek me?' he said, pressing the blade to Eric's neck.

The correspondent leaned into the cold steel, daring Qari to draw it. 'He's not your concern.'

Mullah Maulana panicked. 'Do not do this, Amir Qari. As you said, this man is an errand boy. He is not worth it.'

'Tell me why he seeks me!' Qari demanded.

'Amir Qari,' Maulana pleaded. 'Think of all we have to lose. The freedom of all Pashtun is within our grasp!'

'Save your sermons for your sheep, old man.' Qari withdrew his blade and drove the knife through Eric's flak jacket. 'I will come for you, errand boy. You and your servant.'

Chapter 36

Bethany ditched her glasses before entering the interrogation room. The minor adjustment softened her appearance considerably. 'How are you feeling?' Riorden didn't answer. 'Would you mind if I have a seat?'

Ted watched from the observation room, impressed. Bethany didn't waste any time mounting the tightrope. Asking permission could make Riorden feel as if he were in control of the situation but it also risked feeding his paranoia. It was a delicate balancing act.

'Suit yourself,' said Riorden.

Bethany sat across from the newsman. 'I remember watching you on television when I was a kid. Your reports taught me so much about the world.'

Ted winced. Flattery was way too obvious at this stage.

Riorden's indifference turned to fear. 'Why are you sucking up to me? I've done nothing wrong. There's been a mistake. A big mistake. I need a lawyer. Don't I get a lawyer?'

Bethany slid her hand toward the centre of the table to try to calm him. Ted was disappointed. She didn't have clearance for physical contact. One touch and he would have no choice but to take over the interrogation.

She held her fingertips an inch from Riorden's. 'You're not under arrest, Peter. May I call you Peter?'

Riorden's gaze slowly gravitated from Bethany's hand to her eyes.

Ted was on tenterhooks. 'Don't fight it,' said the spy chief, 'she's your best fucking friend in the world right now.'

The newsman fell under the interrogator's spell. 'I prefer Pete.'

'Yes!' Ted punched the air. Bethany was off and running.

Though he'd trained her himself, Ted couldn't help but marvel at his protégée's patient technique. Most rookies took a sledge-hammer to the cookie jar and walked away with crumbs. Not Bethany. She was going for the whole biscuit. She started with a series of softball questions. *Where did you go to school? Why journalism?* The answers were of no intelligence value but that wasn't the point. Bethany was building a rapport.

Only when she'd prised the lid off Riorden's defences, did she dare introduce more sensitive inquiries. She opened a file and presented him with a selection of press reports tracking the highlights of his SBC career. The earliest clipping dated back to 1991 when 24-hour news was still in its infancy. Riorden's reports from the rooftop of the Dhahran Hilton during the First Gulf War had made him an overnight star. Women swooned over his strong jaw and broad shoulders; men coveted his safari vest and gas mask. His news stud status was cemented when *People* magazine anointed him 'Patriot Pete' after the over-hyped American anti-missile defence system.

The rest of the nineties provided no shortage of conflicts for Riorden to cover: Somalia's descent into anarchy; Sarajevo's tortured destruction; Colombia's drug wars; Russia's power struggles – the newsman had used them all as photo opportuni-ties to feed his myth. But by the early noughties, his star was on the wane. Desperate to appeal to a more youthful demographic, SBC had used the attack on the World Trade Center in New York to introduce a new generation of news talent to the public. Riorden found himself fighting for face time with younger, leaner and smarter correspondents. By 2006 *People* magazine had forgotten all about Patriot Pete and his exploits. That's when the newsman made the ill-fated decision to reinvent himself as Pete Riorden, *investigative* war reporter.

It took exactly one week to tear down what Riorden had built up over nearly two decades. Bethany laid out the headlines tracking his fall from grace.

HAILSTORM PELLETS WHITE HOUSE WITH SHOCKING 9–11 FALSE FLAG CLAIM

BUSH ADMINISTRATION DENIES HAILSTORM ALLEGATIONS

SBC RUNS FOR COVER: HAILSTORM SOURCE MENTALLY UNSTABLE

FIRED! PATRIOT PETE GOES DOWN IN FLAMES

'I was just the front man on *Hailstorm*,' said Riorden, disowning the story that had destroyed him. 'The producers did all the leg work on it.'

'But you did interview the main source over a period of several days,' Bethany pointed out. 'How could you not have realized he was schizophrenic?'

'Because he wasn't,' Riorden insisted. 'That man was as sane as you and me.'

Bethany didn't respond immediately. Ted knew her silence was deliberate. She was attempting to exacerbate Riorden's feelings of isolation so he'd have no choice but to take her into his confidence. 'I believe you, Pete.'

Riorden's eyes softened. 'You do?'

'I know your body of work,' she explained. 'You were a very serious, very experienced war correspondent. I don't believe for a second that you would accuse anyone of wilfully slaughtering United States citizens unless you thought your source was mentally sound.' Bethany waved her finger over the clippings. 'If you ask me, this whole thing reads like a set-up.'

Riorden burst into tears. 'That's what I've been saying for years but no one will believe me.'

Bethany let him cry it out. Ted sat up. Now that she'd cracked him, she could move on to the real purpose of the interrogation.

'Do you have any idea who was behind it?' asked Bethany.

Ted grabbed his head. There was nothing more to be gained from picking the scabs off Riorden's wounded career.

Bethany slid her hand across the table again. 'Who was out to get you?'

'Careful, Bethany,' Ted said out loud.

Riorden looked her in the eye. 'I would tell you if I knew.'

Ted had underestimated his protégée. Bethany hadn't erred by digging deeper into Riorden's pain. On the contrary, by taking an interest in his version of events, she'd won his trust completely.

For the next hour, the newsman poured his heart out to Bethany, giving her a blow-by-blow description of how his life had unravelled after the *Hailstorm* controversy. He bitterly recalled how no one would return his calls or emails. Rival networks regarded him as damaged goods and his colleagues had washed their hands of him. His wife filed for divorce. His children refused to speak to him.

Bethany feigned sympathy through it all, nodding in agreement, adding vitriol where appropriate. By the time Riorden moved on to his post-SBC ventures, he was an open book.

The burgeoning world of online media was a natural landing point for the disgraced newsman. The barriers to entry were low and anyone with brand name recognition had a better than average chance of sticking out from the pack. Riorden's first brainchild was a subscription news service focused on Iraq. Though he had no experience running a bootstrap news operation, it didn't stop him from sinking all his savings into it. He figured he had to speculate to accumulate.

It was a bad investment. It turned out no one was willing to pay for content they could download for free somewhere else. Riorden blamed the omnipotence of 'corporate-owned mass media' for 'silencing anyone who dare put forth an independent journalistic voice'. When the United States turned its attention away from Iraq and back to Afghanistan, he went for broke, folding his Iraq news service and heading to Pakistan to try his hand at yet another subscription venture: Media Intelligence South Asia: MISA.

'What made you think MISA would be financially viable?' asked Bethany. 'The business model had already failed in Iraq.'

Riorden grinned as if he knew better. 'Because MISA offers more than news.'

'Sounds intriguing.' She flashed a slightly flirtatious smile.

The gesture pumped Riorden's confidence. He leaned back and spread his legs.

Though it was a sign that the interrogation was going well, Ted found the newsman's overtly sexual body language unsettling. That was his agent in there with Riorden.

'Reporters, or at least print ones,' the newsman explained. 'Television reporters nowadays are a fucking joke . . .'

'Get to the point,' Ted grumbled.

'. . . good reporters don't simply sit in Kabul and Islamabad talking to officials. They go where the action is. They interview locals, they seek out the opposition.'

'The opposition?' said Bethany.

'Warlords, the Taliban, al-Qaeda. That's the way I always did it,' Riorden boasted. 'So I thought why not leverage those contacts to diversify MISA beyond news gathering.'

'I see.' Bethany played to his vanity. 'It is amazing that no one ever thought of it before.'

Riorden shrugged, though it was obvious he thought his idea was genius.

Bethany scratched her neck with the tip of a pencil. 'Weren't you concerned about a conflict of interest?'

'There's no conflict,' said Riorden. 'The news website is completely separate from the rest of MISA's operations.'

Bethany laid down her pencil. Her curious expression morphed into an indicting scowl. 'I'm not talking about firewalls.'

Riorden sat up and put his legs together. 'Firewalls?'

'The United States government may not always find free speech convenient but it does respect the press's right to talk to our enemies in the name of objective reporting,' said Bethany. 'Free speech is after all a cornerstone of the Constitution. But your activities with MISA are not protected by the First Amendment – Mr Riorden.'

The newsman shuddered at the sound of his surname.

'You are brokering access to terrorists,' Bethany charged. 'You are therefore profiteering from terrorist activities.'

Riorden started shaking. 'I swear I never . . .'

'That's treason, Mr Riorden. Treason against the United States of America.'

The newsman was hyper-ventilating. 'I love my country. I'm a patriot – Patriot Pete! I never even met the Taliban.'

'What about your . . .' Bethany read from the transcript Ted had recorded while eavesdropping on Riorden, '*network of stringers?*'

'It's all bullshit,' Riorden confessed. 'I don't have the money to put stringers on retainer.'

'And yet you offered to broker meetings with the Taliban,' Bethany reminded him.

'It was a marketing tactic,' Riorden pleaded. 'I was lying through my teeth. I swear I don't know any Taliban.'

'So you're telling me you employ no stringers?'

'Not a single one.'

Bethany shook her head. 'But there are news stories on your site attributed to MISA staff.'

Riorden grabbed his chest. 'I am the MISA staff. Those stories on my website, they're rip-offs of reports I found in Pakistani newspapers. The only thing I'm guilty of is plagiarism. I would never betray my country.'

'But you were looking to *hire* staff – weren't you, Riorden?'

'I told you I have no money.'

Bethany leaned over the table. 'What about Emma Cameron?'

Riorden froze. 'Emma was a huge star,' he stammered, 'I couldn't afford a two-bit local stringer, let alone her.'

'Oh, but you had something better than money to offer her.' Bethany rose. 'Didn't you, Riorden?'

The newsman trembled. 'I had nothing to offer her or anyone else.'

'Really?' Bethany produced the computer stick Emma had passed to Ted. 'Then why did you give her this?'

Chapter 37

Serena Hotel, Quetta

A blonde woman surfaced from the pool, her breasts jiggling beneath two flimsy Lycra triangles that left nothing to the imagination. The Serena towel-boys found excuses to hang around and steal glimpses of their nearly-naked guest – clearing empty beer bottles, placing fresh towels on loungers – even though the end of the day was approaching. The western male guests weren't so subtle. They pointed and cat called, as if she were a stripper circling a pole.

'What makes them think they can get away with that?' asked Matt.

Eric cut into his club sandwich. 'Who get away with what?'

Matt nodded at the jeering guests. 'Those numpties, that clueless woman,' he explained. 'Don't they realize where they are?'

'It didn't stop you from causing a scene at Mullah Maulana's.' Eric tucked into the sandwich.

'Look, mate, I'm really sorry about that.'

The correspondent swallowed and wiped the crumbs from his mouth. 'I'm not getting at you. I was just making a point.'

'About what a total arse I am?'

'About western superiority,' Eric corrected.

'I don't think I'm superior to anyone.'

'Bullshit,' said Eric. 'The British built an entire empire on the belief that their culture is superior to everyone else's.'

'An empire that died,' Matt pointed out.

'But the belief in western superiority is still alive and well.' Eric gestured to Jerry. The cameraman was sitting on the other side of the pool, sipping beer through a straw to accommodate his wired jaw. 'Take Jerry for instance. Now, back in the States, he's bottom of the barrel. He watches porn, he smokes, he's got a tenuous relationship at best with soap and water. Bring him to Pakistan however and the yardstick changes. He's a stinking rich westerner with an expense account. People like Jerry don't even realize they're acting offensively because as far as they and the global economy are concerned, they are the product of a superior culture which gives them the right to impose their values and preferences on anyone.'

Brutal as it was, Matt had to admire Eric's candour. Most people didn't have the guts to voice such uncomfortable truths. 'Better watch it, mate, or the PC police will get you.'

'The politically correct are the biggest hypocrites of all,' Eric moaned. 'Have you seen how aid workers live here? Plush villas, cooks, maids and drivers on standby 24-7 – even during Ramadan. They're no different from Victorian Viceroys.' He raised his water glass in mock toast. 'Long live the empire.'

'I lost track of how many diplomats I dragged home from piss-ups in Kabul,' said Matt.

'The East–West dynamic hasn't changed in two hundred years,' said Eric. 'So don't beat yourself up about what happened earlier. Westerners will always think they can come here and get away with murder – until it blows up in their faces.'

'That's still no excuse,' said Matt. 'I should know better, especially with my background.'

Eric scrutinized him. 'How does someone go from being a Special Forces soldier to looking after journalists?'

'I left the military four years ago,' said Matt. 'I take work where I can get it.'

'Why did you leave?'

'It's a long story.'

Eric checked his watch. 'We have an hour to kill before the governor's interview.'

There was only one person Matt had ever shared his Delta experience with – Emma. Maybe it was Eric's loyalty to her or the fact that the correspondent's safety had been compromised, but Matt felt he owed him a truthful explanation. 'There was an operation in Baghdad. I was liaising with a US Delta team. Things went pear-shaped and I left the Regiment not long after.'

'So the Deltas fucked you?' said Eric.

'They didn't mean to,' said Matt. 'The captain in charge of the operation was gutted by what had happened. When I needed work, I went to see him and that's how I ended up with you.'

'I knew it,' Eric said triumphantly. He leaned in. 'OK, Matt. Time to come clean. It was clear in Maulana's office that you're working some other agenda.'

Matt was floored. One outburst and Eric had sussed him as a fraud.

'Tell me the truth,' Eric pressed. 'Why did you come to Pakistan?'

Matt was cornered. Eric was not going to let up. 'You're right,' he confessed. 'I do have another agenda.'

'Tell it to me straight. No bullshitting.'

Matt looked him in the eye. 'I came here for Emma.'

Chapter 38

Riorden was close to convulsing. 'What is that?'

Bethany tilted the storage device to display the SBC logo. 'You know exactly what it is. It's stamped with your old employer's initials. What'd you do, Mr Riorden? Raid the supply cabinet on your way out the door?'

'So what if I did? There are thousands of those things in circulation.' Riorden grew bolder. 'That could belong to anyone.'

Bethany laid the stick on the table. 'This device is manufactured by a firm with close ties to US intelligence. Plug it into a computer and it plants software that enables third parties to read anything stored on the hard drive.' She placed the stick on the table in front of Riorden. 'Your digital fingerprints are all over this.'

'So what?' said the newsman. 'It still doesn't prove anything.'

'We traced text messages on Emma Cameron's BlackBerry to phones purchased in your name. We have CCTV footage of you in Heathrow Airport. We can establish beyond reasonable doubt that you gave this to her.' Bethany paused. 'But that's not what interests me.'

Riorden grasped at the potential reprieve. 'I'll tell you whatever you want to know.'

'How did you get your hands on this information? Who gave it to you?'

Riorden looked at the stick and broke down. 'I don't know.'

Bethany walked around the table and whispered in his ear. 'I advise you to start talking. Especially as I'm the only person in the world prepared to believe you.' She glanced conspiratorially at a light in the ceiling. Riorden's eyes popped as he realized they were not alone.

'Who passed you the information?'

'I don't know,' Riorden insisted. 'It was left for me in an unmarked envelope.'

'An unmarked envelope?' Bethany flaunted her disappointment.

'It's the God's honest truth,' said Riorden. 'Someone left it for me on the seat of a cab.'

'And where did you take this fateful cab ride?' she asked sceptically.

'Islamabad.'

'When?'

'A few months ago.'

'Be more specific.'

Riorden searched his memory. 'Two months maybe. Three? I don't know. I can't remember the exact date.'

'Give me the name of your Taliban contact.'

Riorden jumped. 'I told you, I don't know any Taliban!'

'Someone connected to the Taliban then,' Bethany hounded, 'a middle man, an interlocutor.'

'I don't know any middle men.' Riorden started sobbing again. 'It was left for me on the seat of a cab, I swear.' He appealed to the ceiling light. 'If I knew the source do you think I'd have given the story away to someone else? I'd have published it under my own name, for fuck's sake.'

Bethany glanced at the light. Ted met her eye from the other side. They were both thinking the same thing: Pete Riorden was telling the truth.

Bethany sat down. 'Why the cloak-and-dagger act with Emma

Cameron? The dead drops, the text messages? Why not just approach her directly?'

'Are you shitting me? Emma Cameron wouldn't have touched that story with a bargepole if she'd known it had come through me.'

'You two had been colleagues,' Bethany pointed out. 'Surely she had some regard for you.'

'Please. I spent twenty-five years building SBC into a respectable news operation – slumming through war zones, getting dysentery, sleeping on floors. Do you know how long that little bitch was with the network when they gave her my job? Six months – six fucking months! If anyone deserved to take a fall for a bogus story, it was her, not me.'

'Is that what you were hoping would happen?' asked Bethany. 'That the story would prove a fake and her career would be over?' She wandered the corridors of his twisted logic. 'What if things had gone the other way?'

A maniacal calm settled over the newsman. 'Then I would have owned her.'

'What do you mean – owned her?'

'Imagine if it had got out that Emma Cameron had reported a story that came through me – Patriot Pete, the *Hailstorm* patsy? She would have done anything to keep me silent and preserve her precious reputation. Even work for MISA – and for pennies no less. A media whore like Emma Cameron couldn't go five minutes without being on camera.'

Bethany gathered up her files. 'I think that's enough for now, Mr Riorden. Get some rest and we'll talk more later.' She called the guards to escort Riorden back to his holding cell.

Ted stared at the monitor, a lone tear streaming down his face. The irony was too cruel. Riorden's petty professional jealousy had led to Emma's death.

Bethany joined him in the observation room. 'I'm sorry, sir. I thought the interrogation would give us more.'

Ted collected himself. 'You did an outstanding job.'

'How much longer shall we hold him?'

Ted sighed. 'Until he's out of danger.'

Chapter 39

Eric was visibly shaken. 'What do you mean, you came here for Emma?'

Matt swallowed the lump in his throat. 'I knew her.'

'Knew her . . . how?'

Matt broke down. 'We were going to be married.'

Dozens of emotions flashed across Eric's face. 'I had no idea she was even seeing anyone.' He was speaking to himself as much as Matt.

'I know you were friends but don't think ill of her,' Matt said through his tears. 'Emma had this thing about keeping our relationship separate from her work.'

'Well, she was damn good at keeping you a secret.' Eric sat up suddenly, as if pulling out of a tailspin. 'Your friend who got you this job. Does he know about you and Emma?'

'No one knows – except you.'

'That's why you wanted to know where Abdullah Qari was hiding. You blame him for her murder.'

'I'm sorry. I never should have used you to try and find him. I just didn't know any other way.'

Eric recoiled. 'You can't keep working with us,' he said coldly.

Matt nodded. 'It shouldn't take more than a few days to fly in a replacement.'

'I want you gone tonight,' said Eric. 'We'll return to Islamabad after the interview. You can catch a flight to Dubai when we land.

I don't want you coming back to the hotel with us. Do you understand? You're finished with us.'

Matt couldn't blame the correspondent. 'I'm sorry I involved you in all this.'

Eric stood to leave. 'So am I.'

Chapter 40

Matt observed the governor's guards circling the car. They were nothing like the police escort that had been following them all day. Instead of western-inspired uniforms, the governor's security wore green combat jumpers over tan shalwar kameezes. The biggest difference though was their preparedness. Their weapons were set to fire.

Matt was curious as to which branch of the security services they belonged, but he dare not raise the question in front of Eric. The correspondent had been acting agitated and preoccupied since the pool, and the guards' thorough security check wasn't helping. They were scouring the vehicle for explosives, searching beneath the chassis and inside the wheel arches with hand-held mirrors. When they finished with the exterior, they moved inside the vehicle, probing behind seats and removing the gear and luggage from the boot.

Eric checked his watch. 'We don't have time for this.'

'It is for your safety as well as the governor's,' said the minder.

'We have to be out of here by six-thirty,' said Eric. 'We have a plane to catch.'

'If you miss your flight there will be another tomorrow.'

'We're leaving tonight,' Eric barked, 'interview or no interview.'

The grounds of the governor's mansion were more akin to a 19th Century English country pile than a modern Pakistani residence of state; lavishly landscaped and peppered with statues of

Victorian- and Edwardian-era British generals and Foreign Office luminaries. A sign nailed to an old tree suggested the old occupiers had tried to make amends for their sins.

PLANTED BY HER MAJESTY
THE QUEEN ELIZABETH
5.2.1961

Matt and his clients were shown to the mansion's main reception room. Like the gardens outside, it was a repository for the detritus of Britain's glory days: brown leather Chesterfield chairs, dark wood panelling, antique cranberry glass, heavy carved tables. Two sets of old flintlock rifles with elegant, curving butts were mounted on either side of a tiled fireplace. They were accompanied by their original gunpowder horns and round ceremonial shields. Matt admired the craftsmanship. Someone had poured their blood into the iron.

Hanging on the wall opposite the antique weapons were tapestries of nineteenth- and early twentieth-century battles. One depicted a British royal regiment fighting a group of tribesmen dressed in white turbans and robes. The pale British officers and their tan mercenaries were armed with guns. The locals had only swords and hatchets. They were mounting a courageous if not suicidal defence. One tribesman had drawn a scythed blade over the head of a British officer attempting to reload his pistol. The simple thread work vividly captured the determination of the warrior to defend his homeland against the foreign invaders.

'They are Baluch,' said Naj. 'You can tell from the white turbans.'

The sound of the traitor's voice made Matt bristle.

'They are as ruthless today as they were then,' Naj continued. 'Baluch insurgents have spilled much blood in the name of freedom, including their own people's. That is why the Frontier

Corps is in charge of the governor's security. Only outsiders are to be trusted in this province.'

Matt recalled the guards outside the gate. 'Where do they come from?'

'The FC are Pashtun recruited from the tribal areas and NWFP,' Naj explained. 'The government brought them to Baluchistan thirty years ago to crush a local rebellion. They have been here ever since.'

Matt's eyes narrowed. The FC was from Abdullah Qari's neighbourhood. 'You admire them, don't you?'

'I respect what they are trying to achieve,' said Naj. 'The Baluchistan Liberation Army are animals. The governor must not fall victim to their terror campaign.'

Matt moved his face to within inches of the fixer's. 'But there have to be Taliban sympathizers in the FC ranks; cold-blooded mercenaries waiting to betray the very people who trust them with their lives.'

Naj smiled. 'I would advise you not to repeat that statement to anyone.'

'Or what?' Matt challenged. 'You'll have me sacked?'

Naj stepped aside and whispered: 'Your job is the least you could lose.'

The governor arrived with a full complement of aides. Like the guards outside his mansion walls, he was not ethnic Baluch but Pashtun. 'Thank you, Governor,' Naj fawned. 'We are most honoured to have an audience with you.'

Eric didn't wait to be formally introduced. He barrelled past Naj and seized the governor's hand. 'Let's get started.'

There was no small talk or taking of tea, none of the ice-breaking pleasantries Eric had engaged in earlier that day with

Mullah Maulana. As soon as the microphone was clipped to the governor's lapel, the correspondent ordered Jerry to roll tape. 'There are many reports of human rights violations by the security forces against ethnic Baluch in this province,' Eric began. 'How do you answer these charges?'

The governor cast a disparaging look at the minder. The civil servant deflected the recrimination onto Naj.

'Well?' Eric pressed.

Matt was taken aback by Eric's bluntness. The correspondent seemed to have lost all sense of tact.

The governor pressed his fingertips into a pyramid. 'There are human rights violations in Baluchistan but the security forces are not responsible. Baluch rebels terrorize settlers who have come here from other parts of Pakistan. They kidnap and execute foreigners working to develop the resources of the province for the Baluch people and the nation.'

Eric waved a paper before the camera. 'I have a petition here from the . . .' he knitted his brow and read from it, '. . . the Baluch Academy in Quetta demanding that the government acknowledge extra-judicial arrests of Baluch nationals; the disappearances of Baluch political workers; the humiliation of Baluch women . . .'

Matt's concern was fast turning to alarm. Eric was going to get them all deported and blacklisted if he carried on like that.

'. . . and other atrocities committed by security forces in the province *you* govern.' Eric slammed down the paper. 'How do you answer these charges?'

'A hundred thousand settlers have migrated from Baluchistan because of the insurgent death squads,' the governor protested. 'Baluch terrorists . . .'

Eric talked over him. 'You mean freedom fighters . . .'

'Don't be obscene,' said the governor.

'What's obscene, Governor, is the systematic genocide perpetrated on the Baluch people . . .'

The governor ripped off the microphone. 'How dare you come here and repeat these lies! There are hidden hands at work in this province, outside powers using Baluch rebels as proxies to destabilize Pakistan. This is what you should report. This is what you should investigate. Not terrorist propaganda.'

The governor stormed out of the room. Jerry followed him, with the camera rolling.

Chapter 41

The temperature had plummeted rapidly with the setting sun. Matt squeezed into the front seat next to the minder. The chill from the civil servant was frostier than the air outside.

'To the airport,' the minder ordered. He was more anxious than Eric now to get SBC the hell out of Quetta.

They turned out of the mansion grounds and onto a dual carriageway. Though twilight had fallen, few headlights were switched on. Naj probed the poorly lit haze in fits and starts, exploiting openings created by the mismatched horsepower of donkey carts and petrol-driven vehicles.

Matt looked in the passenger mirror. Their security escort was swerving and jockeying to keep up. 'The police are falling behind.'

'I wait for them and we shall never get to the airport,' said Naj. Something flew over the concrete median and landed in their path. Naj slammed on the brakes, throwing everyone forward. The police truck screeched and tapped them, sending a second shock wave through the tin-can car. 'They came out of nowhere!' the fixer exclaimed.

Matt recovered from his whiplash and identified the apparition; a motorbike carrying two locals. He watched it head off-road into the desert, a plume of dust spiralling in its wake. He plotted the trajectory of the whirling dervish; it was heading for a junction further up the road. The motorbike was using the desert as a rat-run.

Matt searched for it again as they approached the junction. The motorbike was long gone but an even more suspect vehicle had caught his eye – a pick-up truck parked on the far side of the intersection. Four passengers wearing pakols and long shawls drawn up around their shoulders and faces were sitting in the open back.

The truck could have pulled onto the shoulder because of mechanical failure but Matt doubted it. It was no luxury vehicle. If it was broken down, the passengers would be attempting to repair it themselves. As Naj drove into the junction, Matt cracked his window. The pick-up's diesel engine was clicking away.

Matt studied the men riding in the back through his passenger mirror. Their eyes were like lasers and some of their shawls had odd peaks. Matt could think of only one cause for the distortions – rifle barrels. He shifted focus to the front of the pick-up. There were two men sitting in the cab, a driver and a passenger who was either clean shaven or wore his beard closely cropped. The light was too low to make a definitive call.

As soon as SBC was through the intersection, the pick-up driver reached his hand out of the window and rapped twice on his door. He was signalling the lads in back that they were moving.

Matt's paranoia intensified as the pick-up pulled off the shoulder and swerved in behind the police escort. The timing of the move was no coincidence. SBC had been targeted by a kidnapping gang.

Everything pointed to abduction. The lads on the motorbike had marked SBC's vehicle and driven ahead to alert the ambush team. Now the pick-up was moving in to take the prize. The only question remaining was how they planned to separate SBC from its security escort.

'You may want to pick up the pace,' Matt suggested calmly.

'First you tell me to slow down,' Naj complained, 'now it is speed up.'

'Shut up and drive faster,' said Matt.

'Whoa, I don't think so,' Eric protested.

'Are you serious?' Matt turned around. 'All night you've been bitching to get to the airport.'

'If we get into an accident we definitely won't get there.'

Matt checked his mirror. The pick-up was trying to overtake the police. 'Look, mate, I don't want to alarm you but we've got . . .'

Naj hit the brakes without warning again. A sharp pain shot through Matt's neck as his head slammed sideways into the passenger window.

The fixer shoved the heel of his hand on the horn. 'Son of a bitch!'

Matt shook off his daze and looked ahead. A jingly with a covered flatbed had pulled across the carriageway and stopped at a crossing point, blocking most of the road. He craned his aching neck to get a look at the oncoming traffic. There were more than enough gaps to make a U-turn, not that a truck that size needed any.

The pick-up pulled out from behind the police escort and headed up their left side. Matt's eyes darted between the advancing truck and the idled jingly. The throbbing in his neck stopped as his body flooded with adrenaline. The two vehicles were working in tandem. 'Get us out of here now!'

Naj sighed and looked around for an opening.

'Go! Go! Go!' Matt shouted.

Naj grabbed the gearshift but it was too late. The pick-up was alongside them, blocking their only escape route.

Matt was convinced the fixer was doing everything in his power to make them vulnerable. 'Back up!'

'I can't,' Naj protested.

'Do it or I swear I'll tear your head from your shoulders!'

'The police are behind us,' the fixer insisted.

'They'll bloody well get the message!'

'Would one of you please tell me what the hell is going on!' Eric shouted.

Men armed with Type 56 assault rifles started pouring out the back of the jingly. They were carbon copies of the guards from Maulana's compound, right down to their black turbans. Matt turned and lunged over the seatback. 'It's the Taliban!' he said, pushing Eric and Jerry to the floor. 'Stay as low as you can and pull your body armour on top of you!'

The Taliban opened fire on the police. Matt watched the contact unfolding through the rear window. A barrage of automatic bullets ripped through the policemen's exposed cab, instantly cutting down three of them. The survivors rose to respond but they were in complete disarray. Some had tried to fire with their safety-catches on. Others had released them but forgotten to feed a bullet into the chamber. The poor laddies didn't have a chance.

Another blitz opened on the flank. Matt turned to see the men in the pick-up throwing off their shawls. As he'd suspected, they'd been concealing weapons, but not garden variety AK rip-offs. The quartet had serious firepower; Heckler & Koch G3s with over and under grenade launchers.

Matt expected the quartet to finish off the police with a high-explosive round. 'Cover your ears and brace for an explosion!' he warned. But to his astonishment, the men in the pick-up didn't fire an HE round at the police. They turned their weapons on the Taliban!

Muzzle flashes lit the street as the two gangs traded salvos. The cacophony was deafening; both sides firing on automatic. Matt searched for a safe passage out. The car was too light to ram through the vehicles hemming them in and too low to clear the median with any degree of certainty. He and his clients could leg it, but without a weapon of his own, he had no way of covering them as they withdrew.

Matt checked on his clients. Eric and Jerry were lower than a snake's belly. The minder and Naj didn't have that option. Between the steering wheel and blubber, neither man could get below the dashboard.

A wild round shattered the back window and exited through Matt's, blowing it out as well.

'Stay calm!' the minder bellowed. 'The police will protect us!'

'They're dead!' Matt informed him.

'Then I will defend us!' The minder leaned back and reached into his waistband.

Matt's eyes widened when he saw a 9mm Browning emerge from the minder's fat folds. 'Give me that weapon!'

The minder aimed the pistol at Matt's head. 'Stand aside!'

Matt ducked and waited for the discharge. But instead of a bullet flying out, he heard the whistle of an incoming round followed by the thud of a body absorbing the bullet. The minder collapsed on top of him – dead.

'Merciful Allah!' Naj cried.

Matt threw off the corpse and freed the pistol from the minder's warm hand. 'Drive us out of here or you'll be next.'

'Are you mad?' said Naj. 'Drive where?'

'Over the median.' Matt shoved the pistol in Naj's temple. 'Do it!'

The fixer yelped and fumbled with the gearshift. The engine revved but the car went nowhere – he'd thrown it into neutral.

'Open the door!' Matt shouted.

'We cannot go out there!'

'Open the bloody door!'

Eric sat up. His face filled with dismay when he saw Matt
aiming a pistol at Naj. 'What are you doing!'

'He sold us out to the Taliban and now they're trying to
kidnap us!' said Matt. 'He set us up, just like he did Emma!'

'What are you talking about?' demanded Eric.

Matt climbed over the minder's corpse and pushed Naj out of
the car.

'I am innocent!' cried the fixer as he tumbled into the street.

Matt slammed the door. 'Get down!' he said to Eric.

He threw the car into drive, hit the gas and turned the wheel
hard. The battle raging around them was momentarily eclipsed
by the sickening thud of metal slamming into concrete. It was
the axle cracking in two. 'Fucking hell!' Matt shouted as the
chassis buckled.

A camera rose from the backseat and rotated like a periscope.
The red light was on. Jerry had been filming the whole time.
Matt dived over the seats. 'Turn that bloody thing off and stay
down!'

'We need to go back and get Naj,' protested Eric.

'He's with his mates, let him fend for himself,' said Matt. 'I
need to get you two out of here before one of these gangs gets
the upper hand.'

'*Gangs?*' asked Eric.

'One of them's TTP-Q, I'm sure of it. I don't know who the
others are.' Matt poked his head above the parapet. The two
sides were still locked in a fierce exchange. He looked across to
the other side of the highway. Several pairs of steady lights beckoned through the smoke and darkness. They were set high off
the ground – three storeys up by his estimate. He dropped down.
'There's a building across the way. If we can get up to the roof we
can barricade ourselves in and wait until help arrives.'

'We can't go out there,' Eric objected.

'We're out of options,' said Matt. 'On my call, both of you get out of the car and take cover behind the engine block. When I give the signal, run to the building directly across from us. Whatever you do, don't stop and don't look back. Just push your way to the top floor.' He raised the minder's pistol. 'I'll be covering you. Understand?'

Eric and Jerry nodded.

Matt wedged his body against the passenger door. 'Ready?'

'Ready,' Eric confirmed.

'Go! Go! Go!'

Eric opened the door, rolled out and crawled on his belly toward the front of the car. Jerry followed behind but instead of moving on hands and knees, he scooted on his arse with his camera raised above his head, recording.

Matt shoved the Browning into his waistband and dived for the open door. He was halfway through when someone grabbed his legs!

He called to Eric and Jerry, 'Run! Run!' Both men moved out from behind the engine block and bolted into the smoke. Matt braced the doorframe with both hands and kicked up with all his strength. He managed to free one leg, but the other was still in the clutches of the kidnapper. He released his right hand to reach for his pistol, only to find himself sliding backward. The kidnappers were pulling him out of the car!

He landed chin first on the tarmac. Matt's face turned to mince as he was dragged feet first through the gunfire. He thrashed and twisted, trying to right himself. He managed to free a leg and kick the kidnapper in the stomach. He was wearing a black turban. TTP-Q had won the fight.

Matt leapt to his feet and sprinted for the other side of the highway. A yard from the median, his knees buckled. Another kidnapper had rugby-tackled him from behind.

Matt threw off the captor only to have three more pile in on top of him. The crushing scrum was disorienting. All he could see was a collage of bared teeth, beards and fists. One slammed into his nose. The blows kept raining down until blackness fell.

PART III

Chapter 42

Matt awoke to his worst nightmare – plunged in cold darkness, unable to move, see or hear. His lungs couldn't inflate and his nose and mouth were blocked. He was certain he was drowning.

The weight on his chest shifted. Matt gasped but instead of air, sand flew up his nostrils, triggering a coughing fit. His fear escalated to absolute terror. The kidnappers hadn't submerged him in water. They'd buried him alive!

A shove to his ribs disrupted the spasm. Matt's dread eased slightly. He wasn't in the ground. There were people around him, warning him to lie still. He bit his lip to curb the cough. The dried blood on his face flavoured the grit in his mouth, making him gag. Matt tried rolling onto his side for fear of choking on his own vomit, but the movement only invited another kick.

He realized it didn't hurt. Something was insulating his body, a wrapping of some sort. He scratched his nails against it. The material was rough with weft and warp. He'd been wrapped in a carpet; a thin kilim.

His reason restored, Matt systematically unravelled the other conditions of his captivity. He hadn't gone deaf. The kilim was muffling noise. He focused on the dissonance outside of it, isolating individual sounds. There was the rattle of an engine, diesel, light not heavy. The Taliban had lost out. Matt had been abducted by the pick-up quartet. He detected the white noise of wind rushing past. No wonder he was so cold. He'd been wrapped in a flimsy kilim and thrown onto the back of the truck.

The kidnappers' conversation filtered through the layers of carpet. Their dialect was different from the one Matt had heard in Maulana's compound. He could identify only three voices. The contact in the street must have reduced the quartet to a trio.

An object landed on Matt, compressing his lungs again. It was one of his captors. They were using him as a human cushion. He feigned choking noises, figuring it was better to be kicked than suffocate under someone's arse. The pressure subsided and a slip of air was restored.

After a while, the cold retreated. An icy warmth spread through Matt's body, pushing him into a dream state. His life started flashing before his eyes. There were scenes from his childhood; running through the Highlands; watching his mother swing a falcon lure; helping his father mend the wind turbine. The imprints gave way to the accident that had torn him from his parents' idyllic sanctuary – the car swerving into the river; his parents' lifeless eyes; the water swallowing his chest, his chin . . .

Matt shook himself awake. He tried wiggling his toes. They wouldn't respond. He tried bending his knees. They felt brittle, like termite-ravaged wood. He may not have been drowning but he was slipping under. Blood had diverted from his limbs to his core. He was going down with hypothermia.

It could be minutes or hours before he died. There were so many unknown variables. Matt railed against the cold, contracting his muscles to restore circulation. To keep his mind alert, he plotted his escape. His best opportunity would come when the kidnappers unrolled the kilim. Their guard would be down. But there was little Matt could do to outmanoeuvre them at this stage. His limbs were lead, plus he was outnumbered. What he wouldn't give for a weapon . . .

He rocked his hips forward. The body of the Browning dug into his waist. The pistol buoyed Matt's spirits. The kidnappers hadn't bothered to search him. He rocked back – his mobile was still in his pocket as well. A weapon and comms; he had everything he needed to escape. Now if he could just survive long enough to make his move.

The minutes stretched into hours. Matt succumbed to the cold again. With his systems nearing total shutdown, his mind wandered back to the only happiness he'd known since childhood . . .

It was two months before Emma was able to fit Matt into her schedule. By that point, he'd convinced himself nothing would happen. But the moment she opened her hotel door, his instincts overwhelmed his insecurities. He grabbed her and kissed her until her knees weakened. 'OK then,' he said, 'get into bed now.'

They feasted on each other for hours. As lovers, Matt and Emma were mutually narcotic; the more they had, the more they craved. Matt wanted to dismiss the attraction as purely chemical but he knew there was something deeper between them; a longing to connect to something real.

He ran his fingertips along the silver chain gilding her collarbone and stopped at the cross. 'I nearly lost a tooth to this thing,' he said, flipping it up.

She slapped his hand away. 'Then I suggest you get a gumshield because I never take it off.'

'If you're that into religion, we're going to have a lot of disagreements.'

'Relax. I'm no evangelical. I'm just superstitious.' Emma

propped herself up on her elbow. Matt mirrored her. 'I bought this the day after nine-eleven,' she explained, 'and nothing's happened to me since.'

'Were you in New York?'

Emma nodded. 'I was studying for a business degree at Columbia University. I was going to go into banking and make shitloads of money but after the Trade Center attacks, I decided to rescue my country from the scourge of terrorism.' She rubbed her cross. 'Turns out the world needed rescuing from us.'

'I'm glad you changed your mind. I've never met a banker flying to Kabul.' Matt stroked her hair. 'So how did you become *The Satellite Dish*?'

'Ugh!' Emma threw her head back. 'That name is so demeaning. The fucking assholes in PR made it up to boost my Q ratings. The news business is bullshit.'

'It can't be that bad,' said Matt. 'At least you get to see the world.'

'See the world?' Emma balked. 'All I do is stand on rooftops spouting rubbish. Seriously, I can count on one hand how many times I've left the Serena in Kabul. I have no idea what's going on in Afghanistan.'

Matt nuzzled her neck. 'So Emma Cameron is a fraud,' he teased.

She bit her lip.

'I'm kidding,' he laughed.

Emma rolled out of bed and grabbed his trousers.

'I'm sorry,' said Matt, fearing she was throwing him out. 'I didn't mean it.'

She rummaged through the pockets and found his passport. 'This is a little embarrassing,' she said, hiding her face behind it.

Matt sat up.

She lowered the veil. 'I don't know your last name,' she confessed.

'It's Logan,' Matt smiled. 'Now will you come back to bed already?'

Emma sat down beside him and opened the passport. Matt tried to grab it but she whisked it from his grasp. 'Nice mug shot,' she joked. Her light-hearted mood vanished abruptly. 'Wow.' She looked at Matt as if seeing him for the first time. 'Are you really a . . .'

Matt's heart sank. Emma had discovered his shameful pedigree. 'No. I'm not.'

She studied his features. 'You're lying. I can see the family resemblance. OK,' she pretended to look over his shoulders, 'where are you hiding the private jet?'

'I don't have a jet.' Matt took his passport back. 'I don't even own a car.'

'So, you're a frugal billionaire?'

'I'm not even a thousand-aire.' Matt paused. He'd never discussed his family background with anyone. But he didn't want Emma thinking he was someone he wasn't. 'If you really must know, my mum was disowned by her father. So technically, I'm an outcast.'

Emma was intrigued. 'Mind if I ask what she did?'

'Nothing illegal if that's what you're thinking,' said Matt. 'She married my father.'

'Was he like a convict or something?'

'Dad had the audacity to be working class,' Matt explained, 'and Scottish to boot. Not exactly what my grandfather had in mind for his only child.'

'It all sounds very *Wuthering Heights*.' Emma settled in for the yarn. 'So, how did your parents meet?'

'At a ban the bomb rally. Angus and Winnie were always trying to save the planet.' Saying their names brought forth more torpid memories. 'They had this small farm in Perthshire that was totally off the grid – literally. It had a wind turbine and a wood-burning stove.'

'Is that where you were raised?'

'Yeah. Dad taught me how to fix things and work the land. Mum taught me the country pursuits worth knowing,' Matt said wistfully. 'It was great.'

'How did your mother cope? Going from mansions filled with servants to chopping wood?'

'Mum loved the farm even more than Dad. She wasn't beholden to anyone. No one could threaten to cut her off if she didn't do as they said. She lived life entirely on her own terms.'

'I can definitely see the appeal in that.' Emma looked into the distance. 'Do your parents still have the farm?'

'Their estate was auctioned off when I was thirteen.'

'That sucks,' said Emma. 'Were they foreclosed?'

Matt turned stoic. 'They died.'

'Oh my God. I'm so sorry. That must have been awful, losing your parents and your home all at once.'

'It was a long time ago.' Matt took Emma's hand and kissed it. 'You would have liked Mum. She had a mouth just like yours. When Grandfather threatened to cut her out of his will she told him to shove it up his fat old arse.'

'Good for her.' Emma rested her chin on Matt's shoulder. 'There's one thing I don't get. If she hated your grandfather so much, why did she name you after him?'

Matt sighed like he was shouldering the weight of the world. 'She was hoping I'd bring integrity to the family name.'

Emma caressed his face. 'Do you ever think about going back?'

Matt pulled away. 'To the family – never!'

'No,' said Emma. 'To Perthshire . . .'

*   *   *

A jolt tore Matt from his past. The pick-up had turned onto a bumpy track. Ten undulating minutes later, they stopped and the engine cut. Matt did his best to snap himself out of his hypothermic haze. This was his chance to escape.

He tumbled out of the kilim onto the hard ground. Matt tried to get up but his frozen limbs refused to cooperate. Coughing and heaving, he struggled to get his bearings. The earth beneath him was dry and cracked – a desert environment. He shifted his eyes toward the horizon. Artificial lights were visible in the distance. The yellow-orange beacons were grouped around a tall building with two archways. Chain link and razor wire fanned out from either side. The configuration was in line with a border crossing, but which one? The kidnappers could have driven him to Afghanistan or Iran.

They pulled him up by the hair and drew a black hood over his head. Before the cover fell, Matt managed to identify a building approximately thirty metres away – single storey, cinderblock, shuttered windows.

The cab door opened and closed. One of the kidnappers was walking toward him. The man had a distinctive gait; a step followed by a long drag. 'Get up,' a voice commanded in English. Matt tried to obey but he was too paralysed by cold.

The kidnappers seized his wrists and dragged him face down along the ground. The desert rubble dug into Matt's legs, clawing them back to life. He flexed his knees and ankles and willed his wrists to do the same. To operate the Browning, he'd need full use of his hands and fingers.

A door creaked open and Matt was hurled forward onto a hard, unforgiving floor. The kidnappers yanked him up like a rag doll, sat him against a wall and shoved something in his hands. He recognized the object by touch. It was a newspaper. They were trying to establish proof of life.

The kidnappers removed his hood to take his picture. Matt absorbed as much as he could before the flash blinded him. Three armed men were in there with him. All of them had rifles slung casually across their backs but getting shot was the least of his concerns. The floor was covered in blood spats and wads of dirty cotton wool. A table with a torn red vinyl cover and insect-like metal restraining arms was in the centre of the room. A trolley with dirty medical instruments, syringes and a small machine with a cavity probe was standing beside it. He was being held in a torture cell.

Chapter 43

A burst of light obscured the chamber of horrors. Matt regained his vision to find the kidnappers checking the image they'd snapped in the viewfinder. It was now or never. He laid the newspaper on his lap, reached under it to retrieve the Browning and pulled back the slide.

The cocking of the weapon alerted the kidnappers. They reached for their rifles but Matt beat them to the draw. He aimed the pistol and operated the trigger but no shot rang out. His advantage blown, he pulled the slide again and ran for the door, shooting, but once more the weapon failed to discharge.

Matt slammed the door behind him to slow the captors' pursuit only to discover there was another man outside. The figure limping toward the torture cell was dressed differently from the others – instead of a shalwar kameez, his outline was framed in the sharply-tailored angles of western clothing.

The lame man reached for a sidearm when he saw Matt. 'Stop or I'll shoot!' he commanded in English.

Matt steamrolled over him and headed into the desert, searching for cover in the broad, moonlit plain. The border was at least a thousand yards west and there were few compounds in between. A long embankment to the north looked like a possibility, but Matt had no idea what lay beyond.

He ran to the closest compound, dived behind the perimeter

wall and checked the kidnappers' progress. The trio from the house had stopped to assist their lame partner.

Matt pulled his mobile from his back pocket, hit speed dial and cradled the handset in his neck while he worked on the malfunctioning Browning. He released the magazine to check if it was empty. It was stuffed to the gunnels with thirteen rounds. He ejected the top bullet and rubbed his thumb around the base. The rim was completely worn away. 'Lazy fucking git,' Matt muttered. No wonder the pistol wouldn't fire. The minder hadn't alternated the rounds in the magazine and now the top one was too worn to feed into the chamber. He stuck his finger in the magazine to see if it could be salvaged. All the remaining rounds were compressed, indicating the spring was shot.

Matt pounded the magazine against the heel of his hand. His phone call connected as the bullets fell into his palm. 'You have reached 7M operations. Our offices are now closed,' said a recorded voice. 'If your call is urgent, please hang up and redial . . .'

'Fucking hell!' Matt shoved the phone back in his pocket and examined the bullets. They were covered with dirt and grime. He peered around the corner. The trio from the torture room were closing in on his position. He quickly rubbed the rounds clean, cocked the pistol to set the hammer and fed a bullet manually into the chamber.

He aimed for the biggest kidnapper and operated the pistol trigger. The bullet clipped the target's shoulder, spinning him to the ground. The captors left standing responded, spraying the perimeter wall with automatic gunfire. Matt loaded another round into the pistol, fired and took off.

The desert stretched toward the border like an endless chasm. It was suicide to risk a run for it. Matt searched the embankment to the north, trying to establish what lay behind it. He noticed gaps in the rise. His initial assessment had been wrong. It wasn't high ground at all. It was a line of lorries; dozens of them parked right up next to one another. The fuel trucks had long, cylindrical trailers and boxy cabs. He ran toward them, trying to load another round into the pistol, but it was too difficult to do on the fly.

Matt ran between two lorries, only to be thrown off his feet. He broke the fall with his wrists and turned. A man rose from the darkness – a lorry driver holding an AK 47. He'd been sleeping on the ground, guarding his cargo, but now he was yelling, alerting other drivers to the outsider in their midst. Figuring the driver would think twice before firing live rounds around thousands of gallons of petrol, Matt rolled beneath the fuel trailer to escape.

Voices echoed throughout the steel corridors. He crawled on his belly searching for a way out. If he backtracked south, he'd fall into the hands of the kidnappers; stay, and he'd fall victim to the lorry mob. The border lights in the distance called to him. It was the only option he had left.

A pair of feet came trampling by. Matt waited a few seconds, sprang to his feet, and ran through the corridor. Shots ricocheted around him as he traversed the exposed ground leading to the border. He serpentined to throw his pursuers off target. The exertion pushed him to the limits of endurance. His legs threatening to buckle, Matt mined the dormant determination that had once propelled them over the Brecon Beacons into the most elite fighting force in the world.

A siren sounded and a searchlight switched on. Three border guards followed the sweeping beam into the desert. Matt went for broke, jumping into the light, raising his arms and dropping to his knees. The shooting behind him stopped as the guards stepped into the circle, shouting and clutching their weapons tightly. He was still holding the half-functioning Browning. Matt gingerly laid the magazine-less pistol down, laced his fingers behind his head and gestured to his chest. 'The bullets are in my pocket, mate.'

The guards recovered the rounds and marched him back to their station. As they approached the double-arched gate, Matt could see a flag waving on the other side; the black, red and green standard of Afghanistan. The kidnappers had driven him to the Chaman border crossing.

The guards threw him into an empty room and shut the door. Matt rested his head against the wall, took a deep breath and allowed his heart rate to slow. He'd survived a kidnapping attempt and an angry mob. Nothing could faze him now.

The guards returned with three angry-looking men. One had a bullet wound to the shoulder. Matt's heart stopped. The border guards were handing him over to the kidnappers!

This time, the trio took no chances. They replaced Matt's hood, bound his hands and feet with duct tape and frogmarched him back to the torture chamber.

His teeth rattled as his jaw hit the floor but the pain was quickly eclipsed by a boot slamming into his kidneys. Matt arched his back. The contortion only invited another kick to his stomach.

'Stop!' someone commanded. 'Move him there.' Matt recognized the voice – the crippled kidnapper he'd trampled outside.

Matt was hoisted up and roughly deposited on a cushioned surface; the table with the scary metal arms.

The door shut and the room was silent for a moment. Then the footsteps started, the strides were menacing; a heavy drop followed by a long, abrasive slide. Matt had no illusions about what was coming; he was about to be taught a lesson. That's why the trio had been called off; torture was wasted on the comatose.

The hood was removed. An overhead light burned a hole in Matt's vision. He turned his face only to have it forced back toward the glare.

Features slowly rendered on the darkened silhouette looming above him – familiar features.

'How are you, my friend?'

Matt blinked, but his eyes weren't playing tricks. He knew his torturer. 'Khalid?'

Chapter 44

The fluorescent bulb popped. Eric shuddered and looked up. The light casing was overflowing with desiccated insects. He lowered his eyes to the floor. Hundreds of tiny rodent tracks were visible in the talcum dust. Satan himself could not have designed a more fitting purgatory for the correspondent, but Eric couldn't blame the devil for his circumstances. He'd chosen to work with vermin. It was only fitting that he be locked up with them.

The door handle twisted. Eric assumed his victim's mask. The sooner he got through the police interview the sooner he could call McKay.

'Mr Riddell?'

Eric's face collapsed. 'Who are you?'

'My name is Bethany Saunders.' The young spy closed the door behind her. 'I'm with the United States Embassy. I got here as quickly as I could.' She sat down beside him. 'How are you holding up?'

'Where are the police?'

'They're still processing . . .' Bethany consulted her notebook, 'Mr Fitzwilliam I believe?'

'What about the rest of my team?'

Bethany's eyes welled with concern. 'I'm afraid we have no word yet on Mr Logan, but . . .'

'I was talking about my fixer,' said Eric. 'Mohammed

Najibullah? He's Pakistani. We were separated during the attack.'

'I was not made aware of Mr Najibullah but I'm sure the local authorities will give his case the utmost priority. As for Mr Logan, you should know that I've spoken to the ambassador personally. She wants me to assure you that everything is being done to secure his speedy release.'

'Matt's British,' said Eric. 'The US Embassy has no authority to act on his behalf.'

'The British Foreign Office has sought our assistance,' Bethany explained. She took out a pen. 'Now, I know you've been through a terrible ordeal but if you don't mind, I'd like to ask you a few questions about the abduction.'

'Wouldn't it be more productive if we waited for the police to join us?' said Eric.

'The sooner we start gathering information the greater chance we have of bringing Mr Logan home alive,' Bethany explained. 'Time is of the essence in these situations.'

'Then you should get Jerry in here too,' Eric suggested. 'If you debrief us together you'll get the information that much faster.'

'How do I explain this . . .' Bethany removed her glasses. 'When people survive a traumatic, violent incident as you and your colleague just have there's a tendency to inadvertently tailor memories to create a common story. Think of it as an unconscious show of solidarity. By debriefing you separately we have a much better chance of avoiding this phenomenon and assembling an accurate picture of what happened.'

'Did you just make that up off the top of your head?'

'If I sound patronizing, Mr Riddell, I apologize. That was not my intention.'

'How did you know I was here?' he asked.

'The embassy dispatched me as soon as it got word of the incident.'

'How did they know?'

'The Quetta police informed us.'

Eric shook his head. 'The police don't work that fast in Pakistan.'

Bethany nodded. 'That may have been the case before but with the new protocols . . .'

'New protocols, my ass,' Eric snapped. 'There's no fucking bat phone between here and the US Embassy.'

Bethany tried to calm him. 'You are obviously agitated which is to be expected after the ordeal you've been through.'

'Get out,' Eric ordered.

'Perhaps I should give you a moment before we . . .'

'Fine.' Eric stood up. 'I'll leave then.'

Bethany blocked the door. 'If you care at all about Mr Logan's fate, you'll talk to me.'

'I do care. Which is why you're the last person on earth I'm talking to right now,' said Eric. 'Fucking embassy, my ass; the United States doesn't even have a consulate in Quetta.'

'I was in town attending a donor conference on behalf of the State Department,' Bethany explained. 'I assure you, there's no ruse afoot.'

'A donor conference? Really? Who's the sponsor?'

'UNHCR.'

Eric laughed. 'Tell Ted his cover's getting stale.'

The boss's name stripped away Bethany's pretence. Her expression turned as steely as Eric's. 'This is not the place to have this conversation.'

'If I was going to talk, it wouldn't be with some two-bit intern.'

Bethany didn't bite. 'We're willing to cut you a deal if you cooperate with us.'

'You're in no position to bargain.'

'We can protect you, Mr Riddell . . .'

Eric seized her by the shoulders and slammed her against the wall. 'Like you protected Emma?' he scowled.

Chapter 45

Khalid adjusted the lamp. 'You are a mess, my friend. You should not have run.'

Matt was still disoriented. 'What's going on?' he asked. 'What are you doing with those thugs?'

'Their methods lack subtlety but they are not thugs,' said Khalid. 'They are associates of mine.'

Matt tried to reconcile the figure before him with the man he'd worked with in Kabul. 'They don't act like translators.'

Khalid pulled back his coat. His Glock 17 was sitting comfortably in a holster. 'If you'll recall, neither did I the last time we were together.'

Matt rewound the attack on Camp Phoenix; the fearlessness Khalid had displayed while firing at the VBIED, his uncharacteristic attempts to wriggle out of the assignment, the bogus indignation over Julia's dress. 'Fuck me,' said Matt. 'You knew the Taliban were going to target Camp Phoenix that night.'

'I wanted to warn you,' said Khalid. 'But doing so would have compromised my mission.'

'Your mission?' Matt connected the dots. 'You're ISI, aren't you?'

Khalid did not deny it.

'The whole time you were with the British Embassy?'

Khalid nodded.

'Why were you spying on us? You're our ally.'

'You wear naivety poorly,' said Khalid. 'You know, I was surprised you agreed to take Julia to Camp Phoenix for something as trivial as a game of tennis. It did not fit your profile.'

'Racketball,' Matt corrected.

'Always the penchant for detail,' Khalid commented. 'Were you aware that the embassy terminated my employment after I was wounded? My superiors in Islamabad were not pleased. Your ambassador is a very indiscreet man. I was hoping you would intervene and have me reinstated but of course, you'd taken another position.' He looked down at his leg. 'All I have is this souvenir to remind me of my time with the British.'

Matt couldn't see Khalid's wound but he could tell it was festering. There was a note of sour flesh in the air. 'Is that why you came after me? To get a little of your own back for making you come with me that night?'

'I told you I would never forget what you did.' Khalid pulled out a pocket knife. 'I have answered enough of your questions. It is your turn to answer mine,' he said, selecting a blade.

Matt didn't show his fear, but inside he was quaking. The blade Khalid had chosen was serrated; perfect for sawing through fingers.

Khalid rolled him onto his side. 'Tell me, my friend, why did you come to Pakistan?'

'I got a job here,' said Matt.

'And what is the nature of your work?'

Matt eyed the probe sitting on the trolley beside him. 'Same as Kabul. Close protection.'

Khalid winched Matt's hands up. 'You are lying.'

'It's the truth,' Matt winced.

Khalid wiggled the blade between Matt's wrists. 'We can play this game all night if you desire. But sooner or later you will tell me the truth – if you care to stay alive.' He thrust the knife up. A sharp pain shot through Matt's fingertips as the blood flowed back into them. Khalid had severed the duct tape.

The ISI spy handed him the knife. 'You do the rest.'

Matt shook the pins and needles from his hands. 'You scared the shit out of me.'

'Good.' Khalid hobbled across the room. 'Perhaps now you will listen to reason.'

Matt cut the tape from his ankles. 'Kidnapping me and hauling me into a torture chamber is a little over the top, don't you think?'

'A torture chamber?' Khalid lowered himself into a chair. 'We're in a women's clinic.'

Matt reassessed the metal arms on the table. They weren't for restraining people against their will. They were stirrups for pelvic examinations. 'How's your leg doing?'

'Poorly.' The spy regarded the limb as if it were no longer a part of him. 'They will have to amputate if it does not improve.'

Matt jumped down from the table and handed Khalid the knife. 'I wish there was more I could have done for you.'

'I do not blame you, my friend,' said Khalid. 'The Americans did this to me. They have no regard for Pakistanis.' He gestured to the trolley. 'If they did, they would stop selling us those machines.'

Matt took a closer look at what he'd mistaken for an electric shock delivery system. It had a General Electric logo stamped on the side. 'What is it?'

'A portable ultrasound,' Khalid explained. 'Pregnant women come here from hundreds of miles to learn the sex of their unborn children. If the baby is a boy, they celebrate. If it is a girl, they kill it.' The spy paused. 'How could you work for Americans?'

'My clients are journalists,' Matt explained. 'They have nothing to do with what goes on here.'

'I'm not referring to the journalists,' said Khalid. 'The day you arrived in Pakistan you were met at the airport by members of an American Special Forces security unit.'

Matt recalled the red Toyota tailing them down the highway. The ISI had lumped him in with ICON. 'I'm not working with those men. They just gave me a ride.'

'Are you honestly suggesting they are merely a taxi service?'

'They're old . . . associates,' said Matt, borrowing Khalid's terminology. 'We worked together when I was a soldier, but not now.'

'Do you give me your word that you are not a part of their operation here?' said Khalid. Matt crossed his heart. 'A poorly selected gesture, but point taken.'

'Great,' said Matt. 'Now would you mind giving me a lift back to Quetta?'

'You cannot go back there. Your life is in grave danger.'

'Tell me about it. Your spooks damn near killed me.'

'You think I would send spies to kidnap you? The men are SSG Black Storks, the Pakistani equivalent of your SAS,' Khalid explained. 'I was a commander in the unit when I was a younger man. Back then, we trained with American Special Forces.' He patted his Glock. 'This was given to me by a Delta Force colonel during a joint exercise. *Inspired Venture* they called it.'

'I'd love to sit around and trade war stories but if I'm free to go . . .'

'The SSG got to you in the nick of time,' Khalid warned. 'Do you have any idea what Abdullah Qari would have done to you?'

'I knew those were Taliban targeting us,' said Matt.

'Targeting *you*, Matt, not the others. Your instincts were correct. Mullah Maulana is indeed hiding Qari in his compound. I believe he may even have been in the room with you when you lost your temper.'

'How do you know all this?' asked Matt.

'I know everything.'

'Then why are you wasting your time with me?' Matt grew angrier. 'Your Storks . . .'

'Black Storks,' Khalid corrected.

'I don't care if they're fucking pigeons. You should be sending them after Qari, not me.'

'That would play right into the hands of our enemies,' Khalid countered. 'Three years ago when General Musharraf was president, there was another cleric trying to overthrow the government, Abdul Rashid Ghazi, leader of the Red Mosque in Islamabad. You may have heard of it. One of your 7/7 bombers studied there. Like Mullah Maulana, Ghazi's followers were from the tribal areas. He had them running wild, arresting anyone whom they considered impious. Some even engaged in suicide missions. The government tolerated these excesses for fear of making martyrs of the hoodlums. But when they set fire to a ministry building, General Musharraf had no choice but to kick the hornets' nest. He ordered the SSG to storm the Red Mosque. Ghazi and hundreds of his followers were killed. Musharraf's rivals exploited the operation by accusing him of shedding Muslim blood to appease America. Soon, the public lost trust in the general, so much so that when Benazir Bhutto was assassinated, they blamed him for her death – a baseless accusation.' Khalid sighed. 'In the end, General Musharraf made the ultimate sacrifice. He resigned the presidency to heal his nation.'

'He dug his own grave,' Matt shot back. 'I heard about the deals Musharraf cut with the Afghan Taliban. Anyone that soft on terrorists isn't fit to lead.'

'General Musharraf could not abandon the Afghan Taliban without making Pakistan a slave to its enemies.'

'He dropped his pants for the terrorists.'

Khalid lost patience. 'Would you have us be like Britain! Lapdogs who jump when America snaps its fingers!' Khalid regained his composure. 'Pakistan is not a rotting imperialist power, my friend. We will determine our future, not the West.'

'So you're just going to let Qari get away with murder?' Matt hissed.

Khalid's indignation gave way to an epiphany. 'Now I understand,' said the spy. 'You did not come to Pakistan to fight terrorists. You are here to avenge your woman.'

Matt froze.

'I was there at the beginning of your affair,' Khalid reminded him.

'I thought you were spying on the ambassador?'

'And other persons of interest. Your history is quite extraordinary, my friend.' Khalid checked his watch. 'Come.' He waved Matt over. 'There is something I must show you.'

Matt didn't hear him. He was too exercised by the question of how much Khalid really knew about him.

'Hurry, hurry,' said the spy. 'There is not much time.'

With dawn still a few hours off, the desert was dark and tranquil. Not even the wind stirred. Khalid pointed north. 'Those lorries over there supply petrol to NATO troops in Afghanistan,' he explained. 'They have been stuck here for days, waiting for the border to reopen.' He raised his arm. 'It is very dangerous work, hauling goods for NATO. The Afghan Taliban punishes such activities.'

Khalid dropped his arm like a flag. Suddenly, the quiet stillness was shattered by a double boom. Matt recognized the duelling thumps – an RPG deploying. The missile sliced through one of the petrol trailers, igniting the fuel. A black and orange mushroom cloud erupted, shaking the earth violently and throwing flames onto other tankers. The same drivers who'd tried to kill Matt less than an hour earlier ran screaming into the desert only to have the ground before them turn hostile. The Afghan Taliban who'd initiated the assault had come out of hiding to finish them off.

The wind howled as the spreading inferno sucked oxygen from the air. 'Call them off!' Matt urged.

'It's too late!' said Khalid. 'The genie is out of the bottle!'

Human cries punctuated the Taliban's staccato rifle bursts. Some drivers charged their executioners, preferring the swift suicide of the firing squad to the agony of burning alive. Matt had never witnessed such horror. 'This isn't human.'

'Humanity became a casualty of this war long ago,' said Khalid. 'I am going to make you this offer only once. Leave Pakistan tonight. Mourn your woman. Find another. Forget you ever came here.'

Matt turned to him. 'You know I can't do that.'

Khalid nodded. 'Then I shall help you get the revenge you seek.'

Chapter 46

'I take full responsibility, sir.'

Ted pulled the sword out from under his protégée. 'It wasn't your fault, Bethany. I should have known better than to try and pump him for information. Eric's good. And I'm . . .' he paused. 'What was it again?'

'Stale, sir.'

Ted ate the insult. 'Does he know who our informant is?'

'I don't think so.'

'Does he or doesn't he?' the spy chief snapped. He regretted his tone straightaway.

'He had no compunction about saying your name,' Bethany explained. 'I believe had he known the identity of our informant, he would have divulged that information as well.'

'Not necessarily. Eric could have been trying to throw you off the scent.'

'But your name wasn't the only card he laid on the table.' Bethany hesitated. 'He knew Ms Cameron was in contact with you before she died.'

'Are you sure?' Ted was alarmed.

Bethany felt the back of her head. It was still swollen from having been knocked against the wall. 'Absolutely.'

Ted turned a protective eye toward her. 'You're off the case.'

'But, sir . . .'

'If Eric knows Emma came to see me then the people he works

for know it too,' said Ted. 'They're professional assassins, Bethany. They killed Emma. They wouldn't think twice about killing you.' He picked up the phone. 'Damn it.'

'Who are you calling?'

'The Director.'

Bethany put her hand over the keypad. 'What about the laws of physics?' she reminded him. 'Shit doesn't roll uphill, sir.'

'Don't worry. It will come crashing right back down on my head.' Ted pushed her hand away.

'I urge you to reconsider.'

Ted slammed the phone down. 'I will not lose you! We've had too many agents slaughtered already.'

'But we have leverage over Mr Riddell,' Bethany argued. 'He doesn't know who abducted Mr Logan.'

Ted marvelled at her tenacity. Bethany was like a musician on the *Titanic*; playing until the ship went down. 'Neither do we.'

'But he doesn't know that.'

'Whatever impression of ignorance Eric may have given you was an act,' said Ted. 'He knows far more than he lets on.'

'You're wrong, sir.'

Ted was taken aback. Bethany had never countered him so directly. 'Gather your things. I'm sending you back to Islama . . . no, I'm sending you back to the States.'

'May I speak frankly?'

'I've heard enough,' said Ted. 'I've given you far too much responsibility. You need to learn your place. A couple of months sitting behind a computer in Langley . . .'

'I won't abandon you, sir,' Bethany said over him. Ted fell silent. 'I'm not going to jump ship just because we've hit a hiccup.'

Ted was touched by her loyalty. 'This is not a hiccup. I'm toxic, Bethany. And you have a bright future ahead of you.'

'Do you trust me?' she asked.

'Of course,' said Ted. 'It goes without saying.'

'Then trust my decision to see this thing through. Now,' she said, getting back to business. 'Mr Riddell accused us of failing to protect Ms Cameron . . .'

'He's right.'

'But he doesn't just blame the CIA. He was highly emotional. He was flogging himself as much as us,' Bethany observed. 'He feels guilty. I know it.'

'That's not guilt; it's self-preservation. Any regard Eric had for other people died when he stopped being a mouthpiece and started cultivating terrorists.'

'You didn't see him, sir. He lashed out at me, to the point of getting physical. Someone as calculating as you described would never lose control like that.'

'Perhaps he has a tinge of guilt about Emma,' Ted conceded. 'But I fail to see how that gives us any leverage.'

'Because it's not just Emma keeping him up at night,' Bethany revealed. 'He's worried about Mr Logan.'

'Eric doesn't give a rat's ass about his security contractor.'

'Mr Logan is no ordinary contractor.' Bethany placed two folders on the desk and opened the top one. 'This is the list of numbers we lifted from Ms Cameron's BlackBerry,' she said, handing Ted the phone log. 'All the calls were to and from SBC staff, except the messages from Pete Riorden of course.' She pulled out another log. 'This is what we found on her other handset. Since we already knew who'd passed her the computer storage stick, I didn't think it was terribly relevant.'

Ted took the paper and examined it.

'Ms Cameron used that phone to call and text one number almost exclusively.'

'She was engaged,' said Ted. 'It's probably her fiancé.'

Bethany was startled. 'You never informed me of this.'

'Need to know,' Ted reminded her.

'Did she tell you his name?'

Ted looked at her curiously. 'No.'

Bethany shoved the second folder at him. 'We received this early this morning. When I heard a Matt Logan had been abducted I knew it couldn't be coincidence.'

Ted opened the folder. His eyes turned to saucers when he saw Matt's name written on an old military photo ID clipped to the inside flap. The word SECRET was watermarked across the pages. The spy chief scanned them quickly. Nearly the entire dossier had been blacked out with marker. 'MI5 laid a lot of ink before letting this go.' He closed the folder and shoved his phone out of the way. 'Start digging, Bethany. I want to know why the Brits are so sensitive about him. And make sure we keep surveillance on Eric 24/7. If he so much as sneezes I want to know about it.'

'I'm on it,' said Bethany.

Ted settled in with the dossier. 'So, Mr Wonderful. What are you hiding?'

Chapter 47

Khalid pushed the door open with a crutch. Matt jumped to his feet.

'Why are you on the floor?' asked the spy.

'Nowhere else to sleep.'

'I apologize. More comfortable accommodation awaits. Come, let us go.'

'Are you sure that's a good idea?'

Khalid looked at his wounded leg. 'I should make use of it while I still have it.'

'I meant me,' said Matt. 'I'm pretty pale for these parts.'

'You are my guest,' Khalid assured him. 'Pashtunwali dictates that no harm shall come to you.'

Chaman was even bleaker by daylight; bare rocks, dry gravel beds, khaki hills. Black smoke was curling off the smouldering tanker carcasses. The wind had carried the dark phantom over the double-arched border, into Afghanistan. The crossing was still closed to vehicles and livestock but the authorities were allowing foot traffic; men, women and children struggling with heavy bundles in their arms and on their backs. The breakdown in relations between Washington and Islamabad had reduced them to beasts of burden.

Khalid hobbled along on his crutches. 'We shall leave here tonight, by helicopter.'

'Sure you want to hang around here that long?' said Matt. 'That leg of yours isn't smelling too good, no offence.'

'You do not smell of roses either, my friend.' Khalid gestured to the compound in front of them. 'We shall shelter here until sundown.'

Matt recognized it from the night before. The SSG's 7.62 bullet casings were lying on the ground around the perimeter. 'How's the lad I shot?'

Khalid knocked on the gate. 'He shall survive.' A man wearing a black turban greeted the spy with a kiss. His eyes narrowed with hatred when they fell on Matt.

Six more grimacing figures were inside the courtyard, huddled around a wood-burning stove eating kebabs. They'd used daggers as skewers. One of them drew the blunt side of his blade across his throat as Matt followed Khalid into the main house.

Matt bolted the door. 'Those blokes out there, are they the Taliban who attacked the convoy?'

'Yes,' Khalid confirmed. 'Ignore them – Afghans are all bravado.'

Matt was incredulous. 'You're off your head if you think I'm staying here.'

Khalid gathered his crutches in one hand. 'There is nothing to fear,' he said, taking a seat at a table.

'That's not a theory I'd like to test. Those men live to kill Brits.'

'If you want to operate in Pakistan you must learn to embrace paradoxes.' Khalid pulled a phone from his pocket and gave it to Matt. 'Sit down. Look at this.'

Matt examined the screen. It contained a mug shot of a child. The boy was barely into his teens.

'His name is Soheil,' Khalid explained. 'The army arrested him in Rawalpindi the morning your woman was killed.'

Matt recalled Emma's final report. *The alleged car bomber was apprehended early this morning local time* . . . He studied the photo intensely.

'He gave himself up to the army,' Khalid continued. 'The boy claimed he lost his nerve when he saw the minaret. He said Allah would never forgive him for killing Muslims.'

'Did he confess his connection to Abdullah Qari?'

'Yes,' said Khalid. 'This child is typical of the martyrs groomed by Qari; Pashtun, fatherless, effeminate . . .'

'Effeminate?'

'Qari likes young boys.' Khalid did not conceal his disapproval. 'He baits them with Islam, buggers them and sends them to their death.'

'A jihadist *and* a paedophile.' Matt returned the phone. 'All the more reason to kill him.'

'A pervert, yes. But Qari is no Mujaheed,' Khalid corrected. 'Before he wrapped himself in the flag of Islam he was a petty smuggler operating here, in Chaman.'

'But he's a disciple of Mullah Maulana.'

'A marriage of convenience,' said Khalid. 'Maulana required a Nike Stripe for his cause. Qari answered the casting call. He is the least devout jihadist you will ever come across.'

'If he doesn't give a toss about Islam, how did he become Pakistani Taliban?'

'Qari's path to the TTP was by no means a direct one,' Khalid explained. 'After Afghanistan was invaded, smuggling became an even more profitable activity. A handful of gangs soon controlled everything. Insects like Qari needed to join a larger operation or perish. He enlisted in the Frontier Corps.'

'But the FC is military,' said Matt.

'It is also the biggest organized crime syndicate in Pakistan. The FC polices the border crossing here and in Torkham, North-West Frontier Province. You can't transport a grain of rice into Afghanistan without giving the FC a cut of the profits. Qari climbed the ranks quickly, cutting down anyone who interfered with his business. The TTP heard of his exploits and decided he could be useful to them. But they failed to appreciate the extent of Qari's greed. He did not care to share his spoils with other TTP leaders, so he joined forces with Mullah Maulana and formed a breakaway faction: TTP-Q.'

'How does Qari choose his targets?' asked Matt. 'Bombing an army mosque is obvious but why SBC? What did he have to gain aside from proving he could pull off a coordinated assault?'

'The attacks were not coordinated.' Khalid paused. 'Qari did not kill your woman, Matt.'

'Maybe not directly, but he sent the bomber.'

'We thought so too,' Khalid swiped the phone screen and gave it to Matt, 'until we found this.'

Matt studied the new image. It appeared to be a mask lying on a pavement. The heavily bearded face was grotesque. 'What is it?'

'Not what – who,' Khalid corrected. 'It is the bomber who attacked SBC's villa. The police recovered those remains from the scene. As you can see, he is nothing like the scared child who surrendered in Rawalpindi.'

Matt re-examined the image more closely. He could see now that the waxy flesh was no reproduction. It had been ripped violently from a human head. 'There were two local guards on duty.'

'It is not one of them,' said Khalid. 'The day after the attack, the police returned to gather more evidence. They discovered the crime scene had been washed clean overnight.'

'What do you mean *discovered*?'

'The police claimed it was not they who were responsible. That is when the ISI took over the investigation. It is we who ordered DNA tests.' He gestured to the screen. 'That is the bomber. The evidence is beyond question.'

'So he doesn't fit the usual profile,' said Matt. 'He could still be Qari's boy.'

'You do not understand. That man is Baluch. And the Baluch do not take orders from Pashtun.' Khalid swiped the screen again. 'They take them from this man.'

A photo of a white-turbaned, greying figure appeared. The image reminded Matt of the tapestry in the governor's mansion.

'His name is Tansvir Sardar,' said Khalid. 'He is a senior commander of the Baluchistan Liberation Army – a terrorist organization that seeks to secede their province from the rest of Pakistan. Until recently, the BLA confined its terror operations to Baluchistan. But they have become more media savvy. And what better way to gain celebrity than to stage an attack on live television.'

'How can you be sure it was this guy and not Qari?' Matt pressed.

Khalid hesitated. 'We have a Baluch informant who is very close to Tansvir Sardar,' the spy revealed. 'He confirmed the BLA's involvement.'

'Are you positive the attacks weren't coordinated?'

'Yes.'

Matt laid the phone down. 'This informant; has he told you how to find his boss?'

Khalid nodded. 'He has provided very accurate intelligence on Tansvir Sardar's movements.'

'And yet the bastard's still running around free,' said Matt. 'Let me guess, killing him would play into the hands of your enemies?'

'Not in this instance,' said Khalid. 'The BLA has attacked every migrant group in Baluchistan. All of Pakistan wants them dead.'

'So what's the problem, then?'

Khalid sighed. 'The SSG have made several attempts to kill Tansvir Sardar, but alas none has proved successful.'

'He's one bloody man.'

'Every time the SSG moves in, the terrorists know they are coming.'

'Maybe your tout's not as reliable as you think.'

'His information has never been wrong,' said Khalid. 'I believe it is a question of tactics.'

'So change them,' said Matt.

Khalid put his phone away. 'Why do you think you are here?'

Chapter 48

Jinnah Naval Base, Baluchistan Province

The heli pilot started his descent. Matt tightened his stomach but he couldn't stop it from bottoming out. It had been sinking since Khalid had put the offer to him.

It was a straightforward swap. In return for helping the SSG eliminate Tansvir Sardar, Matt would have the honour of drawing first blood. His gut reaction was to hold off. His sights had been set firmly on Qari. He couldn't adjust them on a whim. But Khalid insisted there was no time to think it over. It was either take the deal or leave Pakistan – immediately.

Ten uniformed men were waiting for them on the LZ at Jinnah Naval Base. Matt pegged them as army from their maroon berets. A badge with daggers framed by lightning bolts adorned their left shoulders.

One stepped forward and saluted Khalid as he disembarked.

'I thought you weren't in the military anymore,' said Matt.

'In my country, one never retires fully from the army.' The spy gave the soldier a kiss on both cheeks and turned to Matt. 'Allow me to introduce Major Qureshi. He is the commander of this unit.'

'Good to meet you,' said Matt.

'We have met already,' said Qureshi. 'I am pleased that from now on we shall be working with you rather than against you.'

Matt's stomach churned. He'd signed on to a mission with the same soldiers who only the night before had sat on him, kicked him and beat him senseless.

The SSG entourage led them to a briefing room deep inside the base. A civilian wearing a white turban was waiting for them when they arrived.

'This is Sobhat,' said Khalid. 'The Baluch informant of whom I spoke.'

Sobhat bowed subserviently. The gesture seemed at odds with everything Matt had heard about the Baluch. 'What's he doing here?'

'I asked him to join us for the briefing,' said Khalid. 'It is important you trust him. The information he provides will be crucial to our success.'

Never in Matt's wildest scenarios would he have a tout anywhere near a mission briefing. 'If it's all the same to you, I'd rather he leave.'

'There is nothing to fear,' said Qureshi. 'We know friend from foe.' The commander launched into the briefing with the informant present. He began by offering some background on the target.

Tansvir Sardar was unlike any terrorist Matt had ever faced. The Baluch rebel leader was no fly-by-night jihadist feeding off popular Muslim discontent with the West. He'd spent the better part of four decades fighting for a cause to which he'd lost five sons. The profile made Matt even warier of Sobhat. Warriors like Tansvir Sardar inspired absolute loyalty amongst their men.

Qureshi laid a map on the table. 'Sardar's compound is located here, approximately thirty kilometres from Gwadar. We know from our surveillance that it is guarded at all times.' He moved his finger clockwise. 'The ring of security stretches for approximately twenty kilometres. The roads and tracks are policed by

BLA insurgents but there is informal protection as well. Civilians in the area co-operate with the BLA for fear of reprisals.'

'Now you understand why we have had such difficulty getting close to this terrorist,' said Khalid. 'Assaulting on foot or by vehicle is impossible without alerting the entire area.'

'What about airstrikes?' said Matt.

'Would your military leaders order airstrikes on British soil?' Khalid suggested sarcastically.

'Point taken,' said Matt.

'We believe we have found a solution to this problem,' Qureshi continued. 'Sobhat has told us where the guards are located and when they change over. Our plan is to insert by helicopter during this vulnerable window, fast rope into the compound and take out the target.'

Qureshi seemed very confident of his strategy. Matt didn't know why. It was riddled with faults.

'Do you endorse the major's plan?' asked Khalid.

'No,' said Matt.

Qureshi stepped away from the table. 'Please, elaborate your objections.'

'Well, for starters, there's no element of surprise. Changeover or not, the guards in that compound will hear our helis long before they land. They'll have plenty of time to get into a defensive position. Fast roping is also a mistake. If we're forced to withdraw we can't just crawl back up the rope into the heli. We'll have to leg it through twenty kilometres of heavily guarded BLA terrain to an extraction point.'

'Now that you are familiar with the operations area, is there an alternative course of action you would propose?' asked Khalid.

Matt considered it. 'I suggest we go Black Ops with a tinge of Grey.'

'I'm sorry,' said Qureshi. 'What do you mean by Grey?'

'The plan you just outlined is textbook Black Ops: high profile, high aggression,' Matt explained. 'Those tactics may work against inexperienced terrorists, but not Tansvir Sardar. He's been doing this far too long. If we're going to nail him, we can't let him see us coming. We need to go Grey by inserting covertly.'

'How do you suggest we achieve this?' asked Qureshi. 'As you said, his guards will hear our helicopters before they land.'

'So we target him when he's outside his compound.'

'You think this has not occurred to us?' said Qureshi. 'Sardar's movements are erratic; there is no pattern to them.'

'There's always a pattern.' Matt turned to Sobhat. 'What are your boss's . . .'

'He does not speak English,' Qureshi interrupted.

Matt doubted it but he indulged the major. 'Tansvir Sardar has to have some way to relax – a hobby perhaps.'

Qureshi conveyed the question to Sobhat. The informant's face lit up. He started speaking excitedly.

'What's he saying?' asked Matt.

'Apparently, Sardar flies birds of prey,' said Khalid. 'Falcons specifically. They are his business and his passion.'

'And he's just telling you this now?' said Matt.

'The Baluch are simple,' Qureshi said dismissively. 'He does not think unless we ask.'

'How many guards does he take with him when he flies his falcons?' asked Matt.

Qureshi put the question to Sobhat. 'Four, maybe five men,' the SSG commander relayed.

'Come on, there's got to be more than that,' said Matt.

Qureshi asked again. Sobhat's answer was the same. Matt waved him over to the table and pointed to the map. 'Show us where he goes.'

Sobhat singled out a valley approximately nineteen kilometres from the compound.

'It will not work,' said Qureshi. 'That area is inside the BLA cordon. The civilians will hear our helicopters and inform the terrorists.'

'Is this the only training area?' Matt pressed.

The question was put to Sobhat. The tout confirmed there were no others.

'He's a wanted man,' Matt argued. 'There's no way he'd go to the same spot over and over again.'

Sobhat was adamant; there was only one valley where Tansvir Sardar flew his beloved falcons.

Matt studied the map. Several small farms and a village were within a kilometre of the valley. That translated into a lot of ears listening on the BLA's behalf. An idea clicked. 'We can make this work, lads. We'll insert at night, go to the valley and wait for the target to come to us.'

'But how can we land and still be *Grey*, as you say?' Qureshi challenged.

'Oh, we'll be Grey,' said Matt, 'so Grey they won't even know we've arrived.'

Chapter 49

Quetta, Baluchistan Province

The 7M kidnap and ransom negotiator pulled up to the Serena. The staff had been alerted in advance that the specialist would be gracing their fair establishment and had promised complete discretion. This was not the first K&R guest they'd hosted.

Eric came down the steps to greet him. 'Boy, am I glad you're here.' He extended his hand. 'I'm Eric Riddell.'

'Cut the crap,' McKay sneered.

Eric's grateful demeanour didn't falter. 'We're being watched. Shake my hand.'

The ICON commander took it and yanked Eric in. 'Don't ever assume that tone with me, boy. I do not tolerate insubordination.'

'Fine,' said Eric. 'May I humbly suggest then that you go check in and in an hour, if you're agreeable, I'll come get you and we'll go to a restaurant. I found a clean one where we can talk.'

McKay looked at him as if he were a complete amateur. 'How hard is it to debug one room?'

'I couldn't clean it without arousing suspicion. The hotel is crawling with ISI.'

'And you expect me to trust you to choose a restaurant?' said McKay. 'We'll rendezvous at the safe house after sundown.'

'We have a safe house in Quetta?' said Eric. 'Why wasn't I made aware of this before?'

'I decide what you need to know and when you need to know it.'

'How do I get there?'

McKay put his arm around Eric's neck as if comforting him. 'We'll go together,' he said, tightening his grip, 'make sure no one tails your civvy ass this time.'

There were no street lights in the warren of shops, houses, tea rooms and madrassas; just the dim glow of hurricane lamps and generator-powered bulbs seeping between shuttered windows and beneath closed doors. The stench of cloying spices and old cooking fat hung in the sloping alleyways, clinging to everyone and everything passing through.

Of all the shithole neighbourhoods in Quetta for ICON to have a safe house, Pashtunibad was the last place Eric would have picked. The sprawling slum on the city's eastern edge was a haven for Afghan Taliban – not TTP-Q. 'Are you sure this is safe?' he whispered. 'This place is full of Afghan refugees. They're not exactly our support base.'

McKay kept walking in silence.

'We have no influence here,' Eric protested.

McKay turned around. 'You really don't know dick, do you? Afghans jump to the winning side. And right now, that's TTP-Q. Shut up and keep moving.'

Eric should have realized. After all, he'd been instrumental in driving Quetta's Afghan community into Qari's arms. He imagined the money he'd doled out as ICON's banker spreading through Pashtunibad like a cancer; corrupting the honest, turning brother against brother, breeding death and destruction. He longed for the days when he was just a simple propagandist. Sowing patriotic agendas under the guise of objective network reporting may not have been glamorous, but at least he could go to bed with a clear conscience.

They arrived at a dump on Pashtunibad's western edge. McKay pointed to a compound on the other side. Eric looked at the minefield of rotting rubbish and rusting vehicles standing between them and the safe house. 'I don't suppose there's a way around this?'

'Fucking civvies,' McKay muttered before wading into the garbage.

The safe house was empty and shrouded in darkness when they arrived. McKay lit a lamp and placed it on a table. The walls came alive in the flickering light as, one by one, the ICON commander's loyal ex-Special Forces team stepped out of the shadows.

McKay didn't bother with introductions. 'All right then,' he said to Eric. 'Tell us who took Logan.'

The correspondent scanned the faces around the table. McKay's men wanted to eat him alive. 'Don't you know who has him?'

'This isn't a game,' Carter warned. 'Tell us who kidnapped him!'

McKay raised his hand to the ex-Delta captain. 'Riddell's a civvy.' His tone implied he considered this to be a defect.

'I don't know who kidnapped Matt,' said Eric. 'I thought you might, but obviously I was mistaken.'

Carter opened his mouth. Before he could speak, McKay stopped him. 'Just tell us what happened from the beginning and we'll figure it out.'

'Well,' Eric began, 'we arrived at the airport and went straight to Mullah Maulana's . . .'

'The beginning of the hostage-taking incident, you idiot,' said McKay.

Eric relayed the salient facts as he remembered them; the motorbike flying over the median, the jingly blocking the road, the pick-up pulling alongside them, the shoot-out between the two groups of kidnappers. He purposely omitted Matt's treatment of Naj.

'That can't be right,' said McKay.

'I'm telling you there were two groups trying to abduct us. And that's not all.' Eric paused. 'One of them was TTP-Q.'

'Bullshit,' said McKay.

'With all due respect, sir, this man was probably crapping himself during the contact,' Carter observed. 'I wouldn't trust a word out of his mouth.'

'You Deltas are more tribal than the Pakistanis,' said Eric. 'Matt ID'd them.'

'When?' asked Carter.

'Right before he told me to run.'

Carter scowled at the correspondent. 'And you did.'

'What was I supposed to do?'

Carter was disgusted. 'Stay there and help.'

'I was crapping myself,' Eric deadpanned. 'What use would I have been?'

'What about the rest of your team?' said McKay. 'Did they identify two groups of kidnappers?'

'My cameraman saw only turbans and bullets.'

'Where is he now?'

'I sent him back to Islamabad. I didn't want him underfoot when you were in town.'

'What about the local with you?' asked McKay. 'What did he see?'

'I don't know,' said Eric. 'My fixer got separated from us during the incident . . .'

Carter turned to McKay. 'Sir, I request permission to question this man immediately. As a local he may have helped orchestrate the kidnapping . . .'

'Naj wasn't in on it,' Eric insisted. 'He was wounded during the contact. We located him only this morning recovering in a hospital.'

'That doesn't prove anything.' Carter appealed to McKay. 'Please, sir.'

McKay nodded to the ex-Delta captain. 'Permission granted.'

'I've known my fixer for years,' said Eric. 'If you want to question him, go ahead, but I'm telling you, you're wasting your time. This city has more kidnappers than soldiers. Anyone could have Matt right now; the Baluch, the Afghan Taliban, Qari . . .'

'We own Qari,' McKay growled. 'He'd never go rogue.'

'Really?' Eric challenged. 'He pulled a knife to my throat the last time I saw him.'

'I don't blame him,' said Carter.

'What'd you do to piss him off?' asked McKay.

'I refused to give him more money. Which is why I wouldn't put it past him to kidnap Matt. Qari will stop at nothing to bleed us dry.'

'If you were right, he'd have asked for a ransom by now.' MaKay dismissed Eric and turned to his trusted circle. 'What have we been able to dig up?'

'The 7M ops room received a call from Logan's mobile around two hours after he was abducted,' said Hernandez. 'No one answered and it went to voicemail. We tried triangulating the signal but the call was too short.'

'Never have a civvy do a soldier's job,' said McKay. 'All right, team, here's what we're going to do. Bazinsky, get onto your contacts from the rally. I want TTP-Q to start canvassing their area of operations, see what they can find out about Logan's whereabouts. Carter, you're on the BLA. Find out if they grabbed

Logan or if they know who has him. Ginta, Dietrich, start work-ing the Frontier Corps. If they don't have Logan, they'll know who's trying to buy him.'

'We have our orders,' said Carter, 'let's move.'

The team filed out of the room, leaving McKay alone with Eric. 'There is one possibility you haven't considered,' said the correspondent. 'The ISI. They've been known to abduct a person or two.'

'Don't be a damn fool,' said McKay. 'They don't even know who Logan is.'

Chapter 50

The Cobra attack helicopter turned west toward Gwadar. An Mi-8 followed on its heels. The twin-turbined chopper was capable of transporting up to two dozen troops into battle. On this night though, its great belly was empty.

Matt had been directing the bogus sorties for over a week. The agile Cobra would fly ahead and buzz the valleys around Tansvir Sardar's compound; the Mi-8 would plod in behind and drop a unit of phantom troops. Four more days and the civilians ensconced in the BLA stronghold would be so immune to the chopping of rotor blades they wouldn't even notice when the real operation took place.

While the dummy drops dulled the enemy's awareness of the operation area, Matt and the SSG sharpened theirs, poring over satellite images and other intelligence. The final plan deviated little from Matt's initial proposal; drop two valleys over from the falcon-training site, move into position by foot, wait for the target to show, eliminate it, withdraw and extract.

The operation couldn't have been simpler but the rehearsals weren't going as smoothly as Matt had hoped. The hiccups had nothing to do with personalities. Qureshi's initial prickliness aside, he and his men had taken to Matt as quickly as the Deltas. The problem was down to skills. Despite Khalid's comparison, the SSG was not on par with the SAS. Matt likened the Pakistani unit more to a high-grade infantry than an elite fighting force.

He had a lot of ground to cover in a short time if they were to achieve a successful mission. As he'd already learned, Grey Ops was a completely novel concept to the SSG. Matt worked tirelessly getting them up to speed on covert tactics; teaching them how to move stealthily into position and, more crucially, how to cope with the tedium and discomfort of lying up. Some of the men were eager to broaden their soldiering skills and embraced the lessons wholeheartedly. Others found them frustrating, including Major Qureshi. He was like Matt had once been – obsessed with swinging through windows and banging down doors.

Steadily the skill gap narrowed. But there was one nagging difference that was proving almost impossible to overcome. Whenever Matt threw an unscripted variable into a contact scenario, the SSG would stop speaking English and revert to their native tongue. He couldn't be sat in the middle of an operation unable to communicate with the soldiers around him, so, he gave up on English altogether and devised a basic code he and the lads could relay through the pressel switches on their radios: one click for 'positive', two clicks for 'negative', three for 'stand by', four for 'stand down' and so on.

The code worked brilliantly, so much so that even Qureshi was impressed. The SSG commander rewarded Matt's initiative by designating him 2IC. From that point on, Qureshi insisted they do everything together. Matt understood the logic. An effective 2IC knew his commander as well as he knew himself. Still, he desperately needed time alone. Because even though he'd planned it, Matt had yet to embrace the mission fully.

He found his space on the firing ranges. As lead assassin, Matt required plenty of solo practice. The SSG had given him the Bentley of sniper rifles to play with: a Russian-made 7.62mm Dragunov. Lying prone on the ground, zeroing the telescopic sight, he started to feel like the soldier he once was; confident and full of self-belief. Matt revelled in the minutiae of his technique; changing elevations to gauge the impact of wind and gravity on the bullet's trajectory. The Makran Coast's sniping conditions were deliciously challenging. He eventually gained permission to travel beyond the ranges to vary his practice scenarios even more near the sea and further inland.

Travelling back and forth between the two extremes opened a window to the target's mind. Matt understood why Tansvir Sardar had spent a lifetime fighting for his homeland. The area around Jinnah Naval Base was the most beautiful he'd seen in Pakistan. The Arabian Sea was a kaleidoscope; waking up hoary silver, turning pink and going to sleep a deep, emerald green. Matt marvelled at how he could walk even just a few metres inland and be transported to a lunar desert of bleached mesas and wind-carved conical sculptures.

Unfortunately, the insights only heightened his reservations. If Matt were Baluch, he wouldn't share the land either. The doubts plagued his practice. Even though he'd become adept with the Dragunov, achieving a headshot from 350 metres out, every time he looked through the crosshairs it wasn't an old Baluch rebel he envisioned but Abdullah Qari.

The night before the mission, he lay awake trying to convince himself that Tansvir Sardar was indeed the man responsible for Emma's death. All the rational evidence pointed to it. But he couldn't shake the feeling that Qari was his man. It gave rise to other questions Matt had yet to answer. Had Emma really died in the explosion or had she been killed right before it? Was the sanitized crime scene a cock-up by the Islamabad police? A deliberate tactic by the ISI to take over the investigation? Or had ICON done it to erase 7M's shoddy CP work? The more answers he sought, the more confusing the picture became, until finally

Matt didn't know what to think. He tried taking a step back and regrouping. But distancing himself gave rise to the most troubling question of all. Did avenging Emma really justify working with a country that was aiding and supporting the Afghan Taliban – the very insurgents who were killing British soldiers in Helmand? It was a paradox he would never embrace.

Khalid was waiting for Qureshi in the briefing room. 'Is our guest prepared?'

'He is ready,' said the SSG commander. 'He has fired the weapon at least a thousand times.'

'I'm not questioning his competence. Does he trust us? Does he trust you?'

'We have bonded like brothers,' Qureshi assured him.

'You are certain he suspects nothing?'

'Logan believes he has much to teach us. Such a man sees himself as a knight or a king – never a pawn.'

'Let us hope his British arrogance continues to blind him,' said Khalid.

'Logan will assassinate Tansvir Sardar,' said Qureshi. 'I am confident of it.'

'I do not care who does it.' Khalid hobbled toward the door. 'Just make sure the BLA believes it is Logan who killed their commander.'

Chapter 51

The Mi-8's rear doors opened like an insect's jaw. Matt pushed all his questions aside and walked up the ramp determined to achieve a successful mission. When he reached the fuselage, the mix of aviation fuel and adrenaline hit him like a hammer, smashing his focus. He hadn't smelled the combination since that fateful night in Baghdad . . .

The house had still been ablaze when the Chinook lifted off for the Green Zone. Matt stared into the fiery ruins, wondering how many innocent women and children had perished in the airstrike. He kept the inferno in his sights until the horizon snuffed it. Only then did he look at his team-mates. The Deltas were as gutted as he was. None of them had ever had an operation end so horribly.

A medical team was waiting on the LZ to take Carter to hospital. The Delta captain refused to be stretchered off the heli. 'Logan?' he said, extending his good arm. Matt pulled him up and helped him down the ramp. 'Don't worry,' said Carter. 'I'll write a full report distancing you from this mess. I take full responsibility for everything.'

'I can speak for myself,' Matt insisted. 'Besides, you're not accountable for the regular army any more than you are for the CIA. If everyone had just backed the fuck off and let us get on with our jobs, those civilians would still be alive.'

'Amen to that, brother.' Carter's legs began to buckle. Matt tightened his grip and carried him the rest of the way.

'We'll take him from here, soldier,' said a doctor.

Matt laid Carter down on a gurney. 'Look after yourself. And remember what I said about your shoulder. Doctors don't always know best.'

The Delta captain pulled Matt to him. 'I didn't see the civilians, but I believe you, brother. Whatever happens, I'll back you one hundred percent.'

'Don't worry about me,' said Matt. 'Just be honest about what you saw. That's what I plan on doing.'

The medical team carried Carter away. Matt headed to his quarters for a debriefing with his SAS troop commander. He didn't hold back his criticism. Though he had nothing but praise for the Deltas and their conduct, Matt's condemnation of the broader American military structure was scathing. He lambasted the trigger-happy regular troops and warned that the turf war between JSOC and the CIA could result in future cock-ups. The troop commander thanked him for his candour and promised to pass it up the chain. Matt ended the post-mortem with a request. He wanted to transfer to a Basra-based troop. Rounding up old men from the deck of cards didn't seem like such a bad way to spend his war now.

While the brass processed the paperwork, Matt cooled his heels in the Green Zone. Approval came through after three days. Then, an hour before his departure, the headline hit.

SPECIAL OPERATIONS ATTACK ENDS IN CIVILIAN DEATHS

A human rights group had got wind of what happened. Their information wasn't terribly detailed but the eye-witness reports they'd cobbled together gave an accurate broad-brush picture. Officially, the Pentagon and the MoD refused to comment, citing confidentiality surrounding Special Forces operations. Discrediting of the report was left to 'senior unnamed military sources' who dismissed the Iraqi testimonials as insurgent propaganda.

The story was not front-page news but with rumours circulating through the blogosphere about a JSOC/SAS partnership, the brass wasn't taking any chances. Matt was sent to Hereford. His Squadron OC assured him he'd be back in the war once the whole thing blew over.

But the storm got worse. A classified video of the Apache targeting the house was leaked to the press. Some commentators lauded it as proof of the official version of events. The gun-sight image clearly showed armed individuals on the roof of the house firing at American forces. Unfortunately for Matt, the video also contained audio transmissions between the helicopter crew and the soldiers on the ground.

The press went wild wondering why a Scottish voice was screaming *I repeat there are civilians* on a US Department of Defense classified tape. The speculation grew so frenzied, an MP raised the issue in Parliament. That's when the Squadron OC and the CO of the SAS called in Matt. They wanted to hear from him personally about the events of that night.

Matt wasn't afraid of the Ruperts. He had nothing to hide. But when he got to the CO's office, he suspected that the truth was the last thing they were after. A third officer was also in attendance: the Aide de Camp to the Director of Special Forces – the CO's CO.

Matt stuck to his story. He'd seen a woman and child in the house and told the Apache to abort the airstrike.

'Are you absolutely certain that is what you saw?' asked the Squadron OC.

'Yes.'

'Thank you, Matt,' said the CO.

The Aide de Camp cleared his throat. 'Was this your first operation with Delta Force, Mr Logan?'

'Yes.'

The aide glanced at the CO. 'Perhaps you were disoriented by their protocols? The Americans do have their own way of doing things.'

'It didn't affect my vision,' said Matt.

'Remember yourself,' warned the CO.

Matt readdressed the aide. 'I know what I saw – Colonel.'

The aide picked up a bound report with an American eagle seal on the cover. 'Yet not a single Delta soldier recalled seeing civilians.' He laid it down again. 'Do you think they're being dishonest?'

'No,' said Matt. 'They're honourable men.'

'Then why haven't they corroborated your story?'

'The Deltas were grouped west of me. I had a different vantage point from them.'

The aide seemed disappointed. 'What was your impression of the Deltas, Mr Logan?'

'They were highly professional. Their conduct throughout the operation cannot be faulted. In my opin—'

'No one asked for your opinion,' the CO interjected.

The aide raised his hand. 'I'd like to hear what he has to say.'

It was the sort of contradictory behaviour Matt had come to expect from Ruperts. 'In my opinion the mistakes of that night were a result of the regular forces being ill-prepared and communications errors between the CIA and JSOC.'

'Could you be more specific?' asked the aide.

'As soon as there was a contact, the regular forces panicked and called in air support. The regular troops knew fuck all about COIN ops . . .'

'Matt,' the CO warned again.

The aide rose. 'I'd like to have a word in private with Sergeant Logan.' The OC and CO left the room. The aide gestured to their empty chairs. 'Please. Make yourself comfortable – Matt.'

The congenial turn put Matt on guard. Nothing was more suspect than a chummy Rupert. 'I prefer to stand.'

'Very well.' The aide leaned against the desk. 'It is my understanding that you were selected to liaise with the Deltas based on your skills and,' he paused, 'open-mindedness, shall we say?'

'You'd have to ask the OC about that.'

The aide nodded. 'It's my experience that outstanding soldiers rarely pay attention to military politics, so allow me to enlighten you, Matt. For several years now DSF has resisted attempts to integrate the SAS into JSOC. But the course of the Iraq campaign has forced a rethink. You are no doubt aware that we are struggling in Basra. There is a lot of pressure from government for a victory in Iraq. The army must prove its worth. Bringing the SAS into JSOC's orbit will achieve this.' He produced a prepared statement. 'Now, the army would never ask you to change your story for . . .'

Matt clipped him. 'Good.'

'You're not alone in this,' the aide warned. 'The careers of the men who fought beside you that night are on the line as well.'

'I told you,' said Matt. 'The Deltas did nothing wrong.'

'Sadly, Mr Logan, right and wrong do not factor here. This is an issue of perception. If the public believes that you and your team participated in an operation that ended in civilian deaths, mark my words, it will haunt you. The SAS will distance itself from the scandal by returning you to your regular army unit. I cannot say with certainty what will happen to the Delta troops but it is doubtful they'll emerge unscathed.'

Matt should have seen it coming. The filthy Rupert was telling him to lie or take the Deltas down with him.

The aide gestured to the American report. 'A shame really. Captain Carter speaks very highly of you.'

'Carter was down wounded,' said Matt. 'There's no way he could see the house clearly.'

'Now, if you were to open your mind to the possibility that you couldn't either, this whole episode would be cast in a very different light. I'm familiar with your family, Matt. With your record and your pedigree, there's no reason you shouldn't make an officer one day. Play your cards right and you may even command a sub-unit of this Regiment.' He handed Matt the statement and the pen. 'No one is asking you to debase your integrity. Just acknowledge the possibility that you may have been mistaken, then this whole thing will fade from memory and you and your American friends can go back to doing what you love most – soldiering.'

Matt stared at the paper. If he didn't sign it, he wouldn't just lose his job – he'd lose the only real family he had left. The Regiment. 'I'd like the CO and the OC to witness this.'

The aide smiled. 'Of course.' He called the other Ruperts back to the office. 'Mr Logan is prepared to recant,' he informed them.

The OC was stunned. 'Is this true, Matt?'

Matt looked him in the eye. 'I came to the SAS to be the best soldier I could be. It's the greatest military unit in the world. I earned my place here and I can't imagine what life would be like if I left.' He laid down the statement and turned to the aide. 'But if you think I'm going to lie to save my arse, you're off your fuck-ing head.'

'Mr Logan!' rapped the CO.

Matt lashed out at his commanding officer. 'It's a shame the sergeants' mess doesn't run this Regiment because the officers' destroys everything that makes us great!'

'Pack your things,' said the CO. 'You're RTU'd.'

'You can't return me to unit,' said Matt. 'I'm resigning from the military. The old fellas were right. The Ruperts come to the SAS for a couple of years to further their own careers and ruin the careers of good soldiers who want a life here. I should have seen it coming!'

*   *   *

Three clicks fed through Matt's earpiece. It was Qureshi telling the team to stand by. They were nearing the target area.

Matt stopped regretting his past and fixed his night sights. It was time to take out a terrorist.

The Mi-8 bumped over a ridge and dropped between two cliffs. Matt tried savouring the moment but the old feeling he'd had in the Regiment eluded him. It wasn't fear preventing him from accessing the best of himself. Dread stalked men who had something to lose. Matt's problem was something more permanent. There was nothing left to connect to.

The heli touched down and the rear doors flew open. Matt and the SSG team stormed down the rear ramp into the moonlit desert. The Pakistani Special Forces unit moved like black whispers through the ethereal landscape, deftly negotiating natural obstacles they'd encountered on previous missions. Matt was less agile, awkwardly side-stepping ankle swallowing pits and rocks the size of rugby balls.

A patchwork of mesas ringed with vehicle tracks delivered them into the mouth of the valley. Matt canvassed the falcon-training area through his night sights. It was wider than the maps had suggested; at least two kilometres from head to head. On the plus side, there was ample cover from fire and from view.

Squat, thorny trees with broccoli-like tops ringed the upper slopes. Large boulders and rock formations littered the deep basin. Matt was spoilt for choice.

Qureshi and his men fanned out in a horseshoe pattern to the sides and rear, while Matt moved to a firing position near the head. He stopped to inspect the one remaining branch on a decapitated tree jutting up from the valley floor. It had been stripped of leaves and the bark was scored with hundreds of marks. He ran his finger along them. They'd been carved by something razor sharp – falcons' claws. Sobhat hadn't been telling tales. Tansvir Sardar used this valley often.

Matt found a covering position at the base of a crag. He could lie on his belly in the oblong depression and achieve the most accurate shot. He settled in and checked the ground behind him. He couldn't see hide nor hair of the SSG lads. They'd literally dissolved into the landscape.

Qureshi's voice crackled over his earpiece. 'Red One, are you in position?' Matt responded with a single click of his pressel switch. The SSG commander canvassed the rest of the team. All clicks were affirmative.

As the hours passed, Matt's mind kept wandering to the questions that had dogged him in the run-up to the operation. He cursed his lack of concentration.

The arrival of dawn quickly re-centred him. The valley was very different when viewed with the naked eye as opposed to night sights; only a kilometre and a half wide and much shallower than Matt had estimated. The differences considerably heightened the risks. Tansvir Sardar's guards would be right on top of him and the SSG lads.

Truck engines sounded in the distance. Matt cased the dirt track through his binos. The vehicles weren't heading toward them. He assumed they belonged to the local farmers and villagers.

By eight a.m. Matt was soaking wet with sweat. Although far from midday, his dark green patterned combat clothing was absorbing the sun's heat like a sponge.

The low rev of diesel engines took his mind off his discomfort. Matt got out his binos and waited for the source to show itself. A lorry emerged between two saw-toothed cliffs; a dozen armed, white-turbaned passengers riding in the flatbed.

The vehicle turned onto the track leading to the valley. 'Four or five guards, my arse,' Matt muttered. Sobhat's intelligence had been way off. Instead of outnumbering the BLA two to one, Matt and the SSG now had to fight them on even terms.

The lorry disappeared around a bend. Matt heard the engine cut. The BLA guards were walking the rest of the way. He took stock of their firepower as they came into view. The militia was armed with an array of weapons – AK 47s, old hunting rifles, he even spotted an M16. The only uniform piece of equipment was their radios.

The guards took up position on the high ground overlooking the basin, placing Matt and the SSG firmly inside their cordon. Fortunately, he'd anticipated such a scenario in rehearsals. If Qureshi's men held their nerve they should achieve their objective without losing a man.

A pick-up truck came zooming up the dirt track. Matt tucked away his binos and viewed it through the telescopic sight on his Dragunov. Two people were riding in the cab but the dust circling the windows prevented him from making a positive ID.

The truck stopped approximately six hundred yards from Matt's position – too far to ensure a clean kill. He watched the passenger dismount. The man had a dark beard and moustache. Matt homed in on the driver's door as it opened. The greying figure who emerged had a leather satchel around his shoulders and a long falconer's glove on his right arm. The rifle in his left hand belonged in a museum. Matt's senses sharpened. The target was in view.

Chapter 52

Tansvir propped his Lee Enfield against the side of the truck and pulled a falcon lure from his satchel. Matt watched the preparations unfold, comparing them with those his mother had taught him as a child. The biggest difference was the baton tied to the end of the lure. Rather than leave it bare, the BLA commander garnished his with raw meat to entice the falcon back from flight. It appeared the hardened terrorist was a soft touch when it came to his falcons.

Tansvir lowered the tailgate and retrieved a falcon from its cage. Matt zeroed in on the bird with his sniper sight. The saker was magnificent; a foot tall with grey flight feathers, pale brown belly and yellow-tipped black talons.

The spirited creature flapped its wings and strained at the jesses as Tansvir walked out to a patch of open ground. He stopped approximately two hundred and seventy-five metres from Matt's position – well within targeting range.

Matt brought Tansvir into his crosshairs but held off operating his trigger. A fraction of a millimetre on a telescopic sight translated into several metres over distance and he knew the rebel leader would not be stationary for long.

Tansvir started swinging the lure. As soon as he established a momentum, he released the falcon to the sky, turning and swinging as the bird soared over the valley.

With the falcon roughly four hundred metres into its flight,

Tansvir called it back. The creature ignored the command and landed on a tree. Tansvir threw the lure down and cursed the disobedient bird.

The tantrum was the opportunity Matt had been waiting for. He dug his face into the Dragunov cheek-rest and hit his pressel switch three times to alert the team to stand by. Bringing the target into the aim, he prepared to operate the trigger, but the face in the crosshairs paralysed his finger. Despite everything Khalid had told him, Matt couldn't see the BLA commander as the enemy.

He ignored his gut and took up the first pressure. Suddenly, his sight went black. Matt released the trigger and pulled back his eye. The falcon was flying above him, clutching a small creature in its claws. The hunt had taken the bird through his line of sight.

The stay of execution further eroded Matt's resolve. He wanted to abort but he knew there was no going back. The SSG and the ISI had too much invested in this mission to tolerate anything less than success.

He locked on the target and dropped the sight down a fraction. With the anonymous heart squarely in the crosshairs, he operated the trigger. The round struck Tansvir in the chest, sweeping him off his feet. It was done. Matt had killed the man who'd murdered Emma.

The shot echoed through the valley, making it impossible for the guards on the high ground to pinpoint the source. They started shooting blindly into the basin. Cracks and thumps bounced off the rocky ridges like pin balls, amplifying the battle. Certain Qureshi and his men were answering the guards with rounds of their own, Matt checked the target before falling back to join them. But instead of a motionless terrorist, he found a patch of white rising from the earth.

Tansvir ripped open his kameez, exposing a set of body

armour. Sobhat! The fucking tout had double crossed them. Tansvir had known they were coming.

Matt realigned his shot, determined not to fail again, but before he could discharge his weapon a BLA round struck just inches from his head. Keeping his eye to the sight, he rolled into the rock fold, the Dragunov ready to take out the BLA guard who'd sussed his position. The hillside was still crawling with white turbans; the SSG was performing as poorly as Matt.

He couldn't move without announcing his location to every guard standing above. Another bullet struck near his leg. He needed to find the rebel targeting him and give him the good news. Matt swung around and aimed his weapon toward the back of the valley, his crosshairs jumping from target to target, searching for the threat. He zeroed in on a rifle barrel. It was pointing right back at him but to his astonishment, it wasn't a Baluch wielding the weapon. It was Major Qureshi. The SSG commander had turned on him!

Matt aimed at Qureshi's right kneecap and operated the trigger. The SSG commander fell out of cover, wounded. The guns fell silent as the BLA guards circled him like vultures.

Matt wondered why the rest of the team weren't coming to the aid of their commander. That's when he heard the helis. The gutless bastards were extracting, leaving both Qureshi and him behind.

Matt watched through his scope as six of the rebels hauled Qureshi down the ridge and out of the valley. The rest of the guards followed behind.

Matt lay like a stone for hours, cradling his Dragunov, baking in the sun, waiting for night to descend. He sipped water sparingly to conserve it, but by late afternoon his supply was exhausted and his alertness started to lapse.

The earth was cool beneath his face when Matt awoke. He rubbed his eyes and reached for his rifle. It would be time to head out soon – where to he hadn't a clue.

'Don't move,' a voice commanded. Matt looked beneath him. His rifle was gone. 'Put your hands on your head – slowly.' He raised his arms and eyes. The orange sun sinking into the horizon blinded him to his captor's face but the weapon aimed at his head was clear as day. Matt was staring down the barrel of a Lee Enfield.

Chapter 53

Successive chimes sounded as Matt was marched blindfolded and bound into a building. He recognized the half-tone couplings from his childhood – falcons' bells.

Thrown face first into a sandy pit, he heard the sound of a heavy iron chain scraping against a flimsy metal door as the BLA locked him in. When they'd gone, Matt attempted to discern more of his surroundings. He rolled onto his back and clawed the sand with his fingertips. A layer of felt lined the floor beneath. He stood up and paced his cell; ten feet by eight, with at least six feet of head clearance. The dimensions were as familiar as the bells. He was being held in a falcon's mews.

'Logan,' a voice whispered from across the way.

'Qureshi?'

'I cannot see,' said the SSG commander. 'Where have they taken us, brother?'

'I'm not your fucking brother,' Matt growled.

'Do not be a fool, Logan. The rebels will return soon to question us. We must find a way to escape.'

Matt kicked the cage. 'You tried to kill me!'

'Whatever our differences, we must set them aside now. The Baluch are ruthless. You have no idea what they are capable of.'

'Why did you try to shoot me?' Matt demanded.

'I had no other choice,' said Qureshi. 'I had to do it for my country.'

'Are you off your head? I was trying to kill one of your enemies.'

Qureshi laughed. 'You fool. You *are* the enemy.'

Qureshi hadn't exaggerated the BLA's brutality. Shortly after he was hauled away for questioning, shrieks filled the compound. Matt charted the SSG commander's cruel torture from his cell. The screaming escalated into primordial howls before degenerating into cries for mercy. As the night wore on, the unanswered pleas tapered off to pitiful whimpers.

By daybreak, all Matt could hear was the wind and the occasional chime of falcons' bells. Alone with his thoughts, he inevitably turned them inward. He could rage against Qureshi all he wanted, but ultimately he had only himself to blame for his predicament. He'd signed his death warrant the moment he'd agreed to kill Tansvir. He should have known Khalid and Qureshi would milk him for his skills and then leave him for dead. But he was too blinded by vengeance to see them for what they really were.

The smell of burning breakfast meat wafted into the mews house. Though he hadn't eaten in over twenty-four hours, Matt found it more nauseating than enticing. The metallic, sulphurous odour grew stronger as the guards entered, dragging something behind them. It was Qureshi. Matt could hear the SSG commander's faint gurgles beneath their footsteps.

He knew they'd come for him next. Rather than give them the satisfaction of seeing him beg, Matt rose to his feet and raised his chin defiantly. He may have lost control of his fate but he could still meet it like a man.

A guard entered his cage and untied his blindfold. 'How are you, Logan?'

'What do you know,' said Matt. 'You do speak English.'

Sobhat laughed. 'A language I look forward to practising with you today.'

'Hate to disappoint you but I don't feel much like chatting.'

'Neither did Major Qureshi at first.' Sobhat left the cell and locked it. 'We can be very persuasive.'

The tout walked away, leaving Matt a clear view of Qureshi's cell. He expected to take a modicum of satisfaction from seeing the man who'd tried to kill him brought to heel. But the charred lump lying on the floor evoked only one emotion in Matt – pity. The BLA had literally roasted Qureshi alive. His burns were so severe his operational uniform was indistinguishable from his skin. His eyes had melted in their sockets.

Matt fell to the ground heaving. The burnt meat he smelled wasn't breakfast. It was human flesh.

Chapter 54

The freshly skewered chickens looked like tombstones against the white-hot charcoals. A waiter extracted a carcass from the graveyard and laid it on a plate. Eric watched with resigned repulsion as flies dive-bombed his lunch. They were still swarming when the waiter deposited it on the table along with a cup of tea. Eric examined the bird. There was no distinguishing the insects from the black ash stuck to the crisped skin. He raised his tea glass. It too was awash with soot.

'How's the food?'

Eric lowered the glass. He knew he'd flush Ted out eventually. 'Very ethnic,' he sighed.

Ted walked around the table and took a seat. 'I'm starving,' he said, as if they had a lunch date scheduled. 'What's good?'

Eric slid the plate across the table. 'Help yourself.'

Ted tore a leg from the bird. 'Much obliged.'

He ate with the gusto of a local but somehow avoided looking like a tourist who'd forgotten his manners. Eric couldn't help but feel envious. Ted had mastered his surroundings without losing himself to them.

The spy chief laid down a half-gnawed leg. 'It's good. You should have some.'

'I'll pass.'

'May I?' Ted took a sip of Eric's tea. 'Lost your appetite, eh?'

'The hygiene here does leave something to be desired.'

Ted pulled a photograph from his pocket and placed it in front of Eric. 'I meant for your work.'

Eric was shaken to the core by the old image of himself, standing in a cap and gown flanked by his former best friends, Ted and Emma.

'Remember the vow we made to each other that day?' said Ted. 'We were going to save the world from terrorism.'

Eric returned the photograph. 'We were kids.'

Ted tucked it into his pocket. 'Didn't work out like you thought it would, did it?'

Eric threw down a wad of rupees and pushed back from the table. 'If you think you're going to win me with nostalgia, you're wasting your time.'

Ted followed him out of the restaurant into the busy street. 'Talk to me,' he said in a hushed voice.

Eric kept his eyes forward. 'Get lost before you get us both killed.'

'The ISI won't touch you when you're with me.'

'My ass is covered, thank you very much.'

'If you're referring to your ICON friends, forget it. They don't give a shit what happens to you.'

'And you do? The only reason you're hounding me is to advance your own career. Go scramble over someone else's back because you're not using mine.'

'This has nothing to do with my career,' said Ted. 'You're on the wrong side, Eric. Come back to the company and I promise you'll be forgiven.'

'You think there's a difference?' said Eric. 'Wake up. We're both working for the same master.'

'Not since you bailed.'

'I didn't bail,' Eric countered. 'My job was absorbed. Remember?'

'You were doing communications when you left us; not financing terrorists and getting your friends killed.'

The accusation stopped Eric in his tracks. 'ICON doesn't know you're on to them.' He turned to Ted. 'I'm begging you. Leave me alone. Don't try contacting me again.'

Ted's aggression evaporated. 'My God,' he said. 'You never told them Emma came to see me, did you?'

'They still don't know. It's the only advantage you have. Don't blow it.'

'Help me to bring them down,' Ted urged. 'I'll protect you, I swear.'

'Don't you get it?' said Eric. 'You can't even protect yourself.'

Chapter 55

Matt was still heaving when Tansvir entered the mews house. 'You are the one they call Logan.'

'Yes,' Matt panted.

'You tried to kill me, did you not?'

Matt rocked back on his knees. 'Yes.'

'Thank you for not denying it.' Tansvir brought himself eye level with Matt. 'May I ask whose side you are on?'

Matt shook his head. 'I wish I knew.'

Tansvir stroked his beard. 'A man who does not know where his loyalties lie is a danger to all, including himself.' He stood up. 'Are you not a mercenary who sought to profit from my death?'

Matt jumped to his feet. 'No! I would never kill for money.'

Tansvir gestured to Qureshi's cell. 'Then why did you offer your services to my enemy?'

'I didn't offer him anything,' said Matt. 'The ISI asked me to work with the SSG to kill you.'

'Sending a red-haired devil to Gwadar to kill me?' Tansvir laughed. 'Even the ISI is not that foolish.'

'It's the truth,' said Matt.

'There is no point in continuing this charade. The major confessed to us that you are an ICON mercenary.' Tansvir's face hardened. 'You and your masters will pay for this betrayal a thousand fold.'

Matt's mind was racing. How would Tansvir know about

ICON? He recalled the Baluch protestors from Islamabad. Carter and his mates must have been playing the same game with the BLA that they were with TTP-Q – infiltrating the organization in order to destroy it. 'I work for SBC.'

'Enough!' Tansvir bellowed. 'McKay has sought my assistance in locating you, Logan; a ruse no doubt intended to cloak his wolf in sheep's clothing.'

Matt should have realized Carter and his mates would be looking for him. 'All right,' he confessed. 'I do know people at ICON. But they didn't order me to kill you. The ISI sent me, I swear.'

'You may protest ICON's innocence all you want. It will not change your fate.'

Matt knew he was a dead man. But he wasn't bringing ICON down with him. 'Qureshi was lying to you,' he insisted.

'What would he have to gain from this?' Tansvir challenged.

'I don't know,' said Matt, 'but he was working some kind of angle otherwise he wouldn't have tried to kill me too.'

Tansvir balked.

'If you don't believe me check the shell casings where you found me. They'll match the rounds from his weapon. You can also check his knee, or what's left of it. The bullet came from my Dragunov. I wounded him after he fired on me.'

'If what you say is true, my fighters shall be very disappointed.' Tansvir crossed the floor to Qureshi's cage. 'They have been arguing all night over who should take credit for wounding this animal.' He regarded the dying major with contempt. 'My mother was burned alive by the Pakistanis. I was hiding in the hills with my militia when the army shelled her encampment. It took forty years to put this wrong to right.' Tansvir turned to Matt. 'I shall have my revenge on ICON with or without your cooperation.'

'Go ahead and kill me. But don't blame them for my mistakes.'

'May Allah have mercy on your soul.' Tansvir walked away.

Matt had to buy more time. His eye pivoted to the falcon in the adjacent cage. 'I can help you,' he called to Tansvir. The rebel leader ignored him. 'You're rubbish with that saker.'

Tansvir turned around. 'What do you know of falcons?'

Matt nodded to the saker. 'Enough to get that one to fly to the lure.'

Chapter 56

'Do as you say and I shall kill you swiftly.' Tansvir pulled his dagger from his waistcoat. 'Attempt to escape and your death shall be slow.'

'Where am I going to go?' said Matt. 'Come on. Let me fly her.'

Tansvir unlocked the cage. 'I have always considered falcons an excellent judge of character. They detest all that make men weak: cowardice, fear, subterfuge.' He cut the straps from Matt's hands. 'If you are lying about ICON, as I believe you are, she shall expose you.'

Matt massaged his fingers. 'Just bring me the saker.'

Tansvir retrieved his falconer's gear. 'Why are you so certain you shall succeed where I have failed?'

'Because I know how to handle her,' said Matt.

Tansvir gave his satchel and glove to Matt. 'We carry our birds of prey on our right hand, not on our left as you English.'

Matt slipped the glove on and opened the satchel. 'I'm Scottish.'

'I shall fetch meat for the lure,' said Tansvir.

Matt handed him the falcon's hood and took out the baton. 'Don't bother.'

His audacity amused Tansvir. 'Have you flown a wild saker?'

Matt unwound the lure line from the stick. 'I had a captive-bred peregrine as a boy.'

'Then you do not know what you are dealing with,' said Tansvir. 'The saker will not return to you unless there is a reward waiting.'

Matt looped the line around his left middle and index fingers. 'That's where you've been going wrong. A falcon's like a beautiful woman; give her everything she wants upfront and she won't respect you. Hold back and she'll do anything to please you.'

Tansvir laughed. 'But how does one win her heart?'

'Like any woman's.' Matt opened the saker's mews and thrust his arm inside. 'First, you take her.' The bird flew from its perch to the glove. 'Then you eliminate all distractions.'

Tansvir placed the hood on the saker's head. 'And now?'

Matt grabbed the jesses. 'Free her to her pleasure.'

He walked the falcon outside. Matt didn't think to recce the compound. Escape no longer mattered to him. His sole concern at that moment in time was mastering the untamed creature on his arm.

He removed the hood with his teeth. The bird's eye rotated to its new master. Matt held its gaze, threw the lure straight up, and started swinging counter-clockwise. The looping rhythm coursed through his body into the falcon, bridging the divide between man and beast. At one with the saker, he released it to the sky.

The falcon beat its wings and soared. Tansvir laughed. 'She will not come back. You will see.'

Matt was too consumed by the falcon's flight to listen. 'Ho!' he cried. The bird turned and dove for the lure. Her speed was breathtaking; like a cheetah. Matt's eye fused with the falcon's as the talons opened for the circling lure. But he wasn't ready to gratify it yet. He stepped forward and dropped the line, pulling it from the bird's grasp. Robbed of its kill, the saker recovered and soared skyward once more.

Matt changed tack, turning his body as he dragged the lure along the ground and brought it back up. He lost himself in the dance; swinging the lure, calling the falcon to dive; denying it satisfaction, enticing it to try again. The purity of the creature's instinct and his ability to control it awakened the part of him he'd feared he'd lost forever. There, on the baked plains of the Makran Coast, Matt rediscovered the best of himself – the hunter.

On the fifth pass Matt finally gave the saker its due, allowing it to catch the lure. He took three steps back and tugged on the line. The grateful falcon dropped the reward and landed gently on his glove.

'Most impressive,' Tansvir conceded. 'I thought she would never be tamed.'

'She won't be.' Matt stroked the falcon. 'She belongs in the wild, not a cage.'

Tansvir re-assessed his captive. 'I do not understand. How does a master of falcons fail to kill the prey he stalks?'

Matt kept his eyes on the saker. 'Because I wasn't stalking you.'

Tansvir looked at him curiously. 'If it is not my blood you thirst for, Logan, whose do you seek?'

Matt finally turned to him. 'Abdullah Qari's.'

Chapter 57

Tansvir aimed his Lee Enfield between Matt's shoulders and marched him out to the cliff edge. 'That is enough,' said the rebel leader.

Matt looked down. Two steps and he'd plunge three hundred feet to his death. At least there were plenty of witnesses to his execution. Half a dozen gantry cranes were working full tilt in the bay below, moving goods from a man-made jetty onto diesel-belching merchant ships. Some of the spreaders were holding as many as four forty-foot sea containers in their jaws.

'Why do you seek Abdullah Qari's head?' asked Tansvir.

'Because he murdered the woman I love, or I thought he did, until the ISI showed me a picture of the bomber's face. They told me he was Baluch but that was probably a lie.'

Tansvir bowed his head. 'It is true.'

Matt whipped around. 'So it was you who ordered the attack on SBC's house.'

Tansvir held his rifle in the aim. 'I would never deliberately martyr my fighters.'

'You're no different from Qari,' Matt charged. 'Better finish me off now because if you don't, I promise I'll kill you.'

'I am sorry about your woman, Logan. But it was not I who ordered the attack but Qari.'

'I thought Baluch didn't take orders from Pashtun.'

Tansvir lowered his rifle. 'That was true – until I failed my people.' He walked to the precipice. 'Would you believe that just ten years ago, none of this was here? Soon Gwadar shall resemble Dubai.'

'Why did you bring me here to kill me?'

'I brought you here so that you may understand why I allied my army with Abdullah Qari's.'

'If you had a scrap of honour in you, you never would have joined him.'

Tansvir lowered his eyes. 'I disgraced the BLA and all Baluch when I entered into a pact with that animal. But honour is a luxury when faced with an enemy so powerful it could bring even America to its knees.'

'That's no excuse,' said Matt. 'Pakistan doesn't have that kind of power.'

'I was not referring to Pakistan.' Tansvir laid down his Lee Enfield. 'Do you know why America went to war in Afghanistan?'

Matt regarded the rifle with caution. It had to be a trap. 'I've had enough of riddles.'

'It is not a riddle. Why did the United States invade a broken, landlocked country?'

Matt kept his eye on the weapon and gave the pat answer. 'Because they didn't want it to fall into the hands of terrorists again.'

'You are wrong.' Tansvir grabbed a piece of sandstone and started etching what resembled a hangman's scaffold in the desert floor. 'This is the north and east coastline of the Arabian Sea.' He ran his finger left to right along the top. 'To the north, Iran, Baluchistan and Pakistan,' he dropped his finger down, 'to the east, India.' He drew an oval to the left of the scaffold. 'The Gulf states; Oman, UAE, Qatar, Saudi Arabia, Kuwait, Iraq. Through these proxies and Indian cooperation, America maintains control over the Arabian Gulf and all the oil wealth that travels through it. Ten years ago, however, the balance of power began to shift.' He drew an ellipse running north-east from the right corner of the scaffold.

Matt recognized the outline. 'Pakistan.'

Tansvir pointed to the north-west border. 'You know the Durand Line, yes?'

Matt nodded.

'When the Soviets invaded Afghanistan, Islamabad created the Taliban to keep the Russians from crossing the Durand Line into Pakistan. America supported this arrangement to stop the communist expansion. And they continued to do so after the Russians left until . . .'

Matt finished the sentence. 'Until the Afghan Taliban invited al-Qaeda in and September eleventh happened.'

'A common misperception,' Tansvir corrected. 'America did not invade Afghanistan to defeat the Taliban.' He pointed to his map. 'They did it to stop China from gaining control of the Arabian Sea.'

'China's more than a thousand miles from the coast,' Matt argued.

'Hence why Beijing built the port below us.' Tansvir punched the stone into Pakistan's western shoreline. 'Gwadar is China's gateway to the Arabian Peninsula. And soon, Beijing shall be the dominant power in the Gulf – not Washington.'

'It'll never happen,' said Matt. 'Besides, Islamabad's allied with the Yanks. Pakistan will never choose China over America.'

'In the past, maybe. But that changed when China embraced capitalism.' Tansvir rounded out India's borders into the Bay of Bengal and drew another saddle encompassing Bangladesh, Burma, Thailand, Malaysia, Cambodia, Laos and Vietnam. 'Economies cannot grow without energy. Secure supplies of oil and gas are vital. Before Gwadar, China had no choice but to ship oil from the Gulf through the Straits of Malacca, the choke-point linking the Indian Ocean to the Pacific. Like the Gulf, the Americans control that too. That is why ten years ago Beijing took steps to break America's hold over its energy supply routes by starting a dialogue with Islamabad to build this port. Gwadar allows China to bypass the Straits of Malacca and pump oil through Pakistan directly into Western China.'

'What does Pakistan get out of it?'

'Billions in investment and rents from the pipeline traversing its land,' said Tansvir. 'Washington tried to thwart this arrangement through diplomacy and promises of more aid to Pakistan but they failed. Beijing and Islamabad finalized their agreement on the eve of the War on Terror; August 2001. A month later . . .'

'Are you suggesting that America engineered the World Trade Center attack?' Matt interrupted.

'I cannot tell you who was responsible for nine-eleven. But do you not find it odd that all the hijackers were Saudi and yet America chose to invade Afghanistan?'

Matt conceded the point.

'America believed it could bend Pakistan to its will by controlling Afghanistan,' Tansvir continued. 'All they had to do was destroy Islamabad's proxy army and the country would be theirs for the taking. For this task, they enlisted the mortal enemy of the Afghan Taliban; the northern alliance leader Ahmed Shah Massoud.'

Matt recalled Naj's history lesson at the gates of Mullah Maulana's compound. 'He was killed two days before nine-eleven.'

'By the ISI,' Tansvir added. 'They knew that with Massoud gone, America would have to fight the Taliban themselves – an impossible task for a western army. And while America has been squandering blood and treasure in Afghanistan, China has laid the foundations to become the greatest superpower on earth.'

Tansvir connected the dots on his map. 'China now has ports throughout the Indian Ocean, the Straits of Malacca and the South China Sea. They call it the *string of pearls* and its riches are beyond measure. The oil wealth of the Gulf, hydrocarbons in the South China Sea, a market with billions of consumers and for Islamabad the greatest prize of all – containment of its most hated enemy.'

Matt ran his eye along the string. It was literally a noose around India's neck.

'Now you see why Islamabad will never abandon Beijing for Washington,' said Tansvir. 'For as China rises, India falls.'

Matt still wasn't convinced. 'Why would the Yanks bother with Afghanistan? Why not just invade Pakistan?'

'Not even America is so bold as to attack a nuclear power. America's soldiers and aircraft would be vaporized at the press of a button. Pakistan cannot be destroyed from the outside.' Tansvir raised a fist and slammed it down on the Durand Line. 'But it can be destroyed from within.' He drew in new boundaries encompassing Pakistan's tribal areas, North-West Frontier Province and southern and eastern Afghanistan. 'Pakistan is to South Asia what Yugoslavia was to Eastern Europe; an ethnic tinderbox of false borders. TTP-Q seeks to reunite the Pashtun tribes by creating the Emirate of Pashtunistan.' He moved Baluchistan's western border into Iran. 'This is what Baluchistan will look like once our homeland is reunited.'

'But the Yanks won't be any better off with you in power than Islamabad. And they sure as hell don't want to see the Taliban eating up half of Afghanistan.'

Tansvir looked at him curiously. 'What do you know of ICON?'

Matt grew cautious. 'I told you, I don't work for them.'

'I believe you.' Tansvir looked Matt in the eye. 'ICON fostered the alliance between me and Abdullah Qari.'

'You're off your head,' said Matt.

'Think what a free Baluchistan would mean to America and Britain,' Tansvir challenged. 'Containment of Iran, control over China's energy routes. It is in the West's best interests to break up Pakistan. That is why ICON brought me and Qari together.'

'You're barking if you think ICON supports either of you,' said Matt, 'especially when there's nothing to stop you from jumping to China's side.'

Tansvir was offended. 'And empower the Punjabis and the Persians? The very people who have occupied our lands, murdered our women and children and stolen our birthright? Never, never in a thousand years!' he cried. 'I swear on the graves of my sons; Baluchistan's future is West not East.'

Tansvir believed passionately in his theory. But as persuasive as the arguments were, Matt couldn't imagine a scenario in which Carter and his mates would back terrorists. Infiltrating them to destroy them – yes. Aiding them – never. 'If ICON is supporting you, as you claim, why did you think they'd sent me to kill you?'

'Because I am worth less to them than Qari,' Tansvir explained. 'I punished that donkey for martyring my fighter and now he desires my death. The Americans will not risk alienating Qari to save me. He is too useful. As long as they feed him money, he will do their bidding, whereas the Baluch will never be for sale. The Americans know this.' The rebel leader picked up his Lee Enfield. 'I fear that when Pakistan is no longer, America intends to make Baluchistan a slave of Pashtunistan.' He gave the weapon to Matt. 'I cannot deliver my people from one occupier into the hands of another.'

Matt ran his palm over the walnut casing. It was like holding the weight of the British Empire in his hands.

Tansvir pressed his head to the barrel. 'I am no longer worthy of leading my people.'

With a twitch of the finger, Matt could achieve what he'd come to Gwadar to do. 'You're wasting your time.' He pulled the weapon up. 'I can't kill you. I already tried, remember?'

Tansvir raised his head. 'If you refuse to kill me, then redeem me.'

'How?' asked Matt.

Tansvir took back the Lee Enfield. 'Help me kill Abdullah Qari.'

Chapter 58

Pashtunibad, Quetta

The shops were all shut save for one tea house. The last customers were sitting in broken-backed chairs, arguing furtively over drained glasses. The debate was far too engrossing for any of them to notice the turbaned figure with the long, cloth bundle slinking quietly up the street.

Matt cleared the quarrelling holdouts and continued on his way. He was so close to getting revenge he could taste it. Tansvir had contacted ICON to request a peace summit with Abdullah Qari for eleven that evening, but when the Taliban leader arrived at the meeting house deep inside Pashtunistan, it wouldn't be the BLA greeting him.

Matt figured he wouldn't be the only one lying in wait. ICON wouldn't pass up the chance to take out two terrorist leaders in one go.

A vehicle appeared at the top of the road. Matt ducked into an alleyway. His disguise could stand up to shadows but not the glare of headlights. The car stopped a few yards short of his position and let out a passenger: a woman in a blue burka. She walked unaccompanied up a footpath leading west – the same direction he was heading.

Matt waited five minutes before following her into the darkness. He reached the meeting point at twenty minutes to nine. The area was exactly as Tansvir had described: a rubbish heap opening onto a walled compound with a yellow gate.

He unwrapped his Dragunov from its cloth camouflage and recced the ground through the night scope. There was no sign yet of Carter or his mates. Matt searched for an observation post that would allow him to see people coming and going from the compound and moving into position around it. A rusting jingly on the southern edge of the dump was just the ticket.

He crept through rancid piles of household and commercial waste into the OP. Shortly after nine, the first ICON man showed. Matt panned his crosshairs along the assassin's rifle. *Baby Girl.* The rest of the team followed behind Bazinsky; Carter, Hernandez, Dietrich, Ginta. Everyone was on hand for Abdullah Qari's final curtain call except McKay. Surely the ICON commander wouldn't miss the final act?

A figure walked out of the alley into the waste ground. Matt recognized the swagger. McKay wasn't alone; there was someone behind him. Matt wondered: was McKay leading Abdullah Qari into the ambush?

Determined to take the kill for himself, Matt raised his sight. McKay's pixilated features walked in and out of his crosshairs. He took up the first pressure on his trigger and waited for Qari to show. Matt's veins coursed with adrenaline as the corner of a loose-fitting turban appeared. After everything he'd been through, the moment he'd longed for was finally at hand.

A chin entered the sight but there was no patchy beard. It was shaven. Matt did a double-take. Eric was following McKay!

What was the correspondent doing accompanying ICON to a terrorist summit – and in a local disguise no less? Had he got to know ICON after the kidnapping and was doing some sort of story on them? It fit Eric's MO, but not McKay's. The ICON commander would never court the press.

*   *   *

By three a.m., Qari still hadn't shown and Matt was no closer to figuring out what was going on. Eric and McKay emerged from the compound and headed out. Gradually the rest of the ICON team withdrew as well. Matt watched their faces as they fell back from their positions. Carter and his mates were as dejected as he was.

Matt stayed in position another forty minutes before finally calling it quits. He climbed down from the jingly onto a pile of garbage. The sound of a weapon cocking stopped him cold.

'Drop your weapon and put your hands on your head,' a Yank voice commanded from behind.

Matt laid down his Dragunov. The ICON lads had got the drop on him.

'Turn around slowly.'

Matt did as ordered, expecting to see a familiar face. But the man holding the pistol was a complete stranger to him.

'I know you,' said Ted.

'That makes one of us,' Matt answered.

'You're supposed to be kidnapped. Mind telling me what you've been doing outside an ICON safe house all night?'

'I've half a mind to ask you the same thing.'

Ted reasserted his grip on his weapon. 'What game are you playing?'

'I don't know.' Matt's eyes shifted left. 'But whatever it is, you lost it, mate.'

Tansvir stepped out of the shadows, his Lee Enfield poised to fire. 'Lower your pistol,' he ordered Ted.

Ted obeyed. 'Who are you?'

'I am Tansvir,' said the rebel leader, 'commander, Baluchistan Liberation Army. This man you threaten is with me.'

'With you?' Ted looked at Matt. 'I don't believe it. You're ICON too.'

'How do you know me?' Matt demanded.

'Emma was nothing more than a target to you,' the spy chief accused.

Matt grabbed Ted's weapon and turned it on him. 'Who the fuck are you?!'

'Ted Joiner. CIA.'

Tansvir raised his brow to Matt. 'Shall I kill him?'

'Do that and you can kiss any hope of US backing for Baluch independence goodbye,' Ted warned.

'I already have Washington's support,' Tansvir said dismissively.

'ICON is not Washington,' said Ted. 'They're terrorists.'

'Release him!' a foreign voice thundered.

Matt swung around. His eyes narrowed with hatred as they met the aggressor. 'I should have killed you when I had the chance.'

Naj stepped out of the shadows. 'You nearly succeeded.' The fixer kept his pistol trained on Tansvir. 'I am disappointed in you, Matt. Cavorting with the BLA after everything I told you.'

Matt swung his pistol toward Naj. 'You set Emma up.'

'What?' said Ted.

'I would never allow any harm to come to Emma,' Naj protested. 'I was broken-hearted when she was murdered.'

'Liar!' Matt cried. 'How much did Qari pay you to sell her out?'

'You've got it wrong, Matt,' said Ted. 'Naj is not with Abdullah Qari – your ICON buddies are.'

Matt took up the first pressure. 'He's a fucking tout!'

'He works for me!' Ted cried.

A gunshot ripped through the night. Everyone turned their weapons toward the source.

Bethany lowered her pistol and raised her burka. 'Pardon the interruption, gentlemen, but perhaps we should take this conversation indoors?'

Chapter 59

'Twenty-five years I have been CIA informant.' Naj paused to take a glass of tea from Bethany. 'Thank you, my dear.'

'So being a fixer was just a cover?' asked Matt.

'On the contrary. I was employed by SBC when the CIA recruited me.' Naj sipped his tea then put it down. 'Why did you think I had betrayed Emma to Abdullah Qari?'

Matt felt embarrassed now by his accusations. 'I figured TTP-Q had to have someone on the inside.'

'But I am Mohajir,' said Naj. 'No ethnic group has more to lose if Pakistan is a failed state.' He turned an accusatory eye to Tansvir. 'I abhor any organization dedicated to breaking up this country.'

The rebel leader offered no apology for his secessionist agenda.

'You had access to her schedule,' Matt explained. 'You knew exactly what time she'd be on that roof.'

'So did Eric,' Ted interrupted.

'Eric?' Matt imagined the correspondent in the role of Taliban co-conspirator. It was easier to picture having seen him turbaned up just hours before. 'Do you know what he was doing with McKay?'

Bethany glanced at Ted. The spy chief nodded for her to answer. 'Mr Riddell works for ICON.'

'For spies, you lot don't know much. ICON is ex-Special Forces.'

'And ex-CIA.' Ted laid the picture of himself, Emma and Eric in front of Matt. 'The three of us went to school together. After graduation, Emma went off to become a diplomat. Eric and I had more exciting plans. We wanted to be CIA field operatives – real life James Bonds.'

Matt picked up the photo. He'd never seen that side of Emma – carefree, full of optimism.

'It didn't work out as Eric had hoped. In the spy trade, a face like his is a liability. He's too good looking not to be noticed.' Ted rubbed his head. 'Me and my receding hairline were sent to learn field tradecraft for human int. Eric and his chiselled jaw were pushed into strategic communications.'

'What's that?' asked Matt.

'It's a politically correct term for propaganda,' Bethany explained.

'Is that why he went into journalism?' asked Matt.

'Eric was never really a journalist,' Ted divulged. 'The CIA planted him with SBC. What better way to ensure that the American people are behind Washington's foreign policy than to have an agency man himself reporting on it. Eric's a master at making al-Qaeda seem more powerful than they really are.'

Matt recalled Eric's stand up at the protest in Islamabad. 'Like turning a demonstration into an al-Qaeda nuclear threat.' He returned the picture to Ted. 'So why did golden boy jump ship to ICON?'

'He didn't leave the CIA for ICON,' said Ted. 'Eric left us for the Strategic Support Branch.'

'Who are they?'

'It's a US intelligence agency Donald Rumsfeld and Dick Cheney created in 2002, supposedly as a stopgap against perceived CIA failures over nine-eleven,' Ted explained. 'Of course, it wasn't our competence Dick and Don took issue with; it was our transparency. The CIA simply wasn't authorized to do what the architects of the War on Terror wanted: torture, political assassinations, things the Constitution generally frowns upon.'

'Come on,' said Matt. 'The CIA's been doing dirty deeds for decades.'

The spy chief threw up his hand. 'I'll be the first to admit the company has a chequered past. We've overthrown democratically elected leaders, trained death squads and waged secret wars. But all that's behind us now.'

'Bollocks,' said Matt.

'It's true,' said Bethany. 'Iran-Contra clipped the CIA's wings. We're required by law to disclose all of our operations to Congress. We can't make a move without informing the House and Senate Intelligence Committees. They control our budget.'

'Which basically means they have us by the balls,' Ted continued. 'The Strategic Support Branch doesn't have that kind of oversight. They're funded directly by the military.'

'Is there a difference?' asked Matt.

'Let me put it this way,' said Ted. 'The SSB was up and running for two years before Congress even knew it existed.'

'Who do they answer to then?'

'The Secretary of Defense – period,' said Bethany.

'So they're the Defense Department's spy agency.'

'Not the Defense Department's – the Secretary of Defense's,' Ted corrected. 'The SSB gathers intelligence for JSOC. And Rumsfeld separated JSOC from the normal command structure inside the Pentagon, so only he was privy to what the SSB and JSOC are doing. In Washington they call it "The Secret Army of Northern Virginia".'

'Let me get this straight,' said Matt. 'This wanker basically formed his own army of Black Operators supported by his own spy agency neither of which are answerable to anyone but him?'

'Bingo,' said Ted. 'Imagine what a mess US intelligence gathering became with parallel organizations engaged in human int. We were stepping on each other's dicks from Baghdad to Kabul; working at cross purposes . . .'

Matt recalled the Baghdad bust-up between the CIA and JSOC. 'Targeting each other's assets . . .'

'You get the picture,' said Ted. 'It wasn't long before the SSB wanted to take over the CIA's entire human int portfolio – including paying-off foreign assets. That's how Eric ended up with them. The SSB needed a banker to distribute bribes. His cover as an international correspondent gave him the perfect excuse to jet around conflict zones with wads of cash.'

'Fuck,' said Matt. 'I handed him half a million when I arrived.'

'I bet you didn't declare it either,' said Ted.

'So how does ICON figure into this? Is it just a front for the SSB?'

'More of an outgrowth,' Ted explained. 'By 2007, the architects of the War on Terror could see the writing on the wall. Rumsfeld had been forced to resign as Secretary of Defense and it was pretty clear the Republicans were going to lose the White House and both houses of Congress to the Democrats. A lot of people had staked their reputations and their futures on the Secret Army of Northern Virginia. So, rather than let a bunch of elected lefty liberals gut it, they moved it out of the public domain and into the private sector.'

'How?' asked Matt.

'Simple,' said Ted. 'All it took was a willing parent company to front the corporate structure – a firm that had made a killing on US government contracts and needed to return some favours.'

'Seven Mountains Security,' Matt concluded.

Bethany called up the photo album on her phone. 'Colonel John Earl McKay, Delta Force, recruited by Seven Mountains Security to head ICON's military operations October 2007. McKay brought with him a team of seasoned operators.' She swiped through the slide show. 'Nathanial Lincoln Carter, captain, Delta Force; Emilio Hernandez, lieutenant, Delta Force . . .'

Matt finished the roll call. 'Bazinsky, Ginta and Dietrich.'

Bethany closed the program. 'What do you know about ICON's operations in Pakistan, Mr Logan?'

'Well . . .' Matt played his cards close to the vest, 'from what I've been able to piece together, it looks like they're working on some sort of outsourced government anti-terror task.'

'Could you be more specific?' Bethany pressed.

Matt showed his hand. 'I believe their mission is to infiltrate TTP-Q and the BLA in order to eliminate both organizations' leaders.'

'You are mistaken,' said Tansvir. 'McKay supports us.'

'You said yourself he wanted you dead,' Matt argued.

'Because I am less important to him than Qari,' Tansvir countered. 'With or without me, America still has the same goal: destroy Pakistan and contain China.'

'The Yanks want you dead, mate.'

'You're right,' Ted interrupted.

'See?' said Matt. 'The spook agrees with me.'

'Not you.' Ted nodded to Tansvir. 'Him.'

Chapter 60

'What exactly is he right about?' Matt challenged.

'Everything,' said Ted. 'Except the America part. ICON is not the United States of America.'

Matt wouldn't have it. 'You two obviously don't know McKay. The man's a nut job. He thinks he's fighting some sort of Christian holy war in Pakistan. There's no way he'd back an Islamic terrorist.'

'It is not an uncommon contradiction,' Tansvir argued. 'Suicide is forbidden in Islam and yet we have mullahs sending Muslim martyrs to their deaths.'

'Fanatics will rationalize anything in the name of God,' Ted concurred, 'especially when they're losing.'

'But McKay's not losing. He's successfully infiltrated both organizations.'

'The US has been losing Pakistan ever since Musharraf cut a deal with the Waziristan tribes in 2006,' Ted countered.

'He made a deal with the Afghan Taliban,' Matt corrected.

'No. The Waziristan tribes. Think about it, Matt. Why would Musharraf make a deal with an insurgent group Pakistan created and already controlled? His problem was never the Afghan Taliban. Pashtun nationalism was and is the real threat to Pakistan's sovereignty,' said Ted. 'Considering the whole US strategy in the region hinged on dividing Pakistan, Washington was very concerned with Musharraf's efforts to heal rifts. So the

Secret Army of Northern Virginia hatched a plan to drive him out of power and achieve their ultimate goal. Are you familiar with the Red Mosque uprising?'

Matt nodded.

'The Strategic Support Branch was behind that,' Ted revealed. 'They funnelled weapons and money to the Red Mosque to force Musharraf into an unpopular standoff with the Pashtun. After the mosque was stormed, the pact with the Waziristan tribes went out the window and insurgents started attacking Pakistani military posts in the tribal areas. Musharraf sent the army into Waziristan to stop the uprising, but he couldn't contain it. It spread to North-West Frontier Province, forcing him to deploy more troops – to Swat.'

'The spectre of our army killing Muslims was too much for the people of Pakistan to endure,' Naj added. 'Discontent with Musharraf's rule grew so strong he was forced to declare martial law in November 2007.'

'The Secret Army realized that it wasn't how much blood Musharraf spilled that mattered, but whose,' said Ted. 'That's when ICON blew into town.'

Matt remembered Khalid's description of Musharraf's demise. 'Benazir Bhutto?' Ted placed his index finger on his nose. 'But a Pakistani Taliban suicide bomber killed her.'

'Tehrik-i-Taliban didn't even exist until ICON persuaded all the militant groups in the tribal areas to form an umbrella organization,' said the spy chief. 'The first thing they did after they formed was issue a warning threatening to kill Benazir Bhutto if she returned to Pakistan to campaign for the presidency.'

'Do you have proof that ICON was behind her murder?' Matt challenged.

'I don't need proof,' said Ted. 'Look at news footage of the attack. Bhutto was shot in the head right before the bomb detonated. She was killed by an ICON sniper, not a suicide bomber.'

The sequence was chillingly familiar to Matt – a head snapping, a bomb detonating. 'Emma,' he whispered.

Bethany placed her hand on Matt's. 'ICON used the same strategy to eliminate Ms Cameron.'

Matt pulled away. 'No,' he insisted. 'ICON had no reason to kill her. It was Qari.'

'They had a very good reason,' said Ted.

Matt refused to believe it. 'It was Qari who killed her. Don't try convincing me otherwise because I'm not falling for this again.'

'What do you know about Ms Cameron's work?' Bethany asked gently.

'Not much,' Matt confessed. 'I know she hated it and wanted out of the news business.'

Bethany nodded. 'So she never discussed . . .'

Ted raised his hand to silence her. He turned to Matt. 'Did you love Emma?'

Matt lowered his eyes. 'Yes.' Details of their last walk together on Millennium Bridge flashed through his memory. *I'm working on a story – an important one.* 'Wait,' he said suddenly. 'Emma was chasing a story – a big one.'

Ted and Bethany exchanged glances.

'You know what I'm talking about, don't you?'

'Emma had come into possession of documents detailing ICON's operations in Pakistan,' Ted confessed.

Matt took a moment to process the revelation. 'Did they prove ICON assassinated Benazir Bhutto?'

'Bhutto was just the tip of the iceberg,' said Ted. 'After her death, Musharraf's position was untenable. He was desperate to show the public he was in control of the country, so desperate he asked the CIA to work with the ISI to crush the Pakistani Taliban. It wasn't easy. ICON had done a lot of damage in the tribal areas. But somehow between our drones and the ISI's human int, we started turning the tide. By September 2008, we'd convinced more than a dozen tribal elders to call a truce with Islamabad, but there was a spoiler in the works.'

'Remember, Congress controls the CIA's budget,' Bethany reminded Matt. 'ICON had more than one member of the appropriations committees in their back pocket, members who made sure that a portion of our operational budget in the tribal areas was earmarked for training Pakistani forces – the Frontier Corps, specifically.'

'The FC's training wasn't handled by us,' Ted continued. 'It was outsourced to the private sector. ICON got the contract.'

'The FC has always had a reputation for moral ambiguity,' Naj explained to Matt. 'That is why I warned you not to speak ill of them in the governor's mansion. I was trying to protect you from ICON.'

'ICON knew it would find the perfect candidate in the FC, a Pashtun with no ideological affiliations or moral compass, someone they could pay to be whatever they wanted,' said Ted. 'Abdullah Qari fit the bill to a T.'

'So ICON knew him before he was with the Taliban?' said Matt.

'Know him?' said the spy chief. 'They *made* him.'

Matt was incredulous.

'So Abdullah Qari is a fabrication of this ICON,' Tansvir observed. 'I knew he was a whore.'

'It took nothing to build him up from a small-time smuggler into a major player,' said Ted. 'A couple of raids on NATO convoys courtesy of ICON's insider intelligence was enough to cement his reputation among the Pashtun tribes. The Pakistani

Taliban welcomed him with open arms and all the work we'd done in the tribal areas unravelled. Qari went on a rampage beheading elders we'd brought over to our side. Soon everyone was afraid to cross him.'

Tansvir took exception. 'Not everyone.'

'Noted,' said Ted. 'We tried everything to break Qari's stranglehold over the Pakistani Taliban. Nothing worked until Mullah Omar got involved.'

'The leader of the Afghan Taliban?' said Matt. 'You were doing business with him too?'

'The ISI brought him in without our blessing, of course,' Ted clarified. 'They figured they could use Mullah Omar to convince the Pakistani Taliban to stop targeting Islamabad and start fighting the coalition in Afghanistan. It worked and in January 2009, TTP formally pledged their allegiance to Omar and Osama bin Laden. ICON realized they needed a holy man – someone to act as a counter-balance to Mullah Omar. Enter Mullah Maulana. That crazy cleric had been preaching from the rooftops for years before ICON approached him with a deal: join forces with Qari and he'd receive all the backing and funding he needed.'

'Is that when Qari formed his break-away faction?' asked Matt.

Ted rubbed his temples. 'I'm afraid that was our fault.'

'We were doing our job,' Bethany said defensively. 'In August 2009, one of our drones successfully eliminated the leader of Tehrik-i-Taliban. A power struggle ensued over who would be his successor. ICON leveraged the infighting to form a splinter group based around Qari and Mullah Maulana's Pashtun nationalist movement; TTP-Q.'

'All ICON needed to do was reach into their bag of tricks and manufacture an attack that would turn Qari and his organization from ordinary jihadists into legends.' Ted paused to remember his fallen colleagues. 'The attack on our base in Afghanistan was a real coup for ICON. Not only did they kill our agents and put Qari on the map; they curtailed our drone programme in the tribal areas and made us look unfit for purpose.'

Matt was finally grasping the full spectrum of ICON's evil. Their crimes were indeed worse than a single assassination. Not only were they trying to destroy Pakistan from within, they were waging war on their own countrymen to achieve it. 'If you know all this, why haven't you called ICON out?'

'After our turf wars with the SSB, we didn't rule out the possibility that ICON was behind the attack on our base,' Ted confessed. 'But we didn't have solid proof – until Emma came to see me the day before she died. She had everything on ICON: the attack on our base, details of Bhutto's assassination; profiles of suicide bombers, satellite images of Qari's training camps; GPS coordinates for ICON safe houses, phone numbers, bank accounts, serial numbers of US military weapons and equipment diverted to TTP-Q. She even had receipts for the money Eric delivered to Qari. That's how she knew the information was genuine.'

Matt went numb. 'Did Eric set Emma up?'

Ted looked at Bethany. 'Colonel McKay passed Mr Riddell an encrypted message through a news personality website at three a.m. on the day Ms Cameron was murdered,' said the protégée. 'The message instructed him to make sure she was on the roof for a 12.05 live shot.'

Matt's rage boiled. 'He sent Emma to her death.'

'I don't think Eric knew they were going to kill her,' said Ted. 'The message just gave the time and location, nothing more.'

Matt's old paranoia flooded back. He turned an accusatory eye toward Naj. 'How did McKay know she'd given you those files?' he asked Ted.

'There are no leaks on my team,' the spy chief insisted. 'ICON had Emma's source under surveillance for months. They saw him pass the information to her at Heathrow.'

'Who is the bastard?' Matt demanded. 'I want a name.'

'Peter Riorden,' said Bethany. 'He's a retired war correspondent. Ms Cameron took over his position at SBC when he was fired. He didn't know what he had so he gave it to her hoping to either discredit her or blackmail her into coming to work for him.'

'Who gave him the files then?' Matt pressed.

'That is a question I would love to know the answer to,' said Ted. 'It had to be someone high up in ICON's organization; someone with access to *all* of their operations, not just Pakistan.'

Carter's 7M pitch line cut through Matt's anger . . . *governments, energy companies, mining, engineering, banking, telecoms, media; if it's a player, we look after it* . . . 'They control everything.'

'Now you know what we're dealing with,' said Ted.

'Why haven't you stopped them!' Matt slammed his fist on the table. 'Emma gave you everything you need. You could have brought them down weeks ago, instead of sitting here in bloody Quetta with your thumbs up your arses.'

'They're too powerful to bring down in one blow, Matt. They'll just discredit all of Emma's evidence as forgery. There's only one way to break an organization like ICON and that's piece by piece, country by country, industry by industry.' Ted planted his fist next to Matt's. 'Starting here.'

'I'll help you kill McKay,' said Matt. 'And Qari. I'll help you kill them all.'

'The CIA doesn't assassinate Americans no matter how far they've gone astray,' Ted said firmly. 'But I will expose the crimes ICON has committed here and bring McKay and his men back to the States to stand trial.'

'ICON will get him off and you know it,' said Matt.

'Not if he becomes a liability to them,' Ted argued. 'Everything ICON is trying to achieve in Pakistan rests on one man – Abdullah Qari. Eliminate him and McKay will be left twisting in the wind.'

'I should be most pleased to contribute my fighters to this effort,' Tansvir volunteered.

'You are no better than Qari,' Naj objected.

Tansvir unsheathed his knife. 'You dare compare me with that donkey!'

Matt stood between them. 'Go ahead, rip each other's throats out! Play right into ICON's hands!'

Tansvir eyed Naj and stood down.

Ted spoke to the rebel leader. 'I'm thrilled you want Qari dead as much as we do. But unfortunately, I can't use you.'

'Why the hell not?' said Matt. 'We need all the help we can get.'

'The ISI are already keeping us at arm's length,' Ted explained. 'If I'm found associating with the BLA, the CIA will lose any shred of credibility it has left with the Pakistanis.'

'Fuck your credibility,' said Matt. 'The ISI knows everything. That's why they kidnapped me. So they could convince me to kill your man here,' he gestured to Tansvir.

Ted was floored. 'Are you sure?'

'They wanted the BLA to think ICON had sent me to top their leader,' said Matt.

'It is true.' Tansvir raised a brow to Matt. 'But he missed.'

Ted stood up and silently paced the floor. Finally, he returned to the table. 'Bethany. Please leave the room.'

'But, sir—'

'Plausible deniability. Go.' When she was out of earshot, Ted spoke. 'If I agree to work with the BLA, no one can know about it.'

'Very well,' said Tansvir. 'But before I enter into this partnership, I must have a guarantee of American support for Baluch independence.'

'If you're looking for the kind of deal ICON made with you, forget it,' said Ted. 'But,' he paused, 'I could get you a meeting on Capitol Hill.'

Tansvir was unimpressed. 'Congressmen are bullshit. I want an audience with your Secretary of State.'

'I don't have that kind of pull,' said Ted. 'I'm just a CIA station chief.'

'You have mountains of incriminating documents,' Matt argued. 'Don't tell me that can't buy you some influence in Washington.'

'OK,' Ted conceded. 'You'll have to be patient though. It'll take a while to set up the meeting but you will get it.' He extended his hand. 'You have my word.'

Tansvir shook on it. 'My people have waited sixty years for this meeting. A few more weeks shall make no difference. But if you are deceiving me . . .' He reached for his dagger.

'Put that thing away,' Matt chided.

Tansvir placed both hands on the table.

Matt turned to Ted. 'Where do we find Qari then?'

'He hasn't left Mullah Maulana's compound in weeks.' Ted smiled at Tansvir. 'It seems someone scared the shit out of him.'

'I could call another summit,' the rebel leader suggested.

'ICON won't fall for the same trick twice,' said Matt. 'We need to find another way into the compound.'

'We?' said Tansvir.

'You think I'm going to let you do this thing without me?' said Matt. 'Now, how do we get over those walls?'

Chapter 61

McKay stood at Maulana's office window, binoculars raised. The market across from the compound was packed. He'd been monitoring the build-up since dawn when the vendors arrived to unload their goods. He retracted his survey to the eastern and western perimeter walls. It was bad protocol having so many jinglies and pick-ups parked smack against the compound. But diverting them would have tipped off the authorities and McKay was determined for the exchange to happen quietly.

'You are a fool,' said Qari. 'That Baluch dog does not have your man. If he did, he would have killed him or sold him to the Afghans.'

'Brother Qari, please,' Mullah Maulana urged, 'show more respect for our patrons.'

'Tansvir needs weapons.' McKay lowered his binos and gestured to Eric. The correspondent's flak jacket was bulging. 'Weapons cost money. We'll get Logan back.'

'What if he sends a martyr?' Qari challenged.

'Tansvir's boys are homicidal – not suicidal.' McKay resumed his recce. Maulana's followers were performing ablutions in the courtyard for the midday prayer. It wouldn't be long now – provided the Baluch showed this time. He checked beyond the perimeter. Carter, Hernandez and the two ex-Seals were scattered around the market, ready to intervene if necessary. He moved his sights west toward the loudspeakers surrounding the compound's minaret. Bazinsky was hiding in his perch.

A pick-up turned off the main road into the street. It drove around a UNHCR truck before stopping outside the compound. McKay checked his watch: 11.58 a.m. 'Stand by,' he said into his radio. He nodded to Maulana and Qari. 'You two get going, make sure the old man on the gate doesn't give 'em any trouble. We'll be right behind you.'

The cleric left quickly. Qari trailed slowly behind him, stopping to stare down his nose at Eric before walking out the door.

McKay unholstered his pistol and handed it to the correspondent. 'Best keep an eye on Qari. The crazy fucker's acting all weird. I don't want him going postal on your ass.'

Eric looked at the weapon as if it were toxic. 'You keep it. You're a better shot.'

McKay raised his shirt to reveal another pistol. 'I know.'

'This is not what I signed up for. I'm a banker, not a killer.'

McKay tucked in his shirt. 'Tell that to Emma Cameron.'

Maulana was standing at the gate, peering through the sliding peephole. 'There are two Baluch,' said the cleric.

'One of them Tansvir?' asked McKay.

'No,' said Maulana. 'They are young.' He grew more excited. 'They are taking something out of the back of their truck. A coffin!' he gasped.

The blood drained from Eric's face. Qari's lips spread into a self-satisfied smile. 'Wipe that smirk off your face,' McKay said to the terrorist. 'And you,' he said to Eric, 'stop acting like you're at a goddamn funeral. The BLA had to smuggle him past the police checkpoints. There ain't a Muslim on earth gonna risk eternal damnation by disrespecting the dead.'

Sobhat and another young Baluch warrior carried the coffin into the compound. The lid was nailed shut.

'Who among you is McKay?' said Sobhat.

'I am,' said the ICON commander.

Sobhat lowered the coffin. 'Do you have the agreed ransom?'

'Just hold your horses there, son.' McKay motioned to the guards.

Maulana's men set upon the Baluch and searched them. Neither rebel was concealing weapons. 'So far so good,' said McKay. 'Now let's see the goods.'

Sobhat held out his palm. 'The money first.'

'I'm not paying top dollar for a dead man.' McKay gestured to the coffin. 'Now open that thing.'

The Baluch kneeled and started removing the nails. Maulana stood off to the side, mumbling prayers while they worked.

Sobhat freed the last nail, turned his back to McKay and prised off the lid.

Maulana was the first to see the body. 'We have been betrayed!' he cried.

A shot rang out. The cleric spun as a bullet ripped through his chest.

Sobhat and the other Baluch scattered; both warriors now had rifles in their hands.

McKay drew his pistol. 'You!'

Tansvir sat up in the coffin, his Lee Enfield still hot from having shot Maulana. 'I have come for Qari!' he cried, sliding back the bolt to load another round into the chamber. A bullet struck him in the shoulder. He fell back, wounded but still alive.

McKay looked at Eric. The correspondent was in shock; his frozen hand still clutching his just-fired pistol.

Rifle bursts erupted inside the compound. McKay grabbed Qari and pulled him into cover. 'We've been had!' the ICON commander yelled into the radio as he retreated. 'Fight your way in here!'

Eric followed McKay and Qari through the southern block of buildings. When they reached the courtyard door, the ex-Delta colonel peered outside. Baluch warriors were standing on top of two jinglies parked against the compound walls. 'Four enemy on the western wall!' McKay reported to his team. 'At least eight on the east!' He let go of the radio pressel. 'Fuck!'

The market was in a state of bedlam; people running and screaming, trying to escape the violence before it poured over the walls of Maulana's compound into the street. Vendors grabbed what they could carry – abandoning the rest to looters.

The UN workers who'd come out to shop that morning were the only ones not attempting to flee. The pair had taken cover beneath their truck.

Bethany scanned the vicinity and locked onto a target. She aimed her pistol and fired. The silenced round struck Ginta's thigh, wounding him. 'One down, sir.'

Ted already had Dietrich in the aim. He discharged his muffled pistol into the ex-Seal's shoulder. 'Make that two. Any sign of the others?'

Bethany searched. Carter and Hernandez were rounding the eastern wall fifty yards away. 'Targets out of range, sir.'

Ted pressed the switch on his radio. 'Two down, two headed your way. Good luck.'

Chapter 62

'Roger that.' Matt put down his radio and raised the telescopic sight he'd removed from his Dragunov. As much as he loved the sniper rifle this operation required something more versatile; a hard-hitting assault weapon capable of punching through soft walls and taking out enemies at close quarters as well as from a distance. A BLA Russian-made AK, circa 1990 fit the bill perfectly.

He ran the Dragunov sight up the minaret. The end of a CheyTac barrel came into the crosshairs. 'Goodbye, *Baby Girl*.' He lowered the sight, tucked his rifle into his shoulder, steadied his hands with a few concentrated breaths and focused on the tip of the AK's foresight. At one with his weapon, Matt went for the kill.

The 7.62mm round flew out of his rifle and into the target. Bazinsky fell from his minaret perch into the compound below. Matt used the Dragunov sight to inspect the body; a clean shot to the head. The reckoning he'd come to Pakistan for had begun.

He jumped from the jingly onto the eastern wall and lowered himself into the courtyard. The BLA militia followed behind, guns blazing. Dressed in a white turban and shalwar kameez, Matt was virtually indistinguishable from the invading horde he'd nested in the lorry with all morning. But although he'd adopted the Baluch uniform, he refused to copy their ways. The rebels were pitiless, firing automatic bursts into Maulana's defenceless followers.

Matt scanned for the only target that mattered. There was no sign of Qari in the courtyard. He took aim at the southern block of buildings and waited for the terrorist to emerge. Suddenly, there was a commotion to the north. Matt swung his rifle around. The students from the madrassa were running out of their class-rooms. The child-fighters were armed with AK 47s, M4s and other weapons their hands could barely hold.

'Leave them, leave them!' Matt cried. But the BLA refused to grant the child-fighters clemency, tearing their tiny bodies apart with a torrent of bullets. One boy armed with an AK managed to dodge the BLA fire and operate his trigger, but he was too weak to control the weapon. The barrel pulled upwards and to the right, peppering his comrades with fatal automatic rounds.

More of Maulana's followers came charging out of the mosque, brandishing stockpiled weapons. The four BLA fighters perched on the western wall above sprayed them with bullets, killing at least a dozen. The surviving Pashtun warriors turned to answer their enemy, only to find the fight swinging their way.

The Baluch rebels fell into the courtyard, their backs riddled with bullets. Maulana's followers cheered wildly as their saviours jumped over the wall and into the compound. Matt recognized the invaders from their uniforms – the Frontier Corps. They'd come to help their Pashtun brothers.

Another FC contingent surged over the eastern wall. Trapped in a Pashtun pincer, the BLA grew more savage. A crimson tide washed over the courtyard as the two ethnic groups battled it out. Men lost their footing on the blood-soaked pavement, send-ing bursts of fire into friend and foe alike. Stray bullets strafed the walls, pummelling the adobe bricks. The red dust fused with the rifle smoke, shrouding the combat in a deathly fog.

Matt scrambled for cover behind the ablution pool and peered over the edge with his Dragunov sight. The smoke was too dense to identify anyone clearly. He pivoted east to west, searching for Qari. A window opened in the fog, revealing two broad-shouldered figures pinned down on the southern wall. Carter and Hernandez. The ex-Deltas had come to rescue McKay.

An object crashed into the pool, dousing Matt's sight. He wiped the lens clean and looked in the water. His single-minded focus shattered when he realized what had disturbed his hunt; a child no more than seven, floating face down in a sea of red. The small, lifeless body opened Matt's eyes to the true horror raging around him. This was not combat as he'd known it. It was something far more primitive – ethnic civil war. In Gwadar, the reasons for breaking up Pakistan had seemed so convincing when mapped on a desert floor. But the slaughter he was witnessing obliterated those arguments. No political agenda or national security imperative on earth could ever justify unleashing such carnage. Eliminating Qari would do nothing to stop it. ICON would simply groom another soulless puppet to take his place. There was only one way to put an end to their evil agenda in Pakistan. Matt had to kill McKay.

'Logan!'

Matt looked beyond the pool. Tansvir was crawling toward him. The wounded BLA commander was holding fast to his Lee Enfield.

Matt dragged him into cover. 'Where are you hit?'

'Qari is with McKay,' Tansvir gasped. 'I followed them here. You must finish what we started, Logan.'

Matt raised Tansvir's shirt. The rebel leader had two entry wounds: one in his shoulder, another in his right lung. Matt applied pressure to the ribcage. 'I need to get you out of here before your lung collapses.'

'No. You must kill Qari before he escapes.'

'You'll die if you don't get medical treatment.'

'My body is beyond saving,' Tansvir placed his hand over
Matt's, 'but not my soul. Kill Qari.'

Matt looked into the fading warrior's eyes. Allowing Tansvir
to die in peace was perhaps the only shred of nobility he could
salvage from this massacre. 'I'll kill him – for you and for your
people.'

The tension in Tansvir's face relaxed. 'Thank you, my friend.'

Matt checked his magazine; he still had plenty of rounds
remaining to take out Qari and McKay. He looked about. They
could be anywhere in the compound; the mosque, the class-
rooms . . . his eyes tilted up. Maulana's office!

He assessed the distance between his position and the entrance
to the two-storey building. Getting there off his own back without getting shot would be next to impossible. 'Are you strong
enough to cover me?' he asked Tansvir.

The rebel leader cradled his Lee Enfield. 'I am out of
ammunition.'

Matt raised him up by the collar. 'Do you still have some fight
in you, old man!'

The call to arms roused the dying commander. 'I require a
new weapon.'

Matt spied an M4 and a bag of magazines lying on the ground
next to one of Maulana's fallen followers. He belly-crawled out,
retrieved the stash and brought it back to Tansvir.

'You've got around twenty to thirty rounds here,' he said,
shoving a fresh magazine into the rifle, 'plus spares if you can
manage.' He propped Tansvir up and placed the M4 in his hands.
'You know how to use this?'

Tansvir chambered a round. 'Do not insult a dying man.'

Matt pointed to the entrance of the building housing
Maulana's office. 'I'm going for that door. Give me good covering fire with fast single shots.'

Tansvir coughed. 'I was fighting before you were born.' He laid the stock of the weapon on the pool wall for support. 'I will not fail you, Logan. Do not fail me.'

Matt raised his AK and jumped to his feet. 'Go! Go! Go!'

He bolted for the door, leaping over corpses and pushing past the living. He reached the entrance, placed his back against the outer wall and swung his rifle through the doorway. Two of Maulana's followers were inside, guarding it with M4s. He swiftly disabled the inexperienced fighters with fast double taps to their torsos.

Matt ran past the dead men and down the hall. Bullets trailed his wake as the youths in the classrooms fired blindly at the figure rushing past. An RPG cut through the passage in front of him. The grenade exploded, throwing him against the wall. Plaster rained down as a screaming child came running out of the classroom where the RPG had been fired. Matt picked himself up and looked in. It was like Christmas – boxes of rifles, grenades, mines and other explosives. He ducked inside. Keeping one hand on his weapon, he reached for a satchel of grenades. That's when he saw it: the tiny, burnt torso that had driven the child wailing from the room. The dead boy had been standing directly behind the RPG when it was fired. The back-blast had blown the head and arms from his body.

Matt grabbed the grenades and ran for the staircase leading to the top floor. He peered around the corner before entering the mount of the stairwell. A burst of automatic fire forced him back. He took out a grenade, pulled the pin, tossed it up the steps and hunched down against the wall. The corridor shook as shrapnel fragments exploded in the confined space.

Matt raised his rifle and ran to the top of the stairs. Maulana's office was shut; the hallway leading to it deceptively clear. Matt put himself into the mind of his quarry. McKay was an elite soldier. He'd be prepared to take out an enemy attempting to breach the doorway. There was only one way Matt was going to get a clear shot at the ICON commander. He'd have to tempt him out of hiding.

Keeping his back flush to the wall, Matt closed in on his target. 'Help! Help! Is anyone in there!' he called.

'Logan!' McKay responded. 'Is that you, soldier!'

'I'm wounded!' he bluffed, bringing his rifle into the firing position. 'The BLA are right behind me!'

'Drop your weapon,' said a low, menacing voice.

Matt lowered his rifle and turned. Eric was aiming a pistol right at him. The correspondent's hand was shaking. 'You don't have the guts to kill me.'

Eric steadied his aim with his free hand. 'I killed Emma. I'll kill you if I have to.'

McKay stepped into the corridor. The ex-Delta colonel had supplemented his pistol with an M4. 'Are you out of your mind!' he said to Eric. 'Stand down immediately.'

Eric kept his pistol raised. 'Logan was leading you into a trap. He's not wounded.'

McKay looked Matt up and down. 'Jesus H. Christ. What'd they do, brainwash you, son?'

'I'm not your fucking son,' Matt growled.

McKay raised his hand. 'Place your weapon and ammo on the floor and we'll go inside the office and talk; start unscrambling that head of yours.'

Qari poked his head out of the office. He laughed when he saw Matt.

McKay checked the terrorist with one glance. 'You,' he barked. 'Get out here and guard the hallway.'

'But someone may attack,' Qari protested.

'Don't be such a pussy.' McKay looked at Eric. 'Bring Logan into the office.'

Eric pushed his pistol into Matt's back. 'Drop your gun.'

Matt lowered his AK. 'It's a rifle, you wanker.'

Eric forced Matt into the office and shut the door. McKay tossed the correspondent a roll of duct tape and kicked the chair out from behind the desk. 'Tie him up.' He looked on with his weapon poised as Eric restrained Matt. 'I'm not gonna lie to you, Logan. I'm disappointed. I thought you were mentally tougher than this.'

'There's nothing wrong with my head,' said Matt.

Eric bound Matt's wrists. 'Maybe we should leave the questioning for later.'

'Did I ask your opinion?' McKay spoke to Matt again. 'Don't you worry now, son. I won't abandon a fellow Christian. Once you're straightened out, I'll find a place for you somewhere in the organization.'

'I'd rather die than work for you.'

'Now, that's just crazy talking . . .'

'I know what you've been doing in Pakistan. I know it was you who created Qari,' Matt hissed. 'You're scum, McKay.'

'I guess Tansvir spilled the beans, huh. I know this must seem confusing, but you must trust me, son. This is God's work we're doing here.'

'I wish I believed in your god. Then I'd know there was a hell for you to rot in. What gives you the right to plunge a country into civil war?'

McKay pointed to heaven. 'God gives me the right,' he declared. 'The sooner we crush these heathen nations the sooner his dominion will be restored on earth.'

'Does that divine mandate include murdering Christian women?' Matt challenged.

'I don't know what lies Tansvir has planted in your head . . .'

Matt glared at the ICON leader. 'You killed Emma Cameron.'

'That little traitor?' said McKay. 'She was a poor excuse for a Christian, son.'

'You had no right to kill her!'

'The hell I didn't!' McKay thundered. 'The bitch worked for me!'

Matt's heart stopped. Emma's words flooded his mind . . . *Turns out the world needed rescuing from us . . .*

Eric raised his pistol to Matt. 'He knows too much.'

'Lower your weapon, boy,' McKay ordered.

'He's off his fucking head,' Eric argued. 'You can call in a battalion of shrinks but there's no guaranteeing he won't betray us like Emma did. Face it, McKay, Logan's a security risk.'

McKay walked over to the window and looked at the fight raging below. 'Damn it.' He looked back to Eric. 'Do it.'

Matt braced for certain death.

'God forgive me,' said Eric, as he discharged the pistol.

The shot reverberated through the room.

Eric fell at Matt's feet. 'I didn't know they were going to kill Emma,' he cried.

Matt looked at the window. McKay was lying beneath it – dead by Eric's hand. 'Was he telling the truth? Did Emma work for ICON?'

'She was just a mouthpiece,' Eric sobbed. 'She had no idea what ICON was really doing here until she got those files.'

Matt turned away. 'Everything she told me was a lie,' he whispered.

Eric ripped open the top pocket of his flak jacket and pulled out a wired block of plastic explosive. 'I don't expect you to, but I hope you can find it in your heart to forgive me some day.'

The bomb snapped Matt back to the present. 'What are you doing?'

Eric tucked the explosive back inside the suicide vest. 'I helped create Qari. Now I'm going to destroy him.'

'You don't have to die,' said Matt. 'We'll kill him together.'

'ICON murdered Emma for betraying them.' Eric gestured at McKay's corpse. 'It's only a matter of time before they kill me too. At least this way, my death will mean something.'

'Untie me,' Matt pleaded. 'Let me help you.'

'You don't have to die, Matt. McKay's men think you're one of them.' Eric opened the door and looked back. 'I'll detonate the vest far enough away for you to survive.'

Matt called after him. 'Let me help you!'

Chapter 63

The Delta lads were low. Their operation lay in ruins. The colonel they'd followed through hell and beyond was dead and the terrorist puppet he'd created blown away by a suicide bomber. Like all foreigners before them, their grand plans for Pakistan had yielded nothing but regret.

Matt walked with them into the terminal. 'So where are you lads off to next?'

'We're heading up to your old stomping ground,' said Carter. 'Afghanistan.'

'Piece of shit CP task?'

'Piece of shit training task,' said Hernandez.

'NATO thinks it's about time the Afghan National Army had a Special Forces unit,' Carter explained. 'We're gonna go show them the tricks of the trade.'

'God help the Afghans with you two running things.'

'You're welcome to come with us,' Carter offered. 'All it'll take is one phone call.'

'I can't ask you to stick your neck out for me. After this task, I'll be lucky to get a job guarding Mothercare.'

'Don't be too down on yourself.' Carter placed his hands on Matt's shoulders. 'Most men wouldn't survive one day as a hostage. You survived three weeks and lived to tell the story.'

'I lost a client,' Matt reminded him.

'No one will hold that against you,' said Hernandez. 'It served that reporter right, going to interview a known terrorist without the proper security.'

'I know it's un-Christian but if you ask me, he got exactly what he deserved,' Carter added.

Matt extended his hand. 'Well, lads, I guess this is it.'

Carter pulled him in for an embrace. 'Our flight doesn't leave for another three hours. There's still time to change your mind.'

'Watch your backs in Afghanistan,' said Matt. 'You never know who might be coming up behind you.'

He shouldered his bag and headed to the ticket counter. His flight back to London was one-way, not that he had anything to go home for. Even his memories of Emma were dead to him now. Everything she'd ever told him was a lie.

'Passport,' asked the attendant behind the counter. Matt gave it to him. The attendant opened it. 'Excuse me,' he said, rushing off with the document in his hand. He returned with two policemen. 'What's going on?' Matt demanded.

The police wouldn't say. They hauled him to the back of the terminal and left him in a dark office.

A wheelchair rolled out of the shadows. 'Did you think I would let you leave Pakistan without saying goodbye?'

Matt looked at Khalid's folded trouser leg. The wounded limb had been amputated above the knee.

'I gave you the choice to leave Pakistan when we were in Chaman. Now I am telling you.' The spy wheeled closer. 'Get out of my country and never return.'

'I'll make you a deal,' said Matt. 'I'll stay away from your country if you stop spying on mine.'

'I will not promise that.'

'Well then I guess this isn't really goodbye.' Matt opened the door to leave.

'You will never see me coming, Logan,' Khalid warned.

'One-legged spies are pretty easy to spot.'

As he walked back to the ticket counter, Matt's pocket started to vibrate. It was the mobile he'd been given at the start of his trip. He still hadn't returned it.

Emma's broken chain fell out with the handset. 'Yes,' Matt answered, scooping the cross off the floor.

'Hello, I'm trying to reach a Mr Matthew Edward . . . '

'Who is this?'

'I'm calling from SBC human resources about a life insurance policy.'

'I'm no longer working with you. In fact, I shouldn't even be talking on this phone.'

'I'm sorry,' the woman interrupted. 'I'm calling in reference to Emma Cameron's life insurance policy. You're named as the sole beneficiary, Mr Logan.'

Matt stared at the chain in his palm, speechless.

'It's quite a substantial sum,' the woman continued, 'seven figures. The double indemnity clause was invoked . . .'

Matt slipped the silver cross off the links. Emma really had loved him; so much so that she'd secured his future with her death.

'Mr Logan. Hello, Mr Logan, are you still there?'

He closed his hand around the charm. 'I'll call you back.' Matt ran through the terminal, thinking of the solitary life he had dreamed of for so long. He could buy the farm in Perthshire twice over now, thanks to Emma. But he would never truly earn it until ICON was destroyed . . . country by country . . . industry by industry. 'Hey, Carter!' he called.